THE
PUPPE
BOY OF
WARSAW

Eva Weaver is a writer, art therapist and performance artist, who often explores issues of belonging and history in her work. Like many Germans, she is haunted by the events of the Second World War, which inspired her to write *The Puppet Boy of Warsaw*, her first novel, which was translated into eleven languages. Her second novel, *The Eye of the Reindeer*, was inspired by journeys to Scandinavia, encounters with the Sami people and her work as an art therapist over many years in the mental health services in the UK. She moved to Britain from Germany in 1995 and lives in Brighton.

www.evaweaver.com

THE
PUPPET
BOY OF
WARSAW

Eva Weaver

W&N

WEIDENFELD & NICOLSON

First published in Great Britain in 2013 by Weidenfeld & Nicolson
This paperback edition published in 2020 by Weidenfeld & Nicolson
an imprint of the Orion Publishing Group Ltd
Carmelite House, 50 Victoria Embankment,
London EC4Y 0DZ

An Hachette UK company

1 3 5 7 9 10 8 6 4 2

A CIP catalogue record for this book
is available from the British Library.

ISBN (Mass Market Paperback) 978 1 4746 1714 7
ISBN (eBook) 978 0 2978 6829 3

Typeset by Input Data Services Ltd, Somerset

Printed and bound in Great Britain by Clays Ltd, Elcograf S.p.A.

The Orion Publishing Group's policy is to use papers
that are natural, renewable and recyclable products and
made from wood grown in sustainable forests. The logging
and manufacturing processes are expected to conform to
the environmental regulations of the country of origin.

www.orionbooks.co.uk
www.weidenfeldandnicolson.co.uk

For the victims of war then and now
May this book support dialogue, healing and peace

PROLOGUE

*W*ithout the coat nothing would have happened as it
did. At first it was only a witness, a black woollen coat
with a six-button row, but becoming a pocket-coat made it an
accomplice.

Now it lies gutted, like a boar of its entrails, emptied out
to the very last item. Battered and out of fashion, everything
it once sheltered has gone: Mika and his puppets, the old gold-
rimmed spectacles, the beggar's flute, the faded letters, the
photographs, and, of course, the children. All but the last book
Mika slipped into one of its pockets like a secret. Bound in
dark red leather, no bigger than a notebook, filled with photographs, cut-outs and scribblings, Mika's 'Book of Heroes' is a
sunken treasure hidden in the coat's seams.

When Mika bundled up the coat and stuffed it in a box he
was still a young man. Mika's last night as a bachelor was
the coat's dark night of the soul. Here, untouched by sunlight,
the coat slipped into oblivion, slowly forgotten by all those who
had once held it dear: Nathan the tailor, Grandfather Jacob,
Mika, Ellie, the mothers, the twins, the puppets, and the
orphans ...

Then, Mika returned. No warning, only a flash, then light
like heaven. There he stood, grey as his grandfather, old as good
wine, and next to him, with brown chocolate eyes, a boy the size
and build of Mika at the time when the coat first became his.

1

Measured by the old tailor's knowing hands, cut, stitched and adorned with a row of fine black buttons, this was no ordinary coat. And when the Germans took Warsaw and Grandfather Jacob transformed the coat into a pocket-coat two years later, it found a purpose.

But before the pockets, the armband arrived: a blue Star of David worked on a piece of white cotton, stitched tightly on to the coat's right sleeve like a mark. Look closely and you can still see a dark blue thread where the armband was fixed, an innocent piece of yarn from Mother's needle basket.

Over the years many things have mingled in the coat's pockets and become entangled, but the girl, she changed everything. For her, the coat became a vessel, Jonah's whale, swallowing her whole so she could be delivered safely to the other side.

She was the first child to be smuggled and she smelled of sleep, deep, oblivious slumber and strong, cheap soap. The matron must have scrubbed her from head to toe. At least she would smell nice if captured. Perhaps the fresh, soapy smell would protect her, cast some doubt in a soldier's mind. A cherished memory of his own child, clean, ready for bed ...

That first night the coat sheltered the oblivious girl, folded itself around her as tightly as possible, her curls rubbing against its silky insides like coarse wool. And then she was gone, handed over in a flash, only her smell still lingering for a while like an afterthought ...

PART ONE

Mika's Story

I

New York City, 12 January 2009

After a blizzard, snow glistened under a brilliantly blue sky. New York was magical in the first snow, muted and utterly transformed. Despite the snow, or rather because of it, Mika insisted on walking the few blocks from the subway to the museum. *Snow takes the edge off everything. Like a disappearing act.*

Even after a sleepless night and with pain nagging his left knee the old man hummed: the fresh snow held promise and Sunday with his grandson brought a welcome change to his insular existence. Daniel had arrived early to make the most of the short winter's day and after an ample breakfast Mika had suggested they mingle with the dinosaurs at the Natural History Museum. So wrapped in thick scarves and hats to shield them from the cutting wind, they took the subway exit on 72nd Street and headed north towards Central Park.

Daniel was tall for his thirteen years, lanky and agile with delicate features that radiated curiosity and a pinch of cheekiness. Mika had always been fond of his grandson's unashamed laughter and his black unruly curls. Like Hannah. So like Ruth. Every so often the pair broke into a foolish little dance, kicking the powdery snow into

5

caster-sugar clouds, Daniel with his shoes, Mika swinging his stick. They giggled with delight.

It happened as they walked down 72nd Street towards Columbus. They passed a small theatre – from the outside not much more than a large, shabby red door with a printed sign. Mika noticed out of the corner of his eye a colourful poster, proclaiming in bold letters: '*The Puppet Boy of Warsaw – a Puppet Play*'.

Mika slowed down but didn't stop, despite the cold sweat gathering on his forehead and between his shoulder blades.

The poster's words were printed over a picture of an old black coat lying spread out as if it were about to dance or fly away, a Star of David armband stitched on to the right sleeve. A blue star, he noticed, a Polish one, not yellow like the ones the Jews were forced to wear in other places. And there were puppets, lots of different puppets, sticking their brightly coloured heads out of the coat's many pockets: a crocodile, a fool, a princess, a monkey.

Mika's heart pounded, quick, deep beats like those of a crazy drum. He reached inside his coat, first the left, then the right pocket, fumbling, searching for something. Nothing there but an old crumpled handkerchief, a pencil stub, another pair of gloves. Suddenly vertigo and a strong wave of nausea washed over him and with it a sense of helplessness and rage he feared would devour him like a lion gorging on his insides. His chest tightened and he gasped for air. As he clasped Daniel's arm, his voice sounded thin and strained.

'Danny, please, let's go home. I need to show you something.'

'What is it? Are you OK?'

'Yes, I just need to go back. I'm sorry, Danny.' Mika swayed, clutching his stick, but the images were already flooding in: a small figure, stumbling over an endless field of smouldering rubble; a huge black shape above him flapping like a massive crow; a coat, inhabited by a screaming troupe of puppets, chasing after him, trying to catch him once and for all.

As he leaned against the wall the images began to fade but his knees buckled and he felt himself sliding to the ground, a deep ringing in his ears and then blackness.

He didn't know how much time had passed, but then he felt Danny's hand, patting his cheek.

'Wake up, Grandpa.'

A figure from across the street called out. He couldn't hear what the man was saying. *He shouldn't be on the side-walk if he's a Jew like me. Hasn't he heard? It's forbidden to walk on the sidewalk. Or maybe he's German?*

The stranger crossed the road.

'Here, Pops, take a swig, that might help.' Danny pressed a small silver flask to his mouth. It stuck to his lips.

'Everything OK?' The man from across the road bent over him, friendly, concerned, his forehead all furrows. He wasn't wearing a uniform after all, but a woolly hat and scarf.

Still, never trust a stranger's smile. Must get up. Can't die here.

Danny held the flask to his lips again. Mika took a large swig then coughed.

'You want to kill me? What's that?'

The man laughed.

'Stroh rum, seventy-five per cent Austrian. Perfect for emergencies. Can even bring back the dead sometimes. You're feeling better?'

'Thanks, yes.' Mika shook himself like a dog coming out of water.

'Can you get up?' Danny was right by his side. 'I could call an ambulance.'

'No, I'm fine. Really. Just help me up.'

Daniel and the man grabbed one arm each and lifted him up. Mika's legs felt alien, and somehow far away, as if he were looking through binoculars the wrong way. He stomped his feet a few times on the icy ground.

'That's better, thank you. I need to go home.' His head hurt.

'You're sure you can walk, Pops? Get a cab at least?'

Mika smiled. They had not seen a single car since they stepped out of the subway. Carlessness was part of the magic of the first snowfall.

'No, let's just go. And thank you, sir, for the rum – that should do the trick!'

Danny handed him his stick. They didn't speak but Daniel linked his arm through Mika's, supporting him as they made their way through the snowy cityscape. Mika allowed him, and more than that, he was grateful.

They took the subway and after another short walk they finally reached Mika's apartment block. The elevator took them to the fifth floor. After opening the door Mika quickly unwrapped his coat and scarf and became animated.

'Danny, please go to the wardrobe in the bedroom and bring me that big brown parcel behind the clothes.'

The box had been sitting there for many years. Mika had carefully sealed it up the day before he asked his wife to marry him. He was twenty-eight then and had only opened it once since then, last October, when he had added one last item.

Daniel reached far into the wardrobe and pulled out the package. For a moment he swayed under its weight.

'Have you got bricks in there?'

'No, just bring it over here.' Mika's hands trembled as Daniel carefully placed the box in front of him. His fingers slid over the crumpled brown paper, tenderly exploring every side. Then, with a sudden jolt, he sliced through the cord with a sharp kitchen knife. No need to carefully untie the parcel now – he would never do it up again. He grabbed the box and slowly lifted the lid. The smell was overwhelming, sharp and pungent.

'What is it, Grandpa?'

'I want to tell you about what happened in the ghetto. I want to tell you before I die. I want to tell the truth – to you and to my own heart, to your mother and maybe the world.' With both hands he pulled out a huge coat. Heavy and black. It reminded him of the large black dog he had found the previous week, lying dead at the entrance to Madison Park as if struck down by lightning. But his old coat had life in it still.

He lifted it out and slipped his arms into its dark sleeves. Now, as when he was a boy, it looked too big, and yet at the same time it fitted him like a second skin. And like a shaman's coat, it was easy for him to conjure up spirits and memories of his past in its embrace. He took Daniel's hand and drew a deep breath.

'Did you notice the poster at the little theatre we passed – "*The Puppet Boy of Warsaw*"?'

Daniel shook his head and gazed at his grandfather, whose eyes shimmered with a wild glow.

'Well, they used to call me "the Puppet Boy" in our neighbourhood in the ghetto, but they could just as well have called me "the Pocket Boy".'

'Is that what gave you such a shock?' Daniel asked.

Mika nodded. 'Danny, the soldiers never found the secret world inside my coat, never noticed the pockets within the pockets. You see, this coat has its own magic. But let me start at the beginning. Let me tell you exactly how it happened.'

9

2

I was twelve when the coat was made. Nathan, our tailor and dear friend, cut it for Grandfather in the first week of March 1938. It was the last year of freedom for Warsaw and for us.

Nathan lived in a small corner shop at the end of Piwna Street in the old quarter, close to our apartment. He was known for his great craftsmanship, and people from all over the city flocked to him. He never tired of his needles and threads, sewing like an industrious spider, as if the threads emerged directly from his hands. Those threads, a huge collection of shades and colours he kept neatly stacked on a shelf, held together shirts, trousers, coats and jackets and, as it turned out, could not only alter lengths and sizes, but also change lives.

I remember the shop from the many visits I made with Grandpa before the occupation; the muffled light, the stuffy smell of fabric stored without enough air. Cottons of all qualities and colours, wools and even cashmere, the sad, dusty rubber plants in the window which survived even though nobody ever seemed to water them, and the tinkling of the small bell above the door when we entered. Most of all I remember Nathan's bright green eyes, which

10

were a surprise in the dullness of his shop, sitting like emerald jewels in his wrinkly face, and his bony fingers and fidgety hands, always moving, never still. Did he sew even in his dreams?

This was where it all began, in this small, dusty tailor's shop. My grandfather being measured, then running his hands over the many different materials that were laid out before him like a banquet, letting his fingertips choose exactly the right fabric. He had been promoted to professor the previous month and the tailored coat was his way of celebrating.

Grandpa called me Mika, short for Mikhael, gift of God. Did the shortening of my name make me a smaller gift? I was skinny and not tall for my twelve years but I was quick on my feet and eager to learn. Books lay scattered all around my room, even nestled under my pillow.

I adored Grandpa more than anyone in the world. He had become my best friend after my father died. I called him Tatus or Daddy, and sometimes Grandpa. We were a different kind of family: I had no siblings to fight or plan mischief with, it was only my mama, the old man and me – a triangle of three generations.

When we returned to Nathan's shop a week later, Grandpa couldn't wait to try on his greatcoat. It was like moving into a new house, an exciting and grander place to live.

'What do you think, Mika?' His face lit up in the broadest smile as he moved from side to side in front of the large mirror. He didn't wait for my answer.

'Well done, Nathan, my brother. What fine work! Ah, what is algebra compared to such skill?'

He clapped the tailor on the shoulder, paid and we were off. As we headed home, taking the long route, Grandfather strutted along the cobbled streets of Warsaw, his hands buried in the coat's big pockets.

In 1938 we still walked freely in the city, a place where Jewish culture thrived. It was a beautiful city, our city. All that would soon come to a brutal end.

A professor of mathematics at the University of Warsaw, Grandfather was a clever and proud man and his students adored him. His round glasses and calm low voice made him seem the very picture of a professor, while his tall physique, angular features and thick, black hair, streaked with a flash of white over his left temple, commanded respect. He loved the clarity of numbers, how everything made sense when one spent enough time and attention on them. 'Numbers always work out,' he used to say. But a few months after our stroll home from the tailor, I would discover a different side to him, far removed from algebra, logic and abstract numbers. And then I would learn that numbers could not save us.

The spectre of war had been hovering over us for a long time. Then, on 1 September 1939, the bombing started. Schools had already been suspended so I stayed home with Mother and Grandpa, curled up in the old armchair in our sitting room, my physics books spread around me. I heard the first explosion from the direction of the city centre: a deep thud, then a noise as though something huge had smashed into a thousand pieces, splinters ripping into stone.

I ran to the window. All hell broke loose: a swarm of Messerschmitts droned like locusts over our beautiful city, dropping bomb after bomb, lighting up the sky in sinister orange and phosphorescent yellow. I stood pointing, gasping, until Mother grabbed my arm and pulled me away. We hardly slept that night. Nor any of the nights to come.

After that first attack, bombings followed day and night, relentlessly crashing down on the city. Some

12

attacks lasted minutes, others hours. I couldn't help but watch the deadly fireworks, especially at night. Even after we had blacked out the windows with curtains, bed-sheets and newspapers, I still found tiny cracks to peep through. But we were trapped like rabbits, waiting to be slaughtered.

'Come away from the window, you'll get us all killed!'

Mama worried we would draw the planes to us with our spying, while I thought that if I could keep an eye on the planes, the bombs wouldn't fall on us. It was a foolish thought but on many nights Tatus joined me. What else could we do? After days locked in our apart-ment, our limbs and eyes ached, and we were raw with sleeplessness.

And the hellish noise! I feared our eardrums would burst. Then, when the planes disappeared, the strange emptiness of silence scared us even more. But this was only the beginning. A few days later the 'Stukas' arrived – Germany's fiercest fighter planes, fitted with ear-splitting sirens designed to break our nerve and drive us into submission. I heard them from a long way off before I spotted the first one, circling above us like a sinister bird of prey. Suddenly it dropped out of the sky, nose-diving with breathtaking speed and a high-pitched scream, slid-ing down in a diabolical crescendo.

'We took one down.' I cupped my hands over my ears and shouted.

'Tatus, come, look!' I was hopping up and down but my elation quickly burst like a soap bubble. A second before impact the plane dropped its bombs. Our sky lit up in flames, followed by thick black clouds of smoke while the plane began to climb again. The bastards had hit us and escaped. This was bad, very bad. If they could pull a stunt like that, what else did they have in store for us? That night I did not return to the window.

13

Our small family pulled together tight as glue. Mama still managed to cook a soup or a simple stew most days, while Grandpa entertained me with algebra and geometry. Sometimes we spent a few hours with our neighbours, but mostly we just held our breath, peeping from behind our blacked-out windows, listening to the crackle of the radio. There were fewer announcements now, only Chopin's polonaises and waltzes floated through the ether, reminding us of our Polish heritage and pride. Sometimes the music stopped in mid-phrase, interrupted by a broadcast, but they were never heartening.

We were the first to experience Germany's newest tactic, their 'Blitzkrieg', taking us by surprise with intense, overpowering might and forcing Poland to her knees. Our cavalry had fought so bravely, but what were horses and guns against roaring planes, armoured tanks and mortars? People fell like flies in the fierce onslaught, ripped apart by the explosions, buried under the rubble of their own homes, mowed down by machine-gun fire from planes, when all they had done was go out to fetch some water or barter for food.

On 29 September, after a month of bombing which left the city in smouldering ruins and with no more water to extinguish the fires, Warsaw surrendered. Stepping outside, I emerged into a different world. At 46 Pawia Street, where the Chrotowskis had once lived, only an ugly, burnt-out façade remained. The Karsinskis had lost two of their children and my friend Jacob's house was a smoking shell, his father buried under the debris. The old Rosenzweig couple next door had survived but Steynberg's bakery opposite Nathan's shop had burnt to the ground. There would be no more of Steynberg's fluffy white bread. The cobbled streets were littered with rubble and mangled belongings. And the horses. Their bloated carcasses lay everywhere, black clouds of flies lifting as we passed.

That evening we saw a long line of our brave, wretched soldiers being marched out of town. To see them trudge like beaten dogs, barely held together by their dirty, ripped uniforms, made me cringe. What would happen to them? To us?

The next day the German Wehrmacht moved in. And I tell you, they did not do so quietly. Even their Führer, Hitler himself, arrived to inspect his troops and his new, conquered city. The tanks that had so brutally overrun our country now rolled into our city, their treads clattering over our old cobbled streets. And the marching of their troops, endless squares of helmeted soldiers, goosestepping rigidly as if one body. They reached the Führer's tribune and all heads turned sharply as they passed the man with the moustache, pounding the ground even harder with their black leather boots. The whole city trembled from their force.

The flags went up next, as if the prevalence of the hooked cross should remind us of this new 'Herrenrasse', the blonde, blue-eyed master race that would stamp on everything they deemed low and unworthy. It wouldn't be long before they began to squash us like vermin, like insects, like dirt.

Soon the first directives appeared. Then they continued to emerge, week after week, month after month, never all at once, but drip-fed to us, erasing one piece after another of our freedom, our dignity. First they banished entertainment: from one day to the next those of Jewish blood were forbidden to enter local parks, cafés or museums. Our Krasinski Park was out of bounds, outings to the zoo and Lazienki Park were not allowed any more. Benches and trams were suspended and *'nicht für Juden'* – not for Jews – signs sprang up everywhere.

15

One day as I walked home from school along Freta Street, a German soldier appeared around the corner.

'*Mach daß Du wegkommst. Runter hier,*' he shouted. Before I could even try to decipher what he had barked, he grabbed my shirt and threw me into the street as if I were an old sack. I fell to the ground and could feel blood trickling down my knees. My heart hung in shreds by the time I reached home. That night, Grandfather read the newest directives to me: Jews are forbidden to use public trams, visit restaurants in non-Jewish districts and must not walk on pavements but share the street with cars and horses.

In May, Tatus lost his job at the university. Out of the blue one day they told him to pack his things, and said that his presence was no longer welcome. It wouldn't be long before I was hit too.

It happened during a chemistry lesson. Siemaski, our teacher, had just pointed to the element beryllium on the periodic table, when there were three loud knocks, the classroom door opened and our headteacher Gorski stood there looking all flustered, squeezed between two German soldiers. The soldier on the left was carrying a list and he pushed it into Gorski's hands. 'Read.'

'Abram Tober, Jacob Kaplan and Mika Hernsteyn,' Gorski's voice trembled, 'pack your books, you are dismissed. Go home.'

For a moment I couldn't move.

'*Schnell, macht schon,*' the German shouted. I got up and left the classroom, not looking at anyone. I never saw Abram and Jacob again, nor my friends Bolek and Henryk, who stayed behind.

When I got home, I threw myself into Grandpa's arms.

'*Tatus*, they kicked me out, just like that. It's not fair.' Grandpa hugged me and Mama joined in.

'I know. It's in the papers today: "Jewish children are to be withdrawn from public schools immediately." I'm so sorry, Mika.'

I slumped into a chair.

I considered myself to be both a Jew and a Pole, and Polish figures such as Chopin, the great composer, Copernicus and Madame Curie were heroes to me. Those daring scientists and artists had opened new frontiers, pushed into new territories, and I wanted to see myself following in their footsteps. Sitting in our old armchair, frozen with disbelief, I remembered when Grandpa had taken me to Madame Curie's house in the old town, and although we had not entered the Holy Cross church, it filled me with pride that Chopin's heart lay buried in our beautiful city. Having to leave school was a terrible blow. I was an excellent pupil, I loved school. Bolek and Henryk didn't care about school half as much as I did, but they were allowed to stay. Why? We had spent many afternoons playing games in the streets, Bolek even shared the same birthday with me.

Grandfather tried to comfort me and we spent long days together bent over his old books as he shared his love of mathematics with me. I soaked up his gentle voice, his knowledge and kindness. And algebra was indeed a soothing activity. Yet part of me couldn't accept his attitude of surrender – why did he not fight? He had been at the university for decades and was respected by all. So where were his colleagues now? Why was no one willing to stand up for him?

'I am old, Mika, you mustn't worry about me. But you, my boy, you still need to learn and your mother needs you,' he said, shaking his head. He had no answers and could only lay his hand on my shoulder, light as a bird.

*

17

Weeks passed after we received those directives that lay like a noose around our necks. We held our breath. But just as we began to absorb the shock of our limited world, more orders followed: the Germans wanted us clearly marked and labelled. All Jews had to wear white armbands with a blue Star of David, not less than six centimetres across, on our right sleeve. It had to be sewn on, clearly visible, and of course we had to produce the armbands ourselves. From now on it would always be like that: the Germans created laws, then forced us to make our own ropes to be hanged with. Sure enough, within days sellers waved the hateful armbands from every street corner.

Soon after that we had to register for 'Kennkarten', identity cards, stamped with a large J. J for JEW. How a single letter could change everything. We needed those cards to get our ration books, but our rations were meagre, a tiny fraction of those of the non-Jewish population. Two loaves for the German, one loaf for the Pole, a slice for the Jew. Mother's soups grew more watery by the day. We could not get milk or eggs and never any meat. Clearly the German master plan was to starve us, kilogram by kilogram.

To escape the biting hunger, many tried to get hold of Aryan Kennkarten, but if caught they would be dragged to the Pawiak prison. The rumours of torture and murder surrounding this monstrous fortress gave me such nightmares I'd wake up covered in sweat.

Just when we thought it couldn't get any worse, in October 1940 they gave us two weeks' notice to leave our flats, and most of our belongings, and move into a tiny part of the city that the Germans called the *Jüdische Wohnbezirk*, the Jewish Residential District. The word 'ghetto' was taboo, but whispers ran like wildfire through our neighbourhood and we knew it was nothing more than a huge prison.

Imagine our panic and despair. You could smell fear everywhere, creeping like fog into our homes, hanging thick and sticky over us like a thunderstorm about to break. How could we all fit into this tiny area? There were nearly four hundred thousand of us – an ocean of people trying to fit into a pond, surrounded by a ten-foot-high wall, topped by barbed wire and broken glass.

On 31 October the Germans herded us into this small segment of the Warsaw map, its northernmost corner, bordered to the west by Okopowa Street and our old Jewish cemetery. It had always been a densely populated part of the city, and although many of the houses were proud three-storey buildings adorned with iron balconies, most of the streets were narrow and dark. The Germans had forced all non-Jews to leave the area to make space for us, and as we moved into the ghetto we were greeted by an eerie quietness.

Mama took a long time to sort out what to bring with us. I can still see her in our old flat, picking up this candleholder or that book, forced to choose between a pot and a picture frame. In the end she chose the most precious and the most practical things: a photo album, some books, the silver candleholders that had been a wedding present, two pots, clothes and bedding. She bundled them together and then we joined the march. Our little unit, our tiny family: Mama, Tatus and me.

We marched in silence, carrying our remaining possessions in battered suitcases and makeshift rucksacks on our back. People pulled carts or pushed prams filled with boxes, duvets, cushions and pots, some balancing their precious things on their heads. The streets were lined with Christian Poles, watching our exodus with curiosity or pity, and some with that particular grin the Germans call *Schadenfreude*: joy at the expense of others, less fortunate souls like ourselves. We Jews had so long been made into scapegoats, and the anti-Jewish propaganda with ugly bright posters that compared us to typhoid-bearing lice did the rest.

Most in our sad march kept their heads down. But why? I wanted to face those onlookers squarely even if my look of defiance and hatred was the only thing I could shoot at those who stood ready to take our flats and our belongings. I kept a lookout for Bolek and Henryk. They had not come to our apartment since I'd been expelled from school and now I couldn't see them anywhere. How could they turn against me, believe we were second-class citizens? Cowards. I balled my fists, but the memory of Bolek with his missing front tooth and crooked smile stabbed at my heart.

As we entered the ghetto from the eastern side at Nalewski Street I took a last look back. I was being forced not only to leave behind my friends and my school, but also memories of *chlopek*, hopscotch, *zoska* and the many other games we played, our picnics in Krasinski Park, outings to the lakes with Mama and Tatus, and our lovely apartment. As I entered the ghetto through the gate, I was stripped of my childhood and all I had held dear.

And yet, in a twisted way, we turned out to be much luckier than many. A former colleague of my grandfather was a member of the *Judenrat*, the Jewish Council, and he had found us an apartment that was halfway decent: a little flat on the first floor in Gęsia Street, the street of the goose. Number 19 – I tried to take it as a good sign as 19 May was my birthday.

While we settled into a flat with two bedrooms, many big families had only one room, or worse still, had to remain on the streets until a tiny space could be found for them. Sometimes there were nine people to a single room. We knew we were lucky, but shouldn't a big family have our space?

20

By 16 November the Germans had completed the wall and sealed the ghetto.

I was fourteen years old.

That's when the coat changed. Grandfather, who was not only an intelligent but also a very practical man, decided that if he were ever to be taken somewhere else – because to flee Warsaw was now out of the question – he would need his most precious belongings close to him. Pockets were a great solution: small, large, tiny, hidden in the depths of his coat. The first was a small pocket on the left side, level with his heart. A slit more than a visible pocket, but a pocket nevertheless – for his gold watch, the only thing he had left of his father's. Over time he added more and more pockets: a very deep one on the inside, over his liver, for photographs: my father as a boy and the ones of him proudly holding his baby, me, my mother's face glowing with the broadest smile. Pictures I asked to see again and again.

I missed my father badly, especially in those dark, biting winter nights during that first ghetto year. A toddler, only three years old, I didn't remember my father's death. Mama said I played with my toys while he was dying in the next room from pneumonia, falsely diagnosed.

'The doctor thought your father had a cold and a bladder infection,' she once told me when I asked her many years ago. 'He died within a few days, burnt up like cinders.'

I know she never forgave the doctor, nor herself.

'He would have lived if we'd taken him to the hospital. After he died you stopped talking and clung to your battered red toy train day and night,' she said. The train had been his last gift to me.

By now memories of my father had faded and all that remained were traces of smells and sound: a sharp-smelling soap, sweat, tobacco and what I later recognised

21

as a whiff of alcohol mixed with a deep, gentle voice that quieted me to sleep, 'my good boy, sleep now', a faint memory hidden in my body that I tried to visit as often as I could. I longed for my father's presence, the safety of those embracing smells. By the time I inherited the coat, nothing felt safe any more.

Grandfather added pocket after pocket to his grand coat and one day he thought of creating tiny pockets within the pockets. Then, even if one pocket was searched, they wouldn't find those extra layers. Slowly his coat became a huge labyrinth: this pocket connected to that, but not this one; here was a dead end and this one led from left to right.

While people risked their lives for false passports or dug tunnels between the ghetto and other parts of the city, Grandfather found increasingly clever ways to put more pockets in his coat, until only he knew his way around. He selected his favourite books and added them to the seams. An extra pair of underwear tucked underneath the right side. A second pair of glasses, cufflinks and handkerchiefs on the left.

He wore his coat with pride, and as time passed and the situation grew worse around us, when the weight dropped off us because of our meagre diet, I sometimes thought the coat was the only thing that still held him together.

He spent more and more time in his little workshop, which he kept private from Mother and me. It was really only the apartment's walk-in larder and not much bigger than a large cupboard, but he called it his 'refuge'. I asked him many times what he was up to in there, but he simply smiled, and said nothing.

The coat and Grandfather were inseparable, a hand and a glove. Then in July 1941, two days before his seventy-third birthday, everything changed.

*

When I arrived on the street outside our house he was still alive. A neighbour had run up the stairs to fetch us, breathless and pale, her voice full of panic.

'They shot him, come, quick, quick!' Fear grabbed me like a steel vice. I remember a pause, a lingering nothingness in which I couldn't move. The neighbour could hardly get the words out, her chest heaving.

'He couldn't keep his mouth shut, it was that girl again. He couldn't take it, come quick.'

As gentle and private as he was, Grandfather couldn't remain quiet in the face of all the brutality surrounding us: people being kicked and spat at, hit, taunted, or worse – shot like dogs on the spot, as if it were a game. He refused to get used to the occupiers, to the daily unpredictable violence. That morning soldiers had again tormented the young woman in the house opposite ours. They had dragged her outside, held her at gunpoint and told her to strip. Grandfather was walking up to her, opening his coat, ready to wrap it around her to protect her, when they shot him. Just like that, at close range. My Tatus, the kindest man I knew.

The girl was gone by the time I arrived. Only later did I hear that she had screamed, scrambled for her clothes and then ran off. When I reached Grandfather and bent down his eyes opened slightly.

'Take care of the coat, Mika, my boy …' Barely a whisper. His eyelids sagged and his head fell sideways into my lap.

'Take him away,' one of the soldiers barked. He took another look at Grandfather and hesitated.

'Wait, that's a good coat, get that man out of his coat. Give it to me, boy.'

Then Mother moved. She had stood next to me, frozen like Lot's wife, a pillar of salt, holding my hand tightly. Suddenly she let go and started to wail and scream, throwing her hands up in the air and pounding them on her chest again and again. And as she did so, she inched away from Grandfather towards the other houses.

'*Halt's Maul*. Shut up, woman. Quiet,' the soldier shouted. She knocked at the first door.

'Stop that, you whore, or we'll shoot you!' She did not turn.

In the confusion and with help from the neighbours we eased Grandfather out of his coat. More people gathered. A group of men picked Tatus up and carried him towards the house, and then through the crowd I saw Nathan. I had no idea where he had appeared from, but the old tailor's bony hands quickly helped take the coat and put it on me. I felt stiff and lifeless, like one of Nathan's wooden dummies as I let him drape the coat around me.

It was the first time I had put on that coat. I had asked Grandfather before, but he had refused, saying, 'It brings bad luck, Mika, it is not your time yet.'

The coat's weight was incredible; I could hardly breathe with the weight of my grandfather's possessions around me, the weight of his life. But I needed to hurry, to run – to honour his last wish. The coat engulfed me like a warm, heavy being, and as if the coat had given me a surge of energy, I stumbled out of the soldier's sight and ran upstairs to our small apartment.

I collapsed among our brave neighbours, who risked everything by sheltering me. I was terrified for Mama and for a long time sat frozen and quiet in the kitchen, listening for shouts and heavy boots pounding up the stairs, for the dreaded gunshots, but there was only silence.

Mother came home much later, white as a sheet, dishevelled, supported by Anna, our neighbour. I ran up to her and hugged her fiercely, but her face didn't change. She stared at me from behind an empty, expressionless mask, gently pushing me away. She did not speak, but sat at the kitchen table for the rest of the afternoon, gazing at her trembling hands as if she wondered to whom they belonged. Anna sat with her and encouraged her to drink some tea; hot water with just a few tea leaves, already brewed for a second time. I had seen Mother out there in the street, heard the soldiers call her names, but to me she was a heroine.

Only later would I understand the nature of shame, the terrible things it can do to you. I left Mother sitting at the table and buried my fierce love for her and my grandfather deep inside the coat. I spread it out on the bed and lay down on top, searching for my grandfather's smell, for any trace of his life. But all I could feel were my tears and the rough wool against my cheeks.

That night I felt like a child and, at the same time, an old man.

We couldn't give Grandfather a funeral as we would have in the past, but I suppose we were lucky as Grandfather still got a small grave. Despite the fear that grabbed us when we gathered in public in the Jewish cemetery, quite a few people turned up to bid him farewell. I carried the simple coffin with Nathan the tailor, a neighbour and two of Grandfather's former colleagues from the university who had also been sent to the ghetto. The sun burnt down on us on that July day but I insisted on wearing Grandfather's coat and sweat ran down my neck as we carried the coffin to the old cemetery on Okopowa Street. The men from Hevra Kadisha, the burial society, had wrapped Grandfather in a white shroud and he was buried with his old prayer shawl.

It all happened so quickly – forty-eight hours is so little time to say goodbye. As the rabbi said prayers I stood stock still like the knotted trees in the cemetery, looking at the open grave as if through a veil or a sheet of smoky glass. A few people threw a shovelful of earth on my dearest Tatus's coffin, but when it was my turn it broke me. Mama put her arms around me but I trembled and sobbed, inconsolable.

Months later no proper graves remained: instead the dead were left outside at night on the streets and collected each day, carried away on overflowing carts then thrown into a deep hole. There they would lie, nameless, in a mass grave, tangled up with everyone who had died on that same day.

3

I spent the days following Grandfather's death alone with the coat and its secrets. I lived in his tailored masterpiece, breathed its strong aroma, let it smother and hold me. I felt Grandfather's presence in its heavy and rough embrace and sat hidden in it for hours, the muffled world outside ceasing to exist. Mama let me be and I was grateful. She grieved in her own silent way.

But eventually my stomach rumbled and tightened. I hated myself for it, but a definite sharp pang of hunger gripped me, and so I explored the coat's pockets, hoping to find something edible without having to leave its protection. And as my hands searched their way through the pockets' labyrinth, many treasures slipped through my fingers: a wooden pipe, a pair of spectacles, a small book of poetry. I never knew Grandfather cared for such things. Pebbles, sticky sweets, a fountain pen and objects I could not make sense of, like a piece of fur, scraps of colourful fabric, a paper flower.

Suddenly my fingers touched a cool, curved surface with wire strings attached. I pulled it from the depth of the seams and through the tunnel of the sleeve. It was a perfectly formed little violin. I had never heard my grandfather play but here I held a miniature, built as if for a dwarf or as a child's precious toy. I carefully picked it up, pinched the strings and searched the coat for a bow. I found the bow in another small pocket, this time a slim vertical one, behind the row of buttons.

I spread the coat on the floor, sat down in the middle of it and tried my very first scratchings with the little bow. I imagined Grandfather's hands holding the tiny violin like a newborn, but the sounds I produced were far removed from music.

Later that afternoon I discovered another pocket around the height of the kidneys. Inside it were some letters. A small bundle, neatly tied with a light blue, silky ribbon. They were fragile and pale, as if written by a ghost, someone barely of this world. The ink had faded and the handwriting was barely legible. Slowly I pulled the ribbon, and the letters fell into my lap like moths.

That night, burning a precious candle, bent over the pages, I learned things that transformed everything I thought I had known about my grandfather and father. Grandfather not only had an aptitude for mathematics, but also for language – he wrote beautiful poetry. These were letters to his wife, the grandmother I had never met, written during the first big war. He poured his love and the pain of separation into images and metaphors, and although he hardly mentioned the war, the thin crumpled paper streaked with mud spoke of the horror and hardship of the trenches. He had filled the paper right to the edges with tiny scribbled words, aware of the same scarcity of paper we now experienced in the ghetto.

Grandmother in turn wrote sturdy prose, mainly about her boy, my father: disrupted school days, a knee cut open, and my father's insatiable thirst for adventure stories.

I read wide eyed, hungry to learn everything I could about my father. When the dark gave way to grey morning, I wrapped the letters up and hid them once more in the depths of the coat. Exhausted, I sneaked back to bed.

28

For weeks I left the house as little as possible and the coat became my second home, my cave, my quiet companion. Meanwhile the world outside grew increasingly desperate and hostile. The days when I played with Bolek and Henryk in our streets or in Krasinski Park had become a distant memory. The boy's life I had once lived lay shattered. I had no friends to fool around with and whenever Mother sent me for errands, to barter for something or to join a queue when a rumour sprang up about some fresh vegetables, I saw how terrible things had become: the stench, overcrowding and an overwhelming greyness threatened to swallow us whole.

From within the coat I observed the ghetto as if in a dream: who were these hordes of humans, dressed in dirty, torn rags, always running, pushing, shoving through crowds as if trying to reach the last train home? A grey mass of people mixed with rickshaws, the shouting drivers navigating their way through the chaos, and the occasional small horse-drawn carriage. The one overcrowded tram that still moved back and forth through the ghetto, a sad reminder of the past, carried troves of people hanging on to its sides like refugees on a boat. Instead of a number at the front the tram displayed the Star of David. It was the only line left for us to use.

In those early days everyone was flogging something: ragged street children sold the dreaded white armbands; women vendors squatted over tiny potatoes, carefully displayed in groups of four as if they were precious stones, competing with men who sold coarse brushes or other treasures; a bundle of shirts here, a coat, a precious pair of boots there. A young man guarded a baby carriage filled with books, while others sat on the ground selling whatever they could spare – a pot, a dress, tableware – hoping to bring home a few *zlotys* for bread, for some stinking dried fish or shrivelled vegetables.

Some shops were still open in the ghetto and the black market thrived. In fact, if you did have money you could still buy everything. There was even a sweet shop to taunt us. Beggars, thin as skeletons, squatted outside bakeries and grocers, stretching out their fragile arms, while inside the shop window displayed white bread, or even cakes. What had happened to us, to our beautiful city? People were starving right in front of our eyes, living corpses leaned against walls or simply sprawled on the ground, while passers-by tried to ignore their fate.

Some beggars played music, with a violin or small pipes. Old Marek, a man as huge as a bear with a wild grey beard, dragged around a whole little orchestra in a baby carriage. He always drew a small crowd, but very few *zlotys*.

Worst were the hordes of orphaned children sitting on the pavements, staring with their too-big eyes. They had even given up trying to steal anything. I tried not to look at them.

Then Mama started to build her gardens. After they locked us in, small ghetto gardens began to spring up everywhere. Defiant gardens, we should have called them, spaces where people grew flowers against all the odds, vegetables against despair.

You couldn't see them at first in the overwhelming greyness, but then they appeared everywhere: little patches of carefully tended earth, small cleared pieces of land, protected like babies. People traded seedlings and planted, watered, sheltered, even prayed over them. The 'Toporoal Society' encouraged agriculture and the little gardens managed to keep people alive that bit longer: a cabbage could feed a whole family for days and a few beets would keep you breathing for a while. At one point the former Skra sports stadium was transformed into one big field of cabbages – what use was sport now when we were all starving?

Mother insisted we create some window boxes. Grieving for Grandfather, she needed the earth more than anything to comfort her, to reassure her that life would continue. Slowly against the backdrop of the ghetto's greyness, beautiful flowers emerged. How did she manage to get those seedlings?

'I packed some seeds in October, when we had to decide what to take into the ghetto. Weren't they just as important as pots and pans?' she said when I asked.

After the window boxes Mother built a little garden on our balcony. I laughed at her: a garden on a balcony on the third floor? But she carried up bucket after bucket of soil from the back yard, slowly covering the stone floor with a nice thick bed of earth. And I didn't laugh a few months later when we had green salad and small red radishes to eat.

Word of my grandfather's death and of his pocket-coat spread fast, and soon many requests for alterations found their way to Nathan. He had brought his sewing machine into the ghetto, and night after night he worked in his tiny room in the next street, fitting the inside of coats, shirts and trousers with secret pockets to hold people's most precious things, the tokens of their lives.

One day as I was searching my way around the coat, fingering its secret passages, I grasped something unfamiliar and strange: hard, light and almost round, it sat nicely in my palm. Carefully I pulled it out and found myself staring into a face. A small head moulded from papier-mâché, boldly painted with huge eyes, red lips and flaxen hair. It looked so alive I wanted to kiss it.

My heart skipped a beat: of course, the storeroom! The

tiny larder Grandfather never allowed me in. Why didn't I think of it earlier? That same morning I had found a small key in a tiny pocket near the seam of the coat. I grabbed the head, fumbled for the key and ran to the little room. The key fitted perfectly and with barely a sound the door sprung open. When I switched on the light I gasped: an army of little people was staring back at me.

The tiny room was filled with puppets of all shapes, sizes and stages of completion: there was a king, a girl, a fool and many animals – a crocodile with half-painted teeth, a monkey, and a horse without a tail. Some puppets looked as if they were ready to jump off the shelf; others had limbs missing or no clothes at all. A string spanned the room, pegged with tiny legs and dangling arms, waiting to find the right owner.

Tiny clothes in the making lay spread on a small table, carefully sewn from scraps of fabric. I recognised my mother's apron fashioned into a girl's dress and one of our napkins transformed into a little shirt. The dusty room smelled sharply of varnish. A wooden shelf held small pots of paint and some dried-out brushes in a glass, and right at the back I glimpsed a painted stage, complete with velvet curtains.

And there, perched on a shelf, sat a prince. Wrapped in a crimson cloak, adorned with a piece of rabbit fur.

So, this had been Grandfather's secret. These little people, puppets of his own making, keeping him company. But why had he never shown them to me? Had he been preparing all this time for something special, an elaborate performance? And why had he put just this one unfinished puppet into his pocket?

The memory of a special afternoon with my grandfather only two months before, in May 1941, flooded back to me – the day of my fifteenth birthday when Grandfather took me out for a birthday treat. It was a warm sunny day, so welcome after a winter that had taken thousands of lives with its fierce cold claws, and we strolled along Leszno Street, called jokingly 'the Broadway of the ghetto'. It was not a glamorous street, but many places here still offered some entertainment, cafés spilling out piano music, a few small theatres, a cabaret and even a cinema. Posters plastered the walls everywhere, advertising concerts and shows in bold letters. Not only did the adverts paint some colour on the grey walls, but they also promised to take our minds off our terrible situation, if only for one afternoon.

Leszno Street offered a welcome respite from the overwhelming poverty all around us. You could see smiles on people's faces and the fast pace of passers-by stemmed for once from the anticipation of getting to a concert rather than from being chased by police or a race to be first in line when there was a delivery of vegetables. Of course, such amusement wasn't available to everyone, but some people still had money and better clothes; and although the white armband branded us all in the same way, the superior coats, hats and shoes of the rich gave away the distinctions that had always existed among us.

Mother had stayed at home so that Grandfather could take me on my treat. I soaked up the atmosphere and for a moment I forgot the emaciated bodies we had passed on the way that had become such a familiar sight all over the ghetto.

'I know exactly the thing for you Mika, come.' With this Grandfather led me into a café. I wanted to protest, had he not promised me a show? Then I saw at the far end of the room a poster announcing 'The Thief of Baghdad – a puppet play'.

Grandfather approached the woman behind the counter and to my embarrassment announced, 'This is my grandson, Mika. Please, the best tickets in the house for his birthday treat. *Mazel Tov!*' He smiled first at the woman and then at me.

'Of course. The play starts in one hour upstairs, I am sure he will enjoy it. Happy Birthday, Mika!'

I wasn't sure about this, was such a thing not meant for small children? After all, I was fifteen now, shouldn't he have taken me to a serious play? Grandfather and I sat next to each other in the café waiting, and although the lemonade we sipped tasted lovely I sighed with relief when the woman announced with the sharp sound of a bell that the performance would start in five minutes.

We ventured up the steep, narrow staircase with the small crowd that had gathered, and entered a tiny room with an even smaller stage. Every seat was filled. We sat as if in a living room, but with people we didn't know and no distractions other than the gold-rimmed, luxurious stage. The lights dimmed and the curtains opened to reveal the exotic world of Baghdad, an elaborately painted backdrop of mosques with crescent moons and colourful houses stretching out in front of a mountain range.

Then the puppets appeared: marionettes, moving swiftly and as if by magic, held on invisible strings by a puppeteer-master we could only imagine. The thief's world swept me away and I forgot all my reservations. I glanced at Grandfather and saw the sweetest of smiles on his face – for this short time all the terror and fear had left us. Grandfather laughed and sighed, clapped and bit his lip, as if he were the child on a birthday trip, absorbed by the magic unfolding in the tiny room above a café in Leszno Street, in the Warsaw ghetto, in Poland, in the spring of 1941. It was our last outing together.

Something in the corner of the workshop caught my eye, tearing me from my memories. On a table lay a piece of red velvet cut neatly into two pieces, the same fabric from which the splendid prince's cloak had been made. A tiny dress, with needle and thread still attached, as if Grandfather would return any minute, take up the needle and finish it.

But I was the one who sat and finished the tiny dress that afternoon. I chose arms, hands, legs and feet, attached them as best as I could and carefully sewed the head from the coat's pocket on to the puppet's delicate body.

I slid my hand underneath the dress and moved the whole puppet, its thin arms, legs and pretty head. Looking at me with her big, dark eyes, the puppet bowed to me.

'Hello, my boy, and what is your name? Pleased to meet you. I am Princess Sahara,' I said aloud.

And so began my apprenticeship with Grandfather's puppets.

4

I kept the secret of the puppets to myself and spent more and more time in the workshop. Mother didn't ask me what I was up to in there, and we hardly spoke. Maybe she even knew about the puppets, but grief had swallowed her whole as a lion would a lamb, and yet each evening she managed to cook us a soup from whatever she could buy or barter.

As I retreated into Grandfather's puppet world, the situation outside deteriorated further. Houses were marked with a large 'T' where typhoid had swept through street after street, and the ghetto overflowed with people dragging their few rescued belongings in search of a new place to settle. Many now flooded in from the countryside, their whispered stories full of a horror I couldn't imagine: whole villages massacred, everyone taken into the woods, a single woman surviving to tell the tale. I couldn't look at those refugees who had nothing but emptiness in their eyes.

Before the Germans invaded, we used to have a big apartment in the old town with high ceilings and a large balcony. Our ghetto flat was a mere quarter of the size. After Grandfather was shot I took his room – there was space only for a bed and a small wardrobe, but still it was mine. Three weeks later two families moved in with us.

The first were complete strangers who happened to knock on our door at a time when my mother, utterly exhausted from a day of chasing for food, couldn't resist the pleadings of strangers any more. They were the fifth family to knock on our door asking for refuge during the time it took Mama to prepare a thin soup. She quietly led them through the flat.

'Mika, please collect your things, you're staying with me,' she said, giving me a look that demanded I stay quiet and obey. I threw my few books and clothes on to Mother's bed. How dare she give them my room.

And so Marek, Diana and their three children – a baby boy and twin girls of four, Sara and Hannah, looka-likes with black plaits tied with huge pink bows – set up refuge, sharing my tiny room and bed. I refused to talk to them for some days and the crying of the baby kept me awake at night. Sometimes I heard the girls cry, too.

Then, just when I decided to be nice to the twins, more trouble arrived: this time in the form of my mother's sister Cara, who knocked on our door one afternoon with my two cousins, Ellie and Paul. I remembered them well from a summer we had spent together in the countryside near Cracow, some four years ago. Grandfather, Mother and I had taken a train and bus to meet them.

Back then, Ellie was a small, agile girl of eleven and her cheekiness had me in stitches. Paul, though, despite his six years, had an adult air of melancholy about him that I could make no sense of. Now I wonder whether, somehow, he already knew what lay in wait for him?

That sweltering summer we escaped the city to the lakes. While the adults sat on blankets sipping wine and lemonade, laying out a picnic of delicacies, we built a small wooden raft, dived, splashed and dunked each other. I swallowed lots of water, much more than anyone else, but we had such fun. In my cousin's company I felt part of a bigger something, alive and tingling with delight.

My uncle Samuel was still alive then. A watchmaker from a long line of craftsmen, he was a large man with a nice pair of gold spectacles, who shared a keen interest in astronomy with my grandpa. I overheard them exchanging new discoveries, pondering whether man would ever make it to the moon, while Cara and Mama put their heads together in sisterly fashion, laughing and giggling like children.

I remember saying goodbye – I stood stiff and formal, shaking hands with everyone, not wanting Ellie to see I would miss her. We promised to write but never did. A year later Ellie was fighting for her life. It started with a headache and a slight fever, before her legs turned to jelly, and after two days she couldn't walk any more. She found breathing difficult and so they rushed her to Cracow's children's hospital where she lay for weeks, pale and thin in a too-large bed, as if sculpted from wax. Polio, they called it.

Ellie fought hard and recovered, 'a tough girl, your cousin', my mother said, but we heard she had to use crutches for many months. With great willpower she got back on her feet, but her left leg was weak and so she limped. It would forever be weak, the doctors told her, but she was determined to prove them wrong.

The small girl of my memories disappeared and there in our tiny, dull ghetto apartment, in the summer of 1941, stood a feisty fifteen-year-old, holding a large brown suitcase that was battered and filled to bursting, and grinning at me from ear to ear. For a moment the smile exposed her excellent, straight teeth. I couldn't see any crutch or stick.

'Mika! How are you? You've grown so much.' She could talk – she had shot up like a beanstalk and was halfway between the girl of that hot summer at the Rosnowskie lakes and a fully fledged woman. I kept staring at her until she laughed.

'Cat got your tongue, Mika? It's me, Ellie, your cousin. Remember?'

'Of course, silly, come on in. You must be exhausted.'

She moved past me with her brother Paul in tow, who although tall for his ten years, looked pasty and as thin as a candlestick. Except for his constant coughing and a shy hello, he stayed silent. I sneaked a glimpse at Ellie's legs, which were sticking out from under her blue dress. Her left leg was slimmer than the right and lagged a little behind. Embarrassed, I looked away, glad that Ellie hadn't caught my eye.

Aunt Cara was just as thin as Paul but didn't cough. Her pale face, with bruise-like shadows under her eyes and a colourless mouth, showed the strain and exhaustion of trying to understand what had happened to her family and to the world – all our worlds.

The Germans had declared Cracow the capital of their *Generalgouvernement* early in 1940, planning a Jew-free city. Like all Jews from the city, my cousins and their parents were ordered to resettle and had moved to the countryside, not far from the lakes. Later, hunger drew them to Warsaw, in the futile hope that they could turn some of Samuel's watches into bread. They had tried to find us in the ghetto but without luck. And so, unbeknown to us, they had been living in a tiny room in Sliska Street for some months. So very close to us.

Two weeks earlier Uncle Samuel hadn't come home. The police arrested him for trading on the black market and had taken him to the Pawiak. And the previous day Ellie, Paul and my aunt had been thrown out of their room.

I overheard the story as Cara and Mother talked that first night.

'I haven't heard anything since they took him. I'm so scared, Halina.' It was strange, hearing my mother's name; even grandfather called her 'Mama'.

We had run out of space, so all three of them set up in the kitchen. Their arrival changed everything. I couldn't stop thinking about Ellie. She had grown so much, stood taller than me and was still full of life and adventure even in such a dire situation. The fire and cheekiness in her green eyes drew me in, butterflies fluttered in my stomach, but if I drew near to this fire, would I be burned? At first, I tried to ignore her.

Once they had settled in, we could see that Paul was terribly sick. He lay in bed most of the time, listless and pale as chalk. No one slept well as his coughing cut the night into shreds.

I stole away early in the morning to the workshop, always locking the door from inside. I longed to be in the quiet world of my puppets, at least for a while, where I could fight my fights, find love and a little peace.

It was Ellie who caught me in the end. She cornered me as I sneaked out of the bedroom one morning. She grabbed at my sleeve and stared at me with her magnificent eyes. I knew she meant business but she smiled. God, I loved that broad smile.

'Where are you going, Mika? What's the big secret?'

'Nothing, no secret, I just need some space.'

'Aha, the young man needs space. Come on, Mika, let me in, I'm dying of boredom here.'

I don't think it was the tiny piece of chocolate Ellie offered me that made me give away my secret, but the sudden realisation of how lonely I felt. Although used to playing on my own, growing up among adults, to see the twins play, fight and giggle with each other and observe how gently Ellie cared for her brother left me with a deep yearning. Also, I had only two hands and had grown bored of the same repeating scenarios of two puppets meeting on the little stage. Always two: the king and the girl, the prince and the crocodile, the fool and the horse.

I decided to let Ellie into my world.

'Close your eyes.' I took her hand and cautiously she set foot in the dark workshop. I switched on the light.

'Mika, this is amazing! I thought you were building toy trains, but these are beautiful. Look at that one.' She grabbed the princess, slipped her hand under the puppet's skirt and into her limbs and pranced her around the stage.

'Hello, my boy, why don't you bow your head in front of me, the Princess of Thebes?' she said, addressing me.

'Actually, she is called Princess Sahara.'

'All right. Look at the donkey, it's so cute.'

For a moment I felt a surge of happiness spreading through my body. Ellie was so charmed by my puppets. And so, from then on, every play included two important protagonists: Princess Sahara and the donkey, operated by Ellie, while I took charge of all the other puppets. A perfect four-handed duo was born and there was no turning back.

From then on endless opportunities opened up for us, and for the first time since they had locked us in the ghetto, I felt happy. We laughed, giggled and fought in this tiny, dusty workshop. I let Ellie into the coat's secrets too, and Grandfather's coat sheltered us both, the puppets' company helping us forget the adult world for a while. A world where people created ugly things; like a ghetto for Jews. A world we couldn't understand.

We were an industrious workshop, and Ellie and I spent hours in that little space, building ships and whole forests from papier-mâché, painting landscapes with castles and rivers and stitching tiny costumes from any bits of fabric we could lay our hands on, asking our mothers for yet another handkerchief or napkin. We created more puppets for our troupe – pirates and bandits, a doctor – and let the fool play the tiny violin. Then Kaninkudum, the villain from the deep forest, appeared. His speciality was to kidnap the princess, holding her hostage in the crocodile's den until the prince – ta-dah – helped by the fool and the donkey, came to her rescue.

We fought battle over battle on that little stage and I even got my first kiss. Well, it was the doctor, played by me, who won the princess's heart, while the monkey applauded.

In March, the twins' birthday approached. Through our thin walls I heard them pleading with their parents for chocolate on their big day, followed by muffled sobbing and whispers from the parents. The next morning I took Ellie's hand and pulled her into our secret room.

'Ellie, let's put on a special birthday performance for the twins, they've nothing for their birthday. They can be our guests of honour. What do you think?' She was on fire too and so we wrote invitations, bordered with gold paint, proudly handing them out an hour later. The surprise on the twins' faces warmed my heart, and even Paul, who struggled more every day, smiled broadly. Tatus would have been proud. We invited the neighbours too, and that afternoon Mother took me to one side.

'So, this is what you've been up to all this time? You clever, secretive boy.'

She wrapped me in a big hug and we stood there laughing.

The day before the performance we mixed papier-mâché and created a second girl puppet so there would be a pair of twins in our show. We excused ourselves for rehearsals for the rest of the day, and slowly, in the sheltered dark of the workshop, the play took shape. We quarrelled a lot over the plot but in the end it worked itself out.

The big day arrived. We chose the kitchen as our theatre and, with flushed faces, running around like weasels, we laid out as many chairs and boxes as we could find. The stage with its red velvet curtains sat on the kitchen table and I wore Grandfather's coat, sheltering all our precious puppets as they waited impatiently for their big entrance. The room was then plunged into darkness except for two dim lamps illuminating the stage. Ellie crouched behind the curtains. I took a deep breath and stepped forward.

'Ladies and gentlemen, welcome to the first ever performance of *The Trials and Triumphs of Polly and Holly* – a two-act play in honour of our special guests Hannah and Sara! Happy Birthday. Enjoy the show.'

Much clapping, then silence. You really could have heard a pin drop. I dived behind the set and pulled the curtain. I could hardly make out Ellie's face but I could smell her: spicy with a hint of lavender. Her arm brushed lightly against mine like a cat's tail. A swarm of butterflies took flight in my stomach.

I slipped my hand into the crocodile's body. Ellie made the twin puppets prance around the stage in a sisterly game. Soon we heard giggles, shouts and clapping. Then Hannah shrieked as the crocodile snapped its sharp wooden teeth, then picked up the puppet-twins by their necks and dragged them away. When I stole a glimpse at the audience, Sara was biting her little fists.

What an adventure: we sent the puppet-twins downriver on a raft, into the desert, hid them in a bird's nest on top of the highest mountain before the Witch of the North took them prisoner and held them in an igloo. But, in the end, they arrived safely back home, helped by the

43

prince and the monkey, and holding a basket with magical treasures they had gathered on their travels: a flower that never withered and granted everlasting happiness; an eagle's feather which bestowed on the bearer the gift of flying; and an icicle that would never melt and shone brighter than the brightest light.

We closed the curtain, then stepped forward and bowed, Ellie's hand held tightly in mine, warm and sweaty. I'm pretty sure I saw a tear roll down Mother's cheek but the twins ran up to us, grabbing the pigeon feather, the flower – a gift from my mother's window box – and the handkerchief icicle.

We held on to the magic of that afternoon like a precious jewel, but it wouldn't be long before our small joy was shattered.

A few days later Paul's coughing got worse; it was now a continuous hacking that cut day and night into fearful ribbons for us all. I felt my own chest hurting as I listened to Paul's struggle day in and out. Aunt Cara tried everything to get nourishing food and medicine on the black market, but she could find hardly anything. She even sold her wedding dress for a tiny bottle of some dubious syrup, but Paul still grew thinner and paler every day, fading away in front of our eyes. In despair Aunt Cara took him to the hospital, but the nurses sent them away. Children more poorly than Paul had already taken all the beds, they said.

The only medicine left was our puppets, and Paul asked us again and again to bring out the villain and the fool. And so we did, playing for Paul and the twins, and sometimes Cara and Mother joined us for a while.

One morning I woke early. I turned and saw Mother sitting upright on the edge of the bed. I could see the tension in her back – tight as a bow ready to fire off an arrow.

As if she sensed my waking, she turned to face me. Her eyes were bloodshot.

'It's Paul, Mika … He's gone. He died in the night. I didn't want to wake you.' She turned away and put her head in her hands.

It would have been his birthday next week. There were no sounds from the kitchen.

'What is happening, Mika? What are they doing to us?' I stayed silent – there was nothing I could possibly say. I wanted to see Ellie, comfort her, hold her hand, and yet I dreaded it too. She must have been with Paul, right beside him, all through his last night. They slept on field beds next to each other. Her dear little brother. I did not want to think of him in the same way as the many corpses I had seen in the streets of the ghetto. This was Paul, our Paul.

I think he knew he was dying. About a week before, after yet another puppet show, Ellie had gone to put back the puppets and for a brief moment we were alone.

'You have a gift, Mika. You must play for all the children in the ghetto. When I'm gone I hope I can join you – in spirit, I mean. Maybe I can become a puppet, one of your troupe, the fool perhaps or the knight.'

'Don't be silly, Paul. You're getting better. And when you're stronger you can help me, be a second puppeteer if you like. Now you should rest, I think we've exhausted you.' That was the last conversation we had alone.

For the next days life in our household was suspended. We huddled together in the kitchen like cattle in thick fog, frightened to take another step. Everyone caught in their own world. In the end I didn't find words to say to Ellie but simply hugged her, and she let me. I also hugged Aunt Cara, so stiff she didn't move an inch – embracing a tree would have felt softer. When we returned from the funeral with the rabbi, everyone gathered around the kitchen table. Ellie pulled at my sleeve and whispered, 'Let's get the puppets. Paul wouldn't want us to sit and cry into our tea. Let's put on his favourite show.'

And so, there and then in our kitchen, we put on a silly show for Paul. I did not tell Ellie what Paul had said, but I could barely handle the fool. He wanted to be at the forefront of every scene from beginning to end, to rescue and kiss the princess, fight the dangerous magician, and at the end he bowed five times in front of our little audience.

Ellie changed after Paul's death. The confident and chatty girl vanished and instead she spent all day sitting in our only armchair, which she claimed as her new home, poring over her books, particularly *The Arabian Nights*, reading all thousand and one tales. She hardly spoke. Only when I could persuade her to join me and the puppets, tucked behind the small stage, did Ellie come alive again.

And so we continued: the puppets were our companions, and although our hands animated them, they also had their own lives – and we were amazed at some of the wisdom that tumbled from their mouths.

Word spread quickly about us and soon our neighbours approached us with requests for birthdays, bar mitzvahs, and any other special occasion they could think of. I think Ellie continued for the sake of her brother, because the moment she heard we had another request, she would put her book down and lift herself out of the chair.

'OK, let's go and rehearse, we should think about a new play. What's the occasion this time?'

We usually returned with small gifts: pencils, handkerchiefs or even some bread. But once we were home, Ellie would slump back into her armchair, open her book and, like a diver jumping into deep water, disappear somewhere I could not reach her.

Then, all of a sudden, people from other parts of the ghetto began to drop by our apartment. They knocked at the large front door, and when one of us stuck our head out of the window, they shouted, 'We want to speak to the puppeteer, we've an engagement for you.'

I would put on my most professional voice, deep and a bit hoarse, then rush down and lead them into our flat for further negotiations. My adolescent voice tumbled like a roller coaster, high and crystal clear one day, dropping to a husky, rough sound another. It was a most unreliable instrument, but I had great fun lending the villains my deepest, meanest tones, and the fool my highest pitch.

We sat at the kitchen table and bartered: a puppet show with at least five characters for half a loaf of rye bread. For a second show we would request something special: some butter, an egg or fresh vegetables. Very few could offer those things but we always managed to bring home at least some bread and sometimes, just sometimes, a little more.

One morning, exactly four weeks after Paul's death, I found a note that had been slipped through the front door.

'Dear Puppeteer. We have heard of your wonders and would like to invite you to put on a puppet show for our dear son's birthday. We can provide jam and some sugar as payment.

Yours truly, Marek Wonderblum

I rushed upstairs, assembled everyone in the kitchen and passed the slightly crumpled note around. When it reached Mother she didn't smile.

'Look at the address; it's in the small ghetto. I've heard it's even more squalid and overcrowded there.'

The Germans had divided the ghetto into two parts:

the biggest in the north-west of the city, and the 'small ghetto' to the south. They didn't want to lose Chlodna Street to us and so they built a small wooden bridge between the two parts.

'I'm not sure, Mika, what if it's a trap? Why did the person who delivered this not knock? What if they are an informer?'

We heard many stories about informers these days, traitors selling their soul for a bit of bread, some extra privileges. Yes, we needed to be careful, but this invitation did not smell of such things to me.

'Mother, they are promising us sugar and jam. When was the last time you tasted something sweet?'

She looked away.

'I have to go, Mama.'

'I'm coming too,' Ellie said, rising from her chair.

'That's absolutely out of the question. Ellie is staying here,' Aunt Cara intervened. Something had hardened in her since Paul's death. I don't think she had even cried over him; instead she shuffled around the rooms as if she were wearing an old, heavy suit of armour. Also we still had no news about my uncle. Cara often made it all the way to the Pawiak, only to be turned away.

Ellie said nothing. She knew she couldn't argue with her mother. She slumped back into her chair, picked up her heavy book and disappeared into her world of stories, as if nothing else mattered.

5

I left our apartment early the next day. Wrapped in Grandfather's coat, I reached deep into its pockets for the comforting presence of the puppets. I had decided not to bring the stage or many props – this time the coat itself would be the stage.

On the surface I looked like any other boy, but emboldened by the coat, I strode along at a good pace, ready for my hero's journey through the ghetto. What evil could possibly penetrate my magical coat?

I stepped out into the road and moved swiftly along Gęsia Street. With my mind occupied by thoughts about Ellie and the puppets, I had not noticed how much worse the ghetto had become in the past months. Like our flat, the ghetto was bursting at the seams. There had never been enough space, but now I passed whole families sitting on the pavement, a piece of rug with suitcases on either side marking their small territory like islands. Many, wrapped in rags, begged with thin voices, stretching out their bony hands. Even our puppets were better dressed. And the closer I got to the 'small ghetto', the worse it got: not only were there hundreds of beggars lining the roads, but emaciated corpses lay on pavements or in gutters, flimsily covered with newspaper, or half naked and exposed, many barefoot. Shoes, like bread and warm clothes, were among the most precious items in the ghetto. The dead did not need shoes any more, but no one should have to enter the otherworld barefoot. I counted five corpses on my way, two of them children, maybe not older than six years old.

I reached the wooden bridge connecting the large and small ghettos. When I got to the middle, I stopped. It was forbidden, but I couldn't prevent myself from letting my eyes drift over our lost city – this was the only place where we could see beyond the ghetto, down into Chlodna Street, where trams filled with Christian Poles went right through our ghetto. Chlodna Street was so close and yet unreachable. I rushed on.

When I turned into Krochmalna Street, I saw a thin arm sticking out from under some newspaper like a dry branch. My stomach heaved and I began to run as fast as I could. What would happen to all these people? Would anyone throw a hand full of earth on their graves, speak some kind words? Or would they end up in a hole, thrown in with other bodies, covered with chalk, no one even remembering their names?

Every evening we saw the sad wooden carts trundling through the ghetto, pulled by a few thin men, who picked up the corpses and tossed them into the carts like empty sacks. During the daytime, the bodies lay where they had died, passers-by stepping around and over them. Just another obstacle, one more annoying feature of ghetto life. What had we become?

Chilled to the bone, I pulled my coat closer. Crowds gathered around small fires, others stood in long queues, waiting for a ladle of soup from the soup kitchens that had sprung up everywhere. The soups were thin and no one was fed properly, but for a moment, an hour maybe, it soothed the nagging hunger, kept the wild, raging animal at bay.

And so many children! Dressed in filthy rags, barefoot with matted hair, a crust of dirt covering their small faces, they sat listlessly next to their parents, or worse still, huddled together: clusters of lost souls with round, glassy eyes. Such large eyes in such small faces. I didn't want to look any more. My hand reached for the prince, who lay safely buried inside the coat's pockets.

The stench of misery and despair was everywhere: a mixture of cabbage, dirt, sewage and death; the smell of imprisoned crowds, thrown together with no escape.

I pulled up the collar of my coat and covered my nose. What could I do anyway with my silly puppet shows? Shouldn't I be helping in one of the soup kitchens instead, doing something useful? I tried to pass by like a blinkered horse, but even blindfold it would have been impossible to blank out the stench and the sounds: the beggar's pleading cries, the soft moaning of those too weak to stand, people dying right in front of me, a pedlar's desperate voice trying to sell his last treasures; a lifetime's belongings for the price of a loaf of bread.

I was nearing the end of Sliska Street, just around the corner from the address scribbled on my invitation, when a small bundle caught my eye: wrapped in dirty rags, it was moving from doorway to doorway like a nervous dog, rummaging for food. I approached the figure, but before I could say anything, it flew at me, hissing and growling, followed by a shriek and a flapping of small arms.

'Go away, leave me alone!' A tiny girl stared at me with big, glassy eyes and a wolf's determination. She must have been about five.

'OK, OK, don't be frightened,' I tried to reassure her. I stood still for a moment, and then reached into my left pocket. Very slowly, so as not to startle her, bring on another scream or, worse still, a bite, I pulled out the princess.

'Oh!' She stood stock still, her tiny hands covering her mouth.

'Hello, little girl, what is your name?' Princess Sahara spoke softly.

'Hannah.'

'And what are you doing here all on your own, Hannah?'

'Oh, just looking.'

'But what are you looking for, my dear?'

She hesitated for a moment, suspicious. 'Nothing.'

'Do you want me to help you look? I have very sharp eyes. I can see into houses and inside people's hearts.'

'Oh, I don't know ... maybe.'

'Maybe I can find someone else who can help us look.' With my right hand I pulled out the monkey. For a moment she stared, and then something changed in the girl's face: the subtle beginnings of a smile.

The monkey jumped on to her arm, 'I want to help too! Where shall we look? What are we looking for?'

'My brother, I lost him.' Now words tumbled out of her mouth like marbles.

'What does he look like?'

'Like me, but bigger.'

'How much bigger?'

She put her hand above her head as far as she could reach.

'And what's his name?'

'Janusz, like the man I live with now.'

'And when did you last see your brother?' I asked, bending down to match her size.

'I don't know, a while ago.'

'And your mother and father?' Silence. The girl's face clouded over and she retreated back inside herself. I let the princess take her hand.

'Hannah, do you want to come with me and see a puppet show? Afterwards we can look for your brother.' The girl didn't answer but started to walk alongside me. It was a start, and I had a plan.

'Usually a friend of mine, Ellie, helps me. But today she couldn't come. I really could do with a little help with the puppets, could you do that?' Big eyes again and then a faint nod. I gave Hannah the monkey and the princess and she tucked them carefully into her clothes.

I found the right house and rang the bell. Number nine Sienna Street. A head popped out of a window above.

'We're here for the puppet show.'

The door opened with a click and we slipped in. A man with a smile like a summer's day greeted us. I felt a sharp pang in my heart, remembering my Tatus. The man led us into a dimly lit living room where some chairs were laid out, all facing in one direction, ready for our show.

I felt awkward without the usual stage, but I draped the coat over two chairs and told Hannah to hide behind it, together with the princess and the monkey.

The room filled, and the cheerful father who had sent the invitation sat down next to his son, the birthday boy of nine, who was right in front of us.

I announced the show, then ducked down behind the coat and whispered to Hannah to start. She reached up and pushed the princess over the edge of the coat, bouncing her up and down as if she were promenading with a spring in her step. The monkey joined her and the two began a game of hide and seek, accompanied by some silly babble. Hannah clearly had talent.

Then, with a loud clatter, one of my favourite sound effects – a pot-lid crashing to the floor – I produced the villain, who abducted the princess, leaving a shrieking Hannah and a jumping monkey. What a tumultuous play it was: one minute it looked as if the prince, the doctor and the fool would win, then the villain took over again; but in the end it was the fool who rescued the princess in front of an enthusiastic audience.

Hannah beamed as she bowed with me, and even more so when the man handed me a small pouch of sugar and a jar of strawberry jam.

We left the house, and when we were out of sight, I carefully rolled back the cellophane and opened the jar. A long-forgotten smell greeted us: sweet and full, a whole happy summer in a jar.

'Come, Hannah, have a scoop.'

In a flash she transformed once more into the shy girl I had met a few hours earlier.

'It's OK, Hannah, you deserve it, you helped me out.' I smiled at her and held the jar in front of her nose.

She stuck her tiny finger into the jam and left it there for a moment, not quite sure whether to trust this delicious, sticky substance. Was it a trick? Maybe it wasn't jam at all?

Then she bent her finger, pulled it out and quickly put it into her mouth. She could not hide her pleasure – it was everything it had promised to be.

By now the light had faded; and it was not long until curfew.

'Let me take you home.'

'But my brother ... you promised.'

'We can look for him on the way.'

I took her tiny hand in mine – it weighed almost nothing, was as light and thin as a bird's wing – and she guided me swiftly through labyrinthine backstreets until the road opened out in front of a large, three-storey building – a benevolent, whitewashed creature with too many eyes and a large mouth for an entrance.

'You live here?'

Hannah nodded.

'Yes, and a lot of other children do too.' Pride shone in her voice. She let go of my hand, stepped on to the porch and rang the bell. We could hear its sound echo deep inside the house. Quick running steps, then the door was flung open.

'Hannah! Where have you been? We thought we'd lost you.'

A woman, her flushed face in contrast to her white, starched uniform, a pair of round golden spectacles framing her thin face, scooped Hannah up and lifted her over the threshold. Her delight at seeing Hannah made me smile and she embraced her like a long-lost treasure.

Only then did she notice me.

'And who are you, young man?'

'He is a puppet player.' Hannah was hopping up and down with excitement, her dark curls bouncing. 'I helped him. He's called Mika.'

'What kind of a place is this?' I asked.

'It's an orphanage, dear, and Hannah here is one of our little ones. Would you like to come in? Now that you have brought back our angel we at least owe you some tea.'

And so Margaret, the matron of the orphanage, introduced herself. Very soon a group of children of various sizes, all mouths and tiny hands pulling at my coat, surrounded me.

'Show us the puppets, we want to see them, please,' they shouted.

Standing there in the middle of this shrieking audience, I made up a magic show as the puppets had learned some brilliant tricks by this time. From the pockets' maze I pulled a paper flower, a tiny rabbit I made from the rest of the fur, and the small violin. And for the first time in a very long while, surrounded by this sea of screeching,

55

grabbing children, I felt happy. Hannah giggled and laughed, and when the monkey chased the crocodile she poked her neighbour, saying, 'That's my monkey, I played the monkey!'

At the end of the show the children begged me to be allowed to hold the puppets and so I handed them over one by one. All hell broke loose as the puppets were released: stuck on tiny hands they hopped, shrieked, giggled and chased one another; hitting and hugging, clinging together in small crowds, taking off again to find new companions.

As I moved slowly out of the centre of this wild spectacle, I noticed an older man with a neatly trimmed white beard, leaning against the wall in the corner of the hall, smiling. He stepped forward and stretched out his hand to greet me.

'Hello, my boy, and thank you, what a wonderful performance. The children here have so little but today they have been able to forget everything for a while. I can't thank you enough. What is your name?' His voice was deep and warm like a cello and his smile stretched all the way to his eyes.

'I'm Mika. Children always love the puppets. And who are you, sir?'

'Janusz – Janusz Korczak. Nice to meet you, Mika. I've been looking after the children for some years now but the orphanage has grown so much since they packed us into the ghetto, especially over the last few months. We're completely full already, but how can we possibly turn away a child who comes knocking on our door? We don't have enough food to feed all these little mouths.'

His smile faded and I could see how strained he looked. He shook his head.

'But let me show you around, Mika, so you get an idea of what we are doing here.'

While the children continued to play with the puppets, Janusz led me through the large building. Everything appeared so clean and ordered, it even smelled clean, but my heart dropped with every floor – so many children and so few things to play with. The rooms were packed with simple beds squeezed next to each other and the pictures on the walls were the only spots of colour. A few wooden toys lay scattered among the furniture and there was a small wood burner in the middle of each room. Janusz showed me a classroom: about fifty small wooden desks all crammed into one large space.

'We make do with whatever we can get. The children are happy here, but they are always hungry and it is getting more and more difficult every day. We have over two hundred little ones now.'

He took off his glasses and rubbed his eyes. He seemed tired, worn out.

'You know, Mika, they still want to learn. I'm sure you do too. They are so curious about life. The Germans have taken everything from us, but we will still teach them and be a family as best we can.'

My throat tightened and tears threatened to force themselves from my eyes. I admired this man. Later he became so famous – Janusz Korczak – but even then I could see what a special person he was. Slowly we made our way back to the entrance hall.

From a distance I watched the crowd of children playing with the puppets. It hit me how desperately thin and pale they all were. And although the children and the puppets animated each other for a short while, lending each other colour and joy, when I began to collect the puppets, the spark and colour disappeared, until it seemed as though I were looking at an old, faded photograph. I had to leave.

'I'll come back soon, I promise.' I hugged Hannah,

who clung to me, her little hands grabbing my coat as if it were a lifebuoy at high sea.

'I promise, Hannah.'

Carefully I loosened her grip and slipped out into the evening, rushing back towards our apartment. I would not make it before curfew. What if I was caught? I wrapped my coat tightly around me, pretending it would make me invisible. But that evening I was lucky and did not encounter any police or soldiers.

I was dying to tell Ellie what had happened, but when I returned she completely ignored me, and kept reading her book. So I ended up with Mother in our bedroom, drinking weak tea as I told her about Janusz and his orphanage, Margaret the matron, and the overcrowded conditions in the small ghetto.

She listened with an occasional sigh.

'I'm proud of you, Mika. You made them happy for a while.' She looked away and I heard a muffled sob. 'Your father would've been so proud.'

'Proud of what?' A huge wave of helpless anger rose in me like boiling water. 'Performing a few tricks with papier-mâché puppets while thousands slowly starve? What is there to be proud of?'

I stormed out and hid in the corner of the workshop. Mother's praise made it all the worse. We had just about enough to keep us alive with the extra rations that the puppets earned, and even then we were hungry all the time. But what about all the people I had seen that day on the streets? What about the orphans? What good could my silly puppets do them? And Ellie? What was the matter with her? Had she stopped caring? I flung the coat away from me and buried my head in my elbows. I missed Grandfather, and yes, I missed my father, a strong male presence who would absolve me from this new responsibility that hung like a lead weight on my back and chest. I needed someone else to take over, or at least tell me what to do.

I lay down on the floor and stared at the ceiling, keeping my eyes open to hold back the tears. Suddenly a flash of colour caught my eye where the coat was heaped like a shot animal. The prince. I got up slowly and slipped my hand underneath the fabric.

'So you want to give up?' The prince's fine, silvery voice startled me.

'Well, it's no use, is it? You puppets can't feed these children or get us out of here, all you can do is make them forget their misery for a while.'

'But you know that's not true. It's precious what you do. Didn't you see, they actually laughed?'

'True, but what use is laughter? You can't bite off a piece of laughter and eat it, can you? Maybe we should fight, get some guns and shoot them all: the soldiers, the corrupt police. We are slowly starving to death here and they simply watch us, they don't even need to do anything else. And you know what they did to Grandfather. So what if I make us forget all this for a while? Maybe that's not a good thing after all, maybe it would be better if I told everyone to take up weapons, do something instead?'

'Well, I never said you couldn't!'

'What did you say?' A pause.

'I never said you couldn't tell them to fight.' And with that, the prince bowed and stopped talking.

I was in shock. Where did all that come from? I had heard murmurs about people, fighters hiding in the woods, blowing up railway tracks, shooting soldiers and informers. People who risked their lives: forging papers, smuggling others out of the ghetto and hiding them on the Aryan side, right in the lion's den. There were rumours too that some people in the ghetto were gathering weapons for an even greater fight.

59

I looked at the prince with his innocent smile, then dragged myself back to our bedroom. I lay awake, too excited and terrified to give myself over to sleep. Mother was still with Cara and Ellie in the kitchen, and when she came to bed I pretended to be asleep.

'Sleep well, my prince.' Her hand stroked my face, light as a feather. Little did she know what a can of worms this prince had just opened. I wanted to sling my arms around her neck and tell her everything, but I didn't move.

That night images passed in front of my eyes like clouds flying across a stormy sky. There I was, shooting a pistol from a hiding place, aiming perfectly, policemen and soldiers falling like tin cans at a funfair. Applause all around me, thundering like hail. But then, as I bowed, black fur, snouts and claws surrounded me: the soldiers had morphed into giant rats, their small ears sticking out from under large iron helmets. Scurrying up the staircase, they kicked down the door to our flat, dragged me outside and ripped my coat to shreds with their long claws. Then they beat me to a pulp, leaving me to die on the cobbled streets of the ghetto.

All night my mind wandered between these scenarios, hero and victim, as I slipped in and out of a light sleep.

By the time the subtle grey of morning illuminated our room, I was completely worn out, but also changed. I glanced at Mother, who was still asleep, sheltered for a short while from all the worry and fear.

There was such tenderness in her face and she seemed so young. She meant so much to me and I had hardly paid her any attention in all these months, yet it was Mother who held everything together. It was she who managed to put a pot of soup on the table each day and kept our clothes as clean as they could be. She kept my spirit from freezing over so my heart wouldn't become like the frozen lakes in Krasinski Park. We used to skate on those lakes not so long ago. Right there on the other side of the wall lay Krasinksi Park with its lakes and amusements – unreachable for us now.

Mother was gentle, but also very brave – she had soldiered on with a broken heart after Father died, never complaining. And she had risked her life to honour Grandfather's last wish – that I should have the coat. I pulled the prince from the coat's pocket and put the colourful puppet with its rabbit-fur trim next to her face so it would be the first thing she saw when she woke.

Later that day I found the prince back in my pocket with a note wrapped around it.

'Thank you, my dear; I will always cherish you, my prince.'

After that night of restlessness and visions I realised just how much the puppets infused me with energy, purpose and even morsels of joy – gold nuggets in the dark chaos of the ghetto. From that day I didn't go out without my coat and the puppets and slowly a plan grew in me like a seed germinating in the dark, a seed that instinctively knows that some day it will break through into the sun and grow to its true size.

Over time, I got more and more invitations to put on shows, and one day, nine months after my last outing with Grandfather to Leszno Street, a note came through the door from the very same puppet theatre where I had seen my first show. I ran straight into the kitchen.

'Ellie, they want us to play at the puppet theatre. I can't believe it. It's such a sweet little place. I'd love you to help me.' For a moment I forgot my usual shyness around her. I took both her hands and pulled her out of her damn chair. She looked at me, her eyes so beautiful, and I hugged her.

'Wait, Mika! What's all this?'

I took a deep breath and told her about the day I had spent with Grandfather on Leszno Street: the café, the theatre, the puppets.

'All right, I'll come with you. You're right. I can't stay in this chair for ever.' She smiled – the first time I'd seen her smile since Paul's death.

'Let's get going, then.'

That was the thing with Ellie: it was all or nothing. If she was happy, she burned bright as fire and her enthusiasm lit up everyone around her.

We spent that afternoon back in the workshop. Ellie picked up the princess, slipped her hand underneath its dress, and with the other removed a little crown from the puppet's head. She picked up a miniature brush and swung it like a sword.

'Why don't we do Ali Baba and the Forty Thieves?'

I suspected this was a tale from her thick book.

'What's it about? I don't know the story.'

'Well, it's the story of Ali Baba, who is rescued from forty bloodthirsty thieves by one woman and one woman alone. Not once, but many times, until in the end all the thieves end up being slaughtered. A small, outnumbered group wins against an army of thieves. I think our people could do with a tale like this, don't you think?'

She made the puppet wave the brush as if doing battle. I had to admit it sounded like a great idea. We couldn't make forty papier-mâché thieves, only a few new ones, some wearing soldier's uniforms complete with the hated hooked cross. Risky, but then, what wasn't nowadays?

That evening I played for Grandfather. I ached to see him in the seats when we came out to take a bow. My only comfort was Ellie by my side, back on board with the puppets and our shows. Everyone had laughed and

clapped when the thieves lay slain in pieces and the play
was a big success.

I visited the orphanage as much as I could, performing
short puppet shows for the children in the sickroom, for
a birthday girl or boy, or as a late afternoon entertainment on the marble staircase. Hannah always assisted me,
twisting my story plots or practising funny voices, and
when I peered at her, no matter what horrors I might have
witnessed on the way to the orphanage, she always made
my heart tingle. She had become like a little sister to me.

I also got to know Janusz better and, despite the terrible times, he always had something exciting to tell me.
He loved music, and often his records rose from his old
gramophone and filled the house.

One day he took me to one side.

'Mika, you need to hear more music. They may have
locked us up in this stinking place, but look at us, we still
have symphony orchestras in the ghetto, playing all this
grand music, choirs, plays, even a cabaret.' I told Janusz
about the afternoon with Grandfather in Leszno Street,
the puppet show that so charmed us.

'Ah, yes, I've heard about the little theatre. You know,
Mika, all these musicians, actors and singers can still
touch our hearts, even in such terrible times. It's as
important as bread and firewood. I often think of what
the poet Leopold Staff said, "More than bread, poetry is
necessary at times when there's no need for it at all ..." I
know it's difficult to remember that when we're hungry
all the time, but let's not forget the power of music, and
your puppets.'

'Yes, but we can't eat music, or the puppets. What use
are they in the big picture?'

He looked at me with piercing eyes but gently put his
warm hand on my shoulder.

'My dear boy, if people like you didn't exist, the Germans would already have won, destroyed us in the places that matter.' He pointed to his chest, his heart. 'They would have numbed our hearts, killed our spirit, taken our souls. Your puppets carry a spark and light that keeps us warm. This is precious, Mika. It's all we can do at the moment.'

'But, Janusz,' although no one could overhear us I still lowered my voice, 'there are people out there risking their lives, fighting with guns not puppets, really making a difference.'

He pulled me close and put a finger on my mouth. His eyes darkened.

'Yes, my dear, but I don't want you to be one of them. I need you here. People disappear every day. Snatched then spat out as bloody pulp after the Gestapo has interrogated them. I don't want to hear anything like that about you. And here …' He moved over to a small desk and rummaged in one of the drawers. 'I want you to go and see this concert tomorrow afternoon. A dear friend gave me two tickets, but I cannot leave the children.'

He handed me the tickets. They were properly printed on pink card.

'It's a Mozart concerto. I don't know if this is something you will enjoy, but I think there's nothing quite as moving and rousing as his music. It's bigger than all of this.' With a stroke of his arm he drew a large semicircle in the air.

'No, yes, I'd like to go, thank you very much. Are you sure?' His gift made me feel shy.

'Yes, absolutely, and why don't you take your lovely friend?' He winked at me.

I had told him about Ellie and yes, it would be like a date. I quickly got up, put on my coat and made my way towards the large door. As usual, leaving the children felt like trying to part the Red Sea.

Little did I know when I tucked the tickets into a pocket, a small one inside the seam reserved for important papers, that this afternoon would change everything for me.

It was 14 October 1941. I would never make it to the concert.

6

It happened on Ciepla Street. Deep in thought about how best to surprise Ellie, I turned a corner then stopped dead in my tracks. Two Polish policemen and a Wehrmacht soldier were pointing at an elderly woman holding a large wicker basket.

'*Stehenbleiben!* Stop!' The woman froze.

'So, what's in your basket, woman?' one of the policemen sneered in Polish.

The basket looked heavy and the woman was wrapped in a dark coat which hung over her thin body like a tent. Terror flashed across her face – a panicked animal looking for escape. All of a sudden, I heard the doctor's rational, calming voice.

'But gentlemen, time is marching on and surely this fine woman is only making her way home before curfew to cook some supper.'

Everyone – the policemen, the soldier, the woman and myself – stood as if they'd been hit by a strange missile and all eyes were on the doctor, and on me.

The day before, I had bent some wire into a nice pair of glasses and fixed them to the doctor's little puppet face. The glasses gave him a reassuring air of authority and I had proudly presented him to Ellie. Now here he was, making polite conversation with the very people who had killed my grandfather as if it was the most natural thing in the world.

'What is this?' the soldier barked. But the doctor didn't seem intimidated. He had not seen my grandfather fall, and kept his professional demeanour.

'May I introduce myself. My name is Doctor Shiverwick and I can cure just about anything with my medicines. Would you like to take a look at my bag too?' A pause followed – I swear I could hear my heart thump, skip a beat, then another. The soldier's face changed. Like the unpredictable weather of spring, it moved and twitched, uncertain which way to go. His eyes were a bluish grey, large with surprise, and a small dark blond strand of hair spilled out from under the metal helmet. Soft features: a small nose and mouth, and very pale, milky skin. Suddenly in my mind's eye his complexion turned an alarming red. Would he rip me to pieces right there and then? My nightmares of the devouring soldier-rats appeared before me. Sweat gathered between my shoulder blades and I felt dizzy as if I were on the merry-go-round on Krasinski Square that I could never ride without feeling sick for hours afterwards. I thought I would pass out any minute.

Then I heard a strange noise, and when I looked, the soldier's mouth had morphed into a kind of grimace and a hacking sound tumbled from his lips. The soldier was laughing.

Out of the corner of my eye I saw the old woman seize the moment and start to walk in the opposite direction, clutching her basket to her chest. The doctor and I bowed. My legs were shaking and I felt very weak and alone.

'Boy, come here, *wie heißt du*? What is your name?' The two Polish policemen stared at the soldier, as did I.

'Mika,' I replied. My voice sounded strange, too high and shrill.

'Now that is what I call a surprise. Do you have more of those up your sleeve?' The soldier pointed to Dr Shiverwick, who was still stuck on my hand.

'More puppets? Yes. Some.'

'Well, you'd better come with me, then. I want to see the whole show.'

'But—'

He cut me off and took a step towards me. 'There is no but. *Komm*, follow me.'

He grabbed my sleeve and pulled me along. Dear God! My heart was pounding, sweat trickled in streams down my back, despite the late afternoon cold. Was this a trick, a terrible joke? Would this be my last walk? His hand gripped my coat, dragging me along Nowolipie Street as if I too were a puppet, a marionette pulled by invisible strings.

We reached the Nalewki gate, where heavily armed soldiers guarded the checkpoint iron gates covered with thick barbed wire. I never came here. We had heard far too many terrible stories – of soldiers waiting for the ghetto kids to crawl back through the holes in the wall after a day's begging on the Aryan side, shooting them like sparrows, then laughing and slapping each other's backs with every fallen child. They never bothered to take away the bodies. The children lay there, dead or injured, until the soldiers grew tired of their games. Then, under the protection of night, their loved ones would gather the children in their arms and take them home – not without risking their own lives. If you were found on the street after curfew, the soldiers would shoot you like a stray dog.

'He's with me.' The soldier pointed casually at me. I felt light-headed, my legs like jelly. We passed through the gate as though it were the most natural thing.

And then I was walking on the Aryan side, a German

soldier next to me, so close I could smell him. I remembered everything here. These were the streets of my childhood. I had grown up only a few blocks away, and it was not even a year since they had sealed the ghetto, although it felt like a lifetime. The streets were so much quieter here, and so clean. Where were all the people? But of course, this is how it used to be, before the stench of the ghetto. Before we had to wade through crowds like muddy water; people pushing and shuffling, rickshaws, wagons, horses, everyone stumbling over one another, trying to avoid trampling on those left dying or dead on the ground.

Here, a different world existed, a world I had forgotten and that had forgotten us. How could this be? People promenaded at a leisurely pace, dressed in clothes I didn't even remember, so tidy and clean. And what about Bolek and Henryk, my old school friends? Did they still sit behind their desks, bored, yawning, playing the same old games in the afternoon? These people were getting on with their lives, business as usual, while we barely survived. Did my friends ever think of me? My chest hurt, I found it hard to breathe.

Splashes of colour sprang up everywhere: vegetables of all kinds were still on sale here, displayed on nicely decorated stalls, and there were even flowers. I wished I could grab a bunch and bring one home for Mother and a special one for Ellie. I'd forgotten crimson, orange and purple, except for the puppets and the occasional flower that would pop up in my mother's window box.

The overwhelming colour in the ghetto was grey, all shades of it: ash-grey, rain-grey, mouse-grey, bone-grey – these were our choices. Bright colours were a feast for the eyes, but they were not for us any more, not for us Jews. More than the clean streets and people, these colours that existed so close, right on the other side of the wall, made me ache.

Ah, and here I recognised the bakery where Grandfather and I used to buy our bread: soft, large loaves or perfectly formed white rolls dotted with raisins. Cinnamon whirls too. I swear, I could smell freshly baked bread, but when I looked up, the bakery stood abandoned and boarded up, its façade crossed out with big, rough boards. Its owner, like us, had been forced to leave his shop and move into the ghetto. Was he still alive? Did his profession save him from our painful breadlessness? I had never seen him in the ghetto.

I trudged along as if in a hazy dream, putting one foot in front of another. Surely I would wake up at any minute, emerge like a diver from deep water and take a huge, sobering breath. I could still hear my heart thudding. All of a sudden I felt Grandfather walking next to me. I felt him as clearly as the coat wrapped around me. I kept my gaze on the ground, but there it was: a clear sense of Grandfather's warm presence. I soaked it up like sunshine after a long winter. The pavements looked so different; there were no beggars, no dirt, no contorted broken bodies, only old cobbled stones, polished by centuries of strolling feet.

But the shoes. My stomach contracted like a fist. The shoes didn't match. Instead of my grandfather's soft brown leather shoes with their creases and dark laces, there were knee-high boots, polished to a shine, black as a moonless night.

'*Komm, schon Junge.*' The soldier's sharp voice snapped me out of my trance. Grandfather disappeared. Suddenly I felt colder and more alone than I had on the day they shot him.

The soldier led me around a corner towards a large building. It used to be a school for boys, but as we drew closer I saw the hated German flag, a black swastika on a white and red background, flying from the top of the building, confident, as if it had been planted there for many years. I shivered. We were heading straight into the lion's mouth.

The soldier lightly pushed his gun into my back. Enough to remind me that I was his prisoner.

'Keep walking and be quiet.' He made me climb up a flight of stairs. We entered the building.

'*Heil Hitler!*' the soldier barked, his right arm stretched out stiffly in the Führer's salute.

'*Heil Hitler!*' A less enthusiastic echo sounded from behind a large wooden desk.

'*Herr Sturmführer Barke,*' the soldier addressed the man behind the desk, '*dieser junge Mann hier hat Talent.* This young man has talent – *ein Puppenspieler,* he's a puppeteer. You know we always need more acts for the cabaret. I could bring him to tonight's performance. And before that he can entertain our hard-working soldiers. What about a little matinee?'

Sturmführer Barke looked me up and down as if I were a shabby circus horse. His black cap, adorned with a silver skull and SS runes, sat at a strange angle on his head and my eyes caught the swastika pin on his uniform. For a change here sat a German with green, rather than blue eyes. He did not smile.

'Well, do as you like, but it's at your own risk. Keep a close eye on him and don't waste any more of my time.'

Sturmführer Barke dismissed the soldier with a sharp salute.

'Very well, thank you. Heil Hitler.' With this the soldier put his hand on my shoulder and directed me out of the room. He led me down the stairs, keeping me firmly at arm's length, until we were back on the street. At least he wasn't pressing a gun into my back any more.

I must have held my breath the entire time we were inside the building and I felt dizzy, out of breath. But this, as it turned out, was only the beginning.

7

Having paraded me in front of Sturmführer Barke, the soldier now looked me up and down, taking his time.

'My name is Max. Max Meierhauser. Now come, *und keine Faxen*.'

Hearing his name did not make me any less anxious – quite the opposite in fact. Does one not talk in a friendly manner to a dog before throwing a net over its head? The soldier led me around the corner to a large brick building that had been turned into a soldiers' barracks.

'Here we are, boy.' He opened the door and with a slight push delivered me inside.

The noise and stink nearly pushed me back – truly we had arrived in the devil's den. Through thick smoke I could make out about a hundred soldiers, the rats of my dark fantasies. Here they mingled with each other, sprawled out on long tables, relieved of their metal helmets, their jackets thrown carelessly over chairs. Many played cards: holding full hands in their fists before crashing one card after another down on the table with baying laughter. The smell of sweat and thick cigarette smoke hung in the air, from a hundred sucking mouths, stubs thrown on the floor or left hanging at the corner of their mouths.

The soldiers shouted and swore, and the crowded room reeked of stale sweat and beer. So much beer! The rats clutched their glasses as if they were the Holy Grail. Many gulped the dark yellow liquid down in one continuous swig, applauded by their mates, followed by a hollering for more.

'*Komm hier, Kleine, mehr Bier.*' A buxom brunette rushed to fill another huge jug with intoxicating liquid. As she put it down the soldier squeezed her bottom. She was one of four waitresses serving these men: all had thick make-up covering their eyes and cheeks, and they wore less than I had ever seen on a woman. I was struck by their very red lips. Bright apple red. Coarse laughter erupted from everywhere. *Shoot them or be caught?* My mind raced. *Here's your chance to get back at them.* But of course I was the trapped one here. I could only try to keep a clear head; a tall order as my skull filled with a cold sticky fear. Then one of the soldiers noticed us.

'Well, well, who did you pick up there, Max? Isn't he a little pale around the nose?'

A stocky, red-faced soldier approached us, and before I could turn away, he pinched my nose with his thick wurst fingers. He stank of beer and was swaying slightly.

'Not any more, ha, he's red as red cabbage now! There's still hope for you, boy.' He clapped both his thighs with laughter.

'Leave him alone.' Max's voice sounded surprisingly sharp. 'See for yourselves.' With that Max bent down to my ear and whispered, 'This is your chance, boy. You make them laugh, I'll bring you back in one piece; if you bore us, you know where you're headed. If we like you there will be dinner and a bigger audience this evening.'

And so, on that very afternoon, I played for my enemy and for my life. Max led me to the front and I tried to shake the frozenness from my arms and legs. Is this how the puppets felt when I pulled them from my coat? I asked for two chairs, draped my coat between them, and then disappeared behind the makeshift stage. There it was again, Grandfather's presence, warm and sweet as honey. Was it the sheltering coat hanging like a barrier between me and the crowd, or the coat's reassuring smell? Was my mind playing tricks or was it simply my heart aching for Grandfather, pining to take me far away?

I stroked the silken fabric on the inside of the coat, as if I could reach Grandfather through time, through those pockets he had so carefully designed. I wished I could disappear into one of the pockets, a magic trick that would leave the soldiers gasping.

Max's deep voice brought me back to my predicament. *'Ruhe im Haus! Ruhe! Nun zu ihrer Unterhaltung, Mika, der Puppenspieler* – for your entertainment, Mika the puppet player of the ghetto.' Slowly the room grew quieter. I had all the inside pockets to work with, crammed full with my puppet company, but no idea where to start. I slipped my hand into the right pocket and pulled out the first puppet I found – the princess.

I wiggled my hand into it and made the delicate puppet pace back and forth along the length of the coat. Oh, but she looked like an ordinary girl, the distinguishing crown had disappeared. The princess stopped, as if she herself had just realised. She sighed and threw her little hands up in the air. I put on my highest voice, made her cry and bury her head in her lap. It was risky, no doubt – surely these soldiers wanted excitement and tricks, not some princess crying. But here, trapped behind my coat, it became clearer than ever: it was the puppets who were in charge, not me. I followed them, not the other way round. After I had chosen the first one, the puppets would decide how everything progressed. And this looked terrible. I held my breath; did they even know what was at stake?

All of a sudden, making a loud entrance, the fool appeared. He was an exuberant puppet, proudly wearing a colourful costume stitched together from odd pieces of fabric and a pointed green felt hat, adorned with a tiny bell. The fool performed with a few bold leaps and somersaults; then, with a confident and cheeky gesture, he bowed in front of the girl.

'But hello, lovely lady, what has happened to you?' With a quick movement he pulled a huge handkerchief from behind the girl's ear and blew her nose.

'There, there, blow that lovely nose of yours.' With a loud manly blow, the first laughs from the audience appeared. Hannah would have loved the fool's trick, he was her favourite puppet – maybe because of his colourful clothes or jerky movements or because he never trembled in front of anyone or anything. I needed him now as never before.

'Now what is it that is making your eyes water so much, my dear?'

'I've lost my crown and the key to my treasure box. I'm really a princess but no one will believe me.'

'Well, where did you last see the key?'

'I always wear it around my neck but this morning it had disappeared.' Even from behind the coat I could sense the soldiers' attention flagging.

'Ah, that must have been the work of the evil sorcerer Hagazad. Let me see, he usually leaves something behind.'

With this the fool got down on the ground like a dog and with loud sniffing noises moved back and forth the length of the coat, then up and down the girl. I could hear a little laughter.

'Ah, I thought so!' The fool pulled a feather from her hair.

'He changed into an eagle and must have taken your key to the highest mountain. But do not despair, we can call Hagazad himself when we shake the feather.' With this the fool swung the feather through the air and, hey presto, the sorcerer materialised as if from thin air, spreading his black coat across the stage. I surprised even myself with his roaring voice.

'You little worm, how dare you call me.'

This was the first time I had used Hagazad. I had worked on him for weeks and had only finished the black cape the day before. One week after witnessing yet another random act of violence – this time a soldier hacking off an old Jew's beard and spitting at him – I knew I needed a puppet in my troupe that, although terrifying in appearance, I would always defeat. And so I created Hagazad with everything I despised in the rat: piercing blue eyes, blond hair, a pasty face and a metal helmet like the ones the German occupying force wore.

With Hagazad's entrance, I certainly seized the soldiers' attention.

'Well, dearest Hagazad, this beautiful girl here needs you to return something that we think you might accidentally have taken. You know, just a little key. Nothing you would have use for anyway.'

Hagazad's deep, menacing laughter surprised me. 'And why would I do that?'

'Because, once upon a time, you loved a princess just like this one, isn't that true? But she fell for someone else and ever since you've spent your life seeking revenge, taking everything from anyone you can find. You must be tired of this. Let me free you of this load.'

'Quiet, worm, or I'll break your back.' Hagazad swung

his cape like a torero in front of a bull, but the fool wasn't impressed.

'I challenge you, Hagazad, to a game, and if you lose you must return the key to the princess.'

A pause, then the sorcerer broke into ugly laughter.

'Sure, why not, it'll be fun to eat you alive and spit you out one piece at a time. I'll make a fine necklace out of your polished bones. Let's begin!'

As the fool had suggested this challenge, he needed to come up with a game. He chose a simple one, a game of mathematics. Grandfather had taught me some very complicated equations and algebra had always come naturally to me. And so it happened that the fool challenged the sorcerer to a match of algebra. I had a small piece of slate in my pocket and some chalk, and so the fool scribbled down a long equation.

'There, my dear Hagazad, if you can solve this, the key is yours and so am I!'

Soon enough it became clear that Hagazad was hopeless at algebra, and slowly he transformed into an even bigger fool than our fool could ever be. He stomped, huffed, growled and whirled around, but in the end the fool won. With a fierce hiss Hagazad jumped up in the air, somersaulted then dived behind the coat and out of sight.

The fool proceeded to show the girl a magic trick then proudly presented the key – my grandfather's golden key, which I always kept safely tucked in a small pocket right next to my heart. The show ended with a joyful dance between the princess and the richly rewarded fool.

I had immersed myself totally in the play, but now my precarious situation flooded back to me and cold sweat formed on my forehead. Applause – not thundering, but applause nevertheless. I crawled out from behind my makeshift stage, bowed, lifted my coat from the chairs and wrapped myself in it.

Max approached me out of the undistinguishable crowd of soldiers and clapped me hard on the shoulder.

'Not bad, boy, but I hope you'll give the officers a bit more fire, a bit more Punch and Judy. You know we love the Kasperl theatre.' I vaguely remembered Grandfather telling me about the German puppets and Kasperl, the fool with a long nose and pointed hat.

'But I ought to go home,' I said.

'Never answer back, boy. *Verstanden?*' Max's face darkened.

'Yes.'

With this he handed me a piece of bread and a glass of beer. 'Here, *Milchbube*, this will give you hairs on your chest, drink it down in one go!' He laughed and patted me on the back.

'*Na, mach shon.*'

I didn't want to drink the beer, but a group of soldiers had gathered, like an excited crowd around a circus bear, eager to see its awkward tricks. I put the glass to my lips and drank the beer in one go. It tasted bitter and my stomach revolted. Max gestured to one of the women to fill the glass again.

'One more, *mein Bursche*!' I gasped but had no choice. With the second glass my head began to spin. I had only once tasted beer, when Grandfather let me try a sip one evening, and now that my hunger and fear provided no barriers against the alcohol, it went straight to my head: a balloon floating towards the ceiling, detached from the rest of my body. Then the room seemed to sway, echoing laughter surrounded me and the soldiers' faces merged into one big addled mass. I held myself up for a while then slumped heavily into a chair.

'Ah, you've got a long way to go before you become a proper beer drinker! *Komm*, the officers are waiting.'

With this Max yanked me out of the chair and into

the adjacent room. Maybe the beer was my salvation, but the rest of the evening turned into a blur. I remember more beer being forced down my throat, leaving my shirt wet and stinking, clouds of cigarette smoke surrounding me and five officers sitting right in front of my improvised stage, laughing and joining in with my coarse jokes.

This beer-fuelled puppet show resembled more of a battleground than a story. All I remember is the crocodile snapping at everyone, the fool running around frantically, somersaulting along the length of the coat, Hagazad catapulted high into the air, crashing and falling like a dead bird behind the stage, and all of this accompanied by my various sound effects and the officers' drunken laughter. It must have been entertaining enough, as they greeted the show with enthusiastic applause.

Coming out from behind the coat I remember pleading with Max to show me the toilet and begging him to take me home. Nauseous, weak and dizzy, I had nothing left in me – certainly what little innocence might have remained after the Germans had marched me into the ghetto had now gone.

They wanted me back the following week, a little entertainment after all their hard work in the ghetto. The soldiers' and officers' posturing and laughter made me sick. I had seen them ram guns into women's bellies, spit at an old man, shoot people like my grandfather on the spot for absolutely no reason. And here were these same monsters enjoying themselves without a care in the world, entertained by me.

Yes, I had put on the show to survive, but wasn't I betraying my own people? I felt disgusted with myself and the puppets, which were contaminated and compromised just as I was. What would Grandfather have thought of me now? And of his puppets? I couldn't bear thinking about him. Shame crawled over me like an army of ants.

That first night outside the barracks, before he took me back to the ghetto, Max pulled me close and stared straight into my face. My stomach heaved from his breath, a mixture of beer and cigarettes.

'Don't tell anyone where you've been, understand? I will collect you again next week at the same time at the *Wache*. Wait for me and I'll bring you back here, understood?'

I couldn't move. I had used up all my energy and courage. All that remained was a shell, gutted, dirty, washed out. Any moment now I would simply collapse, a lifeless puppet myself.

'*Verstanden?*' His sharp voice jolted me back and, like a marionette lifted by its strings, my whole body became rigid and stiff.

'Yes, yes, understood. Next week. Here.'

'Good boy.' With this he reached into his uniform, pulled out a loaf of rye bread and thrust it into my hands.

'*Komm jetzt*, I'll take you back.'

As he led me back to the *Wache*, we did not speak and I kept my eyes on the cobbled streets of a Warsaw lost to me. On the Aryan side the stones still reflected the moonlight, while in the ghetto they were crusted over with layers of dirt and misery.

We reached the gates and Max exchanged a few words with the guards.

'*Na, komm schon, Junge, los.*' The guards opened the gate and pointed with their guns in the direction of the ghetto. I took a few steps and crossed over, not looking back. I took a deep breath. How could returning to prison feel like a relief? Yet that night it did.

It was nearing midnight, many hours into the curfew. If the soldiers caught me here they would shoot me so I raced back. More than the prospect of being killed, I was worried about Mother. She would be out of her wits with anguish. And how right I was – the moment I entered the apartment her fists pounded down on me. Right there in the hallway, for everyone to hear. She must have been waiting for me there all night, out in the cold corridor. I had never seen her so distressed, hitting me like a fury, sobbing all the while. I took the blows gladly, they balanced out some of the hatred I felt for myself, but soon her blows weakened and she pulled me close.

'I thought I'd lost you, Mika. Don't ever do that to me again, you hear me? You smell awful, I can smell beer and cigarettes. Where've you been? I'm worrying myself senseless and you've been out drinking?'

'I'm sorry, Mama, please don't ask me. I'm fine. Here's some bread.'

She looked at the bread in her hands with a mixture of disgust and hunger – it was good-quality bread, even I could see that, not like the flimsy watered-down variety we got in the ghetto. I saw that she instinctively understood I had earned it with more than just puppetry.

'Where have you been, Mika? Please tell me. I am your mother!' Her gaze pierced me but her voice had grown softer. I stayed silent.

She placed the bread on a small table in the corridor. It sat between us like a silent, knowing witness. Then she simply left for the only room in which she could have some privacy, the bedroom. And even that she had to share with me.

That night I stayed in the workshop. I spread my coat in the corner and made myself as comfortable as I could. I was chilled to the bone, unable to sleep as the day's events replayed themselves in front of my eyes over and over again like an unstoppable turntable. Towards morning I must have fallen asleep, because then came nightmares more vivid than ever. The rats were everywhere.

I woke hungry yet I didn't eat all the following day. And only at the end of the week, when we had run out of all other things, did my mother cut that bread.

Would I really go back to those beasts as the soldier had commanded? But what choice did I have? Many people in the ghetto had seen my shows by now and, even if I tried to hide, the soldiers could find me if they wanted to. They'd kill me there and then, take me to the Pawiak at least, if not Mother, Ellie and Cara as well. I couldn't risk it.

With Ellie, my secret didn't last long. The morning after my forced performance, she cornered me.

'What's the matter with you, Mika? You look awful,' she said.

'Nothing, I'm fine.' Even to my own ears I didn't sound convincing.

'You're a lousy liar. You look miserable, pale, there are dark rings under your eyes. And you smell. You're different, changed. Please talk to me.'

'Wake up, look around you, we're all changing, everything has changed.' My words jumped out like spitting arrows. I was surprised at my sharpness, yet I meant to hurt her, needed to push her away.

But Ellie persisted.

'Come on, Mika, I'm your friend. Don't you trust me? What is going on?'

'This is not about trust, Ellie, leave me alone. I just need to be on my own.'

This time she looked hurt.

'Fine, but don't ask me ever again to help you with your precious puppets.' She stormed out of the room. I stood like a dog that had been drenched with cold water.

I really cared about Ellie. I often found myself looking at her: longing to pull the band from her ponytail, let it glide through my fingers; wondering how a real kiss would feel. What it would taste like.

Now even our adventures in the workshop were over.

That morning I realised Ellie was the first girl I had ever really wanted. I desired her with all of my fifteen-year-old desperate self, here in this overcrowded apartment, on that gloomy morning. In the middle of the ghetto's misery. And I had never felt as lonely and so in need of her company and comfort as now. Suddenly I heard a loud, ugly laugh inside my head and a chilling voice saying, 'Well done, boy, you sent the slut away.'

This is what had become of me, a Nazi entertainer, a coward who saw rats and heard voices. I grabbed my coat and left the house, wandering the streets aimlessly all day.

For a few days Ellie and I didn't speak. Then one evening she found me in the kitchen on my own. I sat at the table, staring into a cup of cold, thin tea saying nothing. She pulled up a chair, leaned forward and before I could draw another breath, she took my face in her hands. How delicate her hands were; slender, warm and soft. At that moment, I could have placed my whole being in those hands. As if her hands had melted the icecap that had settled over me, everything gushed out.

'I'm so sorry, Ellie. I had to play for them. They took me to the other side and I had to entertain them. He said not to tell anyone.'

It was the first time she had seen me cry. She did not remove her hands.

'Slow down, who are they, and who is he?'

'The soldiers, the German officers, Max.'

'Who is Max?' I couldn't believe how kind she was, looking straight at me, without fear. Such beautiful eyes.

'He saw me in the street – a German soldier. I couldn't

help it. They'd stopped an old woman and then the doctor spoke up.'

'The doctor?'

'Yes, the puppet. I just didn't think. Then the worst thing happened, the soldier liked it. He took me to the other side, into our old neighbourhood, to one of their barracks. You should see how it looks over there. So normal. The streets are empty and clean as if they polish the roads each day.'

Ellie put her arm around my shoulder. Her embrace was like a bridge between my lonely secret and her gentle presence.

'I had to put on two shows for them and now I have to go back again. Ellie, there were so many of them, even SS officers. And they forced all this beer down my throat.'

For a while she simply sat and took it all in while I soaked up her kindness. I really think there and then, that very evening, I fell slowly but surely in love with her.

'It sounds awful. You've been so brave, Mika. Please don't be hard on yourself. It reminds me of what you told me about your grandfather, when he stood up for that young girl. He wasn't as lucky as you. You're still alive.'

I didn't know what to say. Could I really think of myself in the same way as Grandfather? But her kind words stopped my tears.

'Will you help me again in the workshop, then? You don't think I am an awful traitor?'

'Don't be silly. There's nothing else you could have done. And yes, let's think up a new play. By the way, I want to show you something.'

And there, in the dim light of the workshop, Ellie showed me how she had put together two simple puppets using things she had found around the flat and on the

85

streets: a few pieces of wood, a bottle top, some wire and pieces of fabric. Two new puppets greeted me.

With the approach of the following week my heart sank. I hated those soldiers and officers with a passion I had not known before. To be their entertainer made me despise myself. What kind of new play could I make up? Mix in stories from the ghetto and appeal to their hearts? I laughed out loud, catching my thoughts. What hearts? From everything I had seen since they herded us into the ghetto I could never match the word 'German' with 'heart'.

The terror of their daily presence surrounded us everywhere. Like random bullets, their brutality could cost you your life any time, just like that. One minute you might be roaming along Leszno or any other street, the next you're dead. And the daily humiliations: soldiers hacking away at the beards of our old men and rabbis with blunt scissors, forcing an audience to egg them on, kicking and spitting into the rabbis' faces, laughing all the while.

Just the week before, I had witnessed the soldiers making people dance barefoot in the streets at gunpoint until they broke down from exhaustion or humiliation; a mother holding her baby, a few men and two old women. In the end, they simply turned and shot the violinist who had been forced to accompany the dance.

Once I saw something that left me shaken for days. I was ambling along the road when a boy of about fourteen turned the corner into our street. He kept his head down so as not to attract any attention, but I could see he was carrying something under his coat. It wasn't obvious, but if like me you have an eye for coats and what they might hide, you would notice.

Two soldiers approached from the opposite direction.

The taller of the two stopped the boy in his tracks, towering over him like a mean shadow – they were trained to notice anything suspicious.

'*Aufmachen*, open up, *was hast Du da untem Mantel?*' the soldier barked.

The boy looked up, pale as the moon. Very slowly he opened his coat, button after button. The soldier stepped forward, grabbed the coat and ripped it open. Three buttons rolled into the road.

And there they were: two lovely, round loaves of bread. The soldier grabbed the bread and threw it on the ground, then trampled the precious load with his heavy boots until it was crushed to pieces.

'*Aufheben*, pick it up,' the soldier shouted.

'Please. The bread is for my mother. She is sick,' the boy pleaded, his voice quiet and thin. Slowly he picked up some large fragments of what only a moment before had been perfectly shaped loaves.

'Open your mouth.'

The boy hesitated.

'Open your goddam mouth.'

The boy's mouth quivered, but slowly he opened it.

The soldier grabbed some large chunks and stuffed them violently into the boy's mouth, one after another.

'There, eat that.'

The boy coughed and writhed and his face went a dark red. I could see he was struggling to breathe, choking on the bread. I worried that the soldier wouldn't stop. But then the soldier gave a harsh cackle, threw the last bits of bread at the boy and moved on. The boy stood motionless for a while, then scrambled to collect the last pieces of bread from the pavement before scurrying away. I wished I had intervened, but the puppets and I remained quiet. Maybe we wouldn't have been so lucky this time.

And these were not even the worst incidents. I heard about another boy who was shot outright for smuggling a single loaf. And so many smugglers, often children no older that six, risked their lives every day, squeezing in and out through tiny cracks and holes in the ghetto wall. No one would have survived in the ghetto without their bravery, and yet so many were killed.

Finally the dreaded day arrived and Max met me at the *Wache*. I stood with my hands deep in my pockets, clenching them into hard fists when I saw him approach. Maybe he had been there when they shot Grandfather? The rats all looked the same to me in their uniforms – how much blood did he have on his hands?

'So, *Bursche*, I hope you have something new?' He looked down at me; I couldn't make out his expression.

'Yes.' I had decided I would only ever say the absolute minimum. What did this soldier want from me? Was it not enough to take our city, lock us in the ghetto? Yet here I was, being singled out for special treatment. What would be the next thing he would ask of me? I shot him a look that could have killed, but Max didn't notice. He didn't seem to be in a talkative mood either so we didn't speak until we arrived at the barracks.

Here the same spiel was repeated: a short play for all the soldiers and then, when the officers and SS joined us, a longer and wilder Punch and Judy-style show. After they had had their fun, forcing beer down my throat, Max took me back to the *Wache*.

'You're good. Funny. Here, this is for you.' As before, he handed me a loaf of bread. A thin smile crossed his lips.

'How old are you, boy?'

'Thirteen,' I lied. It was none of his business.

'I have a son, Karl. He is twelve.' Why was he telling

me this? I didn't care. I moved swiftly through the gate and did not turn back.

This was the beginning of a terrible routine: I would steal myself away from our apartment with the excuse of a puppet show somewhere in the ghetto, meet Max at the *Wache* and cross to the Aryan side. Mother never again asked about the bread, but took it from me and wrapped it in newspaper to keep it fresh.

As the weeks and months passed, another ugly incident occurred, its memory biting me some nights like a snake. It became quite a popular pastime for the Germans to wander into the ghetto in their leisure time and take photographs for their private albums, like snapshots from an outing to a foreign country. I'd seen them occasionally snap away at our shops, our only tram or the sad market. But now whole film teams visited the ghetto, setting up scenes to depict the glorious life of the Jews – yet another dirty lie with which to fool the world.

They forced people at gunpoint to sit around tables laden with crystalware and water-filled carafes, pretending to merrily enjoy food that the Germans dished up. But no one ever got more than a morsel to eat and, once the filming had finished, the food vanished.

Next door, they transformed a filthy room into a make-shift school. The rats had forbidden all schooling in the ghetto, but for this film they stuck a group of children in decent clothes and told them: 'Pretend this is your teacher. Look smart and eager. *Macht schon.* You'll get bread. *Brot.*'

They filled a hospital ward with the best-looking patients, pinned pictures on the walls and had nurses attend to everyone with medicine and bandages in abundance. While typhoid swept through the ghetto and thousands were dying from lack of food and medicine, the rats showed the world just how well the Jews were living in their ghetto. And maybe the world believed them.

One day while I hunted for some vegetables in the market I stumbled across a group of children queuing at a soup kitchen, dressed in dirty rags and thin as twigs. Instead of trousers one boy had simply tied pieces of fabric around his bare legs with a piece of string. The children shuffled along, staring straight ahead, not even talking to each other. I joined the wretched group, then pulled the fool out of my pocket and stretched out my arm. The puppet dangled in front of the boy queuing ahead of me.

'Well, hello, and what is your name?' The boy turned and stared at me as if I'd slapped him. I smiled. Out came the monkey, who had no fear of jumping all over the children, and soon, as the queue moved slowly along, a little crowd had formed around me, eagerly following my little play. The boy finally smiled, exposing a gaping hole where his front teeth should have been. That's when I saw them arrive: three men in suits and hats, carrying a large camera and tripod, accompanied by a soldier.

'Hey, you.'

I tried to ignore him, but I knew he meant me.

'Come here.'

For a moment they debated among themselves.

'Let's get this boy a proper audience. Come on.' As before, I knew this was a *Befehl* – a command, not a request.

'*Komm.*' They led me along small streets and then, turning a corner, I found myself in Leszno Street.

'Here.' They pointed to the small theatre where I had seen my first puppet show with Grandfather.

'*Jetzt zeig uns mal was.*'

That afternoon they forced me to put on a puppet show for their lying camera. And rather than emaciated children with big glassy eyes and hunger-swollen bellies, they hand-picked the audience for a jolly performance.

'*Lachen! Hier, in die Kamera.*' The cameraman told me to come out from behind the curtain and grin into the camera, showing the world just how gloriously we entertained ourselves behind the ghetto walls. I trudged home like a beaten dog.

These were the days of Mika the ghetto puppeteer, when no one, except Ellie, knew of my double life: Mika, entertaining the children, yet feeding the monster that would eat them all. I couldn't sleep and in the mornings I looked at myself in the mirror with disgust.

Slowly, though, the seed planted by my visions of fighting the rats grew. It wouldn't be long before things took a different turn.

8

It was Ellie who came up with the idea late one night when everyone else was asleep. I had been putting on shows for the soldiers for months now but at least Ellie and I still worked together at other times and we had just finished preparing a new puppet show. Ellie sat on a small chair, with the crocodile draped over her hand. She looked at me, but said nothing. Despite the dim light I could see her eyes, full of fire and something else. When her voice dropped a few notes and she started whispering even though no one could hear us, I started to worry.

'Mika, I've thought of something. Please just listen, don't say anything yet and let me finish.'

Was she going to suggest I let myself be fed alive to the lions?

'You have the protection of a German soldier now; they know you at the *Wache* and they know you have a whole troupe of puppets in your coat. They actually trust you and there is nothing suspicious about you: you're just a harmless Jewish boy who entertains them after work.' She leaned in closer.

'Think about it. You could actually use this, smuggle something back from the other side or out from here under your fabulous coat. Do you know how many people risk their lives every day, to smuggle medicine and food? Even children do it.' She spoke as fast as a train.

'But Ellie, I am just glad to get back home in one piece. Do you have any idea how brutal they are? Do you want to get me killed?'

'Of course not, but maybe this is something we can use to our advantage. I can't go on like this, Mika.'

'There is no we, Ellie, it's just me, me alone and the puppets — me and the damn soldiers. That's it. There's no one to protect me.' My heart thumped as if I was right there with the soldiers. She had no idea what it was like.

'I wish I could go. We're all starving here anyway, so what's the difference? A quick bullet or a long-drawn-out death, it's just a matter of time. We're all going to die here.' Ellie got up and paced around the little workshop like a caged panther.

'If I could, I'd hide on the other side until this whole bloody war is over. Take as many children with me as I could.' She sat down again and grabbed both my hands. Hers were hot and sweaty.

'You know, the other day when you were out, I dropped by the children's hospital. I wanted to make myself useful; I'm going crazy here in the house. Mika, it was awful. They've nothing: no food, hardly any medicine or bandages, even bedlinen is rare. I saw some children lying on newspaper and the nurse told me they now stuff newspaper into the covers. The little ones looked so wretched, sunken eyes with dark circles under them. They just stared at me from their beds. And so thin! What if you could smuggle in some medicine from the other side? Or even smuggle out a child? I heard that people are doing this. There's food over there. The children could be hidden.'

Goose bumps spread up my arms, then across my

whole body. I was no hero – and yet I admit it, I felt excited too. Ellie had touched something in me, an idea that might give me back some self-respect. Could this be the remedy for my shame, something that could turn my wretched situation into an opportunity?

Still, my pounding heart reminded me I was also scared out of my wits. We'd all heard of young people who had been taken to the Pawiak prison then turned up days later, dead and mutilated, in a dark alley. Age provided no protection from the Gestapo, nor from any Nazis.

'You're crazy, Ellie, how am I supposed to do this? Max is always right next to me. He collects me and brings me back. All I have is the damn coat.'

'But you are the Puppet Boy. They know you have a coat full of puppets, they won't search you – and if they do, it has to be only the puppets they find. You can conjure something with all your pockets. You know, like a magician. It's about distraction and timing.' Distraction and timing? Ellie had a nerve. She was also right.

'It's too dangerous, Ellie; really, I don't want to hear anything more about it.' Something shut down in me and I tried to change the subject.

'But you must come with me to the hospital.' I should have known Ellie wouldn't give up that easily. 'You'll see for yourself.'

'I've already seen the orphanage, thank you very much, and I see more misery than I can stomach every day in the streets, isn't that enough?'

'No, Mika. We must put on a show for them. It's different there. A lot of children die every day. They're just kids – sometimes three to a bed.'

My resistance collapsed. Ellie had won and I gave in.

*

And so, a few months after my first performance on the Aryan side, Ellie and I left for the Jewish Children's Hospital in Sienna Street. Like the orphanage, the building was three storeys high with a grand staircase leading to different floors and wards. The nurses moved around like ants, as if their busyness could cover up the lack of resources. Seeing the nurses dressed immaculately in starched white uniforms helped us, for a brief moment, to forget that this hospital sat in the middle of the ghetto – until the stench hit us: no uniform could mask the smell of illness and death, of open wounds and human excrement.

The matron, a tall figure with a stern expression and a deep voice, her greying hair pinched back in a bun, commanded the nurses around her, continuously scribbling with a small stump of a pencil on a clipboard which jutted out at a sharp angle beneath her left breast. Ellie approached her.

'Matron, you might remember me from my visit last week. I have brought my friend Mika; he's the puppeteer I mentioned to you. We've come to entertain the children.' Ellie sounded very adult and efficient.

The matron looked at me and a small smile spread across her face.

'Ah, welcome, young man.'

'We'd like to start with the sickest children first,' Ellie continued. Another smile washed over the matron's pale face.

'Well, they're all fairly ill; we never know who will make it through the night. But some little ones surprise us and hang on for quite a while. I suggest you start on the TB ward – third floor to the right. Most of the children there have been in hospital for a very long time.' With this she spun around to attend to a nurse who had been waiting. The matron's voice sounded coarse and despite a warm smile her authority intimidated me.

We wound our way up the marble staircase. With each floor my heart sank. How much more sickness, poverty and suffering could I witness? Little did I know how those children would surprise us.

The TB ward had about twenty beds squeezed tightly next to each other in one small room. A wood burner stood forlorn in the middle, giving off hardly any heat. The loose plaster on the walls had crumbled, leaving little heaps of white debris on the floor, but as if to assert that colour and life still existed, drawings were pinned up everywhere: simple sketches scribbled with coloured pencils of gardens, houses, butterflies, animals or people holding hands; one fine realistic drawing depicted a nurse bending over a child. At the back of the room one drawing in particular caught my eye: a dark, dense sketch filled with nervous criss-crossing strokes, showing a ghetto street crowded with indistinguishable, faceless characters, like ghosts. Only one figure stood out: a woman with friendly features, wearing a cheery, colourful dress.

The bed next to the drawing belonged to a boy who turned out to be fifteen, like me, yet he must have been half my weight. His cheeks were sunken but he smiled when I approached him. He introduced himself as Kalim.

Like those of most of the children on this ward, Kalim's eyes burned, but this was not from the ravaging fever but from a place deep inside him that was still painfully alive. A place that clung on to life despite the knowledge that he would not recover.

'Hello, Kalim, I'm Mika and this is Ellie. We are puppeteers. Is this your drawing?'

Kalim nodded.

'It's great. What is it about?'

'Oh, that's my mother,' Kalim said, becoming animated. 'One day I'll see her again. Maybe you know her? She has brown hair and brown eyes and often wears this beautiful flowery dress. She hasn't been here for a while now, so I'm asking all visitors if they have seen her. We live in Leszno Street, opposite the café. She's called Stefania. Stefania Goldstein.'

We didn't know his mother; the ghetto moulded us all into a single grey mass, a murky river that rolled through the dirty streets, swelling more and more every day with the debris of so many lives. Somewhere in this river floated Kalim's mother. Maybe she had starved in her apartment, or lay dead in her bed. Maybe she had gone mad – it happened more and more. Just the other day one of our neighbours had run out of the house, naked and screaming. Thank God none of the soldiers was around at that moment, and her daughter was able to drag the woman back in.

I felt wretched, standing among the children's beds, but the ones who could get out of bed immediately surrounded us, while the others shouted, all demanding to see the puppets. And so here we were again, making up one little play after another. Just as we'd seen in the orphanage, the children desperately wanted to play with the puppets on their own little hands, creating their own stories. What a shrieking, lively crowd.

We also visited other wards: the general ward, the one for what were termed 'internal' diseases, but we always returned to the TB ward.

It was a special place where the children knew each other well and there was a real sense of camaraderie and mutual support. Their last stop – for no one would ever leave this ward.

*

One afternoon Kalim told us that he used to play the violin, but it had been sold for two loaves of bread when he still lived with his mother and brother in Leszno. That's when I remembered the tiny violin which had slept in the depths of the coat since those first days after they shot Grandfather. When I pulled it out, Kalim's face lit up, and within minutes the small room had filled with a sweet and cheerful melody. This boy played so delicately and with such passion on this tiny instrument, charming everyone around him. I joined in with the little flute while others sang and beat improvised drums. Ellie and some of the children danced to the music, and for one afternoon we were a colourful troupe.

Later that day Kalim asked me to approach his bed.

'That was fun, Kalim! You play so well.' I smiled at him. Kalim ignored what I said and looked me straight in the eye.

'How do I know there is something else after we die?'

His question caught me off guard. 'I guess we don't really know for sure, but we believe. We hope. We pray. Although I don't pray much, I must admit.'

'I'm scared, Mika!'

'I know.' What could I say?

'You and Ellie are like strange angels, showing up here when no one else bothers to come except the nurses. I always feel better when you're here.'

'I'm not sure about the angel bit, but it reminds me of a verse in the Talmud I like: *"Every blade of grass has an angel that bends down and whispers: Grow, grow!"* We all need each other, Kalim, we all need hope. I love coming here to see you.'

'To this place?'

He tried to sit up but stopped halfway. I could see the exhaustion in his face.

'Yes, because all of you are so brave. I never hear you

98

complain about anything. If I were lying here I'd like someone to entertain me.'

Kalim looked at me. I could see the fever in his eyes, his cheeks burning red.

'I wish I could grow up and play one of those large violas.' He stretched out his left hand and put an imaginary instrument on his shoulder, then drew an invisible bow over the strings.

For a moment he seemed lost in music only he could hear.

'And I would love to hear you. I think you should rest now, Kalim, it's been a long afternoon. We'll be back soon.'

'Will you bring your violin again?'

'Of course.'

Kalim smiled. His eyes were like two dark moons against his pale skin, and his hand lay hot and dry in mine. Ellie waved at him from the opposite corner. She was sitting with some girls on a bed, letting the monkey ride on the princess's shoulder.

The following week we arrived in the late afternoon. We entered the ward and as I glanced at the beds I stopped short. Kalim had shrunk into a boy of about six. It took me a moment to understand: a different boy lay in Kalim's bed and the drawing on the wall had vanished. I reached out to Ellie.

'Where's Kalim?' That moment one of the nurses entered, and ushered us outside the room.

'Kalim is not with us any more. He died. The night after your last visit. He slipped away in his sleep. But that evening he asked me to give you his drawing if he didn't wake up the next day. I said to him "Don't be silly!" but, you know, it is mysterious sometimes, the children do know when their time is coming.'

Everyone missed Kalim sorely and that afternoon our plays were dull and lacked enthusiasm. With every death a fire burnt more fiercely in me, but whenever I imagined one of those children under my coat, beneath the very noses of the Germans, I still shuddered, pushing the thought away.

9

The cruel routine continued: every week they forced me to make up new plays for the officers and soldiers. And always on a Friday, our Shabbat evening; as if they hadn't tormented us enough, the rats took special pleasure in using our Shabbat for their debauched amusement, making me and other Jews accomplices. They introduced more cabaret acts and women, who, caked in thick make-up and with forced smiles, had to kick up their legs in front of the *Herren* officers, revealing much flesh and leaving little to the imagination. It was confusing for me. I hated being there, yet sometimes my body let me down. I was embarrassed by those stirrings in my trousers, ashamed that part of my sexual awakening happened in such a way.

I still got sick from the beer they forced down me and my coat always stank of smoke, sweat and alcohol, but Mother left me alone and never asked again where I had been. Instead, she quietly wrapped the bread and put it away. We only ate it when we had run out of everything else. The morning after, Mama always gave me slightly stronger tea and sometimes even a bit of sugar.

I often felt as if I were staggering through thick fog, confused and numb, and if it hadn't been for Ellie, I would have been completely lost. She helped me make new puppets and think up crude jokes and tricks, trying to make me laugh.

The rats expected new tricks and new puppets each week, but Max had become more relaxed and at times was even friendly. He didn't bark at me any more and after each show he'd clap me on the shoulder with a hearty '*gut gemacht Bürschchen*, well done, boy!' Once, when a couple of his comrades were about to force a third beer on me, he pushed the soldiers out of the way, grabbed me and pulled me out into the backyard for some fresh air.

'I see you don't like our beer. Don't worry now,' he said and smiled, for a moment keeping his hand on my shoulder. Although I still hated him, I couldn't help but feel grateful too.

That night, when he took me back to the *Wache*, Max gave me a piece of cheese as well as some bread. We hadn't had cheese for so long I could barely remember its taste.

'You're hungry, boy?' Max asked. What a stupid question. While the Poles on the Aryan side could barely live on their rations, what the Germans allowed the Jews wouldn't have filled a cat. Starving us had always been part of their plan. I said nothing.

'Look, tell me what you need and I'll see what I can do.'

What did I need? Let me think: freedom, decent food, medicine … did he enjoy seeing me squirm? How could I possibly trust a rat?

'Medicine.' The word tumbled out of my mouth before I could stop it. 'Anything. We have nothing in the ghetto.'

I stopped myself before I could say any more. Thinking of the squalor of the children's hospital made me nauseous. Max nodded but didn't comment.

'Meet you here next week,' he simply mumbled, then he turned, making his way back to the barracks, while I strode through the gate.

The next time I saw him, Max appeared tense and hardly spoke to me in the barracks nor when he dropped me off at the *Wache*. He thrust the promised bread into my hand without a word and left. No cheese that day. Somehow I felt relieved: I couldn't trust a rat after all. But towards the end of the week, as Ellie and I rehearsed another play in the workshop, Mama knocked on the door.

'Mika, I found this in the bread.' She held up a small brown glass bottle filled with tiny white pills.

'What's going on? Where did you get that bread from?' I snatched the bottle out of her hand.

'Please don't ask me, Mama, I can't tell you.'

I closed the door.

'Did that soldier hide the pills?' Ellie asked.

'Yes. But it could be a trap.'

'It could be, but that looks like medicine. It says "Aspirin".' Ellie examined the bottle, pouring the pills on to her palm. 'Let's take it to the hospital.' We still visited the children's hospital each week and those pills, although they represented nothing more than a drop in the ocean, would be welcome. The matron confirmed them as genuine and did not ask further.

One day Ellie said she had a terrible pain in her left leg so she stayed behind while I made my way to the hospital. I spent the afternoon on the TB ward and just as I was about to leave, the matron approached me, tugging my coat.

'Come with me for a moment, please, Mika, I want to ask you something.' Her expression was friendly but I was alarmed. She led me into her office.

'Sit down, dear. We're very lucky to have you here. I've heard wonderful things from the children. Your puppets make such a difference. And last week Ellie told me something in confidence. Please don't be cross and let me finish, I know this needs to remain a secret. I swear on my life that it will stay that way.'

I slid around on my chair and put my hands in my pockets. I itched all over.

'Mika, I've a big favour to ask you. There's a little girl who has just arrived. She is just over two and she is tiny. She was dropped off with a note around her neck saying "Please forgive us, but we can't feed another one, please take care of her, she is called Esther."'

I knew what the matron was about to say and I didn't want to hear it.

'Mika, there's nothing wrong with her but she is so very thin and I don't think she'll survive if she stays here. I've connections on the other side so all I'm asking is that you take her with you when you cross on one of your weekly "outings". Take her to safety. Ellie told me the soldiers and officers know you well by now and won't suspect anything. And you always wear that enormous coat. Esther is so tiny. We can arrange for you to meet someone on the other side and hand her over. That way she can be saved, Mika.'

I sat stiff and numb, speechless, not only because of Ellie's betrayal, but also because of what the matron was asking of me. How could she? How could I, still only a boy, possibly hide another human being under my coat? It was an absolutely ridiculous proposal.

'We can give her something so she goes to sleep,' the matron continued her plea, 'and maybe you can steal away for a moment and get some fresh air?'

It was true I sometimes went outside behind the barracks to get fresh air or to throw up after all the beer. The rats were used to that by now and mostly they left me alone. But not always; sometimes they checked up on me. This woman was simply asking too much of me: to hide a living, breathing being, a little girl, under my coat while I marched with a German soldier into the devil's den?

'I'm sorry, ma'am, but I can't do this.' My throat felt as if it were about to close up at any minute, and my voice sounded hoarse and far away. 'I just can't.'

The matron's smile slowly vanished, her face returning to the friendly but reserved mask I had witnessed before.

'Fine, but I want you to come and meet the girl anyway.' She took my arm and led me up the large staircase to the first floor. I felt sheepish and didn't resist.

Ellie and I had never been to this ward. It was even more crammed than the TB ward, full of very young children, sometimes two or three to a bed, and I retched at the overwhelming smell of diarrhoea and vomit. The moaning and crying made my heart sink even lower. The matron looked around the sea of beds, then led me to a small bed in the corner.

The girl looked at me with large green eyes. She wore a thin nightdress and her wild, reddish curls looked as if they had not been combed for weeks. She sat quietly, clutching a naked, blonde doll. She was tiny.

'This is Esther,' the matron said in a matter-of-fact way.

'Hello, Esther, it's nice to meet you. I am Mika.' I didn't know what to say to this fragile being. The girl didn't answer. Something in her gaze unnerved me. I was sure she knew what was going on and right there it hit me: yes, it was very dangerous but this girl would die if I didn't take her.

'I'll think about it.' I turned to face the matron.

'Thank you, Mika.' Her smile returned, as if she knew I had already made up my mind. The girl stretched out her ragged doll towards me. I reached into my pocket and took out the princess. Esther's smile lit up her whole face.

*

That night, Ellie and I sat in the workshop, plotting the girl's escape as if we were putting together an elaborate new show. But not before I had rained down a long tirade on Ellie, about broken secrets, betrayal, trust and friendship. She just sat quietly until I ran out of steam.

'All right, then, let's think.' I struggled to feel as if I was in charge again. 'Timing is crucial. I need to hand over the girl before my act, before I use the coat as a stage.'

I was holding the princess in one hand and the sorcerer in the other. For now, Hagazad had to stand in for me, his cape the closest thing I could find resembling my coat.

'Yes, or you could bring a suitcase with props and a hand-built stage as a surprise. Then you could leave the coat on and go outside at the first opportunity,' Ellie offered. God, she was smart. Still, I wasn't convinced.

'But I don't know when I will be able to go outside. I mean, the person taking the girl from me will have to be waiting behind the barracks, in the shadows. Do you know how dangerous this is? It won't work, Ellie.'

I could picture it all: the pitch dark behind the building, its access to the road via a small alley ... the area swarming with soldiers, day and night. My heart pounded just thinking about it.

'What if they find out? They'll probably shoot me on the spot or send me to the Pawiak. And what about the girl?'

'You mustn't think like this, Mika.' Ellie tried to comfort me but I was still angry with her for putting me in such a position. I was no hero.

Suddenly I remembered the prince and his passionate speech that had once so surprised me. I reached inside the left inner pocket and pulled him out. He spoke immediately:

'So, what's your verdict, then? You can do something important here. More than just talking and waving puppets around. Come on, Mika, this is your chance. Take it – or forever be ashamed.' Ellie sat quietly, stunned and delighted at the puppet's intervention. I had to admit he had a point.

We planned to do it the following week. No use in waiting any longer, it would only postpone the agony. I would take a suitcase to distract from the coat and pack it with props and painted scenery as a surprise for the soldiers. If I appeared nervous I could blame it on this new scenario. We told the matron about our plan, then busied ourselves in the workshop with papier-mâché, paints and endless replaying of scenarios.

And then the day arrived. Just before I was about to leave with my suitcase in tow, Ellie pulled me back into the workshop.

'I am so proud of you Mika. Please be careful, I couldn't bear it if something happened to you. But I know in my heart you'll be fine.' With this she took my face in both hands and kissed me, right on my mouth. I breathed in sharply. It tasted so sweet and was over so quickly. My first kiss! Truly the best antidote to the icy fear that had kept me awake all night. All the way to the hospital I replayed the kiss over and over again in my mind, keeping at bay any thoughts of the little girl I would carry so soon under my coat.

10

'Come quickly. In here.' The matron ushered me into her small room. Her face was flushed, and she moved more quickly than usual. She laid out a plate for me with a thick slice of dark bread and a piece of cheese – like a last meal. Her smile was betrayed by the tension I could hear in her voice.

'I thought you should eat well before you go, so you don't get too drunk and blurt out something.' She patted me on the shoulder with a motherly gesture. The explanation calmed me a little. Esther lay fast asleep on a stretcher in the corner, her matted hair sticking out from under the sheets like a furry animal.

'Does she know what will happen?' I asked.

'It's difficult to explain to such a young girl. But I told her yesterday she would have a long refreshing sleep and when she woke up, there'd be lovely people taking care of her. Mika, she just looked at me the way she looked at you when you first met her, then gave me a little nod. I think she understands everything.' I remembered that afternoon on the ward well.

'I've given her a sedative. But we need to be careful: it has to last as long as possible, in case something goes wrong, but I can't give her too much as it would poison her tiny body.'

While I ate, the matron picked up a strange contraption from the cupboard. She had constructed a kind of harness to go around my waist in which Esther could lie, her body tightly curled around me, her head leaning slightly against my chest.

'You need to hand her over as soon as you can – breathing might become difficult for her under that coat.'

There we go, now I might even smother the little girl. Panic rose in me like a flash. Yes, sometimes the soldiers handed me a jug of beer before my puppet show. This would need to be my excuse. The reason for my exit.

I finished the bread and cheese. I knew it would do me good but I couldn't taste anything, as if the fear had numbed my taste buds.

'Come now, we need to get ready.' The matron tied the contraption in place and we carefully folded the softly breathing girl around me. She weighed so little, was light and soft as a puppy. I slowly buttoned up the coat. Maybe I looked slightly bigger, but with the huge coat I really could get away with it.

I prowled around the matron's office, practised moving naturally with her: I talked, bent down and spun around without any problem. I only needed to make sure she got enough air.

'Thank you, Mika, you're a very brave young man, I knew I could rely on you. Now go, it's getting late.' She hugged me stiffly, but I knew it came from the heart.

As usual, I met Max at the gate. I arrived a few minutes early and the guard looked at me strangely – a boy turning up at the gate with a suitcase and wearing a large coat was surely suspicious. I would never have dared to come here alone. Max arrived soon after me.

'What's with the suitcase, boy?'

'A surprise; I made a stage and some props.'

Max smiled broadly. 'Well, this is good because we have a guest today, straight from Germany, an important *Offizier wird uns mit seiner Präsenz erglücken!*'

I didn't understand what he was saying, but caught enough to know that someone important would be there. I wanted to run back home, this was crazy; the place would be swarming with soldiers, SS and police.

'Don't worry,' Max said, 'you'll be great.' He smiled. If only he had known.

Esther breathed slowly and regularly, her head leaning warmly against my chest, my heart. Maybe this is how it would feel to be a father? Something warm filled me like sweet tea. No, there was no way back, here was Esther and there was a person on the other side who would risk their life to wait in the shadows for me and the girl.

My stomach tightened and I clutched the prince in my pocket, the soft fur of his coat brushing against my palm. He had fired me up and rightly so – I needed to do my bit, not just wait for whatever terrible thing they had planned for us.

I tried to walk even more upright, breathe deeply, and appear confident. Let them think I was putting on a play in honour of the Herr Offizier.

As we crossed to the other side, Max made small talk. *Important to keep him sweet,* I thought, but the effort put a strain on me and gave me a headache.

'It was my boy's birthday on Monday. He's almost your age. His name is Karl. He wants to be an engineer when he grows up.' I didn't want to hear about his son's plans. We didn't have the luxury of plans – the best we could hope for was to survive the ghetto and this damned war. Was there any future for us? Neither I nor Max knew that evening that only a few weeks later the Allies would bomb his home town Nuremberg. By then his Karl would have other things on his mind than becoming an engineer.

We reached the barracks. As usual it was packed with soldiers and the stench of sweat and beer together with their rough laughter hit me like a wall. Through the dense smoke I could see they had built a small stage for tonight. What if Esther was still with me when I had to perform up there and they noticed her breathing? Then I remembered that this time I had a little stage and props, perfect to hide behind. Besides, all the puppets were now safely tucked into the outside pockets, so I could keep the coat on and wouldn't need to open it.

'Ah, there is our little mascot again. Max, you really like that boy, don't you?' Ignoring his comrade's sneering comments, Max ushered me through the main space to a little room at the back.

'Now that you're a real performer, I think you need a room to prepare yourself. Relax for a while; somebody will fetch you when it's your turn. Good luck.' He lingered for a second as if he wanted to say something else. Then he turned and left.

Stuck in a room where no one was forcing any beer on me, what could I do? Maybe I could steal over to the back exit and, if someone asked, pretend I simply felt sick with nerves, which was not far from the truth.

I opened the door and peeped out. The toilet was back here and no one was watching me. Some soldiers were still putting out more chairs; tonight's visit had attracted a bigger crowd than usual. Quickly I headed straight for the back door. I made it outside, breathing hard. The moment I looked for the dark shadow by the opposite wall, the door opened.

'You want a smoke?' A soldier younger than Max addressed me. I didn't recognise him.

'I saw you last week, you're funny. I like your puppets. I had some myself when I was a boy.' What was it with these Germans and puppets? Did the puppets bring out their sentimental side? I remembered Grandfather telling me about the German Kasperltheater, the old puppet-play tradition.

'I think you're on soon, better get ready.'

I had no choice. I was terrified at the prospect of being so close to the officers with the girl tucked under the coat – my precious, sweet load – but I slid back inside the barracks, rummaged through the suitcase, and for a moment actually thought about the play.

All of a sudden there was a roar of applause. I couldn't resist and peeped out to have a look.

The soldiers and even the officers had scrambled to their feet, clapping as one, as a man in a black sharply tailored uniform entered. He wore a cap with the SS skull insignia and strutted in with large, stiff steps, while military music blasted from the speakers. Everyone stood up, right arms stretched in a Hitler salute followed by three *Heil Hitler!*s, echoing back and forth between the man and the crowd.

The officer, not particularly tall and probably in his thirties, did not have a face that would stand out in a crowd, he didn't even have blue eyes, and yet he exuded something that made me shiver. I returned to the little room trembling, as if awaiting my execution. I would die in this Nazi nest.

After what felt like an eternity, someone knocked.

'Puppet Boy, you're on next. Five minutes.'

Slowly I took the suitcase and left the room. I stood at the back of the main hall, watching the last minutes of the act before my own: a man in a smart suit and top hat doing a musical number. After moderate applause, the compère for the evening introduced me.

'And now, *meine Herren, unser Liebling*, the Puppet Boy of the ghetto.' I cringed but forced my mouth into a broad smile.

I clutched my suitcase and to some applause I set up my new little painted stage in front of the officers, then disappeared behind it. I'd decided on one of the usual Punch and Judy-type shows and was just getting into the swing of it when suddenly Esther stirred. My heart hammered. What if she woke up and cried? My play grew wilder and wilder, and the more I let the puppets scream and fight the more the soldiers laughed. Slowly I sensed Esther's little body growing still again, slipping back into its sedated sleep.

The play was a success; I scrambled out from behind the set and took a bow. Max came over, pushed me to the edge of the first row, ordered a drink from a buxom waitress and thrust a jug of beer into my hand.

'*Hier Bursche, fein gemacht*, well done. Now you can relax. Drink slowly.' It wasn't usually Max who forced beer on me, but unknowingly he had given me my excuse. I drank half of the beer then, a minute later, I clutched my stomach, bent over and pretended to be about to throw up. The soldiers' laughter echoed behind me as I ran outside, but no one followed me.

Quickly now. I scanned the wall, and there I saw it: a shadow, barely visible, a darker patch against the blackness of the wall. I quietly whistled the melody – our secret signal. The reply came immediately. Moving swiftly towards the wall, I made out a slight figure in a long coat – a tall woman. My hands trembled as I unbuttoned my coat, slowly revealing Esther's wild hair, her tiny body. I unbuckled her and had already taken one of her legs out of the harness when the back door opened and a familiar voice cut through the night.

'Everything all right there, boy? You were good tonight.' It was Max.

'Yes, fine, I'm just having a pee. I feel a bit sick. Don't worry, I'll be back inside in a moment.' I tried to keep a steady voice but I was shaking all over. Esther stirred and I had to hold her with one hand. Although I was standing between the woman and Max, my coat shielding her to some extent, if Max came any closer it would be the end. For all three of us. Max mumbled something then left.

The rest of the evening passed in a haze. As I handed over Esther to the shadow she briefly opened her big eyes and looked dozily at me. Suddenly the place she had occupied against my chest felt empty: where there had been her warmth and her steady breathing I felt nothing but an exhausted emptiness, as if I had lost a part of myself. I cautiously patted her hair, saying a silent goodbye.

'Thank you.' The woman's voice sounded hoarse. How fear takes even our voice away ... I slowly moved off, then remembered something. Quickly I stepped back towards the wall and caught the woman just before she slipped farther into the shadows. I pulled out a puppet, one of the twin girls with a dress made from my mother's old apron. I handed it to the woman.

'Please give this to Esther when she wakes up.'

'I will, now go.'

I knew that tomorrow she wouldn't be Esther any more. Not such a Jewish name. She would be called Margaret or Domenica or Ania, tucked in a clean bed by Christian parents.

I rushed back, opened the back door and entered the other world. The atmosphere was heated, the place so smoky and loud I felt dizzy. The compère had just announced a new musical act. I wanted nothing more than to be home, but one of the soldiers from Max's group, the stocky one with the bright red face, approached me, thumped my back, and thrust another jug of beer into my hand.

'Here, boy, drink up.' For the first time I took it gladly,

longing for the beer's power to help me disappear into a fog of nothingness.

I got back late that night. I don't remember much, except that the suitcase felt heavy, as if it were filled with stones. Had a child climbed inside without my knowing, hiding in its dark embrace? Walking back with Max by my side I couldn't stop thinking about Esther, the woman with the hoarse voice who had risked her life, and all the other children still in need of rescue. The hugeness of the task hit me like an avalanche. How could we save all the children? Max noticed me struggling with the suitcase.

'Come, give it to me, I can carry it.'

'No.' My voice was sharp. The handle cut into my palm and the side of the suitcase bumped against my legs, but we Jews could not choose much any more and this was one thing I could refuse. I couldn't bring myself to trust a German's random act of kindness, even if he had given us some medicine. Even if he had a boy called Karl. He could still shoot me on the spot if he wanted to.

'As you wish.' Max's voice sounded flat. Only papier-mâché scenery was packed in the suitcase, along with the puppets, but it felt as heavy as if all the pain of the ghetto were contained inside.

Ellie was waiting for me in the corridor. I could manage only a thin smile before my legs gave way, but she caught me and gave me the biggest of hugs.

'I knew you could do it. You're a hero!' She squeezed me fiercely. She had been afraid for me. Warmth spread inside me and somehow in her arms, in the middle of the night, I found some tears. We sat together until the morning, wrapped in my pocket-coat in an embrace that neither of us wanted to leave.

*

The next time I visited the children's hospital, despite the matron's broad smile, I felt wretched. What was one child when thousands of little ones still lay three to a bed, shivering under their newspaper blankets?

'Every life counts, Mika,' Ellie tried to comfort me. 'What you're doing is important, I'd love to do what you do.' But I wished I could swap with Ellie. She had joined a secret group who forged documents so that more of us could pass back and forth to the Aryan side. Although Ellie put herself forward to go too, the group suggested her limp might draw attention and if she had to disguise herself quickly, her leg might give her away. She fumed for days but in the end she decided to stay with the group.

Over the next few weeks the matron carefully picked out more children for me: they had to be small and thin, not older than three years but not too weak. I didn't envy her job. Two weeks later I smuggled another child, this time a boy called David.

'He might stand a chance on the Aryan side with his fair complexion, blond hair and green eyes,' the matron said. I hoped so.

David kicked under my coat despite the sedative so I needed to hand him over before my performance. I sneaked out the back door. All clear. I whistled. With the answer, I stepped into the shadows, unbuckled the harness and handed over little David. That night the boy disappeared into the strong arms of a man. I rushed back inside and started my puppetry. I had been lucky again.

But even after Esther, David, Abigail, Jeremias, Adam, Zach, Chana, Joshua and a few other little ones, smuggling the children never got any easier. I still woke up on the day of a planned mission as if heavy stones were sewn into my stomach. In fact each time it got harder. So far I had been lucky, but when would my luck run out?

*

One day, although I had no child with me then, I was particularly dreading my time with the rats – I had felt nauseous all day – some of the beets we'd eaten had been mouldy and Mama reckoned they'd given me a stomach ache. It had become a regular joke for the rats to get me drunk and then order me to perform another show in that state. That night, just after I stepped off the small stage, one of the soldiers thrust a huge glass of bitter liquid into my hands.

'*Los, mach schon, schnell, runter damit*, drink it down,' he growled.

'I can't, not today, please,' I pleaded.

He smacked my head hard and for a moment I lost my balance.

'*Lass ihn in Ruhe, Mann!*' I heard Max's voice. '*Komm, gib mir das Glass.*'

Max took the glass out of my hand and pushed me though the crowd towards the back of the room.

'*Ah, der Judenfreund! Willst ihn mit ins Bett nehmen?*' A red-faced soldier sneered at Max, but Max refused to look at him. He took me to the storeroom in which I usually waited for my performances.

'Wait here till I call you.' Why would he do this? I didn't trust Max, but was grateful for the gesture.

Only Ellie's gentle praise and her embrace stopped me shaking after such a night. But how strange and tragic that my first romance was mixed up with such horror. So much terror and fear, for my life, for all our lives, and yet here stood my first love in the middle of the ghetto.

At night one dream plagued me over and over again in my fitful sleep: I stood in the black shadow of the wall, about to hand over a tiny child, when a dark, icy hand reached down from above, snatched my precious load and disappeared into the dark with a high-pitched screech. All I could hear was the child's screams and then laughter; blood-curdling, diabolical laughter. I'd wake up drenched in sweat, longing for Ellie.

And so my double life continued. Max had become more chatty with each visit, telling me about his son and his home town, but I didn't take the bait, hardly listened. What did I care about his life?

During the rest of the week I went to the orphanage, the hospital, put on shows for the lines at the soup kitchens or on street corners. Ellie and the puppets and the children prevented my despair from taking over and I was grateful. Months passed with this fragile routine. Then at the height of summer, the evil shadow that had hung over us unleashed its full force.

II

The last time Max accompanied me to the barracks was in July 1942. I had just finished my puppet show to a beer-fuelled audience when a fat officer with pasty skin grabbed me from behind. His sausage fingers dug into me, both hands holding me by my coat, turning me, then yanking me squarely in front of his enormous body. The uniform didn't flatter him and only the thick leather belt kept his barrel belly from spilling over. When he opened his mouth, the foul stench made me gag.

'*Setz dich*, sit next to me, boy.' His voice was rough and sharp, leaving no doubt that this was an order and not an invitation. He took off his cap and put it on his lap, the SS runes and silver skull glinting in the dull light. Gathering my coat as closely around me as I could, I sat down next to one of Hitler's elite. I had no child with me that evening, which was a wild stroke of luck, considering what would follow.

'*Hier Bursche,* drink.' I gulped the beer down, disgusted by the officer's hideous mass next to me.

'Enjoy, my boy,' he whispered, leaning over me. I retched at the rancid smell of his sweat. 'Move and I'll cut your throat,' his voice hissed in my ear. I sat para-lysed as if there were a deadly spider in my lap. Inside I was screaming. He put his hand on my thigh and slowly

moved it farther up towards my crotch while a new performance, a woman singing raunchy cabaret songs, began
in front of us. It was dark in the audience and no one
seemed to notice. I felt sick to the core and wanted nothing but to run, crawl into bed and listen to my mother's
breathing, or lie safe in Ellie's arms.

Time dragged, then stopped completely. When he
finally took his hand off me I felt dirty and so ashamed.
Once I got back to our apartment, although I had longed
for Ellie, I pushed her away. I didn't want to cry, didn't
want her to know. Not then, or ever.

Max had been friendlier than ever before that evening.
On the way back to the *Wache*, I had noticed a strange
expression on his face; was it sadness, awkwardness or
even pain? He stopped near the *Wache*, just before the
guards could see us. He gave me a bigger than usual rye
bread, a piece of cheese and a glass of strawberry jam.
Then he looked at me with this strange expression, really
looked at me.

'Mika, I would like one of your puppets. When I get
home I want to give it to my boy and tell him about you.
He is a bit younger than you. Give me the prince and I'll
give you another loaf of bread.' For once this sounded
more like a request than an order, his voice softer than
usual. But it left me cold. His boy could die, for all I
cared. My prince? No, the prince belonged to my mother
and me, to our family. The prince gave me the courage I
needed – I would never let him go.

'Any other puppet, but not the prince,' I pleaded.

Max's face changed as if a shadow had fallen over it. A
nerve-racking pause followed.

'Give me the doctor, then, that is how it started after
all.' His voice had returned to giving orders. So, the
doctor would be sacrificed. I pulled the doctor out of my

pocket. His glasses were slightly twisted; I took them and bent them back into a nice round shape. Then I handed the doctor over to Max.

A strange sense that we were saying goodbye stirred in my guts.

'Thank you.' Max took the puppet and put it in his jacket. The doctor, with his white uniform and golden spectacles, disappeared without a word.

'Take care, boy; I won't be coming any more now. Good luck.' With this he abruptly turned on his heels and strode back to the Aryan side. I stood, stunned and shaken. Was my ordeal over? And if so, what about the children?

12

I understood the following day. For when Max asked me about the prince, that was the very night before the deportations started.

I woke on the morning of 22 July 1942 with a headache, as if the Germans were once again rolling their heavy tanks into Warsaw, this time right across my head. I sat up and shook myself. Looking at my outstretched legs under the covers, I remembered last night's nightmare: the officer's fleshy hand creeping like a huge spider up my leg. I squeezed my eyes shut and took a few deep breaths. Somebody had once told me that if you are facing a dangerous animal, never show your fear and just keep breathing. As I counted my breaths, listening, I realised what had woken me: our neighbourhood echoed with screams and the rats' dreaded shouting.

'*Raus, raus. Alle Juden raus. Schnell, schnell, macht schon.*' Their orders were followed by a terrible thumping noise. Boots breaking open doors.

I sat without moving, cold to the core. I glanced at Mother; her eyes were open but she didn't look at me.

'They're coming for us, Mika.' Mama's jaw trembled and her voice was faint. I knew in that awful moment that I did not want to meet any of the rats in my pyjamas, and I certainly didn't want to die in bed. We had heard of old and sick people, men and women, mothers with their infants or those too weak to get up, shot right on the spot in the tepid warmth of their own beds.

'Let's get up, Mama. Quick! Don't just lie there. Let's get everyone together.'

I jumped out of bed as if something had bitten me. Mother said nothing but moved her legs slowly out of bed.

We gathered everyone in the kitchen: Ellie and Cara, the parents with the baby, the twins, Mother and me. The baby, as if she knew what was about to come, screamed her heart out, inconsolable, while the twins sat in the corner, quiet and pale, as if all the mischief had been knocked out of their little bodies.

I moved my chair closer to Ellie. Although we hardly spoke her presence comforted me. I belonged here, right next to her, more than anywhere else.

Mama made tea for everyone. As if it were a final, sacred ritual, she brewed the richest tea we had had since they locked us into the ghetto, adding the last precious tea leaves to her pot. Then, from the farthest corner of one drawer, she took out a small pouch, opened it and let the precious white substance trickle into the liquid, then stirred it gently.

'We might as well have our last tea sweet and remember the sweetness of life.'

I felt so proud of Mama. We drank the steaming tea in silence, our hands cupped around the precious liquid, waiting for the dreaded sound: screeching tyres, boots, the pounding on our door.

Suddenly I felt something move in my pocket. No more than a mouse's wiggle, but worrying still. It was the prince, writhing and moving. With a swift gesture he jumped out of the pocket and on to my hand.

'People of Gęsia Street, do not despair. I am your prince and I tell you, have courage.'

Everyone stared wide-eyed at the prince on my hand.

'Don't be fooled, this may not be the end. We will not be defeated!'

With this the prince disappeared again. Nobody said anything but I could see a small smile on Ellie's face, enough to warm my heart.

Our little community did stay safe that day. The trucks moved on and by the afternoon it was quiet again. But despite the prince's fiery words, we lived in continual fear from that day onwards. Over the next few days and weeks the Germans swarmed through the ghetto like a cloud of locusts, at all times of day and night, spreading terror like wildfire.

Strange, but fear actually has a taste: like blood, sharp, iron and bitter. Now, whatever I ate tasted of fear.

I worried about all the children, but Mother did not want me to leave the flat and Ellie had not been allowed out for a long time.

One afternoon I was sitting alone with Mother in our room. She got up, came over to me, held me by my shoulders and looked directly at me.

'We need to stay together at all costs, Mika. You're everything I have. We can hide this one out.' I felt her fear and her fierce love. I couldn't breathe and shook myself free.

'What do you mean, hide? There are too many of us.'

And what about the children in the hospital and the orphanage? How could Janusz hide his two hundred charges? As far as I was concerned we were all in the same stinking boat, the same rotten ark. What difference would it make to try and hide?

When I looked at Mother again, it was as if a flame

124

had been extinguished. I understood with a sharp ache that she was thinking only of me and her.

'I'm sorry, Mama, but there are nine of us. This is our family now. How can we hide without an attic, with no fake walls? And with a baby that could give us away at any moment? Do you want to kill her off first?'

'I know, dear.' The defeated look on her face went through my heart. 'I'm sorry.'

We had run out of options so we simply stayed quiet and waited, listening out for the trucks. There was no other plan. Going out was too dangerous. They could round you up and shoot you any time they saw you on the street. We heard shooting and screams near by. Reports reached us from neighbours: no one was safe, people were being shot for asking a simple question, for hesitating a moment too long, for being too slow or too quick in getting into the trucks. Some were shot for being too old, too young, or just for having a beard.

One early morning our neighbour Johana pounded at our door.

'They're taking everyone away. If they find you they'll shoot you all.' She spat out the words like bullets.

'They've put up posters; if we come voluntarily they will hand us three loaves of bread and some jam. They say they will resettle us in the East, give us work there. I think we should go.'

We had heard they would either shoot you straight away or herd you to the 'Umschlagplatz', a dirty square surrounded by wire at the north-western edge of the ghetto from which trains departed towards the East – cattle trains. But what did this mean? Like aching bones that know when bad weather is approaching, I felt that this could be worse than anything we had ever known.

'No, we stay.' It was the first time I spoke for all the

125

family. As I held the prince in my pocket, my voice sounded determined and clear. We were staying.

Many others ignored the bad feeling, clinging to the hope of a different, better place, and reported to the *Umschlag*, lured by the promise of bread and jam. Such was the price of our lives now: three loaves of bread and a glass of strawberry jam.

For a week we holed up inside, all nine of us, waiting like trapped animals. Ellie and I spent a lot of time in our workshop – being around her and the puppets kept me from slipping into complete despair. But we were so hungry all the time! We had shared every last bit of bread and now the soups got thinner and thinner.

One evening all of us huddled together around the kitchen table, a single candle casting warped shadows on the walls. Suddenly Ellie's hand gently touched my arm and her deep voice interrupted the tense silence.

'Let's play something, Mika!' I was not in the mood to present yet another stupid story we had made up. Now that I had put on plays for the Nazis, I couldn't reach that precious place of joy and innocent fun any more. As if being around the officers had stolen the puppets' shine, drained them of life and meaning, everything felt stale and false. Still, I fetched the prince from my pocket and he immediately spoke.

'How about tonight we tell a story together?' No one answered, but all eyes were on the puppet.

'A long, long time ago in a faraway place, a boy was born on a stormy April night. When he took his first breath among thunder and lightning, his parents called him Tempest.' With this I took the prince from my hand and passed him to Ellie.

'Tempest was a moody baby, but he grew into a strong boy who liked to climb trees and play knights with wooden swords.' The puppet moved from Ellie to Mama.

126

'Actually, this sounds just like you, Mika. The night you were born, a huge storm lashed over Warsaw.' Mother had broken the puppet's tale and instead began to share the story of my birth. Other scenes from my childhood followed as I wiggled on my seat, glad when she passed the puppet to Aunt Cara, who promptly continued with vignettes from Ellie's childhood. And so, as the prince made the round again and again, everyone, even the twins, shared precious moments until the early hours of the morning. I cherished that night despite my embarrassment; our hearts were wide open and no one held back, as if it was the last time we would all be together. The prince, once more, had been a great helper – if only I could find a way to recover my joy in playing with the other puppets too.

The next night I woke up drenched and shaking, and I knew what I had to do: I needed to see the children's eyes on the puppets again. Whenever their eyes shone, something in me lit up too, became alive again.

I knew Mother wouldn't allow me to go and I didn't ask Ellie as Aunt Cara was even stricter. But very early the next morning I stole away to the orphanage. Mother was still asleep. So often in her sleep she looked peaceful and relaxed, the deep frown between her eyebrows softened, her breathing regular and soft. I scribbled a short note:

Gone to the orphanage, will be back for supper.
Please don't worry and don't be angry, I love you.
Mika, your prince

I rolled it up, took out the prince and placed the note under his arm, as if he were delivering an important pamphlet. Then I tiptoed out of the room, closed the front door and went out into the streets.

The early morning brought with it a light breeze and a blackbird's song. I had forgotten about birds, we hardly heard them any more. Why would they visit us when there were only three trees standing forlorn in the whole of the ghetto and no grass anywhere? I sometimes spotted a flock of pigeons but they never landed on their crossing between our cemetery and Krasinski Park. That morning, however, the brutal shouting had stopped, and instead of the screeching of trucks and marching boots all I could hear was the blackbird's haunting song.

It would take fifteen minutes to walk to the orphanage and I moved swiftly. The bright blue sky opened above me and for a short moment I felt happy to have escaped the darkness and stuffy air of the apartment. Hope stirred in me, as if that bird's song had sung straight into my heart.

But hope was as fleeting as that song. Right on the corner of Leszno Street, I stumbled over an upturned pram. I rubbed my foot and as I lifted my head I gasped. The long wide road, once a place for entertainment, was littered with debris and discarded belongings: single shoes, coats, bags, toys, spectacles, hastily scattered objects that told a silent story of how they had been ripped violently from their owners, kicked around, then abandoned, left behind. Dead bodies, distorted into strange positions, lay where they had collapsed after a deadly shot. And feathers – white feathers ripped from duvets – covered the street, like snow in July.

Everything had changed in these past weeks; I could hardly recognise this as the street along which I had strolled with Grandfather all that time ago on my birthday. Fear gripped me like eagle's claws against my neck. What about Hannah and the other children? What if they had been taken? I raced along the street. As I turned the corner I stumbled over an old man. Wrapped in rags, he lay slumped against the wall, his head hanging lifeless. I bent over him but he wasn't breathing. My eyes caught a small object lying in his lap; a wooden flute, and next to it a single white feather. Suddenly I remembered him: I had listened to his flute the day Grandfather took me to see the puppet show. He had looked ragged even then but his joyful melodies had moved me.

I remembered a bunch of street children dancing to his tunes, hopping and whirling, and for just a little while forgetting their biting hunger. There were no children on the streets now, just a ghostly silence. How had he died? No wound showed the cause of his death. I hope he'd died peacefully. I picked up his small flute, light as a bird's wing, a hollowed-out bone.

'I am taking this with me, old man. You won't need it where you are now. I hope you don't mind.' At that moment a gust of wind lifted the feather from his hand, and tossed it up into the sky, swirling. I took it as a good sign. I blew a few thin notes, then slipped the flute into one of the coat's deep pockets and moved on. That little flute would become an important companion to me. I began to run as fast as I could, wanting to get away from all this death and destruction. I needed the children that day, maybe more than they needed me. When I finally saw the orphanage my heart leapt into my throat. I rang the bell. My relief must have shown when Margaret slowly opened the heavy door, peeping out through the small slit.

'Oh, Mika, what are you doing here? You shouldn't be here, it's so dangerous.'

'Isn't it dangerous everywhere? Please let me come in. I've missed you all so much. I worried about you. How are the little ones?'

Margaret opened the door and quickly pulled me in, but not before she had looked around, making sure no one had seen me. The strain on her face showed; she was paler than usual and she had deep dark circles under her eyes, giving her the appearance of a weary owl. She had lost weight, but her smile shone as beautiful as ever.

'They are as well as can be expected. And they've missed you too, they've all been asking about you. Still, you shouldn't be here.'

Yet after a while she brought me a steaming cup of tea and announced my arrival to the children. Soon we were back to the old routine, surrounded by all the little ones, Hannah helping me with the puppets. For the first time since that fateful day when the doctor had spoken up, I forgot myself completely in the puppet play. The children's sparkling eyes were indeed the remedy I needed. But clouds of worry passed across Janusz's face even though he tried to smile. He looked years older than the last time I had seen him some weeks ago.

'I've nothing left to give them, Mika,' he told me, pulling me into a corner; 'I can't thank you enough.'

Hannah did not leave my side and later in the morning she drew me away from the others. I can still feel her tiny hand pulling my fingers.

'I'm always thinking about you, Mika. You're my best friend.' She took a deep breath. 'Can I marry you when I grow up?' She just came out with it. No more time for being shy or polite, she had held back long enough. The first and only proposal I ever received. And fool that I was, I didn't know what to say. I bent down and took her little hands in mine.

'But we are friends, Hannah, I'll always be your friend.'

'But I want to marry you,' she insisted.

'I can't marry you, Hannah, you're just a little girl, and I am far too old for you. But don't worry; I know you will marry someone nice one day.'

Her eyes brimmed with tears but she didn't let them fall. She clenched her fists and her tiny jaw. Seeing her effort not to cry I realised I had broken her heart. She turned away, but before I left that day she gave me a drawing. A simple sketch of two stick people holding hands under a cheerful sun: one tall, the other little. One wore trousers, the other a red and orange skirt. Both were smiling broadly and a colourful butterfly fluttered between them. She signed it *'For my friend Mika from Hannah – come back soon.'*

That day in the orphanage I was just happy to see the children again, and even the puppets were different: free to be themselves. The plays turned very silly, funny and light-hearted, and I even let the fool play the tiny violin, something I had never allowed the Germans to see.

In the afternoon I suddenly remembered I had stolen away from home and my stomach tightened. I promised the children I would return soon and left quickly.

I rushed back through the streets. Anyone I saw darted like prey, hiding closely in the shadows of houses, hushed like mice. Everyone looked at everyone else suspiciously, not knowing who could still be trusted.

When I turned the corner into Gęsia Street, I froze. One of the feared green German trucks was parked right outside our neighbour's house, ready to take its daily load to the *Umschlag*. The street swarmed with soldiers and SS units, shouting and kicking in doors. My ears rang and my heart pounded so hard I thought it would burst. I stood and watched, rooted to the spot.

Then, with the same efficiency and brutal shouting we had heard all over the neighbourhood for weeks, I saw them move towards our house.

'Raus, raus, schnell, macht schon, alle Juden raus.'

The blood hammered in my ears, echoing their beatings on the door. I stood and stared, my legs trembling. A useless boy with no weapons in his hands.

When I looked up I could see soldiers inside our flat. My eyes followed the intruders from the bedroom to the kitchen. One of them opened the kitchen window, grabbed my mother's beloved window box with both hands and threw it full force into the street. Earth and flowers exploded all over the pavement, leaving shards of pottery, petals and uprooted plants scattered as far as the opposite side.

My stomach heaved. Why the flowers as well? My mother's beautiful garden. Another soldier kicked earth and plants from our balcony, hitting them with such force it was as if he was trying to score a goal. His face shone with sweat and satisfaction, the ugly joy of destruction.

Seeing even those small islands of triumph destroyed made me feel nauseous. I was sick to the core and gripped by an overwhelming desire for revenge: to kill off the rats, once and for all. Yet for all that rage I just stood there, frozen, breathing heavily like a workhorse.

The familiar sound of our front door opening – a click followed by a drawn-out creak – shook me out of my trance.

Then I saw them, being led out of the house one after another: first the parents, holding the twins – how thin they looked in the summer light, the baby clutched to her mother's breast – then Cara, and lastly my mother. Mother was very pale, and although she tried not to look around too obviously I knew she was scanning the street for me. They were all wearing coats despite the July heat and each carried only one suitcase, as ordered by the Germans. Neighbours from both sides of the street joined them, a herd of terrified people, clinging closely to each other.

I thought I could hear Mother talking quietly to the twins, but where was Ellie? Had she come after me to the orphanage or was she hiding somewhere?

In that split second I decided to hold back, although my whole being ached to run over to my mother and join her, to turn myself in and go with her wherever they might take us. But if Ellie wasn't there, I had to find her.

'*Na macht schon, schneller, raus.*' The soldiers' brutal commands echoed down the street. They loaded the group into the truck at gunpoint. All stood tightly packed in the open car, hanging on to each other and the iron bars. The truck sped off with screeching tyres.

The rats would take everyone they rounded up that day to the *Umschlagplatz*. I had seen the *Umschlag* from the second floor of the hospital a few days after the deportations started: it was a fenced-off square, packed to the brim with people, chaos and despair. Later, when the trains had departed, it lay empty and abandoned, cherished possessions left behind like flotsam after a flood: a small suitcase, books, a leather bag, paper, clothes. Our neighbour had told me that they were taking away seven thousand of us each day during these terrible weeks. Seven thousand souls washed away every single day.

Through the mist of my tears something tried to push its way into my consciousness. While my eyes knew instantly, it took my brain some time to realise what I was seeing. It was Max, the soldier. He jumped down from one of the trucks that had just pulled up outside the houses on the opposite side. Without thinking I stepped out from the shadows of the wall and approached the van.

'Max.' My voice sounded hoarse and thin. Before I could reach him, another soldier stepped into my path and pointed his gun at me.

'*Halt, Jude, stehenbleiben,*' he yelled.

Max looked startled, as if he thought I was familiar but did not recognise me. Then something changed in his face.

'Wait, don't shoot. It's the Puppet Boy, don't you remember?'

I realised I had seen the other soldier at one of the

evenings with the officers. Instinctively I put my hand in my pocket.

'Put your hands up,' a thin lanky soldier with sharp features screamed at me.

'Max, they've taken my mother, my aunt and my friends, please don't take them. They can all work.' My voice gathered strength. I could see sadness in Max's eyes but his voice cut like a knife.

'This is how it is now, boy, there's nothing I can do. Orders have changed. And orders are orders. You can be glad we let you go. *Mach dass du fortkommst.* Go.' He had given me a chance to disappear but that was all.

My world collapsed, turned into dust right before my eyes. I couldn't move, just kept staring at Max, this soldier whose interest in puppets led me to live a double life. Suddenly, as brief as the flutter of a butterfly's wing, I saw Max give a tiny wink. I could have been mistaken, but when Max passed me on the way to the next house he whispered, 'I'll see what I can do, meet me at the *Wache* tonight at ten. What's your mother's name?'

'Halina Hernsteyn.'

Then he strode on past as if he had never known me.

Was this a final trap or did he really mean to help us? I turned and stumbled away, my body still trembling. In the *Aktion* Max behaved as a brutal rat like any other, smashing our doors with his boots, yet he'd taken risks before, smuggled medicine for us and shielded me once from the other soldiers' games. But even if he wanted to protect my family now, how could he? He was a Wehrmacht soldier, part of the killing machine, sworn to follow orders. Maybe he felt as trapped as I did? I shook myself. How could I even think this? I loathed them all. As for meeting Max that night, there was nothing I could do but wait and see. But where to hide until then? Nowhere was safe now, and I needed to be at the *Wache* at ten despite the curfew.

I made my way to the *Umschlagplatz*, hiding in the shadows of the walls. I saw traces of the rats' terrifying passage everywhere: people lay shot or bleeding in gutters, even children. Left as they had fallen. And so many broken things. Why did the rats have to break everything? Wasn't it enough to drag us from our homes? I had learnt such different things about the Germans, all that time ago, when we were still permitted to go to school. Had admired their music and poetry, learnt about their philosophers and artists. Seeing the littered streets, who could still believe they would resettle us Jews in the East and help us set up new homes?

As I trudged through the devastated streets, my stomach cramped. A bitter taste sat in my mouth. Arriving at the *Umschlag*, I kept my head low until I found a sheltered spot where I could peep through the wooden fence. I tried to find Mama and the others but there was such chaos, I couldn't see them.

People were running around frantically, searching for their loved ones or sitting alone on their suitcases, mumbling, reading, praying. Others gathered in small groups. I couldn't see any water or food and they had nothing to sit on apart from their luggage: only this bare, godforsaken square of dirt. A place of limbo. Nothing good could come from such a place.

I shivered. After a while I couldn't bear it any more. I needed to run. I did not know where my legs were taking me, but soon I recognised the area: of course, the orphanage, the children.

I pounded at the door. Margaret opened it, her eyes wide with alarm.

'What are you doing here again, Mika?' She pulled me in and hugged me fiercely. I felt the cleanness of her uniform, the warmth and softness of her breasts, and just for a few seconds I felt safe.

'Mika, what is it?' Margaret sounded out of breath.

'They took my mother, my aunt and the twins and their parents. The baby too. I don't know what to do!'

Suddenly tears stung my eyes, but I didn't want to cry. Not here, not ever. If I started I would not be able to stop.

'Oh God.' I could see Margaret's face drain of colour. I took a deep breath.

'Is Ellie here? I can't find her.'

'No, she came earlier, you just missed her. She was looking for you too. She said she would go back to Gęsia Street, to the apartment.' Margaret's eyes were kind, and after the first shock she seemed calm again. I could see the children huddled around Janusz in one of the rooms off the main hall. He was telling a story and held their full attention. Among them I spotted Hannah's curly head. It pained me to remember her innocent marriage proposal to me earlier.

'Thank you, Margaret, I need to go.'

'Take care, Mika.' Before any of the children could see me, I slid out of the door.

I ran all the way back. The stinging pain in my lungs distracted me from the fear and the black hole that was beginning to consume my whole body. Gęsia Street lay deserted and wrapped in an eerie silence. Before I entered the house, I gathered some of mother's scattered flowers, carefully scooping up roots and bulbs. Her beloved garden had been trampled on and flattened, yet her love still lived on in those flowers, as mine did in the puppets.

The front door stood wide open and I tiptoed up the stairs to our apartment. The door was slightly ajar. I found Ellie in the workshop, bowed over a new puppet, a little girl with hair like Hannah's and a dress sewn from her mother's handkerchief. She didn't look up.

'Everyone's gone.' Her voice was empty of all emotion.

'Yes, but I saw Max and he might help us find them.' I tried to sound convincing but my words carried little strength. Her sharp laughter made the hair on my neck prickle. I had never heard her like this.

'Mika, *wake up*. Do you believe those pigs? You talk as if this damn soldier is different, but they are all the same!'

'He did give us medicine, remember? And even if he had wanted to help, what could he have done with the other soldiers around?'

Ellie said nothing and my heart sank. I had to cling to this hope as to a rope dangling over a gorge, but the rope felt slippery and frayed.

I left Ellie in the workshop and opened the bedroom door. There, on the bedside table, sat the prince, as if he was waiting for me. That is when I finally cried.

13

I was risking my miserable life just by being outside after curfew, not to mention hanging around the *Wache*, but I moved swiftly, avoiding the watchtower's sweeping searchlights. I forced myself to be still, cowering in the darkness close to the *Wache*, waiting. After a while I couldn't feel my right foot.

'Your mother and aunt are at this address, first floor on the right.' I had not heard Max approach, despite his heavy boots as he slipped next to me into the shadow. He reeked of cigarettes, sweat and beer, and something else I could not distinguish. Was it fear? Grief? Hatred? He pulled out a small slip of paper and placed it firmly in my hand.

'Don't ever tell anyone about this.' His voice sounded strange. Was he scared?

'What about the others, the twins, the baby?' I asked.

'Don't you ever stop? Forget them. *Verstanden?* The trains have left for today. There is nothing I can do. And you must remain at this address. These streets have already been cleared. You'll be safe there.' His familiar impatience returned.

We stood for a moment in awkward silence. All words failed me. I buried my hands in my pockets, touching the prince's cloak, his fur trim and papier-mâché face with my hot fingers. Slowly I pulled out the puppet Max had asked for on that last evening before the deportations. For his son, he had said. After all this horror, what did it matter? What use were the puppets now? As if to confirm my thoughts, the prince stayed silent and hung limply from my hand. I had lost so much already, if I could at least keep mother and Ellie ... I held out my most treasured puppet to the soldier. Max looked at me, startled.

'Here, you can have him,' I said.

'Are you sure, boy?'

For a moment his voice softened. I nodded. Slowly he took the prince in both hands then tucked the puppet into the depths of his uniform. A weak smile washed over his face. Suddenly he looked very tired.

'Thank you, Mika.' It was the only time he'd ever used my name.

'I can't help you.' He glanced at me with an expression I could not read. Then, for the briefest of seconds, he put his right hand on my shoulder, then withdrew it.

'Go now. Good luck.'

I turned and left the soldier with my prince. My prince stuffed into the pocket of his German uniform. My lovely, treasured prince, who had comforted my mother, fired me up to resist and fight. What was I thinking? Did I feel I owed this soldier something? The moment I turned to leave, a sense of loss cut through me as if some vital part had been ripped from my chest. For a second I wanted to run after him, but when I looked, Max had already disappeared. The loss of the prince left a hole, as if he had been a real person, like the very first time I handed over the little girl Esther to the stranger in the shadows.

I stopped.

'Good luck, my prince,' I whispered into the night air. The sky was clear and the stars were out. 'Don't forget me.' But he was gone. He was only a puppet, after all.

139

I shook myself and rushed back to our apartment.

It was so quiet in our house, all apartments emptied of life. I tried to forget the cattle trucks that were carrying our neighbours to some unknown place. Their last hours at the *Umschlag*. I quietly called for Ellie and found her again in the workshop, bent over in the same position as if she hadn't moved at all. I did not have the heart to tell her about the prince but simply showed her the piece of paper on which Max had scribbled the address: Orla Street 52.

'How do you know it's not a trap?'

'I don't know, Ellie, but my gut tells me he's not playing games. And what choice do we have anyway?'

Ellie didn't reply but slowly got up and fetched her suitcase from the kitchen. Mine was hidden under the left side of the bed. Seeing the empty space next to my suitcase where my mother's had been felt like another blow to the stomach. I pulled mine out and chucked in whatever seemed useful or important: the rest of the puppets that didn't live in the coat, fabric, needles, scissors and glue from the workshop, socks, clothes, knives, an enamel cup and a blanket. The last thing Ellie put into her suitcase was her book of Arabian tales. I couldn't find the photo album, Mother must have taken it. Finally, rummaging for food, I found a loaf of bread, wrapped in layers of newspapers, at the back of the kitchen cupboard: one of the loaves Max had handed to me the night of my last performance. It was as hard as a brick. We closed the door and made our way to the address. We had no plans to return.

When we reached the quarter, all the houses lay empty like gutted fish. No lights shone anywhere, except for the almost full moon. We glanced over our shoulders, ducking through the shadows, but no one was following us.

This was indeed a street the Germans had finished with: everyone here had been deported.

We turned a last corner into Orla Street, but when we found the number, the house showed no signs of being occupied. I squeezed Ellie's hand.

'Shall we try ringing the bell?' I whispered. Ellie shook her head, her lovely ponytail swinging. We looked for small stones.

'Which flat is it?' Ellie's voice startled me, she was so close to my ear. I realised how dear that voice had become to me.

'He said it's the first floor on the right.' I pointed upwards. Not even a sliver of light shone from the pitch-black square of the window. Ellie threw the first stone. She missed. She tried a second time. Its clang against the window echoed in the silence. Nothing. I followed with my smallest stone. Still no reply. We took turns, three, four more stones.

'Shhh! I think I heard something.'

'Ouch!'

I must have squeezed Ellie's hand too hard. There was no light but I could swear the window had opened a crack.

'Mama, is that you? It's me and Ellie.' My whisper sounded too loud but I was so tense. After a pause the window opened farther and I could just make out my mother's silhouette.

'Mika, is that really you?' I could hear the trembling in her voice. This time Ellie spoke.

'Yes, it's us, let us in, quick.' The window closed and we heard light footsteps approaching the front door. It was Mother who opened. She stared at me for a second, as if she had seen a ghost, then threw her arms around me and hugged me tight.

'Come on up, Cara is here too.' She grabbed me and Ellie by the hand and pulled us upstairs.

When Mother opened the apartment door I could see Cara sitting at a table at the back of the room, illuminated only by a small candle. She didn't get up to greet Ellie. Slumped in a chair, she simply stretched out her arms but didn't utter a word. Ellie hugged her fiercely nevertheless.

Later we sat together at the table, talking quietly. That is Mother, Ellie and me spoke, while Cara remained silent. She seemed to have given up any faith in speaking.

'They took us to the *Umschlag* – that awful, godforsaken place.' Mother spoke quietly, looking at me and Ellie while Cara stood with her back to us.

'No water anywhere, and the sun pounding down on us like a curse. We were crammed in with hundreds of people and after a while everyone panicked. The Germans just left us there and no one told us what was going to happen. We looked for you both when they put us in the truck and later at the *Umschlag*; I was crazy with worry and missed you both so much, and yet, if you weren't with us, I thought, maybe there was a chance that you were safe?

'Then suddenly a soldier approached us through the crowd. He was tall and moved quickly. I could tell he was asking for someone. As he came closer I heard him call: "Halina Hernsteyn?" "Yes, over here!" I answered like a reflex. "Come," he commanded, motioning for me to come with him, but I grabbed hold of Cara. "I'm not going anywhere without my sister. And there are twin girls and their parents. We can all work." "No, only you and your sister." There was no negotiating, Mika, it was all so quick. I grabbed Cara's arm and we made our way through the crowd following the soldier. I can still see the twins' faces … and their parents'. Their mother turned, said, "Just go, we'll be fine, do as he says," but God, what will happen to them?'

Mama fell silent for a while.

'Cara and I clung to each other. People stared at us, some with pity, others with their eyes spewing hatred. One woman hissed, "Traitor." The soldier led us through a small exit in the wooden fence, then into a nearby house, where he told us to wait in a tiny room until he came back. He locked us in. We were close enough to hear the chaos in the *Umschlag*, people shouting, trying to find each other ...

'And then, maybe two hours later, the train arrived. The police and soldiers started shouting, *"Raus, na macht schon."* People screamed; no one wanted to get into those cattle trucks. We couldn't see anything from the house and I jammed my fingers in my ears, but I just picture them pushing people into the trucks, locking them in like cattle. We heard a loud whistle, then the creaking of the train's wheels as it slowly gathered speed. Then everything went quiet, so quiet.

'When the soldier finally led us out into the evening, we caught a glimpse of the square. So empty it was unnerving, as if the ghosts of the people still roamed there, searching for each other ... But they were gone, Mika. All gone. The soldier took us to another house until nightfall, then he brought us here. Mika, they took the twins, the baby, everyone ...'

She put her head in her hands.

I felt as if I was drowning. Max was an ordinary Wehrmacht soldier, not a member of the SS, but he was also part of the deadly squad that delivered us to the *Umschlag*. And yet he had taken a risk and rescued my mother, my aunt, let me go. Why? Did he see something of his own son in me? Was there a spark of human kindness left in him that was aching to show itself in one last gesture?

In these terrible days, nothing was predictable any more – logic had been suspended and only the cruel

143

randomness of fate survived. How could we distinguish between the soldier who would remember his humanity and the one who would simply obey orders and kill? I had seen the rats change with the blink of an eye: while their propaganda on brightly coloured posters proclaimed us to be vermin, they would happily listen to our performers, let themselves be entertained by our musicians and cabaret acts one evening, then kill us without flinching the next day.

But didn't we all share the same biology: a pumping heart, lungs, warm red blood? That first night Mother insisted we black out the windows with several layers of newspaper. Then we ate a meagre meal: a thin soup she had managed to cook on the stove from some beets, and half a slice of bread each. Not knowing how long we would be stuck in that place we had to be very careful with our food.

I tried not to think about the people who had lived here before while we ate from their plates, slept in their beds. I cringed at the sight of the children's books and toys that lay scattered in one of the bedrooms.

Mother made me promise not to leave her again as long as this war lasted. And on that first night, drunk with relief at having found her again, I gladly said yes.

We lived like moles in the shadow world of that apartment. Often at night I woke, shivering, sensing a presence at the end of the bed. If ghosts existed, that apartment was full of them. And although I took some puppets to bed with me, I missed the prince. I had given him away, betrayed him. I imagined Max finding a box, wrapping the prince up in tissue paper and sending him with a note to his son in Germany, *From Warsaw with love* ... The thought crushed me.

There was little to do there and our daily routine was more than tedious. Cara sat at the table most of the day, staring at her hands, and not even Ellie could get her to talk. Once a day Mama put a little knife next to her sister and asked her to cut up the potatoes or beets, which she did. Ellie occupied an old armchair and disappeared into her collection of Arabian tales for most of the day, and only if I nagged her enough would she read a chapter to me. I scurried around the other apartments, searching for anything edible. Over time I grew clever at finding the best hidden treasures – once I retrieved a small bowl from inside an oven, filled to the brim with precious sugar, another time a stash of beets buried underneath a pillow. Most days I found nothing but a few crumbs. Sometimes Ellie and I would build a little stage out of the suitcases on the kitchen table and make up a play for Mama and Cara. Sometimes Cara would give a fleeting smile, as elusive as a bird, but enough to make it all feel worthwhile for that moment. Another evening, as I rummaged through my coat, my fingers touched the little flute. I pulled it out and, regardless of the danger that someone might hear us, I started to play a simple tune, then another one and another. Mama, Ellie and Aunt Cara joined me at the table, listening as if mesmerised by the tiny flute's melodies. I remembered the old man playing for the street children dancing to his tunes, as I had strolled along Leszno Street with grandfather, all that time ago ... None of us around the table spoke that evening as we sat, tears in our eyes.

After a week in hiding, cabin fever took hold of me: I couldn't sit still, kept tapping my left foot constantly and gnawed my fingernails to a bloody mess. The silence was suffocating me and I was desperate for fresh air and to see the children in the orphanage again, to find out what was happening elsewhere in the ghetto. And what about the children in the hospital? If the Germans wanted to get

145

rid of everyone who was weak and unable to work, surely the children had no chance of survival?

Ellie tried to persuade me to wait a bit longer, to help her make up new plays, but in this constant cautious whispering, nothing could flourish. The puppets hung lifeless on our hands and our dialogues were laboured and without spark.

I left the apartment early one morning, ten days after our reunion. I didn't tell anyone I was going, not even Ellie, but simply put on my coat and slipped out of the door. I just wanted to run to the hospital and back, but I didn't get very far.

As I moved along Orla Street a German patrol sped around the corner. There was nowhere to hide, I was trapped. The patrol stopped with a sudden screech just a few metres in front of me.

A sharp voice stopped me. '*Stehenbleiben Jude*. What do you have under your coat?' A tall soldier jumped out of the truck, shouldering his gun.

'Nothing.' My voice sounded too high-pitched. The soldier came right up to me and lifted my chin with his index finger.

'*Na schau mal wen wir da haben*, look who we have here … the Puppet Boy!' he said, grinning. 'Don't you recognise him? The milk boy, I know your face. Show me your pockets.' He laughed, but there was no mistaking the fact that he could shoot me right there if he wished to. I pulled out the crocodile and Hagazad, the sorcerer.

'Ah, what an excellent *Zufall* – we'll need some cheering up tonight. Into the truck, boy, you can be our lucky mascot for the day. That'll keep them calm.' My legs buckled as they pulled me up into the truck; they simply laughed.

'What's the matter with you, boy, missing your beer?' I didn't remember this particular soldier but he clearly knew me. I looked out for Max but he was not among them.

That afternoon I would lose yet another part of my soul as I saw what their *Aktion* truly meant from start to finish: the soldiers' boots brutally smashing down door after door, the familiar: '*Raus, schnell, schnell!*' filling the streets with terror, the flame-throwers spitting deadly fire into the houses once their inhabitants had been chased into the trucks. That day I knew in my gut that this operation meant they did not expect any Jews ever to return to Warsaw.

Bit by bit the truck filled with people: women holding on to their children, old people and even men who were still '*arbeitsfähig*', able to work, all wrapped in coats despite the heat, clutching their suitcases, just as my mother had done when she clambered into the truck two weeks earlier. Would they take me to the *Umschlag* as well?

Suddenly the soldier who had spotted me turned and looked directly at me.

'*Komm, spiel mal was schönes, Bube.* Get your puppets out and play for them.' He grinned, his mouth revealing a huge gap in a row of yellow teeth. All eyes were on me. I silently cursed the puppets and my recklessness at leaving our hiding place today. It was one thing to put on a show for the hated officers and soldiers, but not for this terrified crowd being taken to the *Umschlag*. And for them to know that I had entertained the Germans before – that I was on such familiar terms with the rats? I blushed and prayed that the earth would swallow me up.

Suddenly I felt a tug on my coat. A little girl with wild dark curls holding a small red suitcase that could have contained nothing more than a few toys looked up at me.

'Can I see your puppets, please?' She must have been around Hannah's age. The girl's father, holding her

147

hand, gave me a brief nod. There was no turning back.

And so, as the truck hurtled through the empty streets towards the *Umschlag*, I pulled out one puppet after another from the many pockets of my old coat. I fooled around, made up little jokes, and when I finished with a puppet, I handed it to someone: I gave the first puppet, the monkey, to the girl, others to an older boy and some adults. Soon there were eight people joining in the play. There was silly banter, even some laughter, as the puppets hit and hugged each other. Then, with a sudden jolt, the truck stopped. We had reached the *Umschlag*.

'*Raus jetzt. Schnell, schnell.*' The soldier pointed at me. 'Not you. You stay.'

The soldiers placed a ramp against the truck and people started to descend as the soldiers yelled insults at them. The girl's father peeled the puppet from his hand and handed it to me.

'Thank you.' Others followed his example and, in a trance, I accepted the puppets back. They lay in my lap while I watched one person after another leave the truck. I was unable to move, a puppet myself, a witness without power, without a spine.

'Sara, give the boy his puppet back.' The father's voice startled me.

Sara! Like little Sara, one of the twins. God, what had happened to the twins? The girl stretched her hand with the monkey puppet towards me. Everyone was giving me back the puppets, while they were losing everything, and all I could do was sit there like an idiot.

'Take it, please.' I pushed the girl's little hand away. Let her at least take the damn puppet. The girl smiled. She slipped the monkey back on to her hand and let the puppet carry her suitcase. A makeshift gate, covered with barbed wire, opened into the *Umschlagplatz*. How could they fit any more people in there? A few moments later I

148

couldn't see the girl any more – the truckload of people who had just been my audience and fellow puppeteers had been swallowed up by the crowd. The truck skidded away.

Four more times that day I was witness to the truck's gruesome collection and delivery to the *Umschlag* before the soldiers finally let me go and headed off towards the Aryan side and their barracks.

They dropped me at the *Wache* late in the evening and told me to be there again the next morning. I knew I wouldn't go.

When I returned to our hiding place, everyone was in a terrible state, especially Mother. Ellie simply hugged me with a strength that I didn't think possible; Mama followed, white as a ghost. And during that long night I finally told Mother all about my double life, what the soldiers had forced me to do and how I had smuggled children under my coat. What did it matter now? Mother cried and stroked my hand, calling me 'my brave boy', over and over again, until I told her to stop.

We lay low in the small blacked-out flat, but it was hard. We had so little food to live on these days that I sneaked out whenever I could, to get some air, escape from the stuffiness and claustrophobic closeness, and to hunt for food. I stuck to the promise I had given Mother not to stray too far.

I shared a room with Mother, and Ellie slept in the other room. How I wished I could just crawl into bed with her, hold her and kiss her, lie close against the warmth of her body. I knew both of us were restless, and to make matters worse it was the height of summer. There we were, holed up like hibernating bears.

Sometimes we stole a kiss or two when away from our mothers, and over time Ellie read me most of the tales in

149

her book, interrupted by the occasional kiss and awkward fumbling.

Then, one day in early August, I couldn't wait any longer to find out what had happened to the children. While one day merged into another like the grey watery soup that was all we now had to eat, we still tried to keep track of the days on a little calendar I had found. I remember it was the seventh of August and a very sunny day. I left a short note for Mother and Ellie and tiptoed down the stairs. When I opened the front door and the warmth of morning greeted me, I knew it was going to be a very hot day. I ran along Orla, then Karmelicka Street, my senses alert.

I knew as soon as I turned the corner. I knew without even getting close. I knew it in the pit of my stomach. Maybe I had even known before I left the house that morning. The big white building that had sheltered the children for so long sat abandoned and empty, the front door boarded up as if it had been gagged. I stared at the barricaded entrance as if it held the answers, then ran up to it, trying to pry away the boards, get through to the door. I knew it was futile. The splinters cut deep into my hands but nothing could match the pain inside.

They were all gone, my little ones. I had come too late.

14

Maybe this was the end. Surely their end meant mine as well. Now at last the earth would open up and swallow me and the whole damn ghetto. People say that when something terrible happens you lose a part of your soul. It just leaves, drifts away to somewhere far away. I know for sure that a part of me will stay for ever rooted in front of Janusz's orphanage on that sunny August morning – trying to break in to find Hannah, Margaret, Janusz and the children. Waiting with my bleeding hands.

I later learned that the whole orphanage had been deported on 5 August: Janusz, Margaret, the other nurses and two hundred children. Janusz could have saved himself – at the last minute the *Judenrat* had managed to get release papers for him, but at the *Umschlagplatz* he refused to leave and stayed with the children. People were surprised he did so, but not me, they were his children, his life.

Anyone who witnessed the long line of children remembered that they all marched in an orderly row of pairs to the dirty square, dressed in their best clothes, singing one song after another. All the way to the *Umschlag*, led by Margaret, Janusz and one of the boys, playing his violin. People later said they saw them climb calmly, without fuss or resistance, into the cattle trucks. Janusz had told them that morning that they were going on an outing to the countryside. But I think what happened was this: of course the children were scared, everyone was, how could they not be? But they loved Janusz as much as he loved them and so they all decided to play the 'let's-go-on-an-outing' game. Many have since learned about Janusz and his children, it has become a famous story and Janusz a hero, but who really knows about the children, their names and their individual stories? And who is there to remember Hannah, the sweetest, most fiery and determined five-year-old I have ever met?

But this was not the end.

The end came on 15 August, another hot and blue-skied day. I had tried so hard to be patient, to distract myself with the puppets and with Ellie, but I needed to know what was happening around us. I had met a boy around my age on one of my brief trips into the neighbourhood searching for food. He told me that, against all odds, the children's hospital still existed. Ellie, worried for the children, and worn down through boredom, fear and hunger, decided she would come with me.

'But let's make it quick – just an hour or so.' I agreed, glad that she would be with me. We took nothing but my coat and the puppets, leaving a short note for my mother and Aunt Cara. When we reached the hospital and pushed open the heavy doors we knew instantly that the nurses had nothing more to give the children than a kind word here and there. It had been many weeks since our last visit and to see the hospital in such a state was devastating. It stood like a lighthouse among the crashing waves, still a refuge of sorts, but with no medicine or bandages and very little food.

There were only five children on the TB ward who remembered us, and now all the children lay three to a bed. They were so thin I couldn't imagine what was keeping them alive. But even then we raised some smiles as the puppets performed their tricks, and despite their weakness the children still wanted to play with the puppets themselves. I glanced at Ellie. I had not seen her smile much in recent weeks, but here she was, animating the puppets, playing with the children, even the occasional giggle spilling from her lovely mouth. I felt lightheaded – maybe it was hunger – but having her there with me seemed the greatest gift in these dark times.

We stayed much longer than planned – how could we see some children but not others? – so it was the afternoon before we headed back. Everywhere was so quiet. Where once an overcrowded ghetto had buzzed with people and life, there now stood a ghost town. We scurried along deserted streets in a wild zigzag. When we turned into Orla Street we saw it immediately: some houses were smouldering, newly torched, and the front door of our hiding place gaped open like a toothless mouth.

We raced upstairs. The apartment door stood ajar and there was no trace of Mother or Cara. The apartment seemed untouched but the newspaper had been ripped off the windows and lay scattered across the floor. The two battered suitcases were gone and so were their coats. There were no neighbours to bear witness to what had happened here, only the bare rooms and a kitchen table that had been ours for some weeks. Mama's scarf lay draped over a chair, dark red like a fresh wound. I moved towards it slowly, like wading through deep water, picked it up and held it in my hand.

I remember the silence between Ellie and me as we faced each other in the small flat. An eerie, electric pause, as though a large storm would break at any moment. Then her fists began to pound me like hail, releasing the storm. God, she was strong!

'Why did I come with you this morning, why? Why

did we go? Maybe we might have heard them coming, could have hidden. All of us together.'

I stood stock still, letting her fists rain down on me, my arms hanging by my sides like strangers. I could hardly feel her blows and there was a strange comfort in the rhythm of Ellie's 'why' followed by a blow, then another 'why', followed by another blow. I would gladly have stayed there for ever, but eventually her blows diminished and it was Ellie's sobbing that woke my own despair. We sobbed in each other's arms, clinging to each other like a shipwrecked couple. When we finally emerged from this embrace, weary and beaten, we ran to the *Umschlag*. It was deserted.

I can't remember much about the next few weeks. We hid in another flat, scurrying about like stray dogs, searching out any scraps of food that people might have left behind. We huddled together at night, holding on to each other for dear life. I couldn't bear talking about our mothers, but Ellie never stopped.

'They're gone, Mika. They're dead, I know it in my bones. How can the Germans get away with this?' She sat up, her eyes on fire.

'Damn it, doesn't the world know what's happening to us? And what about the people on the other side of the wall? They could see into the ghetto, they saw us being taken away.' I stayed silent, my heart frozen like a lake in winter. But at night all I dreamed about was Mama: I'd see her standing at the stove, stirring soup, humming. As I approached her she'd turn, smile at me. 'Ah, my prince!' But just as I was about to come closer, her face would change – her lovely features fading away. First her mouth, then the nose, her deep brown eyes, until her face resembled nothing more than a clean white surface. I'd wake up screaming, disoriented. Only when Ellie stroked my damp forehead would I calm down. I couldn't stop thinking about Mama. What happened to everyone after those cattle trucks? Where did the rats take them?

Then, on 21 September, our Holy Day of Yom Kippur, the deportations stopped as suddenly as they had started. There weren't many of us left. Like everything the Germans did, the action they had orchestrated had been performed with deadly efficiency. And what a plan it had been: put all the Jews into a tiny area and lock them in; leave them to simmer for a long time so that the weak would be rooted out by fever, typhoid, hunger and cold. Let the *Judenrat* distribute the laws; let them make their own armbands. Put the Jews out of sight, out of mind and let the public outside the ghetto slowly forget about them. Then blame the Jews for the diseases, march in and 'resettle' them – not to the East, but to the land of the dead: with total confidence that nobody would care enough to interfere.

How the deportations could have happened under the very eyes of the Catholic Poles who had once been our neighbours I couldn't grasp. Some could see into the ghetto from their houses. They had stood on the sidelines as the Germans herded us into the ghetto in 1940 and then out again to the dirty *Umschlag* in the wretched summer of 1942 ... hundreds of thousands of individuals: children, men, women, whole families, seven thousand people per day, every day, for weeks. Did they really believe we would be taken to new homes after they saw how we were being treated? Or was it the terror the Germans spread like their deadly gas that paralysed them?

Everything had changed. As if all the life force had been drained from us, Ellie and I trudged through the days without purpose – and yet the sun kept shining. As if to mock us, the weather remained unchanged, untainted. How could the grass still grow in small patches among the grey of the ghetto when all the children were gone? It grew better now than before, undisturbed by so many trampling feet. How could there be such a bright blue sky, when Hannah had been taken without even the comfort of my promise, my 'yes', in her little heart? How could some flowers push their way up through the earth when my mama was gone, her window boxes trampled on?

And the indifferent, terrible sun: how dare it burn down, tan my skin and warm my bones, while my mother was being pushed into the cattle trucks? It was in the heat of summer when they took them. Why did they come in summer? The days were longer then, they could work more efficiently and efficiency was everything for the Germans. *Where are you, Mama? What happened to your clothes, your smile?*

I used to love the sun, but that summer its blazing shine sickened me.

How can you look down on us as if nothing has happened? I raged day in and out. The sun should have darkened, but instead she burnt down over the ghetto with relentless force. One day I couldn't bear it any longer and called the sun to a duel, forcing her to disappear. I was willing to give my eyes for her eclipse – if it meant blindness, so be it. I sat alone in the corner of the backyard of our hiding place and slowly faced the sun directly. I took a deep breath and stared … but nothing happened. My reflexes betrayed me and I couldn't keep my eyes open. Instead, I sat with streaming red eyes, sweating, squinting in the glaring light. Only the sun's shadow, a small dark patch in the corner of my eyes, stayed with me for a while.

It was exactly one week after Mother and Cara were taken.

15

A deadly silence hung over the ghetto and a new phase in this gruesome time began. After two months of deportations only sixty thousand Jews remained. When they locked us into the ghetto in October 1940 there had been over four hundred thousand. Where there had once been overcrowded roads drenched in noise, now there was only the silence of a morgue.

One day, posters appeared ordering everyone to report in to the Germans. Ellie and I debated for a while, but we had run out of food and there was little to forage now, so we reported in. And so, for the first time in over a year, we were separated. Men and boys had to sleep in large, shared quarters near the ghetto wall, close to the German factories on the Aryan side in which we were forced to work.

We would gather each day near the *Wache* and then we were marched through the gates towards the Aryan construction sites and the few factories that were left. Someone was making big money from our tired bones and wretched souls. Most of the work was back-breaking, but at least we received some food, and crossing to the other side each day brought new opportunities for smuggling.

Ellie, like many women, was sent to the *Toebbens–Schultz*

shops on Nowolipie Street and ordered, for twelve hours each day, to clean and repair German uniforms that had been sent back from the Russian front.

'You know, many of the uniforms are like sieves, full of holes, torn and so bloody,' Ellie told me one evening with a smile. It was heartening news. Something was clearly not going well for the rats on the Russian front and our women did the shoddiest job possible on the repairs.

Ellie and I did not see much of each other those days, although sometimes in the evenings I would slip out to the women's quarters next to our barracks or she would come to mine. Short, stolen moments; little pockets of time. We still couldn't talk about our mothers, and the comfort we found in each other's embrace was like a droplet that evaporated quickly in the heat.

How could we go on living like this, drained of all life, hollow to the bone? My nights were filled with endless horrors: my mother's face disappearing, me trying to catch up with the trains, running with burning lungs through the ghetto streets, screaming without a sound leaving my mouth. In the factories, the dark days stretched endlessly, devoid of hope and meaning.

But somehow I did go on, kept working with my head down, attending to the menial brain-numbing task of putting together rough brushes to keep the German Reich clean. After a time I looked up at the boys and men next to me and soon discovered young men, just like me, who were fuelled by a fierce craving for vengeance. One day Henryk, a young Jew from Cracow, leaned towards me.

'Mika, go to the toilet – now,' he whispered. 'Look in the corner near the window. There's a piece of paper hidden in a crack. Go and read it. Don't forget to put it back.'

I did as he said. He needn't have worried about hiding things too well in our draughty toilets – the rats would never search there. I pulled out the tightly folded piece of paper and smoothed it out.

'A Call to Arms! Brothers and sisters! We will not be led like sheep to the slaughter. It is better to die in battle as free people than to live at the mercy of murderers. Rise up. Fight till your last breath!'

It was a reprint of a manifesto by the poet Abba Kovner, written in December '41 when we had all been asleep with false hopes. Before the deportations. I shivered, but the message plunged deep into my heart.

And so I became part of a group that had formed in those devastating weeks after the deportations, the ZOB – the Jewish Fighting Organisation. What an amazing bunch of young people, most of us aged between thirteen and twenty-two, including quite a few girls and women too, all burning with a desire for revenge. We met secretly in our quarters in the evenings. Now we needed to organise our resistance for the last fight, we had no time to mourn the people we'd lost and nothing more to lose.

One night a Polish resistance courier arrived at our barracks, dishevelled and stuttering. He stood as pale as a ghost in front of us, forcing himself to speak. We drew close around him, holding our breath. He'd been in the cattle trucks and had managed to throw himself out just before they reached Treblinka, how he didn't say. Maybe he squeezed through a window, made a hole in the bottom of the truck? He followed the railway lines all the way to the camp, hiding in a nearby forest for days, observing the trains. Crowded cattle trucks arrived daily at Treblinka, spilling out their human load before rattling back empty towards Warsaw after only a few hours. Retching from the terrible stench of the black, thick smoke that hovered above the forest, he finally understood why none of the trains ever brought food or other supplies: the dead don't need to eat. There was no resettlement, only extermination.

Somehow, half starved and mad with grief, he made it back to Warsaw, determined to seek us out and destroy any last illusions about the fate of the Jews. The news spread like wildfire. Extermination – this had been their plan all along, to kill us like vermin. Some of us had known this instinctively, known it in our bones, but this witness changed everything. Now, we had to act.

Whatever happened to that broken man? The one who made it back from that hell with the weight of that knowledge on his shoulders ...

Shortly after this a top-secret mission got under way to smuggle a map of Treblinka, drawn from the man's reports, to the Allies, hidden in a shoe. Miraculously it made it through to England, but by the time the Allies finally arrived in Treblinka, nothing was left: the Germans had covered their tracks with the same efficiency with which they had operated the camp. They had blown up all the gas chambers, excavated the dead and burnt them down to dust. The forest had then taken over again. All of this I only heard much later.

We gathered and planned during the long nights. I made a new friend in the factory called Andre, a tall man a few years older than me, a talented violinist who used to play in Warsaw's symphony orchestra. Like me, he too burned with a desire for revenge. He had lost everyone in the deportations: his parents, two sisters and his grandfather. But it wasn't Andre but an older man, Alexei, who began to talk about weapons. He had been a history teacher in the old days and although his eyes and words were full of fire, his voice was soft and steady like a river. None of his family had survived the previous months.

'Comrades, we need to act and act now. We owe it to those who've been taken from us, their bodies burnt to ashes. We didn't want to believe it but now we cannot turn away from the terrible truth. The time of denial is over.' Although he was unremarkable and could easily have been overlooked, Alexei's calm, determined words quickly attracted a crowd. He fetched one of the few chairs, climbed up on to it and lifted his arm.

'Comrades, the time has come for us to rise up and turn the tables, take the Germans out one by one. We will not be led like sheep to the slaughter ever again. Let us rise and use our weapons, avenge our mothers, children, sisters, brothers, friends and lovers!'

We greeted his speech with loud cheers – its passion penetrated those dark places we thought would never awaken again. Ellie, standing next to me that night, squeezed my hand tightly. Our spirits were high but we had hardly any weapons.

'Some people on the Aryan side are finally waking up too and are ready to support our struggle. You think it took strength to survive until now? Forget what you've known so far; now we need every ounce of our strength and courage to smuggle in as many weapons as we can and prepare ourselves, so we can rise like a blazing flame, a bullet-spitting dragon. We will act as one and take the bastards by surprise.'

Everyone listened spellbound. Alexei took a deep breath.

'They took our belongings and houses, marched us into the ghetto and we didn't resist; they ripped our families from us and we didn't fight. Now there is nothing to lose but our complacency. We need to rise! Stoke the fires and prepare for the fight. Who will take this challenge?'

One hand after another rose. Men, boys, women and girls; Ellie's hand among them. Everyone in our barracks was ready. Wasn't this the only possible choice? Nothing else could retrieve our dignity. And so, after this meeting, each of us had another, secret life – something I had already experienced. Finally I felt a spark inside me.

The next night I confessed to Andre about my puppet shows for the soldiers and about the children: those I had smuggled out and the orphans who had perished. Many changing emotions washed over his face, but when I finished, he clapped me on my back.

'You're a brave boy, Mika; I think the puppets and the coat will come in handy some time soon.' And indeed, it wasn't long before he approached me.

'Mika, I've a mission for you. Your coat is perfect for this.' It turned out that he wanted me to smuggle some of the biggest, most dangerous weapons under my coat. On one occasion I hid parts of a machine gun, another time a rifle and three grenades. How much my grandfather's coat had seen: first it had sheltered the children, their hearts beating as fast as a young hare's, and now the cold steel of weapons. But whatever I carried, the puppets were witnesses, confidants and comrades in this game of life and death.

Then one night Andre introduced me to Mordecai, our leader, a young man of twenty-seven with dark eyes, a thick head of coal-black hair and a wonderful broad smile.

'I've heard about your adventures on both sides of the fence, my friend.' I shifted from one foot to another as he looked at me intently.

'Couldn't you boost morale here a bit with your puppets? God knows we all need it.' I thought of the prince and his fiery speech. So much had happened since then. 'And also,' he continued, 'there are still men and women here who didn't greet Alexei's speech in quite the same way. Maybe they are too timid to fight, but we need every

162

hand we can get. Maybe your puppets could help out a bit?'

'I don't know, I guess I could try.' His request touched a sore place in me, but there was also a glimmer of pride. If Mordecai thought my puppets could make a difference then I would give it a go.

So I made puppets of ordinary-looking men and women like us, and also of soldiers, officers and police-men. I didn't want to get caught with them, so I hid them in the coat's innermost pockets. And slowly a different set of puppets emerged that mixed with my old ones and boosted the whole troupe.

One night after coming back from a gruelling day's work on the Aryan side, I stole back to our old apartment to fetch some materials from the workshop. In the strict curfew anyone caught risked being shot, but I had run out of glue, papier-mâché, lacquer and fabric. I saw myself more than anything now as a puppeteer – a smuggling, resisting puppeteer-fighter, and I needed to stock up on materials. As I entered our old apartment in Gęsia Street, the sight of our kitchen overwhelmed me: the table cov-ered in thick dust, our teapot standing untouched, the chairs at an angle as if Mama would enter any minute, sit down and pour us tea. Her soup pan still sat on the stove. I grabbed some materials from the workshop and rushed back. I knew I would never return.

It became more and more nerve-racking for me: the Germans had not forgotten me and every so often they called on me to entertain the officers and soldiers, with the Punch and Judy style that worked best. But at night I fired up my comrades with very different plays. Here, we sniped at the rat-soldiers, blew them up and beat them to a pulp. Sometimes I mixed my new puppets with the old ones and then all hell broke lose: the crocodile chased the soldiers and the fool battered the officer until he collapsed. I even made a little Hitler puppet, which always ended up in the crocodile's mouth.

One night Andre took me to one side.

'Look, Mika, your plays are wonderful entertainment for us, but they could also be the perfect way of making plans for dangerous operations.' I didn't understand but Andre was excited.

'I'm sure this could work, Mika. It could help us to imagine how to fight the Germans. Let's get all your puppets out.'

And so instead of fantasy landscapes as backdrops, we created a miniature set of the ghetto, complete with street names, a papier-mâché wall and landmarks. We let the puppets live in our small ghetto and rehearsed the best approach for attack and defence: the safest way to get from A to B, what to do if we were cornered by the rats and where an ambush would be most effective. Everyone, even Mordecai, wanted to have a go.

And so we risked our lives every day; smuggling weapons, ammunition and food. Some told me that when they were alone and fear ate away at their hearts, they remembered the puppet shows, the fiery speeches. We also played through all the possible scenarios, so that we were prepared for all eventualities. We often ended up laughing and, needless to say, in the puppet plays we always won.

At night, we all had more work to do – in one big secret movement we dug bunkers all over the ghetto: under housing blocks, shops, synagogues and streets. By the end of December 1942 everyone had two addresses in the ghetto, one official and one underground. Slowly we created a secret city – a city of moles. The bunkers were basic, yes, but with cleverly hidden entrances, air shafts, small ovens for warmth and cooking and stocked with as much food as we could spare or steal. We kept a secret radio going and a printing press in one of the bunkers to help mobilise others for the fight, and in one underground workshop we even created simple automatic weapons.

On the afternoon of 9 January soldiers pushed open the doors to the brush factory in which I worked, and started to sniff around. I didn't pay them much attention – we were so used to being searched day and night. But this turned out to be different.

'Mika Hernsteyn? Is there a boy called Mika Hernsteyn among you? The "Puppet Boy"? Step forward.'

I shivered when I heard my name. Had they finally caught on, did they want to search my coat? My hands were clammy as I stepped forward, towards the soldiers. What choice did I have? Sooner or later one of the rats would recognise me. And sure enough, the soldier facing me was the very same one who had pinched my cheeks the first night Max took me to the barracks. His face cracked into a broad grin when he saw me. I flushed, hoping my comrades would eventually understand – not everyone knew about my double life.

'Come, you have a special assignment.' The soldier took my arm and led me out of the factory. A 'special assignment' was never a good thing under the Germans and this was no exception. The chief of the SS and the Gestapo had arrived in Warsaw to inspect the Germans' progress with the Jews and to report back to the Führer. And so, that very afternoon, I performed in front of the son of the devil himself, Himmler, the most powerful man after Hitler.

Much later I learnt that Himmler gave orders to cleanse the ghetto of all Jews by 15 February; our end was declared that very same January day. But not before the 'architect of the Holocaust', as he was later called, had enjoyed the entertainment of a puppet show.

He sat in the front row, looking so very ordinary: a skinny, ugly man, with a dark moustache and round, gold spectacles. Sitting so closely to me, this monster, his black uniform decorated with SS runes, the silver skull sitting on the peaked cap that lay in his lap. At that time death wasn't the grim reaper, a black-cloaked skeleton swinging a scythe. No, death wore a smart uniform sewn in Germany for the elite of the Reich. I remember his thin laughter as I performed – as usual a crude Punch and Judy-style show.

I could have shot him there and then. The fool clowning around, digging deep into the treasure box, discovering a shiny pistol. Bang! Shot by the fool. It would have been so easy; a chance that would never return. But no, I finished my stupid puppet show and when I returned to our sad barracks I wouldn't talk for days. But soon I would be ripped from my self-imposed silence.

16

On the morning of 18 January 1943 a sharp white frost covered Warsaw, glittering under a steel-blue sky. Nothing about this day could have warned us. The rats moved early in the morning, just after sunrise. The first sound we heard was that of their dreaded trucks, then soldiers swarmed through the ghetto like a giant cloud of locusts. They were back to round us up. But this time we were prepared.

This was our sign to rise and fight: we had sworn that if the rats returned for a new wave of deportations, we would strike back with full force. The *'Übermenschen'*, as they called themselves, had been arrogant, so sure of themselves for far too long, believing they could herd us to our deaths like cattle. Sweep Warsaw *'Judenrein'* – free of Jews. *No*. Here we were, drawn together by a single aim: to kill as many as we could, one bullet for a rat, a grenade for a cluster. We would wear their blood on our hands for a change.

Mordecai gathered us immediately at Mila 18, going over our strategy once more: first we'd set the barricades we had built in recent weeks alight, then spread out and hide around Gęsia and Mila Streets in order to ambush them with our bullets. He put Ellie and me with a handful of others in charge of the hundreds of petrol bombs we had manufactured secretly in Mila 10. We handed them out to our fellow fighters, who then separated and quickly ran to the houses and the streets we planned to fight in.

'Good luck, Mika.' Ellie squeezed my hand hard, looking straight at me. Her hands were dry and hot as if they were about to catch fire. 'Let's give them hell!' She had tied back her wild curls with a red scarf and could hardly contain herself – she was as ready as a bull for the fight.

'Here, take one.' The bottle felt cool and smooth in my hands and I inhaled the petrol's sharp smell. My hand reached into my coat pocket and pulled out my mother's red scarf. I always carried it with me but today I would wear it like a proud flag.

'For our mothers. For Grandfather and Peter. The twins. Today we'll avenge them.' Ellie smiled at me – we were ready. We stationed ourselves on the second floor of an apartment block on the corner of Lubiecka and Mila Streets, together with three snipers: Andrew, Thomas and Adam. We crouched beneath the windows, tense like tigers, waiting for our prey. All of a sudden we heard a group of SS soldiers marching up Lubiecka Street, flanking a tank. Our moment had arrived. We let them come closer, until they were underneath our windows. Then the snipers pulled their triggers almost as one and the first soldiers collapsed.

'Die, you rat!' Ellie screamed, taking a broad swing before launching the petrol bomb down on to the soldiers – my Amazon! Her rage found the Germans unprepared. Here she stood, Ellie, my friend, my love, like Syrena, our mermaid warrior, Warsaw's proud symbol of resistance, swinging not a sword but a petrol bomb. I had never seen her like this and never loved her as much as I did in that moment.

Our home-made missiles rained down on to the tank

and soldiers; they smashed into pieces and exploded into fierce flames. The rats tumbled about like crazed torches; their screams mixed with retaliating bullets that splintered the windows around us. We didn't flinch but quickly changed position and continued to hurl bomb after bomb. This time the Germans responded with machine-gun fire.

'Shit, they got me,' Andrew howled, holding his left arm, his face contorted with pain.

'Get over here,' I screamed, pulling him out of the line of fire. We moved up another floor.

'God, it hurts,' Andrew moaned. 'Still, I've got my right hand and a sharp eye.' Within minutes he was back at a window taking aim.

For three days we were sniping, fire-hurling heroes – a ferocious group, making every bullet count. Then, as suddenly as they had appeared, the troops retreated. This was the first time ever the rats had met resistance: we held up their machinery and stopped the deportations, at least for this briefest moment in this long war. We were ecstatic, and no one could have put it as well as Wladyslaw Szengel, our 'ghetto poet':

From Niska, and Mila, and Muranow
Our barrels bloom with flames,
It's our spring! It's our counter-strike!
The wine of battle is in our heads!

If we had to die, we would die fighting, taking with us as many Germans as we could. We would die with honour and pride, avenging our sisters and parents and lovers – like the nine comrades who lost their lives during these three days.

That evening we gathered in the main bunker at Mila 18, elated, and whoever still had a bottle of precious vodka happily shared it. Some showed off guns and pistols taken from the rats in surprise attacks, and Andrzej dug out a battered record player from underneath his field bed. For that one victorious night we risked music – from waltzes to jazz. It was to be the first and last time I danced with Ellie.

After our brief victory the Germans stepped up their searches at the *Wache*. Every day, before passing to the Aryan side to work, we were randomly strip-searched. Often at gunpoint, facing the wall, we had to drop everything and stand naked under a grey sky in the excruciating cold. And yet many still risked their lives, every day, smuggling weapons and food. It was through such acts of courage that we managed to bring more weapons into the ghetto over the following weeks: hidden in potato sacks, baked into bread, even slipped into a secret pocket underneath a coffin. I continued to hide them in my coat. I felt Grandfather's spirit more than ever in those weeks, as if the coat's very fabric whispered 'courage' to me every time I approached the *Wache*. I was never caught.

Support from the Aryan side and from the Polish resistance grew slowly, but the weapons we received were never enough. In those grim days the idea of fighting sustained us better than any thin soup could; we were hungrier for dynamite than for bread, craving grenades more than potatoes. The truth is, no one talked about hunger any more. We transformed the churning cramps of our stomachs into fiery rage, and hunger's light-headedness gave us courage and a strange kind of euphoria as we talked in detail about how to kill the rats. And we had the help of the puppets, who never needed to eat or sleep and continued to encourage us. Some nights Ellie and I scurried though the empty ghetto streets with a bucket of glue, a brush and rolls of posters, putting up a 'Call to arms' message, mobilising those who had not yet joined the fight.

*

Then, three months later, on 19 April '43, the eve of Passover and the day before Hitler's birthday, the real battle began. We heard them approach from outside the ghetto walls: a sinister, distant rumble, growing louder and louder as they surrounded the ghetto en masse. They sang marching songs as if with one terrible voice, and as they marched closer and closer, the ground trembled beneath their boots. The sound of their approach made the hairs on my neck stand up. Himmler had decided to send two thousand SS, Wehrmacht and police into the ghetto to round us all up in one last, giant sweep, to have Warsaw *'Judenrein'* in time for Hitler's birthday. But even after our first battle, they still hadn't bargained on our fearsome courage.

By now we numbered over seven hundred fighters, mostly young men, but also many women and some children – a half-starved but furious army, equipped with the most basic of weapons: pistols and small handguns, grenades, some automatic firearms and a few rifles. We had only managed to smuggle one machine gun into the ghetto, but had plenty of explosives and petrol bombs waiting to hit their targets. It was this, our ghetto uprising, that would become famous all over the world and ignite other acts of resistance. We were the spark that soon burst into flames in other ghettos, raising people's spirits, urging them to rise up and fight. Never before had Jews resisted the Germans in such a way. We fought hard, wounded the giant's pride. The rats still didn't expect resistance but our fight was desperate – David against Goliath. This ancient story touched my heart deeply as we clung to the hope of this unlikely match. But our weapons did not turn out to be as deadly as David's pebble – indeed, they barely made a dent in the giant's armour. And when the giant finally rose, it was the beginning of our end.

How can I even began to describe those days? The lack of sleep that left us raw, the ever-present fear, the unbearable thirst, the heat and smoke in the bunkers, the noise and the chaos, the deadly snipers … We lived from one moment to the next. With our petrol bombs, pistols and grenades, every shot counted.

This time I was given a pistol and holed up on the first floor of 17 Mila Street, close to our headquarters, together with two other snipers and Ellie. I remember the first rat I took out from up there, a tall young soldier. He was holding his rifle out in front of him, defending himself from any possible ambush from left or right, but he didn't look up. My bullet hit him straight in the chest; he swayed, then fell like a tree without knowing what had hit him.

'Yes!' I couldn't stop myself shouting. Only in my dreams and nightmares had I shot the rats. I could not afford to think about this soldier as a real person. All the terror and grief we had endured in the ghetto had been distilled into this fierce desire for revenge, this bitter flame.

The next afternoon Mordecai instructed two boys to climb on to the roof of 17 Muranowska Street, and raise two flags: the red-and-white Polish flag and the blue-and-white banner of the ZOB. My job was to watch out for any snipers who might take the boys down. They scrambled up on to the roof, trying hard to keep their footing as they held on with one hand and clutched the flags with the other. Jacek, who fixed the flags in place, moved quickly, his body as agile as a weasel's, but when the two began the climb down bullets shot at them from all sides – and it was only sheer luck they weren't hit. But what a boost it gave us to see our flags flying majestically over the chaos below. It infuriated the rats so much they ambushed the house with full force, although it took them some days to bring down the flags. The couriers, often the youngest and quickest of our boys and girls, recovered ammunition, weapons, even uniforms, whenever we hit the rats. I remember one boy, Uziel Rozenblum, who rushed out into the street where two SS men had been shot and brought back two pistols, a gun, ammunition and a steel helmet. He handed over the weapons but kept the helmet. At night in the bunker, he scratched off the swastika and painted a neat white Star of David on it. As he paraded it around the bunker with a broad grin, I couldn't help but smile too.

We fed on such small triumphs, repeating the tale over and over when we came together at night in Mila 18. Like the flags, our spirits flew high for several days, but in the second week the Germans started to burn down house after house, street after street. The ghetto turned into an inferno as they kicked in doors and unleashed their flame-throwers. They tried to smoke us out of our bunkers like foxes in their holes. First they brought in their fierce Alsatians to sniff us out, then the poison gas arrived: listening for cavities, they drilled holes deep into the rubble then put in hoses where they suspected the bunkers to be. When they released the gas all was lost. We could hold out without food, resist the heat, but the smoke and poison gas killed us like vermin.

All over the ghetto we heard the cynical chorus: '*Komm, komm, komm*' as the SS stood, hands on their hips in a triumphant pose, waiting for our surrender. Many of us jumped from buildings to escape the fires, others crawled from bunkers, coaxed towards the fresh air, only to meet their deaths. Anyone not shot was marched down Zamenhof Street to the *Umschlag*.

We fought fiercely and bravely. There were now almost as many women as men among us. Tough, uncomplaining women like Ellie. Our women delivered a special surprise for the rats: as they emerged from bunkers wrapped in coats and caps, they dug once more into their pockets, and with one last defiant gesture they threw grenades straight into the soldiers' faces. Others hid a pistol in their underwear to fire a last deadly shot. These heroines handed death back one more time: if I must die, so will you. For a while those women were able to take quite a few Germans with them, but when the rats caught on, they forced all fighters to strip naked before they were allowed to crawl out of the bunkers.

Sometimes, when the wind was blowing in a particular direction, we heard the tinkling of the merry-go-round on Krasinski Square on the Aryan side. Round and round it went, with its jolly melodies, carrying Polish children while we continued our last fight amid thick smoke, fire, and the sound of gunshots. Did those people who put their children on horses and elephants have no shame, no compassion, no conscience? How could the carousel still turn when for us everything had ended? Their indifference to our struggle was the worst insult. I remembered the old merry-go-round; my mother smiling, waving at me as I sat on one of the horses. A brown one. It seemed a million years ago.

The fires in the ghetto burned for weeks, the flames fanned by strong winds. People threw themselves out of houses, burned to death or surrendered before they were marched in small groups to the *Umschlag*. If hell was an inferno, this was it.

Then Stroop, this last operation's commanding officer, ordered his troops to systematically raze the ghetto to the ground. Where once had stood proud three-storey houses, shops or theatres, where we had fought and hidden all this time, nothing remained but a sea of smoking rubble. A landscape of ashes and ghosts. Except that the destruction of our ghetto demanded much more.

174

Our fierce resistance had caused the Germans losses and huge embarrassment and many of us still hid in bunkers, although we knew we couldn't survive much longer in these conditions. The Germans cut the water supply so our choice was to die of thirst, be gassed or shot. But I cannot speak of the very end: I didn't stay.

Many decided to go on fighting, carrying a capsule of cyanide or a last bullet for themselves. Maybe I was just not brave enough. I didn't want to die like a cornered animal. Or maybe the puppets intervened? I swear that one night I heard the fool whisper from my pocket: 'Your job isn't over, you know. Not yet. You can't die here; we need you to tell the story.'

Was this the voice inside my head, the voice of terror?

17

It was hard to get any privacy in Mila 18, the main bunker, as there were more than two hundred of us crammed in together. It was also hot; the temperature rose every day just that little bit more until it became unbearable. Our bodies glistened with sweat but we had run out of water to wash with, as every drop was precious now in order to quench our burning thirst. Our lungs laboured to extract enough oxygen from the stale air and many of us had developed a constant cough. As in an anthill, activity was always frantic, but we kept our voices down as much as we possibly could. The rats still listened out for any signs of life during the daytime but hardly came at night – were they afraid of the ghost they had created? I had buried my grief about Mother as deep as I could, desperate not to think about her all the time, and only at night did I sometimes awake with tears running down my cheeks.

The bunker was full of young people and hormones raged despite our terrible situation. One evening, out of the blue, Ellie told me she wanted me. She had always been like that: direct and bold. She grabbed me from behind and swivelled me round, then looked straight into my eyes, her voice an urgent whisper. She wanted me inside her, not as a comrade or friend, but the way a woman wants a lover.

'I don't want to die like this, Mika. Not knowing. We need to grow up fast, there isn't much time left.' She took my hand; her grip was firm, her skin hot. I gasped – a wave of excitement, fear and a sudden sadness rushed through me like a current. Weren't we growing up too fast, every day weighing like a month? Some days I felt as old as Grandfather, as if my eyes and ears could not take in any more; other times I still felt like a youngster, bursting out of my skin. Mostly time didn't exist any more as we sat suspended and trapped in the twilight of our underground world. Did I desire Ellie? Of course – but differently now than when she first came to stay with us. I had lost so much innocence and my heart was heavy. It was strange to think about Ellie's naked body and the secrets of sex when we were surrounded by a horror that could snuff us out at any minute. But maybe it was exactly the knowledge that our young lives could be cut short at any time that ignited our need for each other, the most natural thing that reminded us of life, of light, of something beyond the ghetto walls. Many paired off for some private time behind improvised screens, flimsily stitched together from old sheets. I cared deeply about Ellie and in some ways this had been a long time coming – I had been thinking about her in a special way for months. Ellie was the last bit of warmth and life left in my heart. After the first wave of embarrassment, Ellie slipped my hand under her shirt. Her heart was beating as fast as a hare's. Then, manoeuvring awkwardly on the narrow field bed, we made love for the first and last time. Quietly, so as not to disturb anyone, or worse, be discovered and have to face the smirks of our comrades.

Ellie lay in my arms, nuzzled close into my neck, her breath warm and soft. Abruptly she sat up.

'Let's go outside, Mika, I want to see the stars with you. If we are to die down here, at least I want to see the stars one more time.' She looked at me with her large brown eyes. I could see no fear.

It was dangerous. There were four possible exits, all well hidden from the outside. But the Germans could still be out there, listening for underground noises or trying to sniff us out with their dogs. We sought permission from Mordecai and he promptly gave us a mission: to go to the farthest exit, armed with pistols, and observe what was going on outside. According to a small map there should have been another bunker exactly opposite. It was up to us to find out whether there were still survivors. But when we surfaced we nearly forgot our task. It was a moonless night but the stars shone brightly and we could make out some constellations: the Great Bear, Cassiopeia, and Sirius. Ellie gasped.

'It's so beautiful!'

I wrapped my coat around us. It held us like a sheltering embrace, like my grandfather's, our mother's, reaching through time.

Suddenly I spotted a shadow opposite us, climbing over the rubble. In the darkness I could see no uniform, only a small skittish figure. I whistled – the sign all fighters knew. The shadow promptly returned the whistle. We had accomplished our mission.

When we scrambled back down, general excitement greeted us: one of the fighters who had been gone for three days, trying to find an escape route through the sewers, had returned. We joined the crowd that had gathered around him.

'I found a tunnel that could lead us out of Warsaw. With luck we can make it … just to the outskirts, but still …' he said.

My heart leapt, but glancing at Ellie I could see she was not interested. I touched her shoulder, pulled her away from the group.

'We might actually live, Ellie. Down here we'll die for sure, but now we might have a chance together.' I couldn't bear this trap any longer; I wanted to get out – and with Ellie. She shook her head.

'We can fight and die honourably,' she said, 'the world up there has already ended. What's left for us?' She sounded tired, like a very old woman, and when I looked at her I knew she had already decided to stay. She smiled and took my hand.

'But you, Mika, and your puppets … I can see there might still be a life waiting for you. If you make it out alive, you need to tell everyone what happened to us. Do it for our mothers, for our families.'

'Please, Ellie, don't talk like this. Come with me.' My voice was choked. 'At least promise me you'll come and find me when all this is over. Please, Ellie.' I stood there crying, my arms limp, not caring what the others might think.

We only had an hour to decide whether to stay or leave. As it was a moonless night, this would be the best chance for escape we would have in a long while. Ellie put her arm around me.

'I don't think I'll get out of here, Mika. But if I do, I will find you. I promise. I will ask everyone until I find you. If I survive … if this war ever ends and I'm still alive … I'll find you. Please go now.'

I pulled Princess Sahara from my coat and handed the little puppet to Ellie.

'I know you're a fighter, Ellie, God knows you are, but to me you're also a princess. My dearest friend, my comrade, my love. Please be safe.'

The sadness in her face choked me. Then a glimmer lit

her eyes as she reached out for the princess and tucked her under her shirt.

'She's a warrior princess, Mika.' Ellie's voice sounded hoarse but strong. 'Thank you.'

She kissed me one last time, as she had that first time in our kitchen so long ago: her hands even rougher now but so warm, cupping my face gently.

We left half an hour later. There were about twenty of us, making our way through the Muranowski tunnel. I bundled my coat with its precious load into a bulky parcel that I tied on to my back with some rope. It sat there like a big hump.

I lost all sense of time as our little group moved through the endless darkness, crawling on all fours, cutting through barbed wire, wading up to our chests in sewage, trying at all costs to stay together. We moved through this stinking labyrinth, with nothing but a few torches and a flimsily drawn map of the sewers, for over twenty hours, chasing away the many water rats with sticks, trying not to swallow the toxic water. I trudged on as if in a trance.

Suddenly, after so many hours, a faint light appeared. We crawled towards it like shipwrecked sailors heading for an island, not knowing whether we would be met with our death or with the torch of freedom. My heart pounded but exhaustion sat heavily in my bones like lead, and in some ways I didn't care any more. As the light grew brighter we emerged into a miracle: no bullets greeted us on this warm spring day in May '42, only a pale sun shining through the thick forest. And with it, the best soup I tasted in my entire life: potato and carrot, glistening like liquid gold. We had finally joined the Polish resistance and about seventy of its fighters in the Wyszkow forest just outside Warsaw. The fighters, men and women, rugged and armed, clapped us on our weary shoulders, eager to hear our story and desperate for news from within the ghetto. For now we were safe, but my heart was broken.

18

Many hours had gone by. In the sitting room of Mika's apartment Daniel had listened to his long tale while the light slowly faded and the sounds from the street grew quieter. The battered cardboard box that had sheltered the old pocket-coat sat between them.

Mika sat back in his chair, his arms hanging by his sides like dead branches. He was utterly spent. He looked at his grandson, aware that Daniel had not interrupted him once. *Like a true witness*, he thought. Mika shivered and wrapped the old coat around him.

'What happened to Ellie, Grandpa?' Daniel's voice was gentle, quiet.

'I don't know, Danny. The memory of that night with Ellie is one of the few things I've treasured from that god-forsaken place: Ellie's heart beating fast, her sweet breath against my neck, her teasing smile after her proposal. The only thing I do know is this: on 8 May the Germans discovered our headquarters in Mila 18. Those who stayed fought a fierce battle, there is no doubt. But Ellie? I will never know how she died. Did she choke, poisoned by the gas or smoke, or did she die in combat? Maybe she took her own life when there was no other way out, like

182

so many of the fighters? All those amazing young people: Mordecai our brave leader, Ellie … all gone. She was so strong but so damn stubborn.'

Mika looked out of the window at the ink-blue sky. 'We saw the ghetto fires from the forest, a sinister orange light flickering in the distance over Warsaw. Then, on 16 May, it was all over. A huge fireball over the great synagogue at Tomlacke Street marked the end of the whole ghetto. We heard the deep growling of the explosion from our hideout. I heard later that the next day Stroop announced in his report to Himmler: "The Jewish quarter of Warsaw is no more." Everyone they captured was either shot or sent to the camps.

'The sky hung low with dense black smoke for days, a choking darkness that revealed to everyone the hell the Germans had created: the thick clouds engulfed all of Warsaw, not stopping at the ghetto wall but staining the neatly hung washing on the Aryan side too. A courier told us that soot fell like black snow all over Warsaw: over the streets, parks and the merry-go-round on Krasinski Square, as if to mourn us.

'You could say our desperate uprising failed miserably. I lost Ellie and most of my comrades: Mordecai, Alexei, Marek – and yet, I believe the ghetto's terrible fires ignited resistance against the rats in many places all over Poland. In August '44 the rest of Warsaw rose up in "Operation Tempest", a last attempt to shake off the Germans once and for all: the famous "Warsaw Uprising".'

'Did you go back to Warsaw?' Daniel asked.

'Yes, I joined the Uprising in '44 and stayed with a small group of fighters, moving back and forth between our hideout in the forest and Warsaw itself, smuggling weapons and people, forging papers and attacking the Germans wherever we could. But part of me had died in that city together with Ellie. The fierce street battle came too late for us Jews. Why did Warsaw not rise earlier when most of us were still alive?

'I remember those weeks only as a blur. I scurried around, hardly sleeping, an empty husk, held together by my old coat and a stubborn determination to fight the rats right to the very end. Sometimes, on cold evenings in the forest, huddled around the small fires or after a successful mission to Warsaw, I pulled out some of my puppets to cheer up my comrades. They all loved the puppets, but I could not stop thinking about Ellie, Hannah, Janusz and all the little ones. After a while I couldn't bear the puppet's cheerful voices any more and stuffed them back into my pockets.

'In October '44, after sixty-three days of fierce fighting, Warsaw capitulated. The Germans had beaten us once again, hunting down anyone who still hid in our battered city and slaying them without mercy. We lay low in the Wyszkow woods, while the Germans burnt down almost everything that was left. The Russians, on Stalin's command, waited across the Vistula for weeks without acting, until finally, on 18 January '45, exactly two years after our first uprising, the Red Army and the Polish First Army entered the ruins. Our long fight was finally over.

'I was with a small group of fighters that day, drinking vodka from morning to night, but although it heated my muscles and bones, it didn't warm my heart. I felt no joy. Our once proud city and Jewish culture lay destroyed – a wasteland of smouldering ruins as far as the eye could see. Where the ghetto once stood was a giant field of rubble; the old town, the market square and our beautiful synagogues all burnt to the ground. How I managed to keep that coat and the puppets through those times I don't know. I guess the coat became a kind of armour to me yet it felt like a home, the last possession from my earlier life, the last link to my family. I had lost everyone.

'After the war I spent months in a transit camp before I was allocated a tiny room in the outskirts of Warsaw. The coat with all its treasures sat packed away in a suitcase under my bed. Shabby and burnt, covered in bloodstains and dirt, it had become the only witness to all of my trials. I wanted to throw it away but something always held me back.

'I stayed in that room for over a year. Not that time meant anything to me any more; it had ceased to exist, along with Mama and Ellie and all the others. I didn't shave, I hardly washed, and for days I did nothing but lie on the bed, staring at the ceiling and counting the wooden eyes in the beams. If it hadn't been for Jacob, one of the fighters who made it through the sewers with me, I would probably still be there. He told me stories about America, showed me photographs, said we could build a new life there. I couldn't muster any enthusiasm. Where had America been during those last months of the war? In any case, I didn't know anyone in this vast continent. But Jacob didn't give up. He applied for a permit and got me to sign an application too. It took two more years of persuasion and endless paperwork before, in 1948, three years after the war ended, I left for America.

'After two weeks spent below decks, seasick and weak, we were spat out on Ellis Island. "Ellis Island", what cruel irony; me and Jacob, but no Ellie. And when I first sighted the statue of Lady Liberty, her arm raised in a gesture of liberation and defiance, I cried. My Ellie and all the others were lost, while I stood here, breathing, embarking on a new life.

'We queued for hours in an enormous white-tiled hall. I remember holding my battered suitcase so tightly my knuckles went white, and I sweated like an athlete under my old heavy coat. My eyes were fixed on the large clock on the whitewashed wall as I stood in front of the official behind the desk who would decide my fate.

'"Mikhail Hernstein." The clerk's reedy voice and the thump of the heavy stamp is all I recall. I leaned against the cool wall, clutching my papers, "APPROVED" stamped in broad letters over them, a permit to stay in the United States indefinitely. I stared at the papers, sealed by the American eagle. I knew then that I had finally left the deadly past behind. We had made it. Jacob hugged me.

'After weeks at sea, New York overwhelmed all my senses – such bustling and energy, noise and stench; some areas even reminded me of the ghetto and its squalor. For the first few weeks I tagged along with Jacob, from his great-aunt's house to uncles and cousins, sleeping on the floor or on the occasional guest bed. But the more of Jacob's relatives I met, the more my losses crushed me and the nightmares returned: pounding boots, screaming puppets, blazing fires. Always fires. Here I was in a new world, this golden land of opportunity, of milk and honey, but without a single loved one. I wanted to disappear among the masses, to go unnoticed, and yet loneliness bit me like hunger. And believe me, I tried to forget Warsaw. But entering this new world, I learned that one can never rip oneself from the past, from one's memory, nor from the earth on which one learned to walk. Like the blood that flows through our veins, our memories live deep inside us, are carved like hieroglyphs on to our souls.

'I took many odd jobs, lugging vegetable boxes to the market, cleaning factory floors, even meat-packing. I couldn't sleep much and spent most of my spare time roaming the streets, or drinking in dark bars. And more than once the most peculiar thing happened during those first months: I could smell other survivors the way Saint Bernards can sniff out avalanche victims buried deep beneath the snow. I met quite a few men and women who, after a night of drinking, shyly or with a wild fire in their eyes, exposed a blue tattooed number on their arm. Me, I had nothing to show. My wounds are carved into my heart.

'Sometimes I tried to talk about Warsaw, but even with those who had seen more than I could ever imagine, I never got far. I've never told anyone the whole story until now, Danny.

'It took me a long time to find my feet in this new country, and I probably didn't do so until I met your grandma Ruth in the summer of '53. I spotted her at a dance Jacob dragged me to. Before I knew it, she had moved across the dance floor towards me during a round of "lady's choice", beamed her gorgeous smile at me and then asked me to dance. That day changed everything and we soon became a couple.

'As it turned out, Ruth was a Polish Jew, just like me. An only child, she'd been put on a train by her mother only days before the Germans closed the Lodz ghetto in 1940, entrusted to a chain of bribed contacts on an epic journey westwards. When she arrived in New York, Ruth was only eight. She never saw any of her close family again and was brought up by a distant great-aunt in a small apartment in Queens.

'We clung to each other like the lost souls we were and married two years later, but the tragedy of our losses always hung over us. Only when we danced did we feel lighter and truly alive. I had accepted that I would have to earn my living doing menial jobs, but Ruth pierced something in me, and suddenly, as if I could hear Grandfather's voice telling me I needed to study again, I found my mind craving stimulation. I enrolled in evening classes studying mathematics, and then chose astronomy. Just as my grandfather had found security in numbers, I felt safe among nebular constellations, galaxies and the study of the universe.

'Then, completely unexpectedly, in 1966, your mother arrived. We named her Hannah, grace of God. We had resigned ourselves to never having a child, after trying for so long, but there she was, lighting up our lives.

'Before I met your grandma, I still occasionally put on my old pocket-coat, and in those first lonely weeks, the puppets gave me company – only they knew the full extent of my losses. Ever so often I would take them out: the monkey and the crocodile, Hagazad and the fool. I didn't touch the soldiers. I never wanted to see them again. I could never bring myself to play with the puppets again, only laid them out next to each other or held them in my lap – my sad little family.

'The day before I married my Ruth, I packed the pocket-coat away, together with all its treasures. Over the years I told your grandma some things about the ghetto, the Uprising, even Ellie, but I never mentioned the puppets.'

Mika slipped his hand into one of the coat's large pockets, searching for the smaller ones, the secret pockets within pockets. Yes, here they were, his old companions: the crocodile, the monkey, the villain, the fool, the donkey, the girl. Nothing had changed ... but of course everything had changed.

One after another he took out the frail puppets, carefully, as if the sudden light might distress them or reduce them to dust. The puppets had lost some of their bright colours and many of their tiny clothes were ripped, but he remembered them all. He laid them out on the small coffee table, one next to the other. Then, as if emerging from a long sleep, he took a deep breath and looked at his grandson.

A sudden warmth rose in him like pure sunshine. It tasted of gratitude, of love. Of a warmth he hadn't been able to express to his own child. Hannah, sweet little Hannah, now grown up to be a proud, beautiful woman, yet so burdened by ghosts, crowding her shoulders: the ghosts of little Esther, Ellie, Cara and Marek, ghosts she could sense, but never name.

How often had she woken from nightmares, telling him with wide eyes of roomfuls of children she doesn't recognise, stretching out their little hands. He had never explained. As if silence could keep them all safe. Hannah, the baby girl he didn't dare hold too tightly for fear of squashing her, losing her. Today he wanted nothing more than to hold her for ever.

Instead he reached out an arm to Daniel.

'Come, Danny, it's late, let's call your mum and make up a bed for you here.'

Daniel's mouth was dry. A million questions threatened to explode inside his head and yet a terrible emptiness sat in his stomach like a dark hole. He let his hands move gently over the puppets, picking up one after another.

'What d'you think happened to the prince, Grandpa?' The moment the question left his mouth he flinched. But just where should he start? Mika didn't seem to mind.

'I've asked myself that same question many times, Danny. I guess we'll never know. All we know is that the princess must have died with Ellie in the ghetto, and the doctor might not have survived the Nuremberg bombings. Or maybe he did, and is hiding in some battered suitcase, who knows. But the prince? I try not to think about him, or the German soldier. These puppets here are all I've got left.'

Daniel stretched out his hand, lightly touching his

grandfather's shoulder. A moment of silence lingered between them.

'Thanks, Pops. Thank you for telling me all this.'

But unbeknown to both, the long-lost prince and his story were much closer than they could ever imagine.

PART TWO

The Prince's Journey

19

Most of the time the soldier forgot about the puppet that lay squashed inside his uniform. It had once been attractive, but now, just like the soldier, the prince looked beaten and shabby, with his faded colours, flaking paint and matted hair. Only when the raw memories tore the soldier back to the city that his army had left devastated did his hand brush lightly over his left breast pocket, shattering in an instant the illusion that the dire situation in which he found himself was a terrible nightmare from which he'd awake. No, this was as real as the lice that had taken over his uniform, his hair, his ears, the whole carriage – a black crawling pelt that tormented him and his fellows with an insane, raw itchiness. As real as the puppet underneath his shirt. With the men packed into bare cattle trucks that rattled eastwards day and night through an icy universe, this journey marked the end of six bloody years of a lost war.

As he sat huddled next to his comrades, his legs stiff and pulled in close to his chest, images flickered like a silent film across his mind: his first day in Warsaw, straining his neck to catch a glimpse of the Führer as he proudly marched past the tribune; months later, a dapper Wehrmacht soldier supervising the building of the ghetto wall before opening the gates to the streams of Jews that would fill it. Most clearly, though, he remembers the day he met the boy and his puppets, that fateful meeting and the many puppet shows that followed ... Mika. Thin, pale Mika and his puppets. Long before the summer of 1942, before the terrible days of the deportations and his desperate roaming through the *Umschlagplatz* in search of the boy's mother ... before the endless blazing fires, the flame-throwers, the poison gas. The ghetto's last days merged in his mind with the city's last uprising – how his army had beaten and throttled the Polish people of Warsaw. But for what? So much death over ruins, so much useless slaughter.

It had been snowing on the January day when the Russian tanks arrived with their creaking loudspeakers and proud red flags, rolling through a ghost town. He had hidden in the ruins with the rest of the soldiers, and Max remembered the moment they were marched out of there, arms raised in the age-old gesture of surrender. It was all over – or so he thought. For nothing could have prepared him for the white hell of Siberia. All this time the puppet lay tucked away beneath his uniform, right over his heart. The prince, stolen from a boy and his mother, from a city that no longer existed.

Max scarcely moved any more, as if trying to conserve his energy for what might await him at the other end of this gruelling journey. All sense of time had slipped away. How long since they were pushed into the trucks in a cruel reversal of what they had done to the Jews? Weeks had passed, Max was sure of that. Only a dim beam of light fell through a tiny opening on the top of the carriage.

The men coughed and mumbled but hardly spoke, silenced by the biting cold. There were no blankets and not a single suitcase between them. A small wood stove provided a little warmth for those directly next to it, but after only a few days the wood had run out. So they sat shivering next to each other in their filthy uniforms and overcoats, their glassy, red-rimmed eyes the only parts exposed, the steam rising from their nostrils a faint sign of life. Some moaned softly, while others occasionally burst out with a tirade of swearing, like sandpaper rasping in short sharp bursts over wood.

'*Die lassen uns hier verrecken* – they're letting us rot in here! No food, no blankets, we're going to die like dogs,' an older soldier next to Max mumbled.

The layer of ice covering the inside of the wooden carriage grew thicker each day, sparkling like caster sugar.

Max sat in the darkness, leaning against the icy carriage wall, drifting in and out of a feverish sleep, as the wheels' monotonous sounds echoed in his ears; katchunk, katchunk, katchunk ... relentless rotations taking him eastwards, farther away from anything he had known. They had heard rumours about Siberia, its terrible cold and the back-breaking work in the mines and forests. His back already hurt from the lack of movement and the penetrating cold of the ice-covered boards behind him. He rummaged through his coat pocket with stiff fingers. Ah, the little silver spoon. He had carried it in his pocket all these years, its handle decorated with carved roses. It belonged with their sugar bowl back home. His wife had secretly slipped it into his pocket the day he left Nuremberg for Poland. Was the white porcelain bowl still perched on the kitchen shelf? He could picture its intricate decoration, next to the cups and plates. Not knowing his family's fate ate away at Max, and he gripped the spoon and started to scratch away at the icy surface.

'*Was machst du denn?* What're you doing?' the man next to him croaked.

Yes, what am I doing? Max thought, looking at his spoon. *Ridiculous.* But he said, 'Haven't you heard that prisoners have dug whole tunnels with spoons just like this one?'

'Well, good luck to you.'

His comrade's cynical tone hurt, but Max continued to scratch away at the ice out of boredom, and to keep that small flame of defiance alive. And indeed, after some days, he felt slightly more comfortable leaning against the wall as he'd carved out an ice-free space in the shape of a human.

Besides the puppet Max had hidden a photograph in his coat of Erna with Karl as a five-year-old on a short holiday in the Alps – two happy tanned faces smiling back at him. Sometimes he took the photo out and studied it, although he was hardly able to make out their faces in the dim light. Other soldiers had saved letters and one even a pack of cards, but whenever a small group huddled together to play, the play was listless and worlds away from the roaring games of the barracks.

Whenever the train stopped, sometimes after whole days, the heavy door would open and the men would stumble or fall out, blinded by the daylight and stuffing their mouths with snow to quench their thirst. A guard would throw a bucket of half-rotten potatoes at them as if they were pigs. They fought over those potatoes, cursing and spitting, trying to grab as many pieces as they could. But before they could even finish the meagre food, the guards chased them back into the carriage. They never knew when they would eat again. And still it got colder and colder.

Many of the soldiers didn't make it. One night Max glanced at the man perched next to him – Xaver, he had introduced himself to Max on the first day in the cattle wagon. Now the exposed skin of his face shimmered waxen grey and Max noticed that no steam rose from his nostrils. Xaver had coughed constantly for days, his hacking tearing at the raw nerves of everyone around him. He was the first of many deaths before their train reached the depths of Siberia. Some froze to death or starved, others simply stopped breathing, defeated by dysentery or a broken spirit.

'*Raus mit den Toten.*' At every stop the guards ordered anyone who looked as if they still had some strength to lay out the dead next to the railway tracks. Rows of fallen soldiers, stiff like tree trunks. They took the coats but left their clothes.

Once Max had helped carry the dead out of the carriage. He remembered the first time he'd stumbled over one of the many emaciated corpses in the ghetto and his stomach cramped.

A sudden jolt ended the journey, slamming the soldiers into one another.

'*Dawai, dawai! Raus, raus!*' Sharp, commanding voices chased the soldiers out of the carriage. The cold hit them like a fist. Guards, as huge and square as wardrobes, growling thick-pelted dogs by their sides and a glaring whiteness greeted the soldiers. A white nothingness, stretching out as far as Max could see – blinding, sky and earth swallowed up as if they had never existed. In the distance was a line of tiny black dots shuffling through the snow – another load of prisoners who must have arrived shortly before them.

They had reached the end of the line. And now the walk to the very end of the world would begin, step after painful step. The soldiers swayed, like snow-burdened trees, one behind the other, pushing against the ferocious wind. The guards carried large rifles and sinister whips. They loved cracking the cruel instruments on the weaker prisoners who stumbled or fell. If one couldn't get up again the guards were quick to fire a few shots, always accompanied by the wild barking of the dogs. They never fired just one shot – they wanted to make sure the collapsed shape would never rise again.

'I can't do this any more.' A faint voice behind him startled Max. He dug his hand into his right pocket, grabbing a piece of string that lay coiled there like a snake. He pulled it out and wrapped it around himself, leaving a loose end.

'Here, hold this.' He twisted round and handed the end of the string to the man behind. The man grabbed it and, linked by the cord, they trudged on.

After a while the wind picked up even more and with it came a sudden blizzard that made it difficult to see even the person in front.

Hours passed. As the blizzard calmed and the sun began to peep through, a ripple moved through the line of men and they slowed down. Where before they had stared at the ground, counting nothing but the next step, all eyes were now fixed on a black stretch ahead: a line of trees, dark as ink.

Once they entered the forest, it swallowed the men up like Jonah's whale, complete and whole, and with it the pale daylight. They marched through the dense woods and thick undergrowth, towered over by tall fir trees, sometimes having to cut their way through. Hours stretched into days: one behind the other by day, huddled together at night around meagre fires.

One night a drawn-out howling awoke Max and the other prisoners. The eerie sound encircled them, drawing closer and closer. Max saw glittering yellow eyes in the woods.

'The last thing we need,' he mumbled. The guards broke into ugly laughter.

'*Volki, volki*, wolf. For you.' After a few rounds from the guards' guns in their direction, the wolves dispersed but Max couldn't go back to sleep. The next morning the long, wretched line continued its endless march. As the days passed no one kept count of how many men were left behind in the forest, collapsing from hunger or exhaustion.

20

Finally they arrived at the camp: a cluster of scattered barracks perched at the edge of the forest. Max noticed that, unlike the ghetto, the camp wasn't surrounded by a solid wall, only a simple wooden fence and one row of barbed wire. Maybe the Russians didn't expect anyone to try to escape from this godforsaken place? A single watchtower stood like a lone chess piece. Max had arrived in the belly of Siberia, at the very core of the cruel, white wilderness.

As he neared the perimeter, Max saw four guards armed with rifles opening the gate, thick caps sitting on their heads like curled-up cats. Above the gate was a momentous portrait of Stalin, greeting the miserable crowd as they shuffled inside and assembled in the yard. *So this is what the end of the world looks like*, Max thought, letting his gaze glide over the huts amid the sea of snow and forest. The men were assigned barracks and allowed to stretch out on the simple hard bunks for a short while. Max slid into sleep as if he had no other thoughts.

Loud shouting woke him.

'*Dawai*. Outside and all clothes off.' A round-faced guard dressed in a thick fur coat growled at the men, chasing them out into the biting cold with a few sharp cracks of his whip. They stumbled into the yard, standing three deep in a long row.

'*Macht schon, runter mit den Klamotten*, off with your clothes!' Another guard addressed them in wooden German. The men slowly peeled off one layer after another. *That's it.* As if it had only hit him now, as their soldiers' uniforms and shirts piled up in the centre of the yard, Max realised that he and his comrades were prisoners. Prisoners of the Gulag, Camp 267. Prisoners of the snow.

The men stood naked, trying to keep their trembling bodies under control, as anyone who moved or whimpered risked the whip or, worse, a bullet. Not everyone succeeded. Max's teeth chattered while his neighbour seemed to turn into a crow, flapping his arms about wildly, before one of the guards shouted into his face and pushed the butt of his rifle into his chest. A memory rose in Max's mind. One November day he had been patrolling the ghetto streets with Franz, a rough, chubby soldier who had been the butcher in a small Bavarian village before the war, when they spotted a boy, trudging along awkwardly, with his back bent and clutching his coat.

'Bet you he's hiding something,' Franz snarled, elbowing Max. Before Max could answer, Franz barked at the boy: '*Runter mit den Klamottem*. Take off your clothes.'

It was December and the boy shook like a leaf as he tried to protect his nakedness, a heap of clothes lying by his side. He had smuggled nothing but Max noticed he had a limp.

'That's enough, Franz,' Max said, 'let's go.' Franz laughed, kicked the clothes towards the boy but kept his shirt. Slowly he ripped it to shreds.

Now the tables had turned on this first day in the camp, the former soldiers forced to swap their uniforms for filthy stinking rags: jackets ill equipped for the terrible cold, thin gloves and trousers through which the wind cut mercilessly. Seeing that his comrades before him were allowed to keep their underwear, Max hid the prince and his photograph in his pants. They were given lukewarm water and one bar of soap between a group of thirty – the first opportunity to wash, at least a little, for weeks. They were taken into a barely heated room and shaved of all body hair with a blunt knife, then deloused. *At least we'll get rid of some of the lice*, Max thought. But he already knew this fight was futile – lice could survive far better than humans in those conditions. The men fell quiet, barely looking at each other. Then, in a last humiliating procedure, the prisoners were ordered to queue up in front of a small table. A clerk in a striped jacket, clearly a prisoner as well, called the men forward one by one, ticking their names off a register.

'Max Meierhauser?' Max nodded, stepping before the desk. 'Your number.' The clerk handed Max two strips of fabric bearing a four-digit number. That evening, sewing his number on to his jacket and shirt, Max Meierhauser, born in Nuremberg in 1902, became prisoner 3587. Bald and wearing identical clothes, the men had difficulty recognising their former comrades. That night, Max hid the prince and his precious photograph underneath a rancid sack of straw on his bunk and fell into a fitful sleep.

'*Dawai*, get up, *aufstehen*.' A rough voice belonging to one of the huge guards woke the prisoners the next morning. Max grabbed the prince from under the straw and placed the puppet under his shirt.

The guard marched the prisoners outside for roll call. The sky, a velvety black, was strewn with stars and the white band of the Milky Way.

'God, it's the middle of the night,' a pale man next to Max mumbled. The men stood silently, trying hard not to move, waiting for their names to be called. An endless procedure.

'I can't feel my feet any more,' Peter, a tall prisoner who even as a soldier had looked thin, whimpered.

'Just hang in there, should be over soon,' Max whispered.

Some ten minutes later they were marched back into a larger building.

'Thank God, I thought I'd collapse,' Peter said as they queued for breakfast: a cup of grey lumpy gruel and a weak brown liquid which the prison cook passed off as tea.

'Ah, hot tea!' Peter's face lit up.

'Don't get excited,' Max replied, 'looks like hot water to me. Still, at least it's hot.' They had hardly sat down when the guard's voice thundered through the room once again.

'*Dawai*. Out, to work.' They washed down the gruel with the watery tea and stumbled out into the yard. By now the darkness had lifted and a small pink band of light stretched across the sky.

This time the guards dished out a pair of gloves and a cap for each prisoner. Some were given saws, others shovels and pickaxes.

The camp commander, a tall Russian wearing a long brown coat and a thick white fur cap adorned with the red communist star, addressed the shivering crowd.

'You work, you eat. You make the quota, you get food. You don't get your quota, you don't eat. You work good, you live. Forget the life you had before. And don't waste your energy thinking of escape, no one escapes from here. This is Siberia. *Verstanden? Dawai*. To work now.'

The prisoners were marched off in neat rows, armed guards by their side, through the camp gate, towards the dark forest through which they had crawled the previous day. And there they stayed all day, until the faint November sun had set and they could not see their hands before their eyes.

The prisoners returned there the next day, and the next. Weeks merged into months and then years. Years of felling huge dark green fir trees with blunt saws and axes, cutting away branches, scraping the bark until the pale flesh shone through, dragging the trunks through the forest, four men tied to a trunk like tired horses, before the wood was shipped downriver, never to be seen again.

Max and most of the prisoners of Camp 267 had become lumberjacks, slaves to the forest, ten hours a day, every day.

Each morning began with a wearying roll call before sunrise in the bitter frost and a pitiful breakfast of watery gruel, a small piece of rye bread and thin tea. Then the prisoners were marched deep into the forest, bent over by the heavy tools on their shoulders, which over time seemed to become an extension of their weary bodies. The quotas were brutal, and if one man worked slowly all the men on that team went hungry that night.

Accidents happened every day: some, unable to leap out of the way quick enough, were crushed by falling trees; others lost their grip on their axe and sent the blade straight into their leg. Without medicine and in the terrible cold wounds didn't heal well and could fester for weeks. Many prisoners collapsed and those who did not get up in time were shot. Most of the time the men shivered in their damp clothing, wearing the same flimsy clothes day in day out. Once the spring rains started, no one could keep dry, and as hard as they tried, the men could never dry out the jackets in the scant warmth of the barracks. The winters were the cruellest of challenges and their beards glittered with snow, small icicles forming under their noses. If the prisoners' eyes watered the tears froze as quickly as they came and sometimes those tears were red, tears of blood.

Max tried to stay as clean as he could. While some of the prisoners did not bother to wash more than once every two weeks, when they were given hot water, all through the winter, Max rubbed his face clean with snow and, if he could bear it, his arms, chest and legs also.

'We look and smell like pigs – that's what they want, to turn us into pigs, until we forget that we are human. If I can, I'll wash.'

Snow could also be a welcome protection against the lice. Hans once buried his jacket in the snow overnight – in the morning the lice had gathered on one small piece of the sleeve and could easily be shaken off – a trick Max and others took up gladly.

Each day the prisoners marched in groups of thirty into the forest where the Russian guards attached bunches of grass on to the trees to mark the boundary of the prisoners' work: that far and not one step farther. An inch beyond, and the guards would fire their guns. Some prisoners, tempted by berries that grew beyond the boundary or simply unaware of the grass markers, lost their lives that way.

Late one summer's day, as the guards lay dozing on the forest floor beyond the bunches of grass, Martin, one of Max's brigade, took a risk and stepped beyond the boundary to pick some of the orange berries that were treasured by the prisoners for their vitamins.

'Watch out, Martin,' Thomas, a cautious boy of barely twenty hissed. Before anyone could take another breath, Martin collapsed. The guard they called 'Iwan the terrible' for his random cruelty had shot him right in the chest. He died instantly. None of the prisoners spoke for the rest of the day after they were ordered to bury Martin deeper in the forest. From then on they were even more

205

wary around the guards, whose sporadic acts of violence could cost them their lives.

Max was assigned to the felling team, sharing his saw with Anton, a quiet young man who dreamed of going back to medical school once this was all over. He had been pulled out of university after two years and sent to the eastern front. Despite shrapnel in his legs and the horrors his young eyes had seen, Anton never stopped wanting to become a doctor. But his delicate hands hurt – he had never done any manual work.

'It's crazy, four of us do badly what one horse could achieve in no time,' Max grumbled one day as he and three of his fellows pulled a huge trunk towards the river.

'The irony. I've worked with wood all my life, as a carpenter, but I never really thought much about where my excellent wood came from. Now they won't let me do anything else but fell these giants.'

'It's better than logging, though,' Max considered. 'Those poor souls have to balance on logs in the freezing river all day long. If they slip and fall, they'll be crushed. Disappear for ever under the sea of logs.'

No one knew what the Russians built with all that wood or who would pick up the logs farther downstream. One day Heinrich, another of Max's fellows, came up with an idea.

'Why don't we hack messages into the trunks? No one knows where we are, we can't send any post, not even a postcard. But maybe we could get a message through that way?'

'Listen to the dreamer,' Heinz, a stocky man from the north of Germany, sneered. 'We're never getting out of this hell! We might as well forget who we are and that there's anyone else out there.'

But not everyone agreed, and soon some of the prisoners had hacked short messages into the logs using their axes. Had they been caught it would have been the end, but it was summer and the guards barely patrolled their territory.

They fed the prisoners watery soup, a grey liquid with bits of cabbage, beets and rotten potatoes, hardly ever any meat or fat, and with scarcely any bedding, just one thin blanket to share among five and a plank for a bed, the men shivered day and night. Spooned tightly into each other without leaving the tiniest gap, they lay squeezed together like sardines, and every hour one of the men would command, *'Alle umdrehen!'* As if one body, everyone turned. Every night was divided into these hourly intervals of squirming, moaning and the inevitable turn. Max lay at the end of the row, facing away from his comrades. He was colder that way but he preferred not to be caught tightly between two bodies.

Sometimes in the depths of the night Max would pull out the prince, running his fingers over the puppet's cloak and face as if he might find an answer in its delicate features. Then, on one particularly icy night, as the whole bed shook from the soldiers' tremblings and groans, Max started to talk to the prince. He lay with his back to his neighbour, holding the puppet close to his face, pouring his heart out to it.

'I tell you, it's not easy here, my fellow. The gruelling work, and the cold. Bites you like those horrible guard dogs that snarl and snap at you any chance they get. If they get you by the throat, they won't let go, just like the cold – it turns your insides to stone. I'd do anything for a bit of warmth. But you can never get warm in this damned place. It's a giant freezer, Siberia. It snaps your bones.'

'You talking to yourself again, Max?' his neighbour whispered. Max ignored him.

'Maybe we deserve it after the war. After Stalingrad, Warsaw, Cracow, all that killing. And whatever happened to Mika, little prince? He was the same age as my boy.'

Max had never talked to any of his comrades about Mika, how he had helped to rescue his mother and aunt from the *Umschlag*, nor about the puppet shows at the barracks or indeed anything to do with the ghetto. Only two soldiers who had been stationed with him in Warsaw had ended up in the same camp. They did not share the same sleeping quarters and Max did not seek them out.

21

Days in the camp were utterly grim, flowing like a leaden stream, like grey pearls strung together by some invisible force. Endless days, stolen from the prisoners, just as they had taken days, years and millions of lives in every place they had claimed as their Reich. The difference here, in this icy, barren spot, was that prisoners were not killed with German efficiency, but left to rot or freeze to death like some giant experiment in the survival of the fittest. Sometimes the prisoners debated their situation and how they had ended up in such a terrible mess.

'Serves us right,' Hans, one of the four men who shared Max's bunk, muttered under his breath one evening.

'Don't be stupid, Hans, we didn't really know,' Heinz, one of the youngest men replied. 'We did what we had to do – it was our duty, that's all.'

Max joined the debate. 'I've seen enough in Warsaw to give me nightmares for the rest of my life. I've been part of too much. I'll never sleep well again.'

'But we were just following orders! We're ordinary Wehrmacht soldiers, remember. God, look at Michael here, he even fought in Stalingrad, lost four toes and nearly lost his wits. You blame him for the war, for what happened?' Heinz's face was flushed.

'No, of course not,' Max said.

'They labelled him a war criminal for fighting there, while the biggest swines got away.'

Michael was the quietest among them, he hardly ever spoke, but when Max had showed him the prince, Michael's eyes had filled with tears.

'Ordinary soldiers we were. Hitler fucked us over. Promised us a land of milk and honey. Now look what we've got, a white hell. Fed us like fodder to the war machines, that Herr Hitler!' Heinz grew even redder.

'That's true,' Max replied, 'it all seemed so grand and convincing. They fed us their lies and we swallowed them down like sugar cakes. But what about the Jews, the women? Don't you ever think about them?' Max's voice grew louder. 'It was wrong, all wrong. I know it was.' He slammed his hand down on the small wooden table.

'But that's what happens in a war, people die. Look, Max, we weren't SS or SA, we were just ordinary soldiers. We did what we had to do. Now give it a rest.'

The camp included about twenty SS men and officers, held in a separate building; but even here the Führer's elite fought for rank and bullied the other prisoners, still convinced that the German Reich had been a great invention and if only they had had better equipment, if the winter had not been so harsh, they surely would have won the war. Max made sure he stayed away from them.

'Let's sleep; it's no use thinking about all this if we want to survive. It's over, finito, *Schluss, aus.* If we don't rest, we'll die, it's as simple as that.' Heinz slumped on the bench, turning away from everyone.

But sleep didn't come easy for Max that night, nor indeed any night. As on many nights before, he pulled out the prince, clasped the puppet tightly to his chest, and began to talk to it.

'God, all these terrible dreams. I'm in Warsaw again, looking down the long cobbled street. I am alone with the flame-thrower by my side. I've been told to walk from house to house and torch them all, burn them down. And so I do it; I kick in the doors and pump fire inside: one, two, three, four, five, six ...

'In my head are the words they fed me on: "Exterminate the vermin, get rid of the *Ungeziefer*, nothing must remain!" I grip the thrower hard. Its fire roars. I know I'm a good soldier and the Fatherland will thank me. Once the staircase and wallpaper have caught fire, I move on to the next house ... Seven, eight, and nine ... Suddenly my chest hurts, burns as if my heart is on fire. I look down and it is you! The prince, wiggling under my uniform, burning like embers into my flesh. I rip you from my jacket and try to put out the flames, but I can't. You're on fire, your face is melting. Then it changes into Mika's face, then that of my boy Karl, my wife. Then an endless stream of faces I've never seen ... screaming ... Then I wake up ...'

Max fell silent after this.

'We just did our duty, Max. Don't torment yourself.' Anton's hoarse voice startled Max. He did not reply but quickly stuffed the puppet back under the rancid straw mattress and pretended to sleep.

Hope became as scarce as good food and many of Max's companions fell sick and collapsed. In the shadow world of the camp they died in droves, like flies at the end of the summer: many in this first year but most later in 1948, when a particularly fierce winter swept across Siberia. The infirmaries couldn't cope with the sick as typhoid, tuberculosis and smallpox became rampant. The barracks reeked of vomit and oozing wounds, and the constant coughing and moans of the dying kept the rest of the prisoners awake. Many died from sheer exhaustion. The dead couldn't be buried during the winter and had to be stored in a small shed, stacked like wood, until spring, when the relentless frost finally loosened its grip a little.

Max continued to find solace in his conversations with the prince.

One evening in May, he pulled out the puppet and held it close to his face. The prisoners had been ordered to spend all day digging shallow graves in the slightly thawed earth.

'I know they can't feel anything any more, but these guards are treating the dead worse than the logs we harvest from the forest. Just to make sure they're really dead they shoot the corpses as well. In the neck. Or worse, they swing a pickaxe through their skulls. If I ever get out of this place, what shall I tell their loved ones? That they piled the dead on top of each other and left them there all winter? First Willy, then Peter, and now Michael. I'm not sure how long I'll last ...' Max's voice quivered.

'You might not feel anything in that small papier-mâché body of yours, but you know, for me, hope is far more dangerous than despair. It eats away at me like those festering wounds that never heal in this dammed cold. I need to stop hoping, longing for home. They might never let us out of this hellhole. I've become a ghost, a shadow of the person I once was. This place is all there is now.' He slumped forward. As always the prince remained silent and Max tucked the puppet back into the dirty straw.

'What's the use, you never say a word anyway ... every time I look at you I see Mika's face. I should have never taken you from him.'

Life in Camp 267 dragged on. The Russians' plan, they said, was to make the Germans rebuild their ruins. They happily told them the good news: 'You can go home when you've rebuilt everything you have destroyed.' But like the other prisoners, Max knew how impossible this was.

'Damn pigs. How can they expect us to work with nothing in our stomachs and only rags to keep us warm?' Anton hissed, pushing and pulling the saw that was so blunt it hardly budged. If they didn't keep it moving it would freeze and get stuck completely.

'We worked people to death in the camps too,' Max replied. 'What goes around comes around, that's what they say.'

'I heard they even had a slogan above the entrance, *"Arbeit macht frei*, work will set you free." But we weren't the ones who put that sign there.' Anton pushed the saw harder and harder. 'I didn't personally sign the orders to ship the Jews to their death. I never tortured anyone. I only carried a gun and followed orders.' Anton fell into a sullen silence. These exchanges always left everyone feeling as if they had slogged through snow for days yet ended up in the same spot.

One day as Max's squad returned to their quarters exhausted after a ten-hour shift in the forest, a senior Russian guard and three others entered, their heavy boots stomping along the aisles.

'Everything off.' Max froze, the last bit of colour draining from his face in an instant. He was sweating despite the freezing temperature. *Oh no, not this, please God. I should have left it with the prince.* His thoughts raced; he had no time to hide the photograph. *Why today? Why now?*

They were never safe from random searches but this couldn't have come on a worse day as he had slipped his precious photograph of Erna and Karl into his jacket pocket that very morning. Although he had cut a little slit in the pocket's side and had placed it in there, he knew that if they searched him thoroughly one of the three guards would find it.

'Prisoner 3465 – step forward,' the senior guard yelled. Willi's number – a quiet and sensitive man who, like Max, was from the Franken area. The guard moved towards him, holding a small black book right under Willi's nose.

'Is this yours?'

Willi nodded.

'What is it?'

'A Bible.' The guard slapped Willi's face with the book then threw it on the floor and stamped on it.

When Max looked up one of the other guards was holding his photograph. He felt something break inside his heart.

'3587, forward.'

Max moved slowly.

'Is this yours?' The same question, same guard.

'Yes. It's my wife and son.'

'Shut up. There are no women and children in Camp 267.' With that the guard ripped the photograph into tiny pieces that scattered over the floor.

After the guards left, Max fell to his knees and gathered up the pieces, making sure he didn't miss any. Anton put his hand on Max's shoulder. 'I'm so sorry, Max. But at least they didn't make you clear out the latrines for weeks or stick you in solitary.'

Max didn't reply. No punishment could have been greater. He didn't speak for days after this.

Over time Max became less vigilant, and even took his puppet out when the prisoners had a rare day off.

'Who's that little fellow?' Anton stretched his hands out towards the puppet, pretending to pinch the prince's cheek. 'At least someone has red cheeks here. You brought him all the way from Warsaw?'

Max nodded. 'Yes, he's a prince.'

The puppet bowed in front of Anton who bowed back.

'Pleased to meet you, little prince.' They shook hands and Max paraded his prince in front of his comrades, introducing him with gallant handshakes. The prince was in his element. Max even began to fool around in front of his comrades, and as the men clapped and whistled, Max allowed the prince to give a little speech:

'Now, gentlemen, even in a place like this I recommend a serious attempt at cleanliness. Rub yourself clean with snow, air your blankets, open the windows so the foul smell in here vanishes. You don't want to return home looking like a thief, do you?' While the men laughed at first, this last statement reminded them too much of their dire situation.

'Enough, Max,' Hans grumbled.

'I think our prince here needs some companions,' Anton declared. 'How about a whole Kasperltheater, with a princess, a crocodile and a villain. Maybe even a devil. What do you think?'

'Yes, and Herr Tod as well,' Sepp's deep voice boomed.

A whole puppet troupe? That could have potential.

'So, who's in? Who's good with their hands?' A few men raised their hands, wearing expectant smiles. Max delegated who would create which puppet and gave himself the task of making Herr Tod, Mr Death, and the crocodile. Anton would attempt to make the devil and the girl, and Peter the Kasperl itself. The men had no special materials, but all learned to improvise with whatever scraps they could salvage, and some had a good eye for detail.

Max found a piece of wood, borrowed a small knife from Peter, who had smuggled it through all the searches, and began to carve the crocodile's teeth. It was difficult to get fabric and a needle, but in the end there it sat, a snapping, whirling crocodile – with a long, stripy body. In fact all the puppets, except Death and the girl, wore clothes made from the stripy prisoners' shirts.

One night, for his bunkmate Klaus's birthday, Max gathered the puppets that were ready – the crocodile, the girl and Herr Death – and tried his hand at a puppet play. Birthdays were special even in the camp as the men received a double ration of the thin soup and an extra chunk of bread, so each man tried to celebrate at least three birthdays per year.

For his puppet, Herr Tod, Max had carved out deep eyes in a potato head then used a piece of rag rubbed in soot for his cloak and a stick with a small metal piece from his cup for a scythe. Someone had donated their carefully hidden embroidered handkerchief for the girl's dress and there they were: the first puppets in Camp 267.

Max stretched a blanket between two bunks to form a makeshift stage and then the play started. It wasn't Schiller or Goethe but rather a wild chase between the crocodile, Death and the prince. As the prince paraded along the stage leisurely, talking about the finer things in life, Death followed with his sweeping scythe, chased by the snapping, stripy crocodile. Max's fellow prisoners laughed as never before, a deep rolling thunder of laughter, right from the belly. And then everyone wanted to have a go, reaching out and grabbing the puppets.

The evening passed with more chasing, fighting, devouring, hugging and shouting. Once the prisoners had tasted some fun they wanted more.

'How about a Kasperl?' Hans shouted. Kasperl – the famous foolish character with a long pointy nose, peaked cap, enormous smile and apple-red cheeks.

'Peter was meant to have a go at the Kasperl,' Max replied. 'How's it coming along, Peter?'

'I'm sorry, I haven't even started.' Peter sounded defeated. 'I got so sad thinking about the puppets. Used to play with my little girl. She's called Lisa.' A long pause stretched between the two men before Peter took a deep breath. 'OK, I'll give it a go.'

And so, bit by bit, a German puppet theatre took shape with the Kasperl, the devil and his grandmother, a policeman and Herr Tod. The prince stuck out like a sore thumb with his colourful, princely costume amongst this stripy troupe. Not that the puppet seemed to mind.

Max often thought about Warsaw and the plays Mika had put on for the soldiers. How everything had changed – here they were now, grown men, once-proud soldiers who had brought so much death and misery to Poland, to the world, now just bags of bones fighting over a bunch of puppets.

The prisoners worked day after day, year after year, in that dark forest – through the short summers, grey rainy autumns and the relentless winters, with only three days' rest per month, sometimes even less. They never saw anything being built with all the logs they felled and never received an answer to the messages they had crudely cut into the trunks.

The puppets kept their spirits up for a time, yet Max and his fellow prisoners were becoming weaker with every day. More desperate too, as the camp reduced them to bones and sinew, their eyes sunken, their flesh melting away. The excruciating hunger and persistent cold brought out the worst and sometimes the best in the men: some prisoners shared their very last piece of bread, while others stole their neighbour's hidden share in the depths of the night. Some who might have considered themselves to be decent men turned into ruthless scavengers, driven mad by the cramps in their stomach, while others discovered a kindness they did not know they were capable of. As hunger bit harder, Max turned out to be as unpredictable as the weather during the Siberian spring.

One December morning, he woke early with a terrible cramp in his stomach. Hunger, naked, relentless hunger, gnawing away at his insides. It was still dark as he swivelled his stiff legs over the edge of the bed and got up, moving quietly along the line of bunks. He remembered seeing Sepp, one of the men who slept near the entrance of their building, hiding a piece of bread the size of half a palm under his makeshift cushion the night before. Max listened to the man's regular breathing as he carefully searched next to his head. With one swift movement he pulled out the bread and wrapped it in an old rag. Sepp stirred but didn't wake. Max returned to his bunk, ripped the bread into small pieces and swallowed them whole.

A memory flashed before his eyes. How often had he marched past children starving on the ghetto streets, their stick-thin arms reaching out to him? A wave of nausea washed over him and he rushed outside, retching until he brought up all of the stolen bread. An hour later the dull sound of hammer against metal sounded – the camp's wake-up call.

'*Schweinehunde!*' Sepp's voice thundered through the quarters minutes later. 'Which bastard stole my bread?' No one answered but Max felt ashamed to the core, and from then on he shared his meagre rations whenever he could.

Camp 267 was also devastating for the mind; only a few smuggled books made the rounds and in the first two years no one was allowed post.

In the third year, on a cold February evening in 1948, the prisoners were told to assemble in the canteen around the long tables. The guards placed small postcards, printed with a red cross, in front of them, along with a pencil stump for each prisoner.

'Write. You can write one card each month. Keep it

simple. Good words only – no complaints,' the guard bellowed. They might have composed letters or whole stories in their minds, but the men had not actually written anything down for three years.

'Good words, what do they mean? I guess they won't send the cards if we tell the truth?' Max wondered. His hand was shaking. What should he say? How to condense three years' longing into a few crooked lines. In the end, the message read simply: *'Meine liebste Erna, mein Karlchen – I am interned in Russia as a prisoner of war. I am safe and healthy, please don't worry about me. I hope you are safe. I miss you so dearly and hope I can hold you in my arms again soon. Kisses to you both. Your Max.'*

Over the following weeks many of the men fell silent, lost in memories of their loved ones. They had lost the war, but no one knew what had happened to their families back home. Max had heard rumours about Nuremberg's destruction. Had Erna and the boy survived?

It took three months. One evening in May 1948 the prisoners were gathered in the yard. After the evening roll call more names were called out. 'Peter Schreiber. Heinz Bauer. Max Meierhauser.'

Max stepped forward and received a single postcard.

Back in the sleeping quarters he hugged Anton.

'They are alive – Erna and Karl, my little boy. The house is gone, bombed to bits, but they are safe. They moved to a village outside Nuremberg.'

'I'm glad for you, Max,' Anton said quietly. No postcard had arrived for him.

'I'm so sorry, Anton, how selfish of me. You might get a reply soon.'

'Maybe.' Anton's voice sounded flat.

Some prisoners only received a three-line message scribbled by an official. So much life squeezed into a few lines on a postcard. Finally, in the summer of 1948, they were allowed to receive one postcard per month and one parcel per year. Max carried his postcards under his shirt at all times, close to his heart.

22

Early one morning in the summer of 1949, Max pulled the prince out from under the straw. There was a dangerous glimmer in his eyes as if he were running a fever.

'I can't go on like this any more. I am starting to forget, I can't remember my wife's face or my son's. I keep trying to picture them, their features, how they used to walk, their voices, their smiles, but it's just one big blur. God, I've lost them. What shall I do?' He stared at the prince as if he might extract an answer if he waited long enough, but the prince remained silent.

From then on, Max debated with the prince every night.

'Look, I don't think I can survive another winter here. So many of us have died.

'I've become a walking skeleton. I don't want to end up being stored in a shed for months, only to be thrown into a shallow grave in this godforsaken place. What could be worse than staying in this hellhole?'

'You could get yourself shot if they catch you,' Anton whispered.

Does he never sleep? Max thought, irritated.

'Remember when Otto from Hamburg tried to escape last winter? They caught up with him after only three hours,' Anton continued. 'Then there was Peter Karpf from Hamburg. Both of them shot in the middle of the yard, right in front of us. And the group with Rainer and the guys from Munich who tried their luck that first year. They were gone for five days but in the end the guards caught them too with their dogs. Shot them the next day, remember? It's hopeless, Max.'

'But what about Thomas and Stefan?' Max hissed. The pair had disappeared one brilliant blue day last autumn and had never been caught.

'Who knows. But just because the dogs didn't get them doesn't mean they didn't freeze to death. They might've lost their minds, starved to death, got lost or dropped dead from exhaustion. And what about the wolves, you've seen them. Siberia's one big prison.'

It pained Max to hear the young man who had once been an eager medical student sound so utterly defeated. Yes, there were rivers to conquer, an army of Soviet soldiers and officials to avoid and a whole continent to cross. But wasn't all this better than dying here in the camp?

Max had made up his mind. But it would be easier in a group. Luckily, after three more nights of whispered debates, Anton changed his mind. Shortly afterwards Hans came on board. Like Max, he had been a carpenter before the war, and although a Northerner, he was always up for a joke, even in the most dreadful of circumstances.

Camp 267 was as remote as the moon and hence not heavily guarded; the Russians knew that not many would dare to escape during those terrible winters. But there were other seasons too. The summers in Siberia blazed with heat for a few short weeks and the prisoners soaked up the warmth, each sunny day a precious gift for their frozen bones. Summer also brought some colour, a comfort to the eyes and hearts after the endless black and white of winter: brown in all shades, mossy greens and even some berry-reds. Clear blue skies stretched high and wide and the harsh winter winds died down to a gentle breeze. Summer would have been a greater relief still, if not for the Siberian plague: swarms of blood-sucking mosquitoes that arrived in huge buzzing swarms, stinging everyone into a red, swollen pulp.

'Damn flies, you want to suck the last of my blood from me?' Max cursed, waving his arms wildly. 'Worse than the cold, those little devils.'

It made working in the woods unbearable. The prisoners needed all their remaining willpower not to scratch themselves bloody and the guards were even more bad tempered.

'Let's go at the very end of summer,' Max suggested. Anton and Hans agreed and the men started to prepare. They saved some of their bread, a few shrivelled beets, dried berries and a small tub of lard. Anton managed to find two small flint stones – without fire they would not have a chance.

Although they had been very careful, some of the other prisoners got wind of their plans.

'So, it's not good enough for you here, ha?' Sepp sneered. He had always suspected Max of stealing his bread.

'Leave me alone,' Max snapped back. But others supported their little group, sharing some of their precious rations. Then, just a week before the planned date, the Russians stepped up their numbers at the gate.

'We're not going to make it,' Hans whispered, 'they're too many of them.'

Anton also seemed deflated. 'They'll catch us before we can even get out of here.'

'I'm going anyway,' Max mumbled under his breath,

'we'll die one way or another. At least I want to die one step closer to being a free man. I can wait a while longer, but not long. Are you with me?'

It was autumn when they finally tried their luck. Fired up by Max, Anton and Hans joined him. The three men agreed that autumn would be actually the better season as in the summers, with all the snow melting, the ground turned into a sponge and they could have drowned in the bogs of the tundra. Autumn dried out the earth. Autumn would still spare them the snow for several weeks and provide plenty of berries and mush-rooms on their way.

The evening before the planned date, Max wrapped the prince in a piece of cloth and tucked the puppet under his flimsy clothes, together with the crocodile, the girl and the Kasperl.

'Please leave me at least some of your puppets Max, I'll die of boredom here,' pleaded Martin Schneider. Since Martin had had an accident the year before, when his axe had slipped and cut deep into his left leg, he had walked with a heavy limp. And although he longed to join the small group of escapees, he knew he would only hold everyone back.

'Take good care of them, Martin, and maybe they'll take care of you,' Max said, handing over the rest of the troupe: Herr Tod, the devil, the grandmother and the policeman.

'I wish you luck.'

'You too.' The men hugged.

Max, Anton and Hans had studied the movements of the guards carefully and discovered a small window of time, a few precious minutes, in which they could slip unnoticed underneath the fence. Over the previous weeks they had dug a shallow hole, just deep enough to scramble through.

They wore all of their winter clothes: two shirts, a shabby, padded jacket, a cap, gloves and their boots. They managed to collect together one blanket each, a few pieces of hard bread, a handful of dried forest berries, the flint stones and their battered metal bowls and spoons.

Max held on to their most precious possession: a map of Russia that Heinrich, a former geography teacher from Munich, had drawn over many nights on a crumpled piece of paper. Heinrich tried to remember every river, mountain range and forest as clearly as he could. The three men had bowed over the map as if looking into a crystal ball.

'It's a crazy mission,' Heinrich had said, 'you've only got this basic map, winter on its way, and a country to cross that's as big as the ocean.'

'But anything's better than this,' Max had whispered. 'I know one important thing for sure: our direction is westwards. We'll follow the sun by day and at night the stars. We eat what we can find and we're not coming back.'

Seeing Max's determination, some other men in the quarters had chipped in and added small gifts to their supply: a few more shrivelled vegetables, a small piece of dried sausage and even one sugar cube.

Now the sun had disappeared behind the forest and night was fast approaching. The three men lay waiting for their moment.

'Quick, now,' Max whispered. They slipped underneath the fence, then ran straight into the forest, its dense wood offering them the best protection. They could hear the wild barking of the dogs and the shouting of the guards but they didn't seem to be getting any closer.

The three ran and marched all through that first night,

staying close together, keeping each other in sight, and only when dawn began to break did they huddle together in a hollow, covering themselves with a thick layer of branches and leaves.

They were lucky. Very lucky. After a while they could no longer hear the troops pursuing them, nor the bloodthirsty dogs which undoubtedly had been sent after them. Day after day the men trudged on, step after painful step, forest stretching ahead, no end in sight. And although they had all known that Siberia was enormous, they hadn't bargained on its utter boundlessness, its limitless vastness. Siberia was as big and empty as the moon.

The three men trekked one behind the other, never coming across any sign of human life, feeding off their meagre supplies and the berries and mushrooms they found along the way. Although far from home, Max had a keen eye for edible mushrooms.

'They're all the same, the whole world over. Look at that beauty,' he said, grinning, pointing out a huge brown mushroom that grew from the damp forest floor.

Max reached under his shirt and pulled out the prince. He sat the puppet on top of the mushroom and laughed.

'Have a dance on the biggest mushroom in Siberia, my friend.'

'You're sure we can eat that one?' Anton said suspiciously. 'I don't want to die from eating a damn mushroom after all this!'

In the end their hunger outweighed their caution and they ate the whole mushroom raw. No one died that day, but the men's stomachs complained and every so often one of them would disappear behind a tree, clutching their belly. Only after four days, when they were far enough away from the camp, did they dare to light a fire and cook some of the mushrooms.

A few days later the weather changed suddenly and the first snow arrived.

'This wasn't meant to happen, not yet. It's only September,' Anton grumbled.

'Look on the bright side; we'll have water wherever we are going. We can melt the snow and *voila*!' Hans replied. Max smiled; this was why he had gladly welcomed Hans into their group – he was a practical guy, always looking for the positive. But as the snow kept falling it grew colder by the day. The men hardly spoke but kept moving.

'I wouldn't care if I never see another tree in my life again,' Max said.

'You can say that again. But then the forest has given us the mushrooms and berries,' Hans replied.

'And the runs,' Anton added.

After ten days the forest began to take its toll. Hans, who had marched in the middle of the three men, suddenly collapsed, lying sprawled like a dead bird in the snow. He opened his blue eyes, looked up at Max and smiled.

'Hey, Max, I think if I were back home I would miss all this snow. I'd better stay right here. You go ahead with Anton. Good luck.' With that he curled into a ball and did not stir again.

His loss struck Max and Anton to the very core, but they could not afford to stay still. They covered him with branches and moved on. Three days later, Anton, who by now was not only quiet but had gone completely mute, suddenly announced he wasn't feeling well and needed to lie down.

'Not yet, Anton. Please, we can rest later. We just need to keep going a little longer, *na, komm schon*.'

'Just one minute, Max, please.'

Then, just as Hans had done, Anton let himself fall into the snow.

Max tried to pull him up but Anton simply smiled at him and closed his eyes. And just like that, Max lost both of his companions.

Soon it was Anton's turn to be covered with branches, but not before Max had rummaged through his pockets to see whether he was carrying anything useful.

'Look at that, the quietest one and yet he managed to swipe a knife. My apologies, Anton, I am very sad to be leaving you here, but that's a welcome gift.'

Max put the knife deep in his pocket and a short while later he moved on, now wrapped in three blankets, his cap pulled down over his face. To distract himself, he started counting his steps, beginning all over again the moment he lost count: '*einhundertdrei, einhundertvier, einhundertfünf ...*' – he never got very far.

That's when Max began talking to the prince again, in an endless stream of thoughts.

'*Mein kleiner Kerl*, I tell you Anton and Hans chose the easy way out. I wish I could lie down or hibernate until spring, but I've got to go on. But why, why? You tell me. My feet are killing me and I'm so hungry I could eat my own hand.'

His dreams were filled with Nuremberger sausages, sauerkraut and apple cakes.

He struggled on for days through the forest but then, suddenly, a glaring wide space opened up in front him. He stopped and pulled out his map.

'So, we've finally reached the tundra. Easier now to find which way is west, we'll see the sun all day and the stars at night.'

But there was also no shelter and he could easily be spotted from miles away.

'I need some snowshoes, my friend. Otherwise how am I going to cross this white desert?' He pulled out the

228

knife and looked for some branches. A while later he held out two oval shapes.

'Look at these beauties.'

He bound them to his boots and, equipped with two long sticks, he marched out into the open, but not before he'd tied a piece of cloth in front of his face, leaving two slits for his eyes. 'Don't want to go snow-blind, that would be the end of me.'

There was no shelter in this ice desert so each evening he dug himself a hole in the snow, or if the snow had hardened too much, he cut it with his knife into awkward slabs, building a simple igloo. The clear night sky and the Northern Star helped Max, but brought little solace otherwise, as starry nights meant plummeting temperatures.

'Please let me wake up again tomorrow,' he prayed each night, 'for Erna, for Karl. For my comrades at the camp.' He got up again as soon as the sun rose, willing his half-frozen limbs to march on like a puppet, reminding himself that he was his own puppet master and without determination and a strong will he would simply collapse just as Anton and Hans had done.

Late one afternoon a wave of excitement surged through him.

'Hey, *Kamerade*, look, there's something sticking out there on the horizon: it might be a farm or a house, somewhere we could spend the night.'

He marched more quickly than he had for days. The object turned out to be a wooden barn, leaning precariously to one side, gaping holes between its boards, but a shelter nevertheless.

'I need to rest, my feet are all swollen and a bloody mess. I can't go on,' Max said aloud.

Hope and fear stirred in his chest. Where there was a barn, there might be a village close by. Food and shelter maybe. But he couldn't be sure. And what if a bounty had been placed on his head or it was a kolkhoz, one of Stalin's cooperatives, crawling with party officials?

'We'll check out the village tomorrow,' Max mumbled before collapsing on a pile of straw, burying himself under it, wrapped in his torn blankets.

That night his body gave up, crumbled like the hard black bread they dished out in the camp. He curled up and fell into a deep sleep. The barn stood quiet as the grave except for the wind that howled around it like a restless ghost.

The fever started an hour later. Max burned like the sun in Siberia's short summers, and sweat poured down his aching body. He moaned, thrashed his arms left and right as if he were fighting mosquitoes or an invisible giant. After an hour, his arms went limp. Then nothing.

23

With the first light of dawn a miracle occurred. Max lay unconscious, delirious beneath the straw, and oblivious to the creaking barn door, the heavy footsteps and deep voices. Strong hands reached into the straw and lifted his body, carrying him out into the icy morning air and placing him on a sleigh. He would later recall a vague sensation, as if he'd been lifted by celestial beings, angels in fur coats. The men wrapped Max in thick furs before rushing through the empty snowscape on reindeer-drawn sleighs.

After a short ride, the men pulled into a small settlement of tents. They carried their human load into one of the tents and placed him on a low bed of furs. The tent was dim, illuminated only by a wood stove that threw flickering shadows across the canvas. A group of women wrapped Max in blankets, whispering to each other as they smoothed the covers and dabbed his sweaty forehead with a sponge. After minutes the news had spread, and the tent filled with curious men, women and children, all wanting to gaze at the half-dead man. Shortly afterwards a broad, tall man with long black hair and a plaited beard entered. A pointed felt hat sat atop his red face and a cloak, stitched from colourful rags and adorned with numerous bells and shining metal plates, jingled with his every move. The shaman had arrived.

The crowd's murmuring stopped and an expectant silence filled the tent. The shaman put his large round drum to one side, then kneeled down next to Max and let his hand move over the stranger's body, hovering without touching, as if he were feeling the heat over a fire. He reached into Max's pocket and pulled out a small bundle. He unwrapped it swiftly and a broad smile spread over his face as the puppet tumbled into his lap – the prince. He took the puppet in both hands, threw it high up into the air, then caught it again and clutched it to his chest. Then he peeled away the layers of blankets and reached under Max's clothes. With a great flourish he pulled out the crocodile, Kasperl and the girl before gently laying the puppets on Max's chest. The crowd stirred, trying to get a glimpse of the small creatures.

The shaman now took a bundle of herbs from his leather pouch and placed them in the fire. Strong aromatic smoke filled the tent. Then he picked up his drum, painted with pictures of animals and small people, with long strips of fabric and leather attached and a mask-like face sitting next to the handle. He beat it right above Max's chest: boom, boom, boom, as fast as a heart in flight …

Max lay stiff as a log, hardly breathing. Then the shaman's chanting began – rhythmic and low, not a melody exactly but a hypnotic repetition of simple words and notes. A few men and women moved closer around the shaman and his patient, joining in. With a loud shout the shaman suddenly jumped up and broke into a wild dance, beating his drum furiously, stamping his feet, his eyes closed, his head falling back.

Then, as suddenly as it had started, everything stopped. Silence filled the tent and the air was thick with anticipation. The shaman's expression morphed into a grimace and finger by finger his hand rolled up into a giant fist. He kneeled and with a loud thump pounded his fist down on Max's chest, just above his heart, again and again. Then, with a loud slurp, he sucked something out of Max's chest, spitting the invisible substance into a small wooden box, snapping the lid shut. A sigh rippled though the audience. The shaman placed the prince, the crocodile and the girl on different spots on Max's body – the prince over his heart, the crocodile on his stomach and the girl across Max's throat.

Suddenly Max's hand stirred, feeling for the prince on his heart. A murmur of relief ran through the tent and the crowd moved even closer around him. The shaman put his hand lightly on Max's forehead and smiled, then whispered some instructions to one of the older women and left the tent.

Max stayed for weeks in the villagers' cosy tent and slowly he recovered. The villagers were nomads who had been forced to settle there as part of Stalin's plan, accountable to a kolkhoz, a collective farm several miles away. Every once in a while the men would kill one of their reindeer, which fed the whole village for several days. Men, women and even children came to feed Max with nourishing morsels of reindeer meat and warm, smelly potions. In the prison camp Max could easily have counted his ribs, but after some weeks in the tent, he put on weight and slowly grew stronger. One morning he took out the prince. A big smile spread across his face.

'Hey, little fellow, glad you're still with me. Weren't we lucky? I can't remember much after I collapsed in that barn. Do you think they know I've been a prisoner? That I'm German? Do they even care? Or maybe the war didn't touch people here?'

233

As time passed more and more village children gathered around Max's bed as if he were a sideshow. They would sit giggling by his side, pointing at his features, his bright blue eyes, carefully stroking his dark blond hair, his ragged clothes. On such occasions Max would take out all the puppets – the prince, the girl, the crocodile and the Kasperl – and line them up next to each other, then play with his little visitors. Their eyes followed the puppets eagerly and they burst out laughing at the puppets' funny antics.

'I feel so much better,' Max confessed one night to the puppets after the children had left.

'All this good food is bringing me back to life. And of course that strange doctor with his shaggy beard and strange coat. ... Wonder what he thought of you?' Max stretched and yawned, then lay back on the comfortable bed of thick furs the reindeer people had set up for him. But as more weeks passed, Max grew restless.

'My prince, these people have been so good to us, but we can't stay here for ever. I didn't risk everything to spend my time in a cosy tent and grow fat like a bear. I have to see Erna and Karl again. I've lost enough time already.'

That night, one of the elders joined Max as he sat poring over his map. The man took a brief look at the crumpled piece of paper and started to laugh, pointing at one of the rivers that Heinrich had drawn. He pulled out a small branch from the fire and with the blackened end drew a few lines. Within minutes the map showed a very different landscape: the thin snake of the river had grown as if it had swallowed a big beast and the mountain range had moved much farther south. The elder pointed to Max, himself and the tent, then plunged the pencil right into the middle of the map.

'We're only here? How can this be?' Max cried, realising he hadn't reached the tundra at all, but the old man gave him a pat on the back.

'*Sibir. Bolshoi.*' The elder used his outstretched arms to indicate a large circle.

'Siberia is big?'

'*Da.*' The man nodded, then his face darkened and he made a cutting gesture at his throat.

'*Sibir plohaya.*' Whatever the phrase meant, Max knew it wasn't good. Then the scowl vanished and the man smiled again and touched Max's chest at his heart.

'*Sibir karsivaya.*'

'*Schön.* Beautiful?' Max asked. The old man nodded and the two shook hands.

As a goodbye present Max put on a puppet show. At the end he thanked everyone with a deep bow and held up the crocodile, Kasperl and the girl. Then, with a smile, he handed them to the children closest to him. Their smiles warmed his heart, even though Max felt sad to leave behind the puppets that had been created amid the hardship of the camp. The next morning the elders gave him a pair of boots made from reindeer skin and a jacket. It was nearly February now and the snow was deep. Max strode out into the endless white expanse, not looking back.

24

The long journey home from the depths of Siberia to Nuremberg was treacherous and it took Max almost three years and a lot of luck.

With the bitter winter somewhat alleviated by his stay with the reindeer people, Max managed to get as far as Yakutsk in the first year. But in the second winter, no one took him in and except for a few days spent resting in barns and abandoned houses, he kept on trudging through the taiga, exposed to the unrelenting cold. His whole being ached from the endless walking and his breath froze into ice crystals that gathered underneath his nose and in his beard. He sheltered at night under trees or curled up in shallow hollows, covering himself with fir branches. When no village was in sight, he lit a small fire to warm at least some of his body and to melt snow to quench his thirst.

Late one evening he was chewing on a piece of dried reindeer meat, his stiff legs stretched out in front of him. As he held his hands out towards the crackling fire he sensed a presence: a slight change in the air, a pungent whiff of something wild and dangerous. He looked up, trying to see into the dark forest, grabbing his staff. The howling started the moment he got to his feet: high-pitched, drawn out and very close, answered by three or four cries deeper in the forest. Max held his breath. As a branch cracked he saw a wolf's eyes: slits of amber, glistening in the firelight. His heart raced. The wolf drew closer, growling; Max could see its thick grey pelt and sharp teeth. He gripped his stick and smashed it into the fire, sending fragments of burning branches and embers towards the animal. The wolf jumped back a few metres, yapping.

Within seconds Max had decided to run. His trick with the fire had bought him time, but he would have no chance against a pack of hungry wolves. He grabbed the knapsack the reindeer people had given him and scrambled through the forest, frantically looking for a tree to climb. In the pale moonlight between the fir trees he spotted the white bark of a birch tree and instinctively his arms reached for a branch, then another, his feet pushing into the tree as he clambered up as high as he could. The wolves quickly picked up his scent and soon a group of five surrounded the tree, howling and snarling, jumping as high as they could reach, snapping at the air. Max was just high enough to be out of reach and he clung to the tree for dear life, aware that with one wrong move a pack of wolves would be feasting on his body.

The stand-off lasted all night. As day broke the wolves gave up, trotting off one after another into the forest. Max waited another hour before he climbed down, leaden with exhaustion.

One week later he reached the edge of the taiga. He was sick of the endless forest and was sure that this time he really had reached the wide expanse of the tundra. He cut two eye slits into a sheet of birch bark and bound it like a mask in front of his face.

'Might not look nice but I can't risk snow-blindness,' he said aloud.

For the first day he enjoyed being out in the open space but soon his left hip began to throb and despite the aid of his wooden staff, he started to limp. Within days the sole of his left boot had worn thin and Max felt the toes of his left foot beginning to itch and sting. Whenever he sheltered, he unwrapped the rags around his foot and rubbed it hard. White, red and yellow patches had spread across it and the middle toes had gone numb. Two days later blisters formed over the waxy skin and he couldn't feel his little toes any more. He knew the blisters would turn purple, then black. He had seen frostbite in the camp – some of his companions had lost fingers and toes that way. That night, as he huddled in a makeshift shelter, chewing on a piece of dry bread, tears stung his eyes. It wouldn't be painful to lose his numb toes, but he felt sapped by Siberia's relentless cruelty as never before.

It was late spring before his two blackened toes fell off like dead leaves. By then the cold had loosened its grip and the snow had melted.

In February of the third year, Max followed the banks of the Volga and as March approached, he enjoyed the river's dramatic awakening – a deep moaning sound before the ice burst apart, like fragments of the earth's crust, huge pieces of ice gliding over each other, tearing away from the bank. Winter gave way to a volatile spring. A vague memory of a Volga song tickled his brain like a feather, stirring hope and a longing for home. After the first melt, the river gathered momentum, swelling into a raging torrent.

Max kept his distance from the unpredictable bank, but one night under a March full moon, just before dawn, the river breached it. Max gasped and screamed, thrashing about in the icy water, trying desperately to stay afloat as the river swept him along together with branches, leaves and other debris. He had been a fine swimmer once, but as the dark river engulfed him and his soaking clothes dragged him down, thoughts and images rushed through his mind as fast as the river: Erna's smile on their wedding day; baby Karl, his big blue eyes; the burning ghetto; the camp; the tent of the reindeer people ...

Something hit his leg and a sharp pain brought him back to his senses. In the twilight he could see a slim tree trunk drifting a few metres away and with a few desperate strokes he reached it and clung to it. Together they floated for miles down the the swollen stream. At daybreak, Max noticed that he had been swept closer to the shore, and with one last push he propelled himself to the edge. He scrambled up the riverbank, swearing and shaking himself like a dog. When he peeled off his clothes and pulled out the prince from his jacket pocket he gasped: the puppet's papier-mâché head had been squashed and some of the colour had run. It took days for his clothes to dry properly and for Max to carefully mould the puppet's head back into shape.

Max trekked on day after day, month after month, crossing tundra and taiga, the Siberian plain and countless rivers and lakes, willing his bruised legs and frostbitten feet to carry on, his whole body on fire with pain.

He had to stay vigilant at all times – watching out for danger, alert to any morsel of food. Sometimes, tired to the core of walking, he took a chance and hitched a ride. Once he climbed into a truck after overhearing the driver mention that he was heading towards Bratsk. He rolled into the back of the vehicle and hid underneath a tarpaulin behind a stack of wooden boxes, jumping off unnoticed as the truck pulled into the town eight hours later, but not before taking two tins of salmon from the crates.

Another time he stumbled across a bicycle on a little

forest road, leaning against a birch tree. He hesitated briefly but couldn't resist and for days he enjoyed the different pace of his journey. Any vehicle would get him home quicker than his beaten feet. He even tried his luck with a ragged donkey he found grazing in the middle of a meadow. Pleased to have human company and welcoming the handful of water Max shared with the animal, it let him sit on its broad back for a few hours before dumping him off and bolting away at a brisk gallop.

Once, late at night, Max jumped on to the freight train from Novosibirsk to Omsk. He landed in a wagon of dirt-encrusted vegetables and dug himself a hiding place within a mountain of potatoes in the corner. But what had seemed a good idea at first soon turned into a nightmare as the dirty potatoes collapsed in on him like an avalanche. The next morning, before sunrise, he dug himself out, threw a few handfuls of potatoes off the train and then jumped, collecting the scattered potatoes as the train rumbled off towards its destination.

Besides his aching but faithful body, it was the kindness of strangers that saved him more than once: villagers handing him bread and water, a pot of lard or a swig of home-brewed vodka, giving him some vital directions or a bed for the night. Max's instinct sharpened the longer his escape lasted and despite some near-misses with armed farmers and Soviet authorities in the form of an kolkhoz official and a train guard, Max remained lucky.

All the way back home Max kept the prince and his cherished postcards from Erna hidden under his shirt. Most days he rambled on to the prince, and in the evenings he placed the puppet on his knees, pondering the route ahead. By now the prince was definitely worse for wear and the puppet's shiny costume only a distant memory.

*

Finally, in the spring of 1952, Max returned home. He had been gone nearly thirteen years. The moment he set foot on German soil, crossing the border from Czechoslovakia, he worked out how and when he could get to Nuremberg, then sent a telegram to Erna and Karl. He couldn't sit still on the last train journey, marching up and down the aisles, occasionally glancing at fellow passengers in their compartments, then out of the window, searching for anything familiar in the landscape. *How did Erna keep her hopes alive,* he wondered, *never knowing whether I'd come back or not? What about all those wives, mothers, children ... what did they do with their swollen hearts?*

When the train finally drew into Nuremberg, Max started to sweat profusely. He opened the top three buttons of his shirt and fumbled with the puppet's head in his coat pocket. As had become a habit for Max, he shared his agitation with the prince.

'Oh my God. Is that Erna? And that tall guy, my Karl?' he whispered as he spotted two figures craning their necks for the long-lost husband and father as the train pulled in.

The moment the train stopped, Max stumbled out of the carriage towards the pair.

'Erna, Karl!' he shouted, waving his arms like a windmill. Erna spotted him first.

'Max, *mein Gott, bist du das wirklich?*' Her voice sounded shrill and as high as a bell.

'Erna!' Max plunged at his wife. They stood in a close embrace for a long time. A faint scent of lily of the valley wafted off her. Max planted a soft kiss on her hair, which was neatly combed, dark brown streaked with grey, then kissed her on the mouth.

'*Mein Gott!*' Her face was red and blotchy and she sounded out of breath. She wiped away some tears with the back of her hand. 'I can't quite believe it's really you,

Max!' She patted his chest. Erna peeled herself away from the embrace and reached out for their son. Max turned to the young man, who extended his hand. Max shook it, then folded his other arm around Karl in an awkward embrace.

'My Karl!' His first words to his son. Karl had been an eager boy of eleven when they said their bitter farewell. The boy had clung to him, trying hard not to cry. Max had told him he would be back very soon.

'Welcome, Father.' The tall young man stood straight and slightly rigid, shifting his weight from one leg to another, glancing at Max, then back at his feet as if he had lost something. The lanky boy with the cheeky smile Max had hugged all those years ago, at the very same railway station in 1939, had vanished. And yet, there, on platform number four, Max decided to give him his present.

'I brought you something, Karl. Well, more like ... someone.' Max stretched out his hand towards Karl, holding the puppet.

'Oh, thank you, Father, I received the doctor a long time ago.' Karl's expression hardly changed. He took the puppet by the head with two fingers and looked at it.

'Come on, you'll have enough time later, our train is leaving in a few minutes.' Erna ushered Max and Karl to a different platform.

'So we live in Wolkersdorf now?' Max remembered the name from the first precious postcard he'd received in Siberia.

'Yes, it's nice there, you'll see. I think you'll like it,' Erna replied.

Karl said nothing but stuffed the puppet into his trouser pocket and walked behind his parents along the platform.

*

When they reached the small station in Wolkersdorf, Erna linked arms with Max and Karl and the three made the short walk to their small house along the cobbled streets with their quaint buildings. A large hand-painted WELCOME banner greeted Max as they entered the house.

His first bath was a quick one as Max was eager to join Erna and Karl at the kitchen table, but the next day he didn't emerge from the bathroom for four hours. As he sat in the steaming bathtub, rubbing away the last dirt until his skin shone raw and bright pink, he was overtaken by violent waves of sobbing. How could he ever soak away the frozen legacy of the tundra? And even if his bones did warm up again, would the icy place inside his heart ever melt? Warsaw, the camp, the brutal journey home ... Max realised that to soften and soak away those wounds would take more than one morning's bath. He scrambled out of the tub and wrapped himself in the towels Erna had brought him.

'Towels ... white towels ...' he murmured, sinking his face into the soft fabric. When he looked up, he froze. As his face slowly appeared in the steamed-up mirror, like a photograph emerging in a darkroom, he shuddered at his reflection: eyes dull and sunken, his skin an ashen grey, lines where he did not remember any and deep furrows between his eyebrows like a constant frown. His hair, so very short and thinning, showed a streak of white on his left temple.

For days, Max touched everything, picking up even the most mundane objects like an explorer, scrutinising them from all sides: a toothbrush, a comb, a porcelain cup, little knick-knacks he didn't recognise. He tried to ignore the glances Erna and Karl threw at him.

'Look, Erna.' He pulled out the little silver spoon he

had carried with him for twelve years. 'Do you still have the sugar bowl?'

Erna looked at him, tears misting her eyes.

'Max, we lost everything. I don't think you understand, when the bombs fell, we were lucky to get out alive. Who cares about the sugar bowl?' Max looked at the spoon. *He* cared about the bowl. He had brought the spoon home, had taken care of it. It belonged together with the bowl.

'It was 28 November 1944.' Erna spoke quietly. 'It was a small air attack, but this time they got us. You never knew whether it would be your time or not. If not, then we probably would have died during that terrible night on 2 January. But why am I telling you this now, you haven't even been home for long. I'm sorry.'

'No, don't be, I want to know,' Max replied.

'Not now, Max, there's plenty of time.'

Despite the welcome, little turned out to be as Max had hoped, or imagined. How often had he dreamed of embracing his wife. He had stroked the postcards with her delicate writing, re-read them on any occasion he could steal himself away – the one postcard that arrived every few months, having to sustain him and keep alive the delicate connection between them.

But when he arrived back in a village he didn't know with a son he hardly recognised and a wife who was friendly but cool, hope crumbled and all that remained were the brittle bandages of his memories.

Max could not settle. Some days he thought Erna was watching his every move, and whenever he took a short walk through the village he pulled his hat down over his face. And although Karl had stepped into his father's shoes and become apprenticed as a carpenter after the war, he hardly spoke to his father. The young boy of eleven who had admired his father had disappeared.

Max couldn't relax at meals and cut up every bit of food into the smallest of morsels, savouring each piece of bread as if it were his last, munching an apple as if it were the only harvest from a tree.

One day, out of the blue, he shouted at Erna.

'You're crazy. Throwing out bread!'

'Don't be silly, Max, it's only the crust. What's the matter with you?' Erna's voice was sharp and irritated. Max covered his face and began to cry.

'Please, Max, don't cry over a small piece of bread.' Erna's voice softened.

'You don't understand, Erna. A man can't live without bread. We've got such plenty here I don't know what to eat. And yet some of my comrades are still rotting in those camps, with nothing to sink their teeth into. Nothing but watery soup and a tiny piece of stale bread.'

Erna didn't say anything, but he could tell that she was searching his face for the man she had said goodbye to on a platform in Nuremberg all those years ago. Before the war that had changed everything.

Max missed the prince. He had not seen the puppet since he handed it to Karl at the railway station and the place above his heart where he had carried the prince felt empty.

One afternoon, when Erna and Karl were both out, he searched for the prince in Karl's room.

'Ah, here you are, I've looked for you everywhere.' Max held the puppet in front of his face and smiled.

'Had to dig you out from under a pile of Karl's dirty clothes.'

He sat on the floor, gazing at the puppet with wistful eyes.

'You're the only one who really knows me now. Everything's so normal here, I don't fit in. I don't know what's right any more, what really happened. But you, my friend, you know everything. You're my witness. Look at me: I stick out like a sore thumb. I'm not really part of this family. I don't really know these people – my people.' He sighed, hugging the prince to him as he walked through the house.

'Yes, there is my wife, and she is still beautiful, but there's a coolness coming off her like the north wind. Everyone's perfectly nice. Erna cooks my favourite food, the *Nürnberger Zipfel* I told you about. We lie together at night and have even made love a few times. But there's this gap between us, as deep and wide as a gorge. As if she's another country. And Karl? He's polite but jumpy, tiptoes around me, the stranger in the house who can't take too much noise. Karl is nearly twenty-four, he'll leave any minute.'

From then on, Max carried the puppet everywhere in his pocket.

He tried hard to fit in, and after some months he found a job as a carpenter in a small factory in the neighbouring town; but he was tense and edgy around the loud machines and always felt cold. The smell of cut timber gave him headaches and one morning he caught himself looking for bunches of grass, afraid the guards might get him after all. He kept his head down and soon his colleagues gave up trying to make conversation with him.

'He's like the walking dead,' he heard them whisper. After some weeks his hands started to swell and ache.

'Damn cold keeps eating away at my joints. Siberia's found me even here.'

Most nights, Max couldn't sleep, and whenever he woke from a nightmare he got up and sat with the prince in the kitchen.

'I don't know how to go on. How can we go on living as if nothing happened after Poland, after Russia, after

246

Auschwitz? We brought death everywhere we went.'

Max limped over to the stove to warm himself some milk.

'I tried to talk to Erna about Warsaw, about the deportations, but she didn't want to listen. Sat there peeling potatoes, then got up without a word and started to cook.'

Soon silence became their daily companion: silent meals, silent chores, silent lovemaking. Then that stopped as well. Max, like Erna, ached for the proud man who had married his wife a lifetime ago, but Max Meierhauser with his thick moustache, broad smile and warm, strong hands had vanished.

Then, after a few months at work, and despite the much milder climate in Germany, Max started to cough. Day and night his chest shook like an earthquake.

'It's asthma, the doctor says,' he told the prince one night. 'A mean beast squeezing the last breath from me, picking at me like the crows picked at the dead men in the camp. The doctor told me no more wood and dust. *Auf Wiedersehen*, work.' He stared straight ahead. 'What am I going to do?'

The following day, it would be his fiftieth birthday. The aroma of butter, almonds and cream, Erna's delicious *Frankfurter Kranz* which she had baked for the occasion, still lingered in the kitchen. His favourite. He took the lid off the stoneware pot that held the cake and breathed in deeply. Suddenly grief gripped his heart and he had to sit down. On the table was his usual glass of hot milk with honey but today a smaller glass, half filled with water, stood next to it like a younger brother, the old silver spoon by its side.

'I've had enough. I'm just a burden to everyone,' he said to the prince, who was sitting between the salt and the pepper pot on the table.

'Can't even work any more now. Thrown away like a

247

piece of scrap metal.' He picked up the tablets he had tried to forget all night, slowly rolling them in his hands.

'Just one good night's sleep is all I want. What'd you think?' He didn't look at the prince but popped open the packet and dropped the tablets into the water, one after another. The last one made a tiny splash before it dissolved. He scooped three spoonfuls of sugar into the glass and stirred the liquid.

'My old friend the silver spoon. Storm in a teacup, that's what they tell me, I'm blowing everything out of proportion. But what if you're one of those tiny sugar crystals caught in the glass?' He held the glass in both hands, looking at the swirling cloudy liquid.

'So, you're giving up? After all you've been through?'

Max looked up, startled. The prince didn't move but Max could have sworn he heard him talk.

'What do you care? You shouldn't even be with me – you belong to that boy, Mika.'

But the interruption unnerved him. He could wait until after his birthday, enjoy his cake. He got up and poured the water down the sink, gulped the milk, then scooped up the prince.

'OK, but it's not over yet, my prince.' He folded his arms on the table and laid his head down. He had not felt as tired as this since he was trudging over the icy tundra. Erna found him fast asleep in the morning, and when Max woke to the strong smell of coffee, he found a large piece of *Frankfurter Kranz* sitting next to him.

25

One night, after Erna and Karl had gone to bed, Max poured himself another schnapps and put the prince on the kitchen table. His face was flushed and his eyes wide.

'Guess what, I met our old neighbour from Nuremberg. He lives in the next village. Turns out he was in Russia too. Stalingrad first, then they gave him ten years' hard labour in Siberia, just like me, only they let him go in '48. Didn't recognise him at first, but I guess I don't look my old self either.'

They met for Weissbeers and cheap schnapps in the local *Gasthaus* and talked late into the night.

'But there were signs, Bert. Our doctor, Jacob Rosenzweig, he disappeared one night. I heard our neighbour whisper "Dachau". We'd all heard of Dachau, hadn't we? And then the smashed-up shops, the fires, the book burnings. How could I have been so blind? By the time I arrived in Warsaw it was too late, I was part of the machine.' Like a dog hanging on to a bone, Max couldn't let go, kept repeating the same questions. Bert said nothing.

'Did you hear, the Amis paraded the villagers in front of the mountains of corpses left behind in Dachau,' Max continued, 'but did they lose any sleep over what had happened right under their noses? Did they feel responsible, squirm in shame, or did they just go home and cook their Weisswurst?'

Still Bert said nothing. But it wasn't the same when they talked about the snow.

'Death isn't the grim reaper,' Max proclaimed, knocking back his fourth schnapps. 'Death is the north wind, clouds heavy with snow that will bury everything alive. It's the cold that burns your lungs and breaks your bones, snaps your spirit. Makes you want to kill for a place at the fire, even one of those lousy wood burners.'

Bert looked at his hands. His left ring finger was missing.

'My glove had a hole. Couldn't fix it so after three days that was it. My finger turned black and they had to cut it off.'

Often the two men simply smoked and drank in silence, but sometimes Max shared his nightmares.

'So in this dream I'm desperately trying to get somewhere but all I can see is this blinding whiteness. I'm drowning, choking in the snow. But the strange thing is, I'm never cold – it's as if I am already dead. I always wake up out of breath, and don't know where I am.'

Bert just nodded.

'Then there is Mika, the boy I told you about. He's being pushed into a truck. I'm there pushing him in with all the other Jews. Just before the train moves away, I see a puppet peeping out of the window: a princess, her thin arms sticking out through the barbed wire. And like a shadow behind her, Mika's face. Then I'm inside the train. It's so crowded I can't breathe. I try to push everyone out of the way, struggling to get to the small barbed-wire window for some air, but I never reach it. Then I'm back in that terrible cattle truck that took us to Siberia, scratching ice from the wall with my small spoon

… Guess you remember those trains too,' Max mumbled.

'They were the same damn cattle wagons. Those trains that took the Jews to Treblinka were the same ones that shipped us to Siberia.' Max's voice had begun to slur.

'All the evil in the world started with those cattle trains. I wouldn't even put a cow in them now.'

Many nights the men ranted about the German government's lack of support.

'Thousands of us were sent to Siberia, millions, they think, can you imagine? And the few of us who returned were only a ghost of our former selves. We'll never know how many died, the Russians never cared about numbers.' Bert's face was so flushed he looked as if he might explode at any moment. 'We died like flies and now nobody wants to listen. As if we're a stain, some dirty mark on their whiter-than-white jackets. There are still men rotting in the camps while the big fish have all got away – well, some anyway. Hiding their Nazi arses somewhere or even getting re-elected. All this talk about "denazification" – sounds like delousing, if you ask me – but there are still enough Nazis crawling around. It's a shambles.'

Sometimes, after a fair amount of beer and schnapps, Max tried to talk about Warsaw. But Bert always cut him short.

'What's done is done, Max. *Schnee von gestern*, my friend, yesterday's snow. We've suffered enough, Max. I mean, really.'

Even with Bert, Max had reached a dead end.

One clear December night, swaying homewards through the snow after his evening with Bert, Max found himself in a philosophical mood. Taking the prince out of his pocket, he pointed to the snow that lay piled up around them.

'I'm sure there's snow in Siberia that hasn't melted since we were there. That snow has seen everything. Do you think it remembers everything? Or the cobbled streets of Warsaw, will they remember our marching boots, all the blood?' Max looked up at the stars. 'I guess nothing ever goes away. Isn't that terrifying and wonderful at the same time, my friend? Just like those stars?'

That night Max realised he would never be free of the past but would always carry the ghetto in his soul, next to Camp 267 and his home town of Nuremberg, which lay in ruins.

Time passed but still Max never quite settled in the village of Wolkersdorf.

'I'm a city person,' he often proclaimed. 'You can't hole me up in such a small village. I miss the old town, the castle, the city air.'

'I know, Max,' Erna tried to comfort him, 'but it would've broken your heart to see Nuremberg after the bombing. The whole city destroyed, only a few walls standing in the old town and rubble everywhere. One source of water for the whole of the old city. And we had to clear the debris so the Allies could move in for their victory parades. It was terrible … and it stank. They couldn't find all the dead under the ruins.'

Max said nothing but thought of Warsaw, its market square, the beautiful old houses torn down or gouged out by shrapnel. Its citizens also nothing but rubble.

Still, Max wanted to see his old city, and so one day he put on his best suit and made his way to the village's station, placing the puppet prince in his jacket pocket.

After a short journey he arrived at Nuremberg's main station. He crossed the road and strolled towards the old market square. All the way Max gave a quiet, rambling commentary to the puppet about each and every landmark – visible or absent. He didn't care about the people who threw puzzled glances at him – he'd become so used to talking to the puppet it no longer seemed strange to him.

'Look at that station. The façade is still the same, beautiful.' As they walked along the Königstrasse, Max picked up his pace as if pulled towards Nuremberg's centre by an invisible force.

'I don't care any more what people think. No one understands me anyway. I can't go back to the normal world, I'm a freak in any case. I hardly recognise this place.' He glanced at the newly built houses along the road. The longer he wandered, the quieter Max became. He could see the silhouette of the old castle but his eyes searched in vain for the butcher's to the front of the town hall.

'God, it's all gone. Must have been bombed to bits.' He felt dizzy and sat down on a doorstep. He set the prince on his lap.

'Just look at the things they've built instead. Ugly. No soul.' He studied the sober buildings.

'What are you looking at?' he snapped at a woman who peered down at him and his prince. 'Never seen a puppet? Well, we've come a long way together, him and me,'

The woman sped away. Max struggled to his feet and moved on. As he turned a corner the cobbled road opened up into the large market square, flanked by colourful houses and the impressive façade of a large church.

'Ah, now, at least our proud Frauenkirche still looks like it did back then.' As he neared the church Max saw scaffolding flanking the church on both sides. His heart sank.

'Our Lady didn't make it either, then.' He approached the intricately carved wooden door.

'Let's go in.' He pulled the brass handle and opened the heavy door.

Max felt as small and insignificant as a mouse as he

entered the majestic cathedral. As he took a few steps into the belly of the church, he realised that although the façade had remained intact everything else had been badly damaged in the bomb raids. Even six years after the end of the war, there were repairs being done everywhere. Max looked around.

'I swear there was an angel with a huge sword right here. So many of the sculptures are gone,' he whispered.

He moved along the aisle, looking up at the red sandstone columns that stretched overhead, supporting the gigantic roof.

Gobbles you up whole, this place, he thought, *columns as high as the tallest fir trees in Siberia.*

Max stopped in front of a flickering field of candles.

'They light them for the dead, you know,' he explained to the prince. 'But just how many would we need to light?' He stared at the candles until his eyes began to water. Then he reached for one of the thin white candles, lit it and placed it in a small metal holder next to the others. He stood quietly for a moment, then stretched his hand out for another candle and lit that one too. Then another. And another. And so on, one after another, with the same steady rhythm. Max lit every candle until none was left.

Max sat with the prince for hours at the back of the church, watching the flickering candles, the afternoon light pouring through the tall glass windows, dripping streams of light over him in every imaginable colour.

'I could stay here for ever.' Max sighed. 'Maybe … with this sea of light, I could get over it. It makes me feel calmer inside.'

As the afternoon light faded and his stomach started to rumble, he picked himself up and made his way back to the train station.

26

A week later, Karl announced he wanted to become a journeyman carpenter, try his luck that way. He was twenty-five by now and fully apprenticed.

'But you won't be able to come home for three years and a day!' Max exclaimed. Tradition forbad journeying craftsmen to come within fifty kilometres of their home town.

'I know, Papa. But I can write. I just need to see the world and get out of this stuffy village. You of all people should understand.'

It was true; not only had he survived his epic journey back from Siberia, but when he was Karl's age, he had done the same, and as a child, Karl had often asked him for stories about his journey.

'Do whatever you need to do, son.' Max kept a brave face. 'It's just ...' He didn't finish his sentence as Erna put her hand on his arm. He understood his son's restlessness but couldn't bear to lose him again so soon.

So Max and Erna hugged their son goodbye and Karl set off on foot in full traditional costume: a black broad-brimmed hat, waistcoat, bell-bottom trousers and *stenz*, a curled hiking pole.

'He'll be fine, Max,' Erna said. Max nodded but didn't reply.

Years passed. Karl wrote letters from all over Germany and phoned once a month on a Sunday.

Then, one day, out of the blue, a particularly beautiful envelope arrived – thick paper adorned with golden writing. Max and Erna opened it together.

'You wouldn't believe it, he's getting married!' Max had locked himself into the bathroom to talk to the prince.

'My son, my boy, he's tying the knot. Look at her, isn't she beautiful? And clever too. So young and she's already a doctor. Maria, she's called.'

After the wedding Karl and Maria visited twice a year – at Christmas and in the summer. Days before their arrival the house would smell of soap and apple cake but the short visits often disappointed, as the pair only stopped over briefly before travelling to places with more exotic names, such as Venice, Rome and Salzburg.

Then, seven years later, their first baby was born – a little baby girl they called Mara. Max cradled her in his arms like the most precious parcel as she gurgled and squirmed.

'She's so beautiful,' he marvelled, 'just perfect.' Tears streamed down his face. Erna smiled but Karl looked embarrassed. Over the next months, then years, Max followed Mara's progress like an eager dog chasing a ball.

'Can she walk yet? How about her teeth? Has she said anything yet?'

Max wanted to know anything and everything about his grandchild and it pained him deeply that he only ever saw her twice a year. Indeed, little Mara touched a place no one else could. Whenever Mara was around, Max hummed, made up songs, carved little animals, and even built a doll's house for his grandchild; the one child he would be able to see growing up.

*

Max pieced it together from the few words that tumbled from Karl's mouth down the phone line three days after Mara's third birthday.

'Papa … we had an accident.' His son was struggling to speak. Max's heart contracted like a fist.

'We'd been to the sea near Kiel, just a Sunday picnic. We were singing in the car … Then this truck behind us …' His voice broke. 'It ploughed into us. Our little Ford had no chance. I'm OK but Maria is dead, Papa, she bled to death in my arms. They didn't get there in time.' Karl sobbed.

'And Mara?' Max's heart hammered.

'She has a broken leg. She's in shock. Hasn't said a word since.'

'Please just come home, Karl. We'll take care of you.'

Karl and Mara stayed for a few weeks, and even after they returned to Hamburg they visited as often as they could. One day, amid his grief, Max remembered the puppets of Siberia. Hadn't he and his comrades found some escape during that terrible time by making puppets out of a few rags, potatoes, a piece of wood and some straw? Even when they were cold to the bone and ravenous as wolves, hadn't the puppets nourished at least their spirits? He stomped into the kitchen, plundered drawers and cupboards and gathered together bits and bobs: a tin-opener, a sieve, a few forks and a nutcracker. As he bound them together with wire and string, bent the forks into crooked shapes and adorned the sieve with strips of a towel he had cut into ribbons, strange creatures emerged. As his hands moved them across the kitchen table they sprang into life; and right there and then he put on a play for his granddaughter. That afternoon Mara smiled for the first time since the accident and even Erna stood laughing in her apron, not bothered by his raid on her kitchen.

But the prince stayed in his pocket, for he feared Mara's innocent questions might pierce his heart.

Mara grew quickly. She never sat still, made up songs with her bubbling voice, ran around the garden, chasing birds, looking for bugs under stones – she was the sunshine in the family. Her strawberry-blonde curls bounced on her shoulders, and she screamed when Erna tried to tie her hair into orderly plaits. Mara's eyes reminded Max of the colour of the Siberian lakes in autumn, a dark, near-emerald green.

Max loved his granddaughter dearly and yet so much life choked him. While his little Mara ran about giggling, in the ghetto a Mara with that same brimming life-force had been squashed like a worm, her bright flame extinguished with a single blow. Those children haunted him, at day in his granddaughter's presence and at night in his fitful sleep. Always two Maras lived with him: his own granddaughter and a Mara whose life he had helped to snuff out. Mara's eyes and the eyes of another. Always a double following him like a shadow, a twin of dust and ashes.

Max's mood changed like the seasons or the phases of the moon. Some days he joked with Mara, letting her sit on his lap, telling her stories, then all of a sudden he would grunt at her like an old bear that had been disturbed in its sleep. And yet, over the years, Mara had found a way into his heart and helped him collect new, precious moments: her open arms as she ran towards him; questions that rolled from her mouth like coloured marbles, tumbling into his lap. Why is the sun hot? How much does a heart weigh? Where do we come from? Why do we die?

'Maybe I'm being given a second chance?' he said to the prince one night.

But still Max held his breath. Was Mara really the

eternal sunshine she seemed to be? Sometimes when he glanced at her, he could see how much she still hurt. Deep inside her heart lay a place like an empty nest. Her mother had been taken and nothing could replace her. But still she kept smiling for her Papa and her Opa.

One day Mara was sitting on his lap in the garden while he read from a book.

'Do you think it was my fault, Opa?' she asked suddenly.

Max was taken aback. 'What do you mean?'

'Did Mama die because of me?'

'No, of course not, sweetheart! Don't ever think such a thing.' He hugged her hard. That was when Max decided to introduce Mara to the prince.

'I'll show you something, Mara.' He pulled the battered puppet from his pocket. Mara's face lit up.

'Can I play with him?'

'Sure you can, here.' Max handed her the prince, and within minutes Mara had made up a little show.

The prince seemed to revel in being made to dance by a child's hands once more, like Sara's before and Hannah's, the orphans' – it had been so long.

One day Max decided to buy Mara a puppet of her own: a Kasperl. Mara slipped her hand into the Kasperl puppet, making it jump up and down, begging Max to tell her more stories.

'Please, Opa, this one again.' And Max did.

From then on, every year on her birthday, Max presented Mara with a new puppet, sometimes even two, and by the time Mara turned ten, she had a beautiful collection of her own, complete with a Kasperl, his companion Gretl, a crocodile, a princess, a villain, a policeman and a monkey. Max even built a little stage for her.

*

His granddaughter's visits kept a tiny spark burning, but often at night the tormenting demons of Warsaw and Siberia returned to haunt Max.

'The war has drained everything out of me, my life; gutted me like a fish. I just don't know how to live with all this guilt and rage that's churning around inside me. No one wants to hear me speak about the war – the neighbours, Erna, Karl. They say I was just doing my duty. But I know I'm guilty. I knew no good would come of the deportations east. And yes, I tried to protect the boy's mother and aunt; yes, I took that risk. If Peter hadn't kept his mouth shut I would've been found out. But in the end it came to nothing. They were caught and sent away just like all the others. And didn't I set fire to those last hiding places with my flame-thrower? I'll never know whether the boy made it out alive.' He sat bent over, holding his head in his hands, heavy as the world.

'I feel like I'm floating on a sheet of ice. I've broken away from people and although I can see everyone, I can't steer myself back to land. Even Erna and me, we hardly speak …' Max fell silent for a long time, gazing at the prince.

'And yet I do still love her. And I do love Karl. And my Mara. You. I just can't show it well. Maybe you can show Mara at least?' He wiped his eyes and took himself off to bed.

Only Mara could glimpse behind his mask. Max made up story after story for her, and after some time he even told Mara snippets about his life and his escape from Siberia.

'What happened next, Opa?' Everything was one big adventure for Mara, and sitting on his lap, fooling around with the puppets, she made Max laugh. Those summers with her Opa lit a deep passion within her and she understood that with the puppets she could reach behind the barriers into people's hearts.

27

In the first days of spring 1969, Max's cough got worse. Once the coughing took hold of him he couldn't stop. The doctor's prognosis was short and grim: three months if he was lucky. In the end Max lived for five. It was the tree in his chest that gave up; the cancer had already taken over the lungs and spread to his kidneys and bones.

'Death doesn't scare me,' he whispered to the prince one night, 'I've looked it in the eye so many times. But I need Karl to know my story. And you, my friend, can't come with me wherever I am going. You need to stay here and tell the tale.'

Erna sighed and rolled over – she had heard Max many times in the depths of night, pouring his heart out to the prince. It filled her with deep sorrow that she was less of a support to him than an old, shabby puppet.

'But I do love you, Erna.' Realising that she was awake, Max tried to reassure her.

'I know, Max,' she said, but she knew that the gulf between them could never fully be bridged. And now, after so many years of waiting, they had run out of time.

Erna broke the news and Karl and Mara came immediately. Then something extraordinary happened. Within the space of a few days all of the carefully composed distance and formality between father and son melted away. In the presence of the cruel hourglass, they shared their truths – father to son, son to father. It was as if the tall, blue oxygen tank by his side helped Max to shift memories from his innermost being, then gently release them from his lips into the ears of his son. He talked about everything: about Warsaw, the ghetto, Mika, Siberia, the camp, the comrades who didn't make it and the long journey home.

And this time Karl really listened with his heart open wide. He became like a boy again in that room at the end of that summer, receiving the stories of his father. Some days he cried.

'Papa, there's so much I want to ask you, so much I still want to know.' Karl poured out his love for his papa. Both admitted regrets and resentments in one last flood of emotion. Feelings. They were both so full of feelings now, carrying them willingly on their tongues, in their eyes, in their breath. Finally. There was no time to waste.

But still Erna held back, bringing food and hot tea, cushions and medicines. She was there to help, to make everything as comfortable as she could, but her eyes stayed dry. She would cry alone.

One morning, just as the light in the room changed from grey to golden, Max produced the prince from under his pillow and fixed his eyes on his son.

'Karl, I want to give you this dear friend of mine. Please treat him well. He might not look like much, but he's been my companion, a witness to all my trials. This puppet has more life in him now than I do. Let him be a comfort to you and Mara.'

'Thank you, Papa, I'll take good care of him.' Karl took the puppet with both hands and stared at it for a long moment.

'Please tell Mara my story when she's old enough – and I mean all of it. I want her to have the prince.'

Max was struggling to speak now, coughing, wheezing.

'And Karl, there is something else. The boy's name is Mika. Mika Hernsteyn. Karl, please try to find out what happened to him. It eats away at me, not knowing. Always has. I should've searched for him. Please, Karl. Maybe he's still alive.'

'I don't know, Papa … It was so long ago.' His voice sounded slightly strained but Max knew it was only fear.

'Please, Karl. I really wanted to be a better father, be there for you. I wish they'd never sent me to Warsaw. I'm so sorry. Please forgive me if you can.'

Karl said nothing. Not about searching for Mika, nor about forgiveness. How could he forgive? It wasn't up to him, and most of those who could possibly forgive were dead. Instead Karl told Max he loved him.

In those last days Mara often sat on Max's bed, her two small hands animating her puppet company for Max. She had brought her entire collection and made up one story after another with such passion and fury, as if her lively plays could infuse Max with new life. But Mara also knew about death and in some small way her plays were also a reminder that life would go on.

Max died in the early hours of a bright September day. At the funeral Karl found himself holding on to the puppet buried in his pockets, his fingers gliding over the prince's face.

Days later, after the funeral, when Erna was putting away one of Max's jackets, she noticed a little lump. She reached inside the pocket and her face twisted in disgust.

'What is this?' She pulled out a piece of hard, mouldy bread. This is when she finally found her tears.

*

Karl and Mara moved into a small, tidy apartment in the city of Hamburg. The first night after the funeral, Karl stuffed the prince into the bottom drawer of his bedroom cabinet. Many weeks passed before Karl one night dug frantically among his socks for the puppet.

'OK, my friend, Mara needs you!' Dangling the prince in front of his face, he continued: 'She's been crying in her sleep, asking about you. Off you go, but I tell you, Mara doesn't need to know everything you've seen. Understood?' The puppet hung limply from his hand.

In the morning Mara awoke to find the prince sitting on a pillow beside her. She hugged the puppet hard.

'Where've you been? Papa told me Opa wanted you in his coffin with him.' She stroked the prince's head, his crown and fur trim, then let the prince gently glide into her pocket. Her hands, like Mika's and Max's before her, would often touch the puppet briefly throughout the day, just to reassure herself that it was still there. Whatever Mara wore, she always made sure the prince changed pockets with her clothes.

28

Mara remained a single child and Karl a single man. He protected her like a precious flower, but somehow she didn't flourish. Most days she brushed off her loneliness, but at night it weighed like a boulder on her chest and she found it hard to breathe. After her thirteenth birthday the situation got worse. The doctors said it was asthma: a tightness around her heart – just as Max had struggled for air, for space around his heart.

Mara visited her mother's grave every week. Brushing along the dense yew bushes that bordered the cemetery, she always arrived with green, scented hands that smelled strong and bitter – like sadness or grief, yet strangely comforting. She would talk about her papa, school or the pigeons she had seen courting high up on a street lamp.

Most of the time Mara played on her own. Besides the puppets, she also owned toy animals of all sizes: a deer, a zebra, a tiger, a giraffe and quite a few bears – all of which became her willing audience, neatly arranged in rows in front of her, ready for another performance. And she did have a knack with the puppets, which was confirmed by the local children whenever they were invited to see a show.

'You know, little prince,' Mara said one afternoon, 'often I feel I belong to a different tribe. I just don't fit in.'

As lonely as Mara may have been, she loved the company of books: their smell and weight, and the way each one, once opened, carried a whole world inside itself. Week after week, shelf after shelf, Mara feasted on books from her local library. She spent adventurous times with Karlsson-on-the-roof, fought a deadly dragon with Prince Lionheart, dreamt of Pippi Longstocking's crazy house, trembled in Bluebeard's chamber, and enjoyed a journey down the Mississippi on Huckleberry Finn's raft. Sometimes she read aloud with the prince for company on her lap.

'I think I'm through with the children's library. I wonder what the adults are reading?' she proclaimed one day out of the blue. She promptly marched downstairs to the adult library and discovered a whole new world.

And so it happened that Mara found herself one afternoon sitting on the floor of the history section with a large book in her lap, names and blurred black and white photographs tumbling before her eyes: *Auschwitz*, *Buchenwald*, *Mauthausen*, *Treblinka*. Names that rang shrill in her ears although she did not know why. She sat completely still and yet her heart was beating like a drum.

'What is this?' she whispered, her startled eyes trying to make sense of what she saw. She leafed through the whole book, then pulled out another. Barbed wire, walking skeletons wearing striped uniforms, corpses in fields, lying mangled in heaps, barracks, soldiers ... She lifted her head and stared straight ahead. These books were windows into a terrible place she did not know whether she should know about. With a quick gesture she snapped the books shut, left them lying on the floor, and rushed out of the library. Her legs felt stiff and alien as she ran, as if they didn't really belong to her. She hiked for miles, all the way to the harbour. There, she sat on a bench watching the huge vessels drawing into the harbour, others leaving. She did not speak to anyone and only left long after the sun had set.

That night she took out the prince and placed the puppet on her pillow.

'I don't know what all this is, but it scares me. Just last week Papa forbad me from watching this film *Night and Fog*, but when I came in to say goodnight I caught a glimpse: people, lots of people, shuffling along like ghosts in a line. They looked like zombies: almost naked and so thin – like walking skeletons. They didn't even look human. Then today in the library I realised it's all true.'

What Mara had glimpsed fuelled a hunger in her, a fierce need to see into the abyss of the human heart. And over time she unearthed photographs, drawings, stories and even poems of those who had survived and could still speak. She learnt the name of that darkness: 'Holocaust'. It tasted bitter and foul in her mouth. What people can do to one another.

But no one wanted to know. At school Mara learnt about Barbarossa and the hundred-year war, but not much about the man with the moustache.

'How could this happen?' She talked long into the night, fretted, questioning herself and the prince.

'Would I have joined up to the *Bund Deutscher Mädel*, proudly marching along with my starched uniform and orderly plaits? Or would I have risked my life, printing secret leaflets? Would I have had the courage to pick up a gun and join the resistance?'

It devastated her that she would never know.

'And what about all those *Mitläufer*, all those people who marched with Hitler and applauded his speeches, his war. Some of them didn't even call themselves Nazis so maybe it is true that some of them didn't know what happened to the Jews. I suppose they just thought of themselves as nice, civilised citizens. But weren't they accomplices as well? Helping the Nazis to run their deadly machine by saying nothing or singing their stupid songs? How could they just ignore their Jewish neighbours being snatched away at night, their colleagues, shopkeepers, friends disappearing – just like that? And what about Grandad? My Opa, what did he do in the war?'

Mara was caught in a current of questions that whirled around like driftwood. There were no answers.

One evening she poured out all her questions to her father.

'God, Mara, all this happened such a long time ago! And you're a young girl, you had nothing to do with this dark time.'

'But I'm German, I'm made from the same blood and bone as the people who created those camps, aren't I? How could this have happened?'

Karl looked at his hands.

'It was a bad time, Mara. Very bad. But Germany isn't just that.'

'Yes, I know our country has brought music, art and poetry to the world. Philosophy even, I know that, Papa! I know about Bach and Goethe, Schiller, Schubert, and all the others. But how can we have created such lovely poetry and music and then produced this terrible slaughter? I heard that the Nazis made some girls play marches and waltzes in Auschwitz for their fellow prisoners on their way to the gas chambers. I just don't understand!'

Then one night, shortly after Mara turned fifteen, the past finally emerged. Maybe it was the balmy air or the soft velvet of the approaching night that made Karl open his heart as he sat with Mara on the veranda.

'Mara, you often ask me what it was like then, in the war and before that.'

Mara looked at him with wide eyes. She moved closer.

'Well, Hitler called the place where we lived, Nuremberg, the "most German of all German cities", and that's why all those huge rallies marched through our town and why they built the rally grounds, the Zeppelin field, there. All of Nuremberg was buzzing with excitement as we prepared for the big rallies. Two uncles, Heinrich and Herbert, travelled all the way from Hamburg and slept on blankets in our hallway. I even wet my pants because I didn't want to leave my spot, waiting for the Führer to march by. My heart swelled with pride as we watched the parades thundering down the cobbled streets. The next day we went to the Zeppelin field. Imagine thousands and thousands of people marching in formation, singing as one. And at night there was the magnificent "dome of light", hundreds of beams lighting the sky. I even had a good time in the Hitler Youth, singing those Horst Wessel songs, marching with my friends. How could we boys have known it was all so wrong, such poison? They seduced us, fed us lies every day. By the time we found out, it was too late. So yes, I did admire my papa in his uniform, I was sad and proud when Mother and I saw him off on his journey to Poland in 1939. But weren't all of us proud of our fathers? It wasn't long before the war started.

'The Allies bombed Nuremberg in August '42 and in '43. We were in and out of our bomb shelter. Our lives had been spared but we were worn out; raw and edgy from so little sleep. Then, on the third of October 1944, the sirens began to howl again. We grabbed blankets and rushed into the shelter. Soon we realised this night would be different. The droning of the planes started as usual, but this time it didn't stop – it was as if a whole hive of wasps had swarmed over the city and was waiting for the kill. Then bang!! A massive explosion and the earth shook as if a giant had stomped his foot right above us. Everyone screamed. There were about thirty of us down there. If the bunker collapsed, would we all be buried alive? Outside there was nothing but silence.

'Mother cried. I kept my head in my book. I stared at the words, but never got beyond the first sentence.

'A tiny girl with a huge big pink bow in her hair moved around the shelter like a restless cat, joining groups of cowering people, making up little stories and songs to comfort everyone. Me, I could think only of myself, needed all my energy to stop myself from shaking. I clenched my jaw so tight it hurt. I wasn't proud of myself.

'At some point I nodded off. Then finally the morning came and with it the screeching siren that gave us the green light to abandon our shelters.

'Someone pushed the hatch and miraculously it opened. One after another we crawled through the hatch. When I scrambled out I couldn't recognise anything. There were fires and rubble everywhere. Nothing had been spared, every house in our street had been burned down or lay smouldering. Bombed to bits.

'I looked up at our house – what was left of it. At first I couldn't understand. Then it dawned on me: the whole front wall was missing! We could see into our kitchen and my room as if it were a doll's house. On the kitchen table stood an egg in an eggcup and some bread on a plate left over from our evening meal. For the first time I noticed our wallpaper: big fleshy flowers, burgundy on a cream-coloured background. I rushed away and threw up.'

Mara sat, hardly breathing. She didn't dare speak for fear her father's stream of words would dry up.

'We moved into an apartment in Wolkersdorf, a

village in the countryside outside Nuremberg. Weeks later nearly all of the old town was destroyed in the space of a few hours. We heard the sinister swarm of bombers approach, ready to drop their bombs on our city. The sky blazed orange all night, the bombs crashing like distant thunderstorms.

'Those who were still holding out in the city needed all the luck they could get. What a lottery! Otto, one of my school friends, survived the inferno, while our neighbours, the Müllers, never even made it to their shelter.

'I'm glad Opa Max didn't get to see his city in such a state. By the time he returned, most of Nuremberg had been cleaned up and ugly new buildings constructed like a quick plaster on a wound.

'The last months of the war were chaotic, we were all just hanging in there, trying to get enough food, foraging in the forests. And then one day a draft notice arrived, calling me to the front for Hitler's "total" war. Boys as young as thirteen were now being drafted in a last desperate bid. It was your quiet Grandmother Erna who protected me from this madness. I was told to report to the village hall the next day. Mother took one look at the notice and said, "Pack a bag, Karl, light enough so that you can carry it on your back for a while. We're leaving tonight."

'We spent the next few months hiding with different people in the countryside. Turns out my mother risked her life and mine doing so as deserters were killed as *Vaterlandsverräter*, traitors of the Fatherland. But if it wasn't for her, I might not be here at all.

'One day we came across an orchard. Mother tried to pull me away but I had already seen it: four bodies – two soldiers and two boys of about my age, maybe even younger – swaying in the wind with cardboard signs around their necks bearing the word *Deserter*!

'Mother grabbed my hand. "We're not going to end up like this, OK? Don't worry!" But I couldn't forget these swollen faces, the strange angle at which their heads hung. Those bodies could have been me and Mother.

'In the last crazy weeks of the war, the Gestapo set up so-called "flying courts martial" along the roadside, executing any soldiers heading home without the necessary authorisation. Some roads were lined with soldiers hanging from lamp-posts and trees.

'Your grandma never talked about all this afterwards, about her bravery. I doubt she even told my father about it, but I know in my bones that she saved my life. Not many youngsters survived the madness of those last days.

'Then one warm April day it was finally over. Hitler had killed himself and Nuremberg was nothing more than a smoking pile of rubble. On 20 April 1945, the birthday of the Führer who was no more, the US Army marched into the city and held a victory celebration at the Zeppelin field. They covered the giant swastika that had loomed over the tribune with the American flag, and later that day they blew the hooked cross into a million pieces. The Third Reich was finished, over.

'When we heard the Americans were coming, everyone panicked and hid their last precious things, buried their silver and porcelain, jewellery and even photo albums. I had only salvaged a few books from the rubble that had once been in my room. I never found the puppet Papa had sent from the East, the doctor. We had nothing precious left.' Karl poured himself a glass of wine.

'You know, I was scared what the Americans would do to us, but in the end they were quite friendly, handing us chewing gum and packages of sugar and coffee. But our lives had been turned upside down and everyone's morale was at zero. I mean, we had lost the war and we were surrounded by ruins.

'One day the Americans put up posters showing photos of the camps. Buchenwald. Auschwitz. Dachau. "These shameful deeds – Your Fault!" were the words plastered over them. I didn't know where to look, what to feel. How could I have known? All Papa sent us from Warsaw was a small puppet and a letter saying he missed me. I had no idea about the ghetto, the camps, what was happening to the Jews.

'And Papa was still missing – we had not heard from him since the end of the war. It took a whole year before we found out what had happened to him, then another few months until we got that first postcard from Siberia. For years all we'd get were those flimsy postcards, a few lines squeezed on to a card. I think that's when I lost my connection to Papa, the feeling inside.'

Mara moved closer to her father.

'It must've been so hard. The bombings, the shelter, not having Opa around. All of it.' Mara laid her hand on his shoulder.

'It was, Mara. That's why I don't talk about it much. But maybe it's important to get it all out; at least your Opa thought so. He told me everything. And there's so much more. You know, Mara, just before Opa died he asked me to tell you the story of the prince. His puppet.'

A long pause stretched between them. Mara looked at her father.

'Please tell me, Papa.'

And so Karl began. They sat until deep into the night and Karl did not stop until he had told Mara everything.

'When Opa died he asked me to look for the boy, the Puppet Boy. He was called Mika Hernsteyn. But I didn't have the heart to search for him. I don't think he made it.'

Mara had finally found some pieces of the giant jigsaw puzzle. But still there were few answers. Her nice Opa had been a soldier in Warsaw's ghetto and now there was a boy with a name ...

A week later Mara started to knit. At first it seemed harmless; just a pair of blue and white stripy socks.

'I'm glad you've found something to amuse yourself with other than history books,' Karl said, and he smiled when she showed him the socks. But soon Mara wouldn't leave the house without her needles and she became a ferocious knitter, devouring ball after ball of yarn. Everything went into her knitting: her loneliness and fury, all her unanswered questions, the more elaborate the patterns the better. Complex starry Norwegian patterns to swallow her sadness, white mohair an antidote to agitation; a coat knitted with needles as thick as brushes to shield against guilt and shame. Like a spider creating jumpers instead of webs, Mara knitted her wool all day long and the repetitive movements filled her head with a fluffy, cocoon-like emptiness.

'I know it's an endless task,' she explained to the prince one night, 'but isn't the list of murdered people endless too?'

Sometimes in the evenings, Mara put the puppet on the windowsill and, opening the window, looked up at the clear night sky. She did not know how often Max had sat with his prince looking at the star-studded skies over Siberia, Max pointing out the Great Bear and Cassiopeia to the puppet. That and the huge hazy band across the sky. '*Schau, kleiner Kerl*, it's the Milky Way!' he used to say. Whenever he saw it, a deep sigh sprang from Max's chest – just as it did now from Mara's.

29

Slowly Mara grew to be an adult. When the time came to choose what she should do with her life, Mara decided to train as a nurse. Maybe being there for others could help her answer those difficult questions about the human heart …

She moved into a small apartment next to the hospital in the neighbouring city of Bremen. She took her puppets with her but stopped carrying the prince around. Instead she sat him on her bookshelf, slightly bent forward with his legs dangling, between Herman Hesse's *Steppenwolf* and Saint-Exupéry's *The Little Prince*, while neatly boxing up the rest of her puppets and storing them together with her knitting under her bed.

Mara worked hard, and as the months and then years passed, the prince gathered a layer of fine dust, his muted colours fading even more. And yet Mara's passion for puppets never completely disappeared. Once she had passed her exams, she started to create animal glove puppets: her first, a lion with fur around its papier-mâché head, followed by a zebra, a wolf then a giraffe. Soon she had a whole troupe.

As a nurse, Mara specialised in working with children. One evening, after a difficult day on the cancer ward, she pulled out her old puppets from underneath her bed. She cleaned the dust off the prince's cloak, polished his little crown and painted new apple-red cheeks and lips on his face.

'There you go!' she said, making up a short play on the spot.

When Mara took the prince into the hospital he was in his element, as if acting in front of a crowd of sick children had always been his favourite occupation. Soon she added her animals and the rest of the troupe, bringing a bit of lightness among so much suffering.

Many years passed. Twenty years to be precise. Then, on a sunny day in July on Mara's fortieth birthday, she sat the prince on her hand.

'I've thought about it. I want to be a puppeteer, my prince. Nothing else feels right any more. You puppets bring so much joy and fun to people. I'm going to make this my job!' From then on she lived and breathed puppets. And during all that time she never forgot the story her father had told her – about the boy from Warsaw, Mika, and her Opa Max. The story about what had happened in the war. This was the story she wanted her puppets to tell.

Mara got stuck in, working long days and sometimes nights, modelling, sewing, creating more and more puppets, painting backdrops, carving props and writing the lines for her play. She had a vision and she hung on to it like a dog with a bone.

Often late at night doubts would push their way to the surface.

Will I get the story right? Do I even know all the pieces? I know I mean well, but perhaps that's not enough? How can I really show the desperate situation in the ghetto using a bit of cardboard, plywood and some puppets?

For weeks Mara slept badly but she didn't give up. She

took particular care in creating a puppet of Mika as she imagined him. As he would be the main character, she made this puppet larger than the rest.

Then one autumn day, with the puppets and props nearly finished, Mara realised what was missing – she had to see the city for herself, feel the place, and maybe find out something about the boy too.

And so the following week, Mara packed a small suitcase, put the prince into her coat pocket and set off for Warsaw.

'We'll make a good team, you'll see,' she whispered as she squeezed into her seat in the small plane. Sipping an orange juice, she gazed out of the small window, admiring the endless field of white clouds. *Like Siberia, only softer.* For a moment her thoughts wandered to her grandfather. The secrets he never shared with her, his escape from Siberia's brutal claws.

On the train journey from the airport into Warsaw, Mara calculated that if her father had told her the truth about Opa, the prince had changed hands about sixty-six years ago. In 1942, right here, in Warsaw. Her hands found the fur trim on the prince's coat. She smiled, reassured by his presence.

She arrived at Warsaw's Centralna railway station, a grey, ugly square of a building that smelled of burned rubber. She took the first exit then stopped dead in her tracks: a colossal, multi-tiered building crowned with a large antenna stretched up into the bright blue sky in front of her.

The Palace of Culture – a gift from the Russians to the Polish people. 'The Russian Wedding Cake', they called it. Mara had done her homework, studying the travel guide thoroughly. She checked into the Polonia Palace hotel, one of the few buildings that had not been destroyed in the war. She dropped her luggage in her room and within minutes found herself back on the street. She placed the prince in her coat pocket and, clutching a travel guide and map, made her way north. Wherever she looked, grey high-rise tower blocks flashed neon signs and sported large advertising boards on their rooftops. Between the concrete giants, cars zoomed along broad avenues, revving their engines.

Reaching the farther corner of the Palace of Culture she found a plaque, marking where the wall had stood: *MUR GETTA* – GHETTO WALL 1940–1943. But there was no wall, not a single brick, only rusty iron letter-markings among the cobbled stones, like lines on a map. This was the beginning of the ghetto walk. Poring over her map, Mara roamed northwards, street after street.

Where once proud three-storey buildings with iron balconies had stood, only high-rise tower blocks with sad squares for windows remained, interrupted every now and again by ultramodern steel and glass skyscrapers.

Then, all of a sudden, Mara found herself opposite some of the old apartment blocks. They stood like blind witnesses with boarded-up windows, a small birch tree growing from the balcony of one, sticking out like a feather on a hat. But there was nobody home there. Hadn't been for a long time.

At the corner of that same street Mara found another plaque, marking the spot where one of the main ghetto gates had stood, the entrance from Zelazna Street. A photograph mounted underneath the plaque showed soldiers patrolling the gate, flanked by a sign spelling out in bold letters '*Seuchengefahr*: Danger of epidemic – keep out'. That was how the Germans justified the ghetto to the Poles on the Aryan side, she knew. She was close to the spot where there used to be a wooden bridge connecting the small and the big ghetto. Chlodna Street. Farther up were some houses that stood higher than the others. There had been so much rubble left after the Germans razed the ghetto to the ground that, instead of clearing it away, new houses, even whole estates, were constructed right on top of it.

Nothing left of the whole ghetto, only a metre of overgrown rubble? Mara thought to herself. *Do the people here ever think about what their houses are built on, sense the ghetto's ghosts late at night, trying to find their way out?* Mara looked out for a bench but couldn't see one. She stuck her head back into the guidebook.

It told her that after the ghetto uprising, the Germans systematically razed the ghetto to the ground. The rest of the city was destroyed during the big Warsaw Uprising in 1944 and in the time up to its liberation in 1945. Warsaw had 1.3 million inhabitants before the war. When the Red Army moved in, only one thousand people emerged from the rubble. During the entire German occupation over 400,000 Jews perished.

Mara began to feel faint. She didn't know what exactly she had hoped to find here, but there was nothing, nothing at all. She shivered and pulled her coat closer. All of a sudden she remembered an image of Nuremberg's burnt-out buildings after the bombings she'd seen in one of her father's books. 'A ruin is a ruin,' she had thought then, 'it breaks your heart.'

But what do you do if there is not even a ruin left? Only grass. And houses that stand a bit taller than the rest of the city?

Mara shook herself. It was still not even lunchtime. She pulled a chocolate bar from her pocket and took a large bite, then headed on towards the location of the former Pawiak prison, making her way along Dzielna Street. All of a sudden the remains of the prison's entry gate greeted her: a barbed-wire gate, cut off in midair. In the centre of the empty prison yard, stretching its branches towards the sky like bare arms, stood a lone tree, covered in name-plaques nailed to its trunk like a metal cloak. A tree of remembrance, a monument to those who died.

As she silently read the plaques, she realised that her eyes were searching for the boy's name. Mika, Mika Hernsteyn. His name wasn't among them. She took a deep breath and went a few steps into the Pawiak's belly. The damp and musty air hit her and she patted the prince's head in her pocket.

She wandered along the dark corridor. The cells' heavy iron doors stood wide open and Mara entered each room. Glass vitrines displaying fragments of the prisoner's lives were displayed on all sides: faint pencil drawings of faces and landscapes, letters, photographs, postcards, a hand-made chess set modelled out of bread, dice cut from wood, a tiny set of hand-drawn playing cards, knitted bags, a musical composition. Everything laid out like treasure. The last traces of those who had endured this dark place. What happened to the woman in the photograph, the chess and card players? The composer? In one of the cells Mara found out about the tree in the yard – an elm tree, the only witness to what happened in that place, and one of the few things that survived all the destruction.

In one of the last cells Mara crouched over the glass vitrines for a long time, deciphering letters and postcards, staring at the black and white photographs. None of the letters mentioned Mika's name. As for the blurry photographs, she did not know. She gazed at one message, sprawled pale pencil marks on a small grey postcard, a missive from a prisoner of Auschwitz to his beloved in Warsaw, written in clear, polite German. A wave of nausea shook Mara and she found it hard to breathe.

As she emerged from the Pawiak's dark bowels, she gulped at the fresh air. The light had faded but the sky still shone an intense cobalt blue. *Wie Samt. Soft as velvet*, Mara thought, looking up. Cut loose from somewhere, a bright red balloon meandered higher and higher, dancing into the expanse of Warsaw's autumnal sky. She watched until she couldn't see it any more.

'Let's call it a day, I think we've seen enough.' Only now did she notice her wet cheeks. She had been worried that once she started she might not be able to stop crying. But walking back to the hotel, she let her tears run freely, grateful for the anonymity of this city where no one knew her.

That night Mara dreamt she was a dog, a large grey mongrel, searching for Mika amid a vast labyrinth of prison corridors, sniffing, scurrying in and out of every cell to no avail. As she emerged from the prison she looked up. And there, high up, was Mika, clinging on to a single balloon, moving closer and closer to the sun.

The next day, after a huge breakfast of marinated fish, cheese and cereal, Mara made her way north-west, heading towards the remembrance monument once again. Today frost covered everything in a sparkling whiteness.

She could see the grey monument from afar, but the moment she arrived, a bus full of tourists parked and spilled its load. The colourful group swarmed around the monument like butterflies, snapping pictures from all sides. They kept their voices low but she recognised the southern German accent. She wished she had come later.

She sat down on a bench, reading from her guide-book: 'The Remembrance monument for the heroes of the Warsaw ghetto Uprising was created from a huge slab of grey basalt the Nazis brought from Norway in anticipation of their victory.' One side of the monument depicted a wretched march of the ghetto's people, moving as if pressed down by a storm: cloaked men, children hanging on to their mothers, a rabbi clutching the Torah; on the other side men and women of various ages stood tall, raising their weapons towards the sky like torches – the ghetto fighters, the heroes. Small stones, candles and flowers lay at the base of the monument as if washed up there by the sea. Mara was tempted to add a stone but hesitated.

The next stop on her walk was the bunker monument, at the site of Mila Street 18, the resistance's main retreat, where Mordecai, their leader, and about two hundred fighters fought their last battle before the Germans blew up their refuge. All that remained of the bunker now was a simple grass mound surrounded by grey housing blocks. The grass shimmered like caster sugar in the morning frost as she slowly moved up the steps. On top lay a large granite block with a long list of names chiselled into it: the names of the fighters. Mara stood as stiff as the stone, reading every name.

All those brave fighters buried beneath the rubble. Should we be even standing here? She snapped her travel book shut, walked down the steps on the other side of the mound and marched on, this time towards the former *Umschlagplatz*, the place where thousands were gathered, to be taken to Treblinka, the extermination camp a few hours to the east of Warsaw. Mara dreaded what she would find there. The former *Umschlagplatz* was not really a square any more, but rather a white marble memorial resembling an open cattle box car. As she moved through the gap in the wall, as if entering the belly of the car, she found herself in front of an unpolished wall engraved with names. A list of 448 Jewish first names chiselled into the stone from A to Z. Mara stood alone in front of the marble edifice, her lips moving as she read the names from left to right: from Aba to Zygmunt, Abel to Zanna, Abigail to Zlata,

Anna to Zofia, and all names in between. She looked for Mika's name. No Mika but Mikhail. She sat down. So many names she had never heard of. It was hard to imagine the *Umschlag*, that dirty square that for so many had been the last piece of Warsaw earth they saw, and yet Mara shivered. She pulled her coat tighter and her hands reached for the prince in her pocket.

'Where to now, my little friend?' She let her fingers glide over her map. She knew where to head next: the old Jewish cemetery on Okopowa Street.

She got up and made her way to the north-eastern part of the city. She came to a small gate, paid the entrance fee and stopped in front of a large map of the cemetery, searching for the spot that marked the memorial to Janusz Korczak. She moved swiftly through the cemetery and soon found it. There he was, the old man, tall and commanding, carved from black stone, his precious load of children in tow, surging forward as if against a strong storm. Small piles of stones lay scattered at the base, left by visitors.

'Love and Respect'. Mara read out the simple words that adorned the sculpture.

The morning's walk had moved Mara but she was no closer to finding out about the boy, Mika. She remembered that there was an archive at the Museum of Jewish Heritage, the Ringelblum archive. Maybe she could find Mika there. But it wouldn't be that easy. Although the people were friendly at the archive they told her she couldn't just walk in here and find someone. It would take time. Weeks maybe, or months. Mara's heart sank. They promised to write to her, took her address and Mika's full name. She couldn't give any other details. By now the sun cast long shadows, dark blue like ink.

She decided to go back via the old town. As she

approached the castle, she encountered crowds of tourists, babbling in dozens of languages, streaming towards the heart of the old town. In the cobbled market square, tour guides holding up their umbrellas gathered their excited flocks, pointing out details on the colourful façades. *Such a different atmosphere here,* Mara thought. *So touristy – all sweet and Continental.* She strolled towards the middle of the square drawn by an intriguing statue: a mermaid, swinging a sword over her head like a fierce warrior – Syrena, the symbol of Warsaw.

Her guidebook told her that the old city had been rebuilt stone by stone from drawings and photographs after the war. It took years, and the people danced and cried in the square all night when it was finished.

Leaving the square, Mara meandered through the old town's quaint streets, past the castle, back towards the modern centre. She recognised the white two-spired church from her book; the place where Chopin's heart lay buried under a marble slab. His body lay in Paris, but he had wanted his heart to return to his home country. Mara stood for a moment in front of the white marble slab surrounded by flowers, a relief of his face – Fryderyk Franciszek Chopin, his Polish name.

Leaving Chopin's heart under the cold marble, she made her way back to the hotel, collapsing on the large bed. It would be another year before, one afternoon, Mara stumbled across an article about Chopin's anti-Semitism. 'More subtle than Wagner,' the journalist wrote. *What comfort is that supposed to be?* she thought. She had loved Chopin's music all her life.

Mara scribbled in her notebook all the way on the flight back to Germany, filling page after page with ideas and sketches. The next day she went straight to work on her puppet play about Warsaw during the occupation. Then three weeks later the letter arrived.

'Nothing. They found nothing on Mika, nothing at all,' Mara said out loud after ripping open the envelope with the colourful Polish stamps. However, the letter did state there might be a small chance he had survived: he might have emigrated after the war to Israel or America as many others did. The letter gave her the address of another archive detailing displaced persons.

That night Mara sat bent over her computer, typing furiously.

'There, let's see what happens now.'

This time the answer didn't come by letter, but via email.

The archive had nothing listed under Mika Hernsteyn, but a Mikhail Hernstein left Warsaw for New York in August 1948. Could this be the same Mika? She tried the online New York telephone directory, without success. *Guess he could have gone anywhere in the US*, she thought, returning to her play.

In time Mara realised that if she were really to do the story justice she would need more than just her two hands. She needed help to change the lights, get troops of Nazis marching and manipulate all the puppets. It wasn't long before she had a little group gathered for breakfast, and then for the first rehearsal: Rainer, an enthusiastic sax-ophonist and redhead, Martin, a former boyfriend with a voice as deep as a well, and Sibylle, Mara's oldest friend, one of the very few people she had connected with in her childhood. After a month of rehearsals the play was ready – *The Puppet Boy of Warsaw* by the 'Black Elk Puppet Theatre troupe' as they proudly named themselves.

Puppet Boy showed first in one of Bremen's commu-nity halls, and after some good reviews, it moved to a small theatre. Papers and radio programmes talked about the show and it was the focus of much controversy: a puppet play about the Holocaust? And not only that, but what authority did this German puppet troupe have to address the history of the Warsaw ghetto? But as harshly as some critics judged the play, and Mara's troupe, others approved of it and hailed *The Puppet Boy of Warsaw* as a groundbreaking piece.

Over the next three months the four puppeteers toured all over Germany – from Hamburg to Düsseldorf, Frankfurt to Nuremberg, Munich and many smaller places in between. Indeed, *The Puppet Boy of Warsaw* turned out to be an unexpected success.

One day, when Mara and the Black Elk troupe had just returned from Munich, an email landed in her inbox with an invitation to put on the play at a puppet festival in the South of France. Spain followed a week later, then Italy and Greece.

During all this time, Mara was so busy that she didn't have time to continue her search for Mika. Then, one late September day on a rare trip home, Mara jumped up from her computer desk with a big leap. Grabbing the prince, who always sat at her desk next to the computer if not on tour, Mara danced through her sitting room like a whirling dervish.

'I can't believe this. We're off to the Big Apple, the big NY! There's a puppet festival and they invited us. All of us!

'Everything is big there, my prince, you'll see.' She hugged the prince close to her heart.

They left three weeks later. To play in New York meant more to Mara than playing in any other place before – not only for the sheer excitement of the pulsing city, but for a hope that stirred in her heart of finding a link, a connection to the boy, the old man who once owned her cherished puppet.

286

PART THREE

Homecoming

30

Pale light falls through the milky glass of the north-facing window, illuminating the black and white marbled pattern on the linoleum. No one in the room is aware of the traffic's constant murmur, interrupted only by the occasional siren – the familiar backdrop to life in Manhattan. The small room is a place outside time, a place of limbo, of waiting; quiet but for the monitor's regular beeping and a machine pumping oxygen into Mika's lungs, its plastic bellows folding and unfolding like an old accordion. Propped up and wrapped in starched sheets, the old man is held firmly in the large hospital bed's cool embrace.

Mika floats beyond time and space, his whole being broken open by the events of the past few days: a brightly coloured poster of a puppet show; a mysterious phone call; an outpouring of his past to his grandson followed by a walk around the block; the dance under a street lamp among the whirling snowflakes; the iron cramp and white-flashing pain in his heart; Danny's face in the ambulance as he held his hand...

When Daniel rang, Hannah had just prepared a pot of strong black tea, ready to settle on the couch for a

289

late-night thriller. The news struck her like a blow, contracting her solar plexus, leaving her breathless.

'What do you mean he's in hospital? What happened?' She had an eerie sense of standing outside herself, noticing her high-pitched voice, a hysterical slant.

'In the snow? In the dark? What the hell were you doing out in the snow? He was what? Dancing?' A wave of anger washed over her. Then she remembered she was talking to her son.

'Sorry, Danny, are you all right? Where are you? I'll come immediately.'

She rushed downtown to the hospital as fast as she could, cursing the snow and her father's recklessness.

Since then, the hours had merged into one another like a sluggish, grey stream. Except for those long hours in which she listened to Danny retelling her father's epic tale: his childhood in Warsaw, the ghetto, the puppets, the fires, the deportations, while the old man lay unconscious, kept alive only by a machine.

Hannah sits close to Mika's bed. Her hands move restlessly over the coarse black coat that lies draped over her legs. She has not let go of it since she found it on her father's bed, waiting like a loyal animal. Not since she reached into its secret pockets and passages, retrieving the tokens of Mika's past. Nothing could make her let go of the coat now – this witness to her father's life that has finally found her, come home.

On her father's bedside table lie a pair of golden glasses, a small wooden flute, a bundle of letters and six puppets, sitting next to each other like a colourful theatre troupe on parade. Even now, two days later, she continues to stroke the objects as if they were precious pets. Sometimes she reaches out to touch Mika's hand.

'Daddy, can you hear me?' Her voice is gentle and

quiet. She is not sure whether to keep speaking to him or to be silent. She finds it difficult to talk – not that she can't find something to say, she just doesn't know where to start. The dam held for so long and she isn't ready for a deluge, for everything pouring out just like that.

She is glad she is not alone. Grateful for the presence of Danny, her boy. She stretches her hand out towards Mika, then for a moment holds back.

Danny sits flicking through a magazine. He moves in and out of the room like a restless weasel, doesn't know what to do with himself. He gets his mother cups of coffee, glad to leave the room even for a few minutes, strolls along the corridors, buys himself a Coke from the machine and then another one. He can get away with it today, Mom doesn't notice.

Despite the sterile environment, Daniel is glad to see Grandpa in the hospital bed, tucked under a clean white sheet. And even if it's with a machine, at least he's still breathing. He looks at Mika and for a second he thinks he can see the old man's eyelids flutter as if they are about to open. In that flutter he remembers the phone call.

'Mom, I need to go back to the flat to check Grandpa's answer machine.'

'Why?' His mother looks somewhat alarmed. 'What is it? Can't it wait?'

'I completely forgot – when Grandpa woke up in the ambulance he said, "Danny, someone called, check the machine," just before he slipped away again. He squeezed my hand. It must be important.'

His mother says nothing for a while, then sighs, puts her hand in her pocket and pulls out a few notes.

'OK, but take a cab and come straight back.'

'OK.'

Danny takes the money, glances at the old man who lies still, unchanged, then leaves the room. *It will be good to get out of this place*, he thinks, *I hate hospitals*. He takes the lift, goes through the heavy glass doors into the cold and waves down a yellow cab.

'Where are you off to, then?' the cab driver asks, smiling at Daniel through the rear-view mirror. Daniel gives him the address, but says nothing else – he is not in the mood for conversation. He slumps into the black leather seat, sighs and watches the snow-changed world pass by. The traffic is slow. Although the streets have mostly been cleared, people are still driving as if the ground were thick with ice: slow, cautious. The driver's beeping and swearing make Daniel feel edgy.

Finally the cab pulls up in front of the apartment block.

'Could you wait here? I won't be long,' Daniel says, already half out of the cab.

He lets himself in through the main door using the code, then heads for the elevator. He kicks the silver elevator doors that bear a mocking 'out of service' sign, then races up the five storeys, sweating and swearing. He hesitates for a moment before putting the key into the lock. Daniel has never had the key before. It was always Grandpa's.

He rushes straight to the answer machine, which flashes red and nervous like an alarm clock, '5', '5', '5', then presses the playback button. His mother. He skips forward. Mom again, checking in with Grandpa. The third message is about him: 'Hi, Dad! Can Danny spend Sunday with you? Hope you're well, call me please!" Sunday seems as long ago as last summer.

Why didn't Grandpa delete these? Keeps everything, the old man. Daniel is aware of just how cluttered the place has become since Nan died. *She kept the ship clean, now everything's a mess. He can't let go of anything.* A deep female voice with an accent he can't place startles him. She sounds nervous, anxious even.

'This is a message for Mikhail Hernstein. My name is Mara Meierhauser. If you were ever known as the Puppet Boy of Warsaw I would love to talk to you. I am in New York at the moment with my puppet troupe, the Black Elk Puppet Theatre. We're playing at the Triad on 72nd. You can reach me on this number.' Daniel grabs a pen, takes down the number, then listens again, compares the number, and punches it into the phone. He doesn't know what he will say if the woman answers.

'Carmen Hotel, reception. How can I help?'

'Could you put me through to Mara Meier... Meierhauser please?'

'One moment please.'

Daniel's heart thumps.

'She's out, I'm afraid, sir. Can I take a message?'

'No thanks, I'll call again.'

He puts down the receiver, looks at it for a moment as if it is an alien thing. Expects the phone to ring again.

Perhaps I should have left a message. But what would I have said? The 'Puppet Boy' is in hospital? Surprised, Daniel notices a flash of anger stabbing through him. He tears the note with the number from the piece of paper, puts it in his pocket and leaves the apartment. He rushes down the five flights of stairs, taking three steps at a time. He's flying, feels light headed.

'Back to the hospital, please.' Slumped in the cab's soft seat, Daniel is grateful to have the same driver, who won't expect him to talk.

Who the hell is this Mara Meierhauser? He plays the message over and over in his mind, thinking about her name.

The moment the cab goes over a small bump it hits him like a slap in the face: Max Meierhauser, the German soldier. Suddenly it all makes sense. He's sweating. For the first time in days he feels hot. His heart is racing too.

'Here we are.'

'Thanks.'

Daniel pays the driver, gets out and goes through the hospital doors.

When he enters his grandfather's sickroom a nurse is about to change Mika's drip. Daniel tries to still his breathing and grabs a chair.

'Are you all right? Did you find anything on the machine?' Hannah asks.

'I'm OK.' Once the drip is reattached Daniel counts the drops until the nurse leaves. He pulls his chair closer to his mother.

'It's crazy, Mom, there's a message on the machine from a woman who wants to talk to Grandad. Says she's called Mara Meierhauser. That's the same surname as the German soldier Grandad gave his prince puppet to. She says she's in New York with her puppet troupe. I called the number but she wasn't there.' The words spill out like a runaway train, he can't stop. 'I didn't tell you this, but Grandad had already collapsed that morning on the way to the museum just after we passed this little theatre on 72nd. Later that day he asked me whether I'd seen a poster – something about a puppeteer in Warsaw. Maybe she's involved in that show?'

'Slow down, Danny. You're sure? How would she even know his number?' But his mother sounds breathless too. 'Then again, if he picked up the phone message ... You know, he never did tell me anything about his life in Poland, his childhood. Nothing. He was a closed book. When did this Mara call?'

'I don't know, some time after you called him to ask about Sunday.'

Hannah gets up, paces around the room, looking at her father.

'Do you think we should call her?'

'Maybe, but not now, Danny. You're exhausted. We'll call again in the morning. I talked to the nurse, there's a relatives' room down the corridor with a bed. Why don't you get a bit of sleep? I'll stay here.'

Sleep sounds good, he thinks. He feels so raw it hurts.

He keeps his clothes on but once he is horizontal he is out like a light, the night swallowing him whole.

'How's Grandpa?'

Daniel looks tired and dishevelled as he enters Mika's room. The morning light reaches through the blinds to his grandfather's bed. He tries to make sense of his dream: hollow trees, broken eggs and a whole troupe of puppets coming to life, first whispering, and then shouting at him. He can't recall their words. He looks at his watch and frowns.

'Guess I overslept.'

'Glad you caught up on some sleep, honey,' his mother says. 'No change with Grandad. But I checked out the puppet shows on the Web and there's one at the Triad, *The Puppet Boy of Warsaw*, with a troupe called the Black Elk Puppet Theatre.'

'Oh my God, that's it!' Danny is wide awake now. 'Grandpa mentioned the poster when we got back to his apartment. I guess that's what started everything off. But it all makes sense now. He'd just seen the poster when he collapsed that first time. I should go and check it out.'

'Guess you should. There's a matinee at twelve.'

Daniel's watch says it's ten past ten. He glances at the puppets lying on the table, picks up the crocodile.

'I'll take this one with me. See you later, Mom, wish me luck.'

31

This time he takes the subway. He remembers exiting on 72nd with his grandpa. Was that really only three days ago? Did Grandpa suggest they come up to check out this theatre ... or did he stumble over the poster by accident?

It is 11.30 when he arrives at the little theatre. He buys a ticket, sits himself on a stool in the foyer bar and orders a Coke. There's hardly anyone there and he wonders why they even bother.

Just then a group of boisterous schoolkids a bit younger than him spill into the foyer like a torn bag of candy.

Finally the bell rings. He enters the auditorium and chooses a place in the front row. He picks up the booklet on his seat, flicks through it. There's her name again: Mara Meierhauser. But before he can read further the lights dim and the curtain opens.

The set is a jumble of three-storey houses in all shades of grey leaning over cobbled streets that disappear into the distance. Daniel puts his hand in his pocket, looking for a lozenge, and finds the crocodile. He wonders what he is doing there.

Just then the first puppet appears. Small and a bit worn-looking, it's wrapped in a dark red robe, a small crown sitting forlorn and lopsided on its head. The puppet sits down on a little chair to the side of the set and starts talking.

'Good day, ladies and gentlemen, *meine Damen und Herren, mesdames et messieurs*. So, you want to hear my story? The things I've seen, the places I've been? Well, I am quite old now and much of my glamour has worn off, but I tell you, I've had a life. Seen places and things you can't even imagine. Picked up tales in many twisting tongues – enough to understand your human hearts. Throughout my humble puppet life I've been applauded, forgotten, lost and, yes, found again.' The puppet jumps up and stands on the chair.

'I was born in a small workshop under the clever hands of a boy called Mika in the Jewish ghetto of Warsaw in the winter of 1940. Mika took his time with me, modelled my papier-mâché head into a princely shape, and painted my face with fine brushes, mixing shades of pink for my two cheeks and for my eyes the colour of the sea on a sunny day. He made my costume, all sparkling with golden seams and shining stones, and a matching crown for my head. I know the colours have faded and I look a bit shabby, but wait until you hear my story.'

Hearing his grandfather's name, Daniel feels queasy. *She's got it all wrong. It was Mika's grandad who made the puppets. Jacob. And she's missed a crucial thing here, the Germans shot the old man, didn't they!*

'Mika always wore a black coat, as big as a tent,' the prince continues. *And you know why? It belonged to his grandad, you moron.* Daniel's heart is beating fast and hard.

And then he appears, a boy-puppet in a huge, black coat. A Mika puppet, taller than the prince.

'They call me the Puppet Boy,' the puppet says. He slowly opens his coat, showing off some smaller puppets that stick their heads out of tiny coat pockets. This is just freaky: Mika the puppet. The puppet speaks with a lower voice than the prince but still with a slight accent. Daniel shivers; it's the same voice as the woman on the phone – Mara Meierhauser.

The Mika puppet introduces two sisters and a brother, then his mum and dad. *No! That woman has no clue.*

'In November 1940 the Germans built a wall and locked all the Jews of Warsaw into a tiny part of the city, the ghetto,' the prince announces while a wall is pulled by invisible strings across the stage until it encircles all the houses. More and more puppets appear, crowding together like grapes.

And so Mika's story unfolds in front of Daniel as told through Mara Meierhauser's eyes: Mika playing with his puppets on the ghetto streets, in front of soup kitchens and in cellars. Daniel watches as Mika whips a miniature puppet from his coat which talks back at a German soldier before that same soldier – a deep male voice with a strong German accent – grabs Mika by the scruff of his neck and pulls him off stage. The curtain closes. *At least she's got something right.*

When the curtain opens again the stage is transformed into the soldiers' barracks with long rows of tables, soldier-puppets lying about drunk or hitting their beer jugs against the benches. At first sight they all look the same with their bulging beer guts, red faces and uniforms adorned with hooked crosses, but when Daniel takes a closer look he notices the details: one soldier has a sharp eagle's nose while another is pale and thin as a pencil. The story twists and turns: the soldiers wreak havoc on the streets, kick, shout and shoot everyone in their way, dragging people to the *Umschlag* and on to the trains.

In Mara's version Mika hides with his mother and siblings in an attic while his father is rounded up by the soldiers. *Does she not know about Grandpa's mother and the soldier hiding her?*

The show ends with smoke and noise, the ghetto uprising and Mika crawling out of the ruins with his mother and siblings in tow. *Alive. You wish. That would be easy.*

The little curtain closes. It's as quiet in the audience as the morning after the blizzard. No one claps. Seconds later three performers step out from behind the set and the spell is broken. Two women – one tall, blonde, the other dark haired with glasses – with a man between them. They hold hands and bow. All are dressed in black: black trousers, black turtlenecks, and black shoes. Then applause falls like hard rain. The three puppeteers smile, bow again and gesture towards the puppets and the technician at the back. The dark-haired woman holds the prince, bows with him and steps forward.

'Thank you. Please come and meet us in the foyer, we're happy to answer any questions.' Daniel wonders which of the two is Mara. He isn't so sure about the voice any more. His heart hasn't stopped beating fast all the way through the play and now, with the lights on, and the puppeteers so close by, his heart is in his throat.

He waits, is the last to leave the small auditorium. The children have spread out in the foyer, chatting and giggling. Daniel puts on his jacket, sits down at a small table and nibbles away at the stale peanuts. *This is too weird, Grandpa's in hospital and this woman is putting on a puppet show about his life without even knowing half of it.*

Minutes later the performers and the technician are in the foyer, mingling with the children and the other members of the audience. The tall blonde woman stands alone with a Coke in her hand while the brunette is surrounded by a group of children. He strolls up to the woman with the Coke.

'Excuse me, are you Mara Meierhauser?'

The woman smiles at him. 'No, dear, I am Sibylle, that woman over there is Mara.' She points at the women with brown hair.

'Thanks.' He moves away before she can ask him anything.

I should go home, this is just stupid. He moves past the children, walks through the front door. The cold hits him like a wall but he welcomes its sobering effect. He decides to wait exactly five minutes.

The sidewalk has been transformed into brown slush. He stomps down the road with extra-large steps, enjoying the splash of the dirty snow. A bagel shop catches his eye and his stomach starts to rumble. He's hardly eaten anything over the past few days. He considers buying a bagel but then thinks again about the German woman, selling her grandfather's story to those gullible kids. Still, he wants to meet her – he knows that's what his grandpa would want him to do.

Daniel turns, walks back to the theatre and enters the foyer.

'Come on, kids.' The teacher ushers her students into a corner and starts counting.

She is alone now, Daniel thinks. *Just stay cool, I can always slip out of here.* But his heart betrays him, beats as crazily as a drum. He takes a deep breath, approaches her from behind, his hands in his pocket, trying to swagger, look casual.

'Are you Mara Meierhauser?' he says.

'Yes, I am.' She turns and smiles but he can see she is nervous. Was she nervous with the kids too?

'I'm Daniel Hernsteyn,' Daniel says. He's never seen blood drain so quickly from a face. She looks white, and spooked like a horse after a fall, a panicked rabbit.

'Daniel ... Hernsteyn?'

300

'Yes, Danny, actually. You left a message on my grand-pa's answer machine?'

'Yes, yes, I did. Oh my God. And you're his grandson?'

'Yeah. But he's in hospital. He had a heart attack three days ago.'

If it is possible the woman looks even whiter now. She moves to a group of chairs and sits down.

'You all right?' he asks, following her.

'Yes, I'm OK; I just didn't expect this when I didn't hear from your grandpa. How's he doing?'

'Not sure. He's unconscious. He's on a machine.'

'Oh no,' she looks at Daniel directly, 'I'm so sorry to hear that. I hope he gets better soon.'

'Yes, so do I. So, you wanted to talk to him?'

'Yes.' She sounds shy now. 'I don't know where to start, there's so much to say. Do you have some time?'

Daniel nods.

'Shall we find a place where we can sit for a while?' Mara asks.

'Sure, there's a bagel shop just down the road,' Daniel replies, turning towards the exit.

'Sounds good. I'll just tell my colleagues.' She gets up, talks to the tall woman, then disappears and returns a few minutes later dressed in a dark blue coat and a ruby-red scarf.

They venture out into the road and walk the few hundred yards to the bagel shop without speaking. As they enter, a waft of freshly baked bread greets them like a warm hug. They peel off their coats and sit at a table near the window.

'Choose whatever you like, please, it's on me,' Mara says. The waitress brings the menu. Daniel hesitates.

'OK, then, thanks, I'll have cream cheese and lox and a Coke,' he says.

'I'll have that too. You don't call it salmon here? We

call it *Lachs* in German. Same word.' She smiles. Daniel wonders whether that is supposed to make him feel better. The waitress takes their orders and they sit in silence.

'I'm so glad you came. I've been looking for your grandad for a long time. There's something I want to give back to him.' She isn't smiling now and her voice sounds hoarse. She reaches into her coat pocket and pulls out a dark red bundle. It's the prince, the narrator of the show. She puts the puppet on the table facing Daniel and adjusts the little crown.

'So is this ...' Daniel stretches his arm towards the puppet but doesn't touch it.

'Yes, it's the same prince – the puppet your grandad gave my grandfather in 1942 in Warsaw. Did he ever tell you about that?'

'Yeah, he told me some things, but only a few days ago. Before that he never told anyone anything about it, not even my mother.'

Then suddenly it all spills out.

'The Germans took everything, why could he not have let Grandpa at least keep his favourite puppet? How could your grandfather take it? My grandpa was only a boy. And by the way, Mika lost everyone in Warsaw, your play is wrong; he was the only one to get out of that hell alive. No one, not one of his family, survived.' Daniel's voice is louder than he wants it to be and his cheeks have turned a fiery red.

'That's awful.' Mara's voice is thin and she looks down at her hands. 'I'm so sorry.'

Daniel glares at her but she still doesn't look up. After a while Mara takes a deep breath and lifts her head.

'Look,' she speaks quietly, bending forward, 'there's nothing I can do to change the past, but I want to give you this puppet at least. Please take it back to your grandad. The prince belongs to him.' She looks at Daniel with her large dark green eyes and pushes the puppet towards him. A fierce anger surges through Daniel like a bolt of electricity. *That would be easy, wouldn't it? As if that could wash away everything.* He breathes in sharply but tries not to sound too severe.

'Thanks, but you'll have to do that yourself. Grandpa's at the Downtown Hospital, room 215. Visiting hours are from one to five in the afternoon, and seven till eight in the evening.' He thinks he can see Mara flinch but she doesn't betray anything as she speaks.

'OK, I will do that.'

Just then the waitress arrives, placing the plates on the table with a grand gesture.

'Two bagels with cream cheese and lox, one Coke and one beer. Oh, how sweet,' she says, looking at the prince, but before she can touch it Mara puts the puppet back into her pocket.

'Thanks,' Mara says. The waitress leaves and they sit in silence. Daniel takes a few sips of his Coke but neither of them eats.

'You say it happened only a few days ago, your grandad having the heart attack?' Mara breaks the silence.

'Yes, on Sunday. I was pretty shaken after he told me the whole story about Warsaw, so he said I should stay over. Mum was cool about it, especially with all the snow. I didn't say anything to her about Grandpa and his story, but she still picked up on something, said my voice sounded kind of funny. When I put down the phone I heard Grandpa saying: "I'm just popping out to get some air. Could you make us some sandwiches?"

'I couldn't believe he wanted to go out into the dark and the snow on his own, so I said, "No way, old man, I'm coming with you!" He fought me but after a while he gave in, picked up his walking stick, pulled on his fur cap and off we went. We took his usual route around the block. He looked funny, hitting the new snow with his stick.

'All of a sudden he stopped under a street lamp, looking up at the falling snow. Then he stepped right into the centre of the light as if it were some kind of spotlight and let go of his stick. He started moving, as if he were dancing to some music I couldn't hear. Slowly at first, then faster and faster, lifting his arms towards the sky, whirling and spinning with the snowflakes. I guess I should've stopped him right there, but I just stared. It was so strange and beautiful, the way he kept looking up at the sky, flakes melting on his face. He was smiling the whole time. And then he fell.'

Slowly Daniel feels his anger dissolve like the snowflakes on Mika's face.

'I didn't know what to do, I was pretty freaked. I tried to get him up but nothing worked. I called the ambulance and, well, you know the rest. Think it wore him out, all that talking about the war.' Daniel sits back, takes a big gulp from his Coke.

'I'm so sorry.' Mara's voice sounds croaky. Daniel looks up and catches her gaze. Tears are running down her face, two silent streams. She doesn't wipe them away and for a moment she puts her hand on his arm, light as a butterfly.

Suddenly there is an opening, an opportunity.

'I'm not sure Grandpa would want me to tell you lots about him, but I guess if you're doing this puppet play you need to know what it was really like for him.' He puts his hand in his pocket and pulls out the crocodile.

'Well, here's one of his old puppets.' He slides his hand into the crocodile, snaps its mouth open and shut.

'Oh my God, it survived? How amazing,' Mara says, stretching her hand towards the crocodile. *She looks like a child*, he thinks.

'Grandpa managed to keep a few puppets hidden in

304

his coat. But when he arrived in America he stored the coat for years in his wardrobe and only brought it out a few days ago.' He slips his hand out of the crocodile and puts the puppet back on the table like an invitation. Mara strokes it with her fingertips.

'And what about the prince, what's his story? How did he survive?' Daniel asks.

Mara reaches into her coat, pulls out the prince and slips her hand under the velvet robe. 'Well now, Danny.' She speaks with a low voice, sits the puppet next to her plate facing him.

'Let me tell you what happened to me ...'

The afternoon dissolves as they talk for hours. Mara tells the prince's story until Daniel's ears ring, then the tide turns and Daniel pours out as much as he can recall of his grandfather's tale. He never intended to, but his grandfather's story is like a flood that forges its own path. As Mika's story unfolds, Mara slowly sheds the defensiveness that has become second nature to her: the price for being German and speaking about the war. She feels herself crumble; fate finally catching up with her.

'Can I get you anything else?' The waitress's voice startles them both. As if emerging from deep waters, Mara looks at her watch.

'Oh my God, is that the time? Let me pay and then I'll tell my colleagues to cancel tonight's show. I'll be in the hospital in an hour or so. Do you think they will let me in? Or shall I come tomorrow?'

'No, I'm sure it's fine, come tonight. If anyone asks just say you're a friend of the family.'

'Thanks, Danny.' She looks away. 'Shall we get these wrapped up?' Neither of them has touched the bagels.

32

Mara stands in the flower shop opposite the hospital among an abundance of colours, unable to choose. Flowers for Mika, the old man who was once a boy in Warsaw. The pocket boy; the Puppet Boy. She picks up a bunch of pink roses, then puts them back. Orange gerbera. Too bright. In the end she chooses a big bunch of bright yellow roses. For life.

She enters the hospital, hurries through the labyrinthine corridors, and finally finds the room: 215. Standing on the threshold, knocking at the door, she tenses. A woman with a thick head of dark curls sits at the bedside. She turns and, on seeing Mara, gets up. Comes straight towards her and embraces her.

'Thank you for coming. I'm Hannah, Danny's mum. Mika's daughter.'

Danny sits close to the bed. He smiles at her. 'Hi, glad you're here.'

Mara shifts from one leg to another; her hands are clammy. The friendly reception chokes her. She feels more comfortable standing, but is also grateful for Danny's gesture, fetching her a chair. She clings to every piece of friendliness from these people into whose lives she has catapulted herself. She feels out of place, out of her depth. As if she has somehow broken a taboo.

'Thank you,' is all she can manage. *What am I doing here, a German puppeteer with a dead soldier grandfather on my shoulder?* she thinks.

Glancing at the old man, Mara stands still now, rooted as a tree. Daniel fetches a vase for Mara's flowers; they look extra bright in the room.

Suddenly Mara remembers why she is there. She reaches inside her pocket and hands Hannah a small parcel.

'Here, I would like you to have this.'

'Thank you.' Hannah receives the parcel with both hands. Daniel peeps over his mother's shoulder.

Slowly, from beneath layers of thin blue tissue paper, a piece of matted fur emerges, then some dark red velvet, a head with big painted eyes, a little dented crown. The prince.

'Oh my God, he's so tiny.' Hannah holds up the puppet, then slowly slips her right hand underneath his robe.

'Is this really the puppet my dad gave to that soldier … I mean, your grandfather? The old prince from Warsaw?'

Mara nods. A lump has formed in her throat. The prince, alive under Hannah's hand now, turns his head from Mara to Daniel, then to Mika. The puppet is silent. Hannah moves closer to Mika's bed and, leaning over him, lays the old prince next to her father's right hand.

Mara can hardly breathe. Her eyes are streaming, releasing the lump, her heart burning.

'Daddy, this woman here, Mara, has brought back the puppet you gave to a German soldier in Warsaw. A man called Max. Mara is his granddaughter. It's the prince, Daddy.'

The old man lies still. He looks as if he is drowning in so much whiteness, except for the puppet, a spot of colour like an accidental splash on a blank canvas. The prince, his crimson robe and matted fur collar, apple-red cheeks and delicate smile. His head could fit perfectly into Mika's palm like an egg.

All three stare at the prince, his little head facing Mika's hand, his body limp like the old man's under the sheets.

Mika's world has shrunk to a white cubicle suspended in time: a bed, a milky window, a muffled universe. He remembers the surging flash cutting him down like a tree as he danced among the snowflakes. He feels submerged, under water, under a sheet of ice. A line of poetry crosses his foggy mind like a crow soaring across a snowy landscape: *'Now my ladder's gone ... I must lie down where all the ladders start: in the foul rag-and-bone shop of the heart.'* Something inside him repeats the line like a broken record: *rag-and-bone shop of the heart ...*

As his body lies still, memories form a collage, a kaleidoscope of images. He is fourteen, wrapped in his grandfather's coat, queuing in the tedious lines of the ghetto; then taller but very skinny, standing in a long line of sea-beaten immigrants in a white-tiled hall on Ellis Island; his first dance with Ruth, a bright spring day in 1952, an old dance hall in lower Manhattan; three years later, his foot crushing the wine glass at his wedding, remembering not Jerusalem but Warsaw's end, as if the shattering of the glass might break the wall around his heart once and for all. Ruth, so beautiful in her cream-coloured wedding dress. Lace.

Then Hannah, a tiny, wriggling bundle, a full head of black curls sticking to her skull, a bright purple birthmark in the shape of a moth, adorning her back. He holds her, kisses her back, right on the moth wing. Little Hannah, her smile, sweet as honey, who slipped into their lives on a hot summer's day in 1966 in their apartment on the Lower East Side – a late surprise. Hannah, 'favoured grace', 'grace of God'. Her first steps, almost one year to the day she was born, on a sunny day in Central Park. A carousel ride for all of them. Holding Hannah on his lap, his arms firmly wrapped around her, Ruth bouncing up and down next to him on a purple horse. All three laughing with delight, his heart for once flying light.

Now his heart contracts as he sees his daughter, a thirteen-year-old, transformed into a Belsen girl by her own hand. Hannah shrinking until she is as pale and thin as a ghost, a shadow puppet. Like the ghost of his other Hannah.

Suddenly Mika's mind jolts and he finds himself in the stuffy heat of the Mila Street bunker, lying on a small field bed next to Ellie. He wants to keep hold of her but is pulled backwards as in a vortex: his grandfather turning in his new coat in front of Nathan's mirror; Ellie at their door with her old suitcase, smiling; Mother's fists raining down on him after the first night with the soldiers; then Ellie's fists after the Germans had taken everyone; the prince lying next to his mother's face, a message in his hand; the princess-puppet, his last gift to Ellie, then Ellie's face disappearing as he climbs down into the sewers. Max, the soldier, the prince dangling between them ...

Slowly the flood of images subsides and voices enter his consciousness. He can hear Danny, lovely Danny with his black curls, then Hannah, her voice gentle but strained. He tries hard but he cannot understand what they are saying. He is aware of another voice in the room, a woman's voice. She doesn't address him but he senses her presence. Then it's Hannah again. 'Daddy,' she calls to him. His girl. He feels a slight weight next to him, cool and smooth, then fur touching his fingers like a breath. Something is trying to push itself into his consciousness, is calling without a sound, without words.

*

309

The three figures gather around Mika's bed. They have stopped talking, only look and wait. Then subtly, like a trick of the imagination, Mika's finger lifts. The ring finger first, the little finger follows, then all four, the thumb remaining on the sheet as if it is too heavy. Mika's fingertips move over the puppet's face like those of a blind man exploring the features of a loved one, fluttering over the fur collar, the velvet cloak, coming back to the face. Mika's eyes remain closed but a sigh shudders through his body.

And suddenly he knows. Knows without a doubt: this is his prince. No, he hasn't dreamt it; he recognises the textures and fabrics, the delicate features of the puppet. His prince has come home. The old puppet has returned to his bloodline. Not that a clear thought like this is able to cut through the fog inside his head, but a distinct feeling spreads from his heart like a radiating sun: this is a reunion. And more than that, it is a homecoming. Whether it is the puppet that has come home or himself, he is not sure. But does this matter?

Something inside him decides to return. To come back, like the prince, if only for a while. He takes his first unaided breath for days, rattling, slurping. His eyes twitch and the urge to open them is overwhelming. Mika senses little pockets of energy emerge from deep within him like air bubbles floating to the surface of a pond. His right hand reaches for the prince, squeezes him lightly. He opens one, then the other eye.

He can make out three figures – Danny, the last sweet face he saw before the darkness fell; and Hannah. He aches for Hannah, wants to reach for her, touch her. And there is another woman he has never seen. She doesn't smile, looks as pale as a ghost. What did Hannah say? The woman's called Mara? As the fog in his mind lifts, the magnitude of what he is being told hits him. The soldier's

310

granddaughter? He flinches, closes his eyes again. How can this be?

'Daddy, can you hear me?' Hannah's voice is as soft as silk. Mika strains to open his eyes, succeeds. Hannah's face is so close he can smell her – the familiar mixture of her skin and her perfume. Danny's voice startles him.

'Grandpa, you're all right?' Mika looks at Danny, opens his dry mouth, but only a croaking emerges. He is so tired.

'How are you feeling, Daddy?' Hannah bends over him. She looks strained, concerned.

'Okhaay,' he whispers, hardly recognising his own voice. He tries to smile. 'Still here. Who's that?' He lifts his hand to point at Mara but it hardly moves.

'This is Mara, Dad. A puppeteer. She's brought back your prince puppet.' Hannah holds the puppet up in front of Mika's eyes. His smile grows broader and his right hand lifts higher. Hannah guides his hand underneath the prince's velvet cloak until the puppet is propped up on his hand.

'Helllooo.' He moves the prince gently, turning its head from Hannah to Danny, bows slightly, then moves it to face Mara. He lingers for a moment. Mara smiles now, but he thinks he can see tears rolling down her face. The prince nods at her and gives a tiny wave before turning back to Danny. He gestures for him to sit on the bed. Danny perches on the edge of the mattress as Hannah props Mika up with some pillows.

'This prince is for you, Danny. For you and Mom,' Mika whispers. He looks at Hannah, smiles. 'Keep him safe ...' his breathing rattles; 'he's come a long way, that prince.'

'It's OK, Daddy, don't strain yourself, rest.' She strokes his cheek. *I've never been so tired*, he thinks. Danny takes the prince from him, puts the puppet over his hand.

'Thanks, Grandpa, I'll take good care of him.'

'Sleep, my friend, I'm safe now and so are you.' The prince's hand softly strokes Mika's cheek before Danny puts him into his shirt pocket.

EPILOGUE

The coat is clearly not popular here: old, shabby and soaked with history, it's like a lion in a library, a dangerous beast among the clean order of the hospital. Yesterday the nurse looked at it as if it were crawling with lice. She would have dumped it if she could. But Hannah stood up to the nurse and so the coat stayed in the room.

Hannah is exactly what an old coat needs: kind and fierce, all rolled into one. She strokes the coat, like a pet, a little absent-minded maybe, but with enough affection to feed its old soul. It isn't asking for much, this old coat, just not to be thrown out – and never to be put in a box again. All it wants now is a hook on a wall, a nice coat hanger in a spacious wardrobe, a chair to be draped over, a corner of your heart. The best thing would be a place with a view. A place where it can rest and belong.

So, whenever you see an ordinary coat, think about what might linger in its folds, what memories might be hidden in its pockets. It might whisper to you at night. There are many more stories sewn into its sleeves and many treasures harboured in its seams.

Mika's Book of Heroes

Adina Blady Szwajger – Nurse

A young nurse in the ghetto children's hospital who, the night before the Germans deported everyone, acted on instinct and, with a broken heart, spared some of the illest children the journey to the gas chambers. She simply put them to bed with a bitter drink of morphine and they slipped into their eternal sleep in the presence of their favourite nurse and a bedtime story. Later she fought in the resistance.

Sylvin Rubinstein – Russian cross-dresser

Resistance fighter and entertainer who performed a flamenco act with his twin sister all over Europe and the US before the war. While performing in Warsaw in 1939, he was caught up in the German occupation and was forced into the ghetto. His twin sister and mother were deported, while he survived. He escaped the ghetto and became a famous resistance fighter in Poland and Germany, fighting as a woman and becoming involved in many assassinations of Gestapo and SS officers. He has been living in Hamburg since the war ended.

Janusz Korczak – Polish-Jewish children's author, paediatrician and child educator

He wrote widely on child pedagogics and ran an orphanage in the Warsaw ghetto. Despite receiving release papers, he did not leave his two hundred children and staff when the whole orphanage was deported to Treblinka on 5 August 1943. All perished.

Hanush Hachenberg – poet and writer, who, as a thirteen-year-old, was an inmate of Terezin

He wrote poetry and plays for the children's magazine Wedem. After being taken to Terezin he wrote a puppet play, *Looking for a Monster*, about a king searching for old bones. He was deported to Auschwitz and killed there when he was fourteen.

Irena Sendler – child-rescuer of giant proportions

Irena, a Roman Catholic social worker, helped rescue about 2,500 children from the Warsaw ghetto with her secret organisation, consisting mostly of women. They smuggled children to the Aryan side and placed them with Polish families – she herself smuggled about four hundred children, recorded their real surnames and with whom they were placed and buried these lists in milk bottles in her garden under an apple tree. Through this action, some of the children who survived the war could be reunited with their families – others at least knew their real Jewish names.

In 1943 she was caught, tortured by the Gestapo and left for dead in the forest outside Warsaw. Miraculously she survived and continued to fight in the resistance. She stayed in Warsaw after the war and died in May 2008 at the age of ninety-eight; in interviews she said she always felt she could have done more.

Hakina Olomoucka – painter of the Holocaust

Hakina survived the Warsaw ghetto, Auschwitz and Ravensbrück. All the way through she managed to paint and draw, hiding her art whenever she could. Her paintings are perhaps the most chilling depictions of the horrors, showing the rawness of pain, loss and the abysmal conditions with such clarity. Her fellow inmates asked her to tell the world what had happened to them should she survive – and she did so in the endless images that poured out of her. She lives in Israel and still paints today.

Nivelli – the Great Magician

Born in Berlin in 1906, he survived Auschwitz, while his parents, wife and children perished. He was forced to perform for the Nazis and even had to teach them some of his tricks. He emigrated in 1947 to the US and continued to perform there with his second wife. He died in 1977.

Sophie Scholl – activist within the White Rose non-violent resistance group in Nazi Germany

She was convicted of high treason after being found distributing anti-war leaflets at the University of Munich with her brother Hans. They and several other members of their group were executed by guillotine. She was twenty-one years old.

The Rosenstrasse protest

A non-violent protest in Rosenstrasse ('Rose Street') in Berlin in February and March 1943, carried out by the non-Jewish wives and relatives of Jewish men who had been arrested for impeding deportation. The protests escalated until the men were released. It was a significant instance of opposition to the events of the Holocaust.

The Edelweiss Pirates, Edelweispiraten – a youth culture group in Nazi Germany

They emerged in western Germany out of the German Youth Movement of the late 1930s in response to the strict regimentation of the Hitler Youth.

ACKNOWLEDGEMENTS

*W*riting this book has been an incredibly rewarding and challenging journey and I feel extremely blessed to have such wonderful people supporting me.

I am most grateful to my coach and mentor Dr Eric Maisel. You supported me beautifully with your invaluable wisdom, kind guidance and humour, helping me navigate each and every step and challenge in the long process of writing this novel.

A huge thank you to Charlotte Robertson, my agent, for putting your trust in me and 'Puppet Boy' and for supporting me in such a special way. I will always treasure the faith you have in me and your huge enthusiasm.

A warm thank you to everyone at Orion House and especially to Kirsty Dunseath for your thorough edit, which helped to bring out the shine and make the book what it is now.

A big thank you to my early readers, Eva Coleman and Sophie Fletcher, for your thoughtful feedback and to all my wonderful friends and colleagues who read all or parts of the manuscript along the way, or who simply encouraged and believed in me: Dee, Betsy, Tim, Kirstin, Gabriele, Natasha, Bob, Erin, Linda, Mark R., Emmanuelle, Kathy, John, Mags, Stevie, Mikhail, Charlotte S., Chloe, Caroline, Johanna, Amy, Cici, Laura and my colleagues at the D. – your support means so much to me.

Thanks to all my writing buddies from Eric Maisel's Deep Writing workshop in London, Paris and Prague for cheering me on throughout the process and to Mark and Jennix from my little writing group. I am also very grateful to all the artists who gathered with me at BLANK studios in the autumn of 2008 in whose company I found the seed for 'Puppet Boy': the coat with many pockets ...

Thank you to Mary Buckham for an early edit that steered me in the right direction and to Antony Polonsky, Professor of Holocaust Studies, for his generous endorsement.

Finally, a big thank you to my parents Erika and Karl Heinz for sharing their stories with me.

AUTHOR'S NOTE

Sylvin Rubinstein, the resistance fighter mentioned on p305, died on 30 April 2011.

324

THE
PUPPET
BOY OF
WARSAW

Reading Group Notes

In conversation with Eva Weaver

What made you write this book?
I guess even after years of working with the theme of the Jewish Holocaust through performance and poetry, I still felt a strong need to attend to this in a substantial way. More than sixty million people died as a result of the Second World War, six million of those Jews – children, women, men, systematically killed. *The Puppet Boy of Warsaw* is an attempt to give those numbers a human face.

Who or what was the biggest inspiration to you when writing your novel?
The resistance and resilience of the Jewish women, men and children in the ghetto has deeply moved and inspired me for a long time – how in the deepest despair and horror people rose to risk their lives daily to help each other. Also, I was moved to hear how in the overcrowded ghetto, musicians, singers, dancers, actors, artists still put on productions, concerts and theatre pieces. The power of the arts to strengthen the human spirit even in the most horrendous circumstances has always intrigued and fascinated me.

What is the significance of the puppets?
The puppets allow Mika to tell his stories with a certain distance; he can hide behind them like a mask. The puppets are in some ways metaphors for the will to survive and the power of survival and resistance in general. The puppets come to life in times of biggest challenge, when most needed. They comfort, entertain, exclude authority and call for resistance.

Why do you tell both Mika's story and the story of Max, the German soldier?

I could have written two separate books, but I felt that these stories somehow belonged together and together would create a more powerful story. I was shocked to hear about the extent of just how many German soldiers had been taken to Siberia after the end of the war. As many as one million are estimated to have perished in the Siberian gulags. We have little evidence for their deaths, as the Russians did not keep precise records. The historical facts were not available to me while I was still in Germany and are only slowly emerging now. This is a different side of this terrible war that I felt I wanted to attend to as well.

Is Max ever able to acknowledge his guilt?

Of course! Max believes in his duty to the fatherland, but he is not without a conscience. Through Mika, Max becomes unable to continue to see a homogenous mass of Jews. We witness his struggle with guilt and shame throughout the book, particularly of course in the second part.

Do you think your novel is realistic? Could something like the coat belonging to Mika's grandfather have existed?

In my research about how people have resisted and have smuggled people, babies, children and adults out of ghettos and camps, I have come across many extremely creative and amazing ways. I know for sure that quite a few people did create secret pockets in coats to hide very precious objects.

Can a non-Jew write about the Holocaust and, in particular, from a Jewish perspective?

I have known from the beginning that to write a book about the Holocaust as a non-Jew – and not only that, but as a German woman – is something that will be questioned and sometimes contested. I have written this book not as a historian, as a political activist working for reconciliation or with a particular agenda, but as a storyteller, humanist and artist who believes passionately in the power of story and art to help us attend to, deal with and sometimes transcend and heal terrible trauma.

Do you think that Germany still has a debt to pay to the Jewish people? How can such a debt be paid?

Germany and its people, as well as Jews everywhere, will for ever carry this wound. I do not believe that it can be ever simply paid off or be 'made good'. I believe that the only way forward is genuine, open dialogue, an exploration on both sides of how Jews and German non-Jews have been affected by the Holocaust and the horrors of the Second World War. It is crucial for Germany and Germans to acknowledge their guilt, without defending themselves, and ask for forgiveness. This guilt and shame about the Holocaust sits deep in our bones and requires much soul searching, bearing witness, but also self-forgiveness, especially on the part of my own generation, which has been affected but has not carried any direct guilt.

For Discussion

— Before reading this book, what did you know about the Warsaw Ghetto and the Holocaust?

— The puppets' company helped us forget the adult world for a while. A world where people created ugly things; like a ghetto for Jews. A world we couldn't understand.

In what way do the puppets allow Mika and Ellie to escape from the oppression of the Nazis?

— What other forms of art – music, stories and performance – allow the Jewish inhabitants to cope with pain, grief and suffering?

— Mother was gentle, but also very brave – she had soldiered on with a broken heart after Father died, never complaining. And she had risked her life to honour Grandfather's last wish – that I should have the coat.

Which other everyday acts of heroism do men, women and children achieve in the Warsaw Ghetto?

— Yes, I had put on the show to survive, but wasn't I betraying my own people? I felt disgusted with myself and the puppets, which were contaminated and compromised just as I was. What would Grandfather have thought of me now?

How does performing for the Nazis change Mika's relationship with the puppets and with his family?

— Why does Max help Mika? Does Max's friendship with Mika allow him to acknowledge his own role in the oppression of the Jews?

— Ellie decides to stay in the ghetto, as a part of the Warsaw resistance, but Mika decides to escape. Why do you think each of them make these different decisions?

— Everything had changed – here they were now, grown men, once proud soldiers who had brought so much death and misery to Poland, to the world, now just bags of bones fighting over a bunch of puppets.

When Max is in Siberia, he begins to talk to the puppet prince. How do the puppets give Max and the other German soldiers courage?

— When Max returns to Nurnberg after the war, he is only a ghost of his former self, and his wife and son treat him differently. Why, after the Second World War, can nothing ever go back to the way it was before?

— What does the reader learn from Mara's visit to Warsaw sixty-six years after the Ghetto was created?

— How is Mara's puppet play different from Mika's real experiences in the Warsaw Ghetto?

— As Mika's story unfolds, Mara slowly sheds the defensiveness that has become second nature to her, the price for being German and speaking about the war. The author of *The Puppet Boy of Warsaw*, Eva Weaver, is German and not Jewish. What challenges do you think she must have faced when writing this book?

— In what ways does this book suggest this generation should go about healing the wounds of the Holocaust and the Second World War?

Further Reading

Fugitive Pieces by Anne Michaels
Homecoming by Bernhard Schlink
Mila 18 by Leon Uris
Once, Then, Now, After all by Morris Gleitzman
Schindler's Ark by Thomas Keneally
The Cellist of Sarajevo by Steven Galloway
The Book Thief by Markus Zusak
The Boy in the Striped Pyjamas by John Boyne
The Pianist by Wladyslaw Szpilman